GW00858491

# 50 GRADES
# OF SHAME

*Bootfall*

*Or*

*From Riches to Wearing the Rags*

By

TERRY RICE-MILTON

*To all who appreciate good manners, true values, humour, a touch of fantasy and good sex (sorry my little joke there - with emphasis on the 'little').*

# CONTENTS

# ACKNOWLEDGMENTS

To all friends and relations that I may have bored or upset over the years, especially my darling wife, Anna.

# 1

"I want the ball to my feet, you f.....g bozo, not in my f.....g nuts. How did you make it into this f.....g football club anyway? Does Daddy own it or something? Hey Donnie, where did they get this thick twat from? Did you take a bung from his family or something? That's the third time he's done it, and every other time he gives me a f.....g hospital ball!"

It was Monday morning in the third week of September and a gloriously sunny day, for late summer. We were at the training ground of Premier League side Barcaster United, and the abrasive, insulting language came from the mouth of hardy professional Rory Stafford. The victim of his abuse was a promising youngster on the team's books, Paul Bastable and long-suffering chief coach and manager, Donald Mclaren.

Humouring Stafford, the coach replied, "Leave the wee laddie alone, big guy. You know you make him nervous. Can you not see he's in awe of you? Don't you think it would make things easier for him if you were to encourage him a wee bit instead of lambasting him all the time? Since when were you Mister Perfect? You were a youngs..."

But Stafford cut him short, saying, "Yeah, yeah, I get the picture. It's just that he's hitting the ball too high or too hard, not just once but every f.....g time!"

"Aw, cut him some slack, Stafford, and curb your language in front of these young lads," the coach said, more forcibly this time, with a stronger hint of his Scottish brogue. "Besides, it's your own fault you're training with, or should I say, 'coaching' the kids. If you had learnt to check that temper of yours, you wouldna' be suspended in the first place!"

To which Stafford replied, "If it hadn't been for that left-back's f.....g diving and award-winning acting performance, you mean. He was doin' it all game... didn't you see him...? All over me like a cheap suit."

He was now talking about the antics of Castertown Rovers' expensive Italian import, Oscar di la Scala, whose jaw had drawn the attention of our hero's elbow, resulting in a 'Red Card and 3-match Ban for Rory Stafford' as the headlines read in all of the Sunday newspapers; and not to mention a painful stay in hospital for Sr. di la Scala, having his jaw rebuilt.

"You'd know about cheap suits then, would you? Look Stafford, normally I would agree with you about him making a meal of it, coupled with his usual efforts to get people sent off, but you used your elbow on his chin. It was a disgrace! It was so obviously deliberate, everybody saw you connect, and it was on live television for God's sake!" Mclaren replied angrily. Then he continued more calmly, "When someone is as talented and as skilful as you, there is no need to carry on in that way, nor to foul-mouth the referee for that matter. What kind of example is that for the captain to set? It *is* called the

BEAUTIFUL game after all, but you turned it ugly with a capital 'U' on the day. Not only that but we'd made a great start to the new season, the team had settled into a pattern of play we'd worked hard on pre-season, and the new players had 'bedded' in really well. We got maximum points from our first six games and were sitting pretty at the top of the table. Everyone, from the kit guys right up to the good folk on the board, was ecstatic, life was a dream. Then you go and do something daft like that! We could only manage a draw on Saturday, and that was with the help of a 'dodgy' penalty. So... am I supposed to feel some sort of sympathy for *you*...? Not bloody likely! Y'see, I've given you the benefit of the doubt so often in the past, for the sake of the team, and the good name of Barcaster United; but your behaviour has got progressively worse and what you did was a total disgrace; not something I could say was 'unfortunate', or that it is a 'man's game' for the benefit of the TV cameras. For once I could not condone it in any way."

All this took place in full view of the younger players, whose aspirations and good habits are drawn from being on the same pitch as seasoned professionals such as Rory Stafford. A player whose distribution of the football is almost magical at times and whose mid-field skills and ball-winning abilities, although quite often overly physical, have been coveted on numerous occasions by several top level clubs. Though, credit to him, his loyalties have always been with his local team – childhood favourites Barcaster United, for whom he signed as a schoolboy just before his final term at Barcaster Comprehensive School.

"I thought that bringing you in to be with the youngsters would work for you and the boys alike. Giving you a 'reality check', and calming you down a little by taking you back to your roots; and also giving them the chance to rub shoulders with, yes, and learn from the biggest star in the game today. You've done alright out of football and this is a good opportunity for you to give something back. These kids are the future of this football club, they need to be nurtured and encouraged, not destroyed by someone they admire and want to emulate on the football pitch. You were not always the richest player around, Stafford. You started just like these youngsters, some of them from the run-down council estates in Barcaster. They aspire to be where you are now, on top of the pile, living in £3 million's worth of landscaped real estate, in the most beautiful part of northern England. It is a big gap between 'sink estate' and 'real estate' and that is something *you* would do well to remember, laddie. There's an awful long way to fall... Eh?" Donald Mclaren stopped his tirade, thinking that he had taken the wind out of Rory's sails. However, Rory launched into one of his own.

"Have you done with me? A'ya trying to f...k me head up with ya clever words, ya sophisticated ways, and ya f.....g Grammar School education? You think y'are so superior? Well I'm..." But before he could finish, Donnie launched into him again, grabbing him by his arms this time and stabbing Stafford in the chest with the forefinger of his right hand.

"Listen to me, hard man, this is about *you*, not me, but since you brought it up, here goes! See, nobody gave me anything; I had to drag myself up by the bootstraps. I lost my father in the war and my mother reared myself, and my four brothers, on her own, insisting on a decent education for all of us, to give us a start in life. We all worked hard at it and got good results in our exams first. Only *then* did I come and make my mark in football, playing for and then managing the biggest team in the land... Not bad for a wee laddie from the 'Gorbals', eh? And in Scotland it was *not* Grammar Schools, it was the academy system." The coach paused then added in his heaviest Gorbals accent, "By the way!"

Rory hesitated for an instant, as if some of what Donnie said had sunk in, but nothing seemed to have got through. Instead, he picked up his track top, booted the nearest ball into the distance, and stormed off in a flurry of foul language and abuse at anyone who was in his way.

Leaping into his open-topped, British racing green Aston Martin Volante, with the biggest and widest alloy wheels, and biggest and noisiest sports engine (this was the 'spec' he gave to the salesman when he bought the car, plus the 'no expense spared' addendum), he drove out of the training facility at breakneck speed, wearing the shirt, shorts, and trainers that he had been playing in.

## 2

Rory Stafford's first port of call was the Cow and Gate pub where the landlord was Ronnie Grubbe, sometimes known as 'Foody'. An ex-footballer himself and a former team-mate of Rory's whose athlete's muscular 'six-pack' was now a beer-swiller's 'firkin sized barrel'. On seeing Rory, he started to pull a pint of Strang's 'Old Griptite' best bitter, Rory's favourite 'brew'.

"How are you, you old bastard?" said Ronnie as he handed him his pint.

"Shut up and gimme that f.....g phone, and less of the 'old', y'twat!" Rory snorted before he downed more than half the glass of beer.

"Yeah, I'm fine too, thanks for asking. Who climbed up your arse and left a deposit? Please tell me, I want to thank them for making my day!" Ronnie carried on talking but Rory took no notice as he dialled up the number of his 'bookie', grumbling and cursing under his breath as he did so.

"Y'ello, who's that...? Eh...? Stop f.....g about and put Micky on. Hello Micky, tell that c..t to stop pissing me off, he's asking to be chinned... What do you mean, like the Italian? F..k off! He was asking for it anyway, for all that spitting and them f.....g wind-ups. I reckon I did everybody a f.....g favour!"

As Rory said this, Ronnie Grubbe chipped in. "Well, you've sorted out the spitting bit, and he certainly won't be pulling faces for a while!"

To which Rory replied, "Shut up, gobshite, and pull me another pint, and I'll have one of them cardboard envelopes you try to pass off as pasties. Yeah, Micky, I'm still here. Look, put two grand on Bishop's Brick to win the 2.30 at Chepstow. What price is it? 9-4? That's fine, I'll take it." There was another pause, then Rory exclaimed loudly enough for everyone to hear, "I tole ya before, I'll be round soon," and more softly now, "yeah and it'll be cash. Shit, Micky, y'know I'm good for it. Anyway, I've been busy." He paused again, listening to Micky. "What do ya mean on hospital visits? Shut up about that twat! Just don't forget that f.....g horse, that's all!" At this, he slammed down the phone and asked Ronnie where his pasty was.

"It's still in the microwave, cooking. 'Ere, I don't know how you modern 'athletes' get away with eating all this fast food crap! It's bound to catch up with you sometime, I know it did me," he said jokingly, patting his enormous belly.

Rory jibed cruelly, "That's 'cos you 'et ten times as much as the rest of us, and *you* had to stop f.....g playing 'cos not only were all the people *on* the park faster than you but just about everybody off it too – even the ol' bird with the Zimmer frame!"

To which Ronnie replied, "Oh, it's alright for our

hero to have a crack at Ronnie, but not the other way round, ay? Anyway, something is chewing at you more than the usual; you're already on your second pint, what's wrong with you? And while you're at it, why are you still wearing your training kit?"

"F.....g 'ell, Foody, you don't 'alf sound like me mum. What's with all the f.....g questions?" But before he could answer, the 'ching' of the microwave oven signalled for Ronnie to go and collect his friend's pasty.

"There we are, sir, and what would sir like with it, a first class stamp or the usual fruity but ever so wickedly spicy H.P. brown sauce?" Ronnie teased as he placed the pasty in front of Rory. "Something is niggling you more than usual after a normal Monday morning training session."

Rory took a breath of resignation and continued more calmly. "That's the trouble Ronnie, it wasn't a normal training day, anything but," he answered. "F.....g Mclaren has got me in training with the youth squad, f.....g schoolboys! He calls it coaching while I'm serving out me suspension. Good for them, and good for me; 'ow is it good for me? I'm a senior pro, for f..k's sake."

Ronnie interrupted him. "Look, Rory old mate, he's trying to keep you involved, to pass on your experience to the lads, and to stop you wasting your time elsewhere, like here for instance."

"Na! I reckon he wants me out the way of the first team squad, so that he can bring on my eventual replacement. They're probably working on a new system, 'cos they couldn't play the same way without me, it could never be as effective without me," Rory said in all seriousness, catching a glimpse of his own handsome reflection in the mirror behind the optics. Approving, he continued, "Anyway, he gave me a right 'coating' this morning, right in front of them 'kids'. He reckons I was giving them a hard time, I was only asking for the ball at me f.....g feet from some skinny little shit. Not too much to ask, surely. He hit me in the 'cobblers' once, for f..k's sake!"

Ronnie fixed a drink for a customer further up the bar, and when he returned he reiterated to Rory, "No, mate, I reckon he's trying to teach you a lesson. You've been in some scrapes in the past on and off the football pitch and he's done his best to sort things out 'cos you were always special to him, but this is the worst yet, you actually put someone in hospital this time. You've always had a hard edge to your game, but this went beyond that. Don't y'see? Donnie Mclaren has always traded on his teams being hard but fair. His role model *and* for many of his contemporaries was Brian Clough, he told him once he liked to see football played with a smile. He always said he judged us on how well we played the game and just like Cloughie, he despised cheats or anybody who hassled the referee for that matter. Don't you remember? Donnie was always saying things like 'in the spirit of the game', or, 'play up and play fair, do I not like cheats' (Attributed to Graham Taylor, I think you'll find...*ed.*). A bit of his public school upbringing, ennit?"

"Ah, no, no! Yer wrong there! It's the acne... acma... academical system...in the Gorbals, where he came from. That's what he told me."

"Do what? Are you sure he wasn't talking about

kicking you in *your* Gorbals like that young lad? The man went to a 'posh' school somewhere in England! I remember everybody talking about it when he first came to Barcaster, because he isn't your normal 'run of the mill' football manager."

"I'm tellin' ya, he went to a f.....g academy in Scotland, he told me so this morning, when he was peelin' me off," Rory insisted.

Then Ronnie said, more seriously now, "Never mind that, though. I reckon it's getting more personal with him now, he's covered your arse for you in the past, but a nasty streak has come more into your game. He probably thinks you are past your best and losing it a bit."

"Shit, Ronnie, you do talk some crap. I'm only twenty-nine, I'm playing the best football of my f.....g life, and every team in the Premiership has made an offer for me at one time or another in the last couple of years." Rory preened himself in the mirror once more, and continued, "I'm the 'ottest property in football at the moment."

*Yes, and don't you know it,* the barman thought as he pulled himself away to serve a pretty young girl at the top of the bar.

"Alright darling, what can I get you? Excited, or just the usual?" he asked, almost hopefully.

She faked shyness, and asked for two Bacardi Breezers, and as Ronnie placed the drinks in front of her, said just loud enough for him to hear, "You *could* introduce me to the gorgeous blond with the legs over there, if you like," nodding in Rory's direction.

Ronnie was quick to put a dampener on it,

answering, "Do yourself a favour, love. Don't go there, you'll be messing with fire, and anyway he's a married man."

"I notice you didn't say 'happily' married man," the girl said pointedly.

Ronnie very quickly snapped back at her, "No, but I did say don't go there!" with heavy emphasis on 'don't'.

Ronnie moved back to where his friend was at the bar, and Rory asked, "Where were you telling her not to go, mate?"

"Oh! That poxy new club down the road. I was warning them that they get the wrong sort in there!" Ronnie cleverly improvised. "They charge a f.....g fortune for their drinks too, so only the likes of you and your 'lardy' friends can afford to go there!" Then realising his 'faux-pas', he added, "When I said 'the wrong sort', of course, I meant present company excepted, and I..."

"It's alright, Ronnie mate, I know what you f.....g mean. I only go in there meself, when there's somethin' special on, anyway," Rory said nonchalantly. And then more seriously, "But tell me, do ya really think ol' Mclaren has got it in for me 'cos of me suspension? He was really mad this morning, I thought he might smack me one. He grabbed me so tight by the f.....g arm, it made me eyes water!"

Ronnie took a deep breath and adopting a stern look, said, "Rory, how long have we known each other? I reck..."

Rory, interrupting him, said, "I don't know but it's a f.....g long time 'cos you 'ad 'air then!" Ronnie carried on, ignoring Rory but wincing at the same time.

"Now, let's see. I was at your Confirmation, and when I was thirteen you came to my bar mitzvah! I've still got the 'cutting'... It was in all the papers." Ronnie laughed, but realising that his little joke had gone over his friend's head, he continued. "No, but seriously, you were a kid just making it, where I'd been a first team regular for a few years by then. But all the time I've known you, you've not really cared about other people's feelings. You only ever did just enough to get by in that regard and fortunately your talent normally made up for it and that was what kept everybody happy, especially Donnie Mclaren. But as I said before, you've been upsetting more and more people lately and now their patience is being stretched, and don't forget you won't be playing forever." He paused, then carried on. "Of course, you know what hurts old Donnie the most *is* he almost regards you as the son he never had. Remember, he hadn't been at United long when he brought you in. So as I said before, you always had a special place in his thoughts, it's like he reared you, as near as damn it! So he feels it that extra bit harder when it's you who lets him down. Even you can understand that."

Rory considered what Ronnie had said but before he could answer, the door flew open and in burst a few of his pals from the first team squad, straight from their morning's training stint. It was Charlie Boyle, who called out, "Here he is, lads, the man of the moment. Where have you been, Rory? Did you pull a 'sickie' today? No, don't tell me, let me guess. You were making a hospital visit, impressing the gentlemen of the press and scoring a few 'brownie' points! We missed you out there on Saturday, mate. Donnie has got us playing more defensive and that's not our style..." At this point his voice trailed off, because Dominic Cousins, team captain and one of its more articulate members, grabbed him by the arm.

"Leave it out, 'Lance-it'. Don't wind him up. It's not funny, anyway. Seriously, where were you today, Rory? The boss hasn't banned you from training with us, has he? Surely he doesn't think you'd be a bad influence on us lot, does he? Sorry mate, only joshing. Where *have* you been this last week?"

Rory, who had been staring open-mouthed at Ronnie up to this point, suddenly turned round and greeted his friends.

"Hello lads, I didn't notice you come in. How was training? Bet you missed me organising things, didn't you? You're just in time to buy me a drink. Who's gettin' 'em in?"

The response from the boys was disbelief and Ronnie was dumbfounded. Rory had not caught a word of what either Charlie or Dominic had said. In fact, one minute he'd looked as if he was in a state of shock, the next he had carried on like nothing had happened.

It was Michael Kelly, the young midfielder recently transferred from neighbouring club and Premiership rivals, Castertown Rovers, who went to the bar and ordered 'orange and sodas' all round.

Rory Stafford had a reputation as a big drinker inside and out of the club, and he wasn't about to lose it now. He shouted, "Don't take the Micky, Michael. I want a real f.....g drink, a man's drink, not that 'wee

wee' that you ladies sip! I'll 'ave a pint of 'Griptite', Ronnie."

"What makes you think I was getting you one? Anyway, are you sure you shouldn't be having a lady's drink, Rory? Isn't that your car out there? I'm not thinking of you so much as those poor unfortunates who might have to share the road with you later on," Michael said, with more than a hint of rancour in his voice.

Rory chose to ignore his young friend's words, and carried on drinking, then enquired almost mockingly, "By the way Michael, what did you write about me in ya piece for the Mercury this week?"

Michael was the brightest and youngest of the bunch, and following his controversial move from the less successful of the local teams to the *more* successful one, was asked to write a weekly article on his experiences of life at his new club for the local newspaper, the Barcaster Mercury.

"As a matter of fact," Michael started, "nothing! How could I? You were banned from Saturday's game and the next two. Besides, I said it all in last week's article. It was quite embarrassing. Everybody wanted to speak to *me*, seeing as how I was forever singing your praises in my previous pieces. I suddenly found myself trying to defend the indefensible. It was really awkward. Here I was, the new kid on the block who had so admired this blue-eyed, blond soccer hero as a teenager..."

Ronnie cut in, "'Ere, steady on, son. You'll have us thinking you're on the turn or something!"

Ignoring Ronnie, Michael continued, "...That I

became a 'Judas' by crossing town to play in the same team as him. What happened between you and that Di la Scala was indescribable. I can't believe your arrogance, even now, what with a three-match ban and the possibility of a criminal charge hanging over you, not to mention the disruption to the team! You carry on as if nothing had happened! What's wrong with you?"

The others remained respectfully silent as Michael delivered his salvo. It was almost inconceivable that the lad who had run the gauntlet of hostility from the Castertown fans – being branded a 'Judas' by them – so he could move across town to play on the same turf as his idol, whose praises he sang more than anyone else's, in his newspaper articles, should now turn against him so vehemently. Michael pushed past Rory and the others by the bar and made his way to the toilet. Ronnie noticed tears in his eyes.

Dominic Cousins broke the silence. "Have a word with him, Rory boy. You've burst his balloon now, he'll be asking to go on the transfer list next. We can't afford to be without him *and* you in our mid-field. You are, I mean, *were* his inspiration. By the way, have you been to apologise to Di la Scala yet? Knowing that you had would help bring Mikey round a bit. He must think you enjoyed messing up the Italian guy's face, so why don't you go out of your way to say you're sorry, eh?"

"Yeah, it would calm the situation all round. Here, you know *how* you can do it, don't you? Put an apology in Michael's next article, everybody in Barcaster and Castertown reads it," Charlie Boyle submitted encouragingly.

"Great idea, Lance-it. He's right, Rory, both sets of 'fans' read his articles and you can put the record straight. That is brilliant, Lance-it, you're not just an ugly face!" Dominic agreed heartily, and quickly downing his drink, continued. "Now get the drinks in, and get us a proper f.....g one this time."

Charlie responded, feigning indignation. "Here, hold up, I'm not ugly. I'm told I've got some very attractive features and besides which, I'm always getting compliments for me shapely bum!"

Before he could say any more, Dominic commented, "Yeah, mostly from the boys!"

Meanwhile, Rory thought about it. "'Ere, I'm not sure I want to apologise to that Castertown c..t, remember he was the b.....d who done me f.....g groin in a couple of years ago," he contended, then continued. "I *would* like to put it right with Michael, though. He's a good kid. I know I give 'im a lot of f.....g stick, but I don't like to see him upset and you're right, Lance-it. If I *was* to make an apology, and that's a big f.....g IF! The best way would be through one of Michael Kelly's famous Mercury pieces."

Just then, Michael re-emerged from the men's room and hearing the tail end of what Rory said, asked, "The best way is through one of my Mercury pieces... To do what?"

Dom Cousins promptly pitched in. "Well, Rory was wondering if he could use your article in this week's Mercury to publish an unreserved apology for the pain and inconvenience that he has caused to all concerned by the 'incident' that took place during the game between Barcaster and Castertown a week last

Saturday, or words to that effect. Anyway, he'll leave the details and the exact wording to you, 'cos you're better qualified than him. Ain't that right, Rory!" He winked at Michael as he passed.

Rory was nonplussed and had no time to react either way, but this was exactly the effect that Dom was hoping for. Michael was visibly moved, and went over to Rory and offered him his hand and said, "That will go some way towards restoring my respect for you and calming down the hostile press, not to mention getting them off my back. Honestly, I'd almost changed my mind about the 'beautiful game' and gone back to my studies. That's how bad I've felt."

(Michael *had* intended to take a degree in media studies before being persuaded to join Castertown Rovers after his A Levels).

"Tell me about it, mate. I was 'ardly able to go out the door last week for trippin' over f.....g press and TV blokes. It's alright though 'cos I trained with the 'kids' at their f.....g patch. 'Ere Ronnie, I bet that's why Donnie had me in with them. To get the media off me f.....g back."

Michael thought about remonstrating with Rory again over his arrogance, but bit his lip and let it pass, consoling himself with the thought that he had got as much of an apology as the world was likely to hear from Rory Stafford. Better still, he had 'carte-blanche' to print it using his own words.

Meanwhile, Ronnie handed Charlie his change for the drinks he had bought and turned towards Rory, agreeing. "Yeah, probably, as well as all that other stuff we were talking about. It gives him a bit of a breather too; that's why he was there with you, I reckon. I'm guessing that the club's main training ground has been like a cauldron, hasn't it lads?"

Charlie checked his change and confirmed Ronnie's thoughts. "You're not wrong there, Ronnie. So Donnie's been over with you at the kids' playground, eh Rory? Is that where you were all last week? He *is* a clever b.....d. Did you hear that, fellers?"

Dominic backed up Ronnie. "Yeah, he is more likely to have done it for a quiet time for himself than to take the heat off you, Rory. When you think about it, he takes his responsibilities very seriously, so he would want to keep us players focused on the next game. Though how the press boys haven't tracked the two of you down God only knows!"

"That's the beauty of me driving the f.....g beast, 'ennit? They can't keep up wi' me for long, can they?" Rory said, with an expression of superiority. "I always drive right past, keep going 'til I've lost 'em, so they've no idea where I end up, do they?"

Charlie could not resist a dig, so he baited Rory. "Very clever, Rory Stafford. Y'know, you'd make a great contestant on that show 'Universally Challenged'."

Rory took the bait and correcting him, said, "You mean 'University Challenge', don't you, Lance-it?"

There was a solid chorus from the others. "No, 'Universally Challenged'!"

Ronnie Grubbe chimed in. "Whilst you're at it, you could always try 'Get me a celebrity I'm out of here'." Nobody laughed so with a sigh of disappointment he carried on serving. (I thought it was quite funny, that's why I left it in...*ed*.)

Rory groaned, shrugged his shoulders and addressing them all, shouted, "I'm not hanging around here to have the f.....g piss taken. I'm f.....g off!" He picked up his car keys from the bar, turned clumsily, tripped and nearly fell headlong into the door in his hurry to open it.

Rory was planning to visit the betting shop next, but on reaching the car park, at the rear of the pub, he spotted the girls who had been in the bar minutes earlier. They appeared to be admiring his car. He crept up on them as quietly as his present state would allow and when he was a foot or so away, he suddenly jumped out in front of them, calling, "Aye, aye, what's going on 'ere, then? I 'ope you weren't thinkin' of nickin' the beast!"

The girls were taken completely by surprise and made as if to run off, but Rory, calming them, said, "It's alright, girls. I was only having a laugh, I f.....g need one. Everybody's 'avin' a go at me today."

The prettier of the two was the one who had admired Rory's legs at the bar and she was the first to speak.

"What do you mean, having a go at you? By the way, nice legs, but do you always go to the pub in shorts and trainers? What is it... a fashion statement?"

She had recovered her senses very quickly. A little too quickly for Rory's liking and he answered, "You wanna know a lot. What's this, the f.....g Spanish Imposition?"

The girl and her friend both sustained a giggle, and

she continued.

"I'm just being friendly... *And* complimentary. Oh, and that's the Spanish *Inquisition*, by the way. Also, you should learn to take flattery with grace."

"That's it, carry on, 'ave another swipe. They're all trying to put me right today and which one of you's Grace anyway?" The girl turned to her friend almost doubled up with laughter, but managed to control it enough to face Rory again.

"What do you mean put you right? Are you in trouble, or have you just had too much to drink? Which is it?"

"F.....g 'ell, now *you're* sounding like me mam too and I've only just met ya. Well I ain't met ya, I mean I don't know ya, I mean we ain't been introduced yet, tell ya what, why don't ya tell me who you are, 'cos you know who I am, right?"

The girl offered her hand to Rory and with her other one gestured towards her friend and said, "Ok then, start again. The tall, statuesque blonde on my right is my work-mate, Sally Farnham. I, the slightly shorter, darker one, am Linda Morris and we work together for an advertising company in that large modern office block over there by the bus station. And you, sir, are?"

"What the f...k was all that?" was all that Rory could muster in reply, bending down to pick up his car keys as he did so.

The taller, blonde girl winced and pulled at Linda's arm, saying, "Come on, Lin, he's so rude. Why are you bothering with him? He's a typical northern yob. We should be getting back now anyway."

Linda had other plans though. Although it was against her better judgement she saw Rory as a challenge and was 'up for it'. She patted Sally on the arm and gently pushed her in the direction of their place of work, then turning towards Rory, she asked, "Are you really so rough and tough or is it a front for deep-seated shyness? I'll bet you're a big softy deep down inside. I'd love to know. As I was saying, my name is Linda Morris, and I'm in advertising. So who are you?" She offered Rory her hand again, this time he took it, steadying himself as he did so.

"Are you sure you're not taking the piss?" he asked. "Anyway, I thought you were 'anging around 'cos you knew who I was!" he continued conceitedly. "I thought ya might be after an autograph or something."

Linda was puzzled; she remembered what Ronnie had said at the bar, but he hadn't said who Rory was, only to avoid him. He did not come over as the 'brightest star in the galaxy', more like 'the one rock on an otherwise golden, soft, sandy beach', but curiosity had got the better of her. She was fascinated, and decided to find out more. Besides, she was beginning to get 'stirrings' of a decidedly physical nature as she held onto his hand and admired his tall, athletic frame and natural blond good looks. "Oh yes, and what would the 'or something' be? I'm sorry but I don't know you. I am quite new to the area, our company relocated and Sally and I moved with them from down south; the rents and rates are so much cheaper up here, apparently. So who are you then? Are you the local deejay or are you an actor from one of the 'soaps' they make up here?" she enquired quite innocently.

"Now I know you're taking the pee, I 'ave played fifty-two f.....g times for England, for f...k's sake. Everybody knows Rory Stafford."

At this point Linda withdrew her hand and once again quite innocently, asked, "Played what fifty-two times for England?"

"Football, of course. F.....g football!" he replied curtly.

For a second Linda caught herself, thinking that perhaps he *was* the brightest star in the galaxy and half apologising for not recognising as much, replied, "Ah, football. I'm sorry... Rory, I am not a soccer fan. I have two brothers who both play rugby for Richmond Park, so we are very much a rugby family. Still, at least I know who you are now. Come to think of it, I do recognise that name, it has been in the news quite a bit recently. I can't remember for what exactly. Has there been a big game or was it a transfer, something like that? Come on, put me out of my misery. What was it all about?"

Rory was silent for a second then said, "You don't want to know. It was nothing important, anyway."

Linda thought, *It must be something controversial, something bad. With this ego, if it was good he would want to talk about it.* But she judged that he was being uncharacteristically guarded. *So what has he done?* She decided to pursue it further, realising that she would maybe have to massage his ego if she was to get any more out of him, and thinking that it might just be worth it anyway.

"Never mind, but I think I would like to get to know you better. How about a cosy drink somewhere?" she asked as she moved a little closer to him.

"Well I'm not going back in there," Rory said sulkily.

"That's alright," Linda reassured him. "I know a little place not far from here, it's cosy and it's quiet."

"Where's that then?" Rory enquired, his ears pricking in anticipation.

"Oh, just a little place I discovered when I first came up here," she teased.

Rory was almost dribbling now; this was a classy lady, and she seemed to be coming on to him 'big-time'. He liked the way she played him along a bit. Not like all the others, like 'groupies' – couldn't wait to have him in their pants! So not one to miss an opportunity to engage in exercises of an amorous nature, he declared, "Well, I'm sure I have nothing too pressing in my diary for the next few minutes, so let's carry on! But 'ow do we get there? I've had too much to f.....g drink really and I usually leave the 'beast' here in Ronnie's car park."

"Maybe I could help there. My youngest brother often loans me his sports car, though not so often now that I live up here, so maybe *I* could drive you. After all, as I said it's not very far."

Rory thought about it, and then said, "Well if it's not far and we don't drive through f.....g town, that's ok!" He handed Linda the keys, and she reassured him that they would not be going through town.

"It's up this road and just before the outskirts of town, actually."

They got into the car. Linda started up the Volante and carefully pulled into the traffic going out of town.

# 3

The first thing Rory noticed was the shortness of Linda's skirt and the tan of her gorgeous, shapely legs as she confidently shifted up through the gears in her Jimmy Choo shoes with the ever so spiteful high heels. He remembered that the first remark Linda had made was about *his* legs! Suddenly it dawned on him that he was sitting next to one of the most attractive girls he had ever met, dressed in the classiest, most tasteful clothes he had seen outside of his own wife's expensive wardrobe. She was so different from all the others, a different class – she was really 'posh'; not like Posh Beckham – *She don't even speak posh,* he thought. Linda looked and smelt a million dollars and here *he* was, just as he had left the training ground – sweaty, probably smelly, and dressed in 'footie' shirt, shorts, and trainers!

His eyes travelled slowly and reluctantly up and away from those fabulous legs until they alighted on the curve of her bosom. *Nice way to fill a bra,* he thought, *if she's wearing one.* He couldn't really tell, because, although her neckline was fairly low cut, her arm movements impaired his view. Just as he was cursing his bad luck Linda pulled the car to a halt in front of a large block of luxury apartments, sending Rory forwards and slightly sideways on to the dashboard with a bump.

"I'm sorry, I should have told you we were here. Are you alright? This is my flat... shall we?" She gestured towards the large front door and started to get out of the car.

"'Old on a minute, we can't leave it here, everybody'll see it!" Rory exclaimed, pulling himself together and rubbing his elbow.

Linda got back into the car, thinking, *Of course... he's a married man!*

"I'm sorry, we don't want any passing fans to spot it, do we? We can put her around the back, out of sight."

"Na, I was thinking of vandals. Kids get jealous and scratch expensive motors like this. It happens to all us top stars."

*God, is there no end to his vanity?* she thought as she re-engaged the clutch and drove the speedster to the car park at the back of the flats. *Never mind, I'm sure he makes up for it in other ways. He smells so masculine, just look at those legs, and his hair is naturally blond, not out of the bottle like our dear Sally's. Hey, steady on there, Linda old girl, let's not get too carried away! Sorry... too late for that, I'm afraid.* She switched off the engine and handed Rory the keys. They studied each other as they got out of the car. Linda led him up the steps to the rear entrance of the building, as she turned the key and opened the door she gave him an encouraging push on his backside. *Great buns, too!*

Rory reacted in kind and gently squeezed her rear,

at the same time backing her roughly against the wall.

"No, not here!" She gulped. "My flat is only on the second floor."

She took his hand and they sped up the stairs together. Once inside the flat, they could not keep their hands off each other and soon their clothes formed a trail that led into Linda's bedroom and right up to the king-size bed.

Rory stopped her at the edge of the bed and they grasped at each other's bodies wildly. She licked the sweat from the nape of his neck and ran her fingers through his wavy blond locks. Rory in turn roughly kissed her shoulder and her beautifully moulded breasts.

He pushed her forcefully backwards onto the bed, struggling in his haste to touch every part of her perfectly formed body. Linda, who gasped as he became more savage with each frenzied touch, was lifted to hitherto undiscovered heights by the experience. Although his flesh felt so big inside her she thought it might split her. Their movements covered every inch of the enormous bed. *So this is what they mean by a bit of rough!* Rory was like a wild animal and pounded his manhood relentlessly until he finally exploded inside her. Linda held his full weight between her thighs and thought that she would suffocate until the moment he released his flood inside her, at which point all her senses seemed to react at once and she experienced what felt like several orgasms at once.

They were both drained from the sheer physicality of their lovemaking, and it took a long time and much deep breathing before either was able to say anything. Rory, rolling limply onto his back, was the first to speak.

"That was f.....g great! I reckon it was more physical than a whole morning on the training ground!"

"God, Rory you say the nicest things," she uttered sardonically, still catching her breath, as she lay prone and exhausted, perched precariously on the edge of the huge bed.

"Seriously, where did you learn that? I've never experienced anything like that before, and I've certainly had my share of it."

Linda raised her eyebrows, paused, drew another breath and replied, "Oh, I just go with the flow, you know." She continued, "Thanks for the compliment, though." She was thinking, *That's the nearest thing to a real compliment I guess you're capable of, and yes, I guess you do know what you are talking about but let's not spoil the moment, Linda old thing. And seriously though, I did just go with the flow, no pun intended.* (None taken...*ed.*)

Before either of them spoke again, the phone rang in the other room. Linda, dragging herself slowly from the bed and into the lounge, picked up the receiver. "Hello, Linda Morris spea... Oh, hi Sally! What do you mean what am I doing? Well, I didn't answer my mobile because it was off! I came home straight from the pub, ye...es with you know who. How could I what? Sally, *you* are beginning to sound like his mother... What? Oh, just a joke. Anyway I can't talk, he's still here. Well of course I brought him home, I didn't want to be seen out with him, and apparently he's a married man. Anyway I told you what the barman said. Curiosity got the better of me and the flesh was weak... well mine was... Oh, nothing... just thinking out loud." Linda was thinking to herself, *I still don't know what he is supposed to have done.* She continued, in a whisper now, "It was fantastic, but I'll tell you more tomorrow. No, I won't be coming out tonight, I'm sore... er... sort of tired." She tried to cover up her gaffe by laughing it off, but she knew Sally had picked up on it. "Of course I'm alright. As I said, I'll tell you more tomorrow. Bye. Oh, by the way, Sal, what did you tell Guy? That's ok then, I should be over my ladies' problems by tomorrow. Thanks, you're a real friend." Linda put down the phone and returned to the bedroom, bumping into Rory on his way back from the bathroom.

"Good, you found your way around alright. Would you like a cup of tea or coffee? I'm having tea myself."

"I could murder a cup of tea, me mouth's like the Sari Desert."

Linda was about to correct him but instead asked him, "Would you like it in a mug, and how do you like it? With milk and sugar?"

"A mug of sweet, milky tea would be great!"

After a few minutes Linda returned from the kitchen with two large china mugs of steaming hot tea. Rory was looking into the mirror on the chest of drawers, running fingers through his hair and checking his face for spots when he caught sight of her still-nude figure as she sidled up to him on the bed. He took the mug from her and took a deep gulp of the hot tea. It was good, just how he liked it and he'd finished his before Linda had made a start on hers. She reached out for a robe to cover her nakedness and asked, "Would you like another one, Rory?"

"Yeah, please, that went down without touching the f.....g sides! Could I have a bit more sugar wiv it this time?"

Linda made her way towards the kitchen, drinking from her mug as she walked. *The charm school didn't do a very good job and his grasp of the language is limited, but then with* his *talent you can dispense with conversation!*

When she returned with the second mug, Rory was reclining on pillows propped against the bed head. It was impossible to ignore his manhood even though he had it half covered by the sheet now. She handed him the mug and pulled the cords on her robe together. She would not be able to do it again, though he looked like he was capable.

"Enjoy your tea, I'm going to take a shower."

"Don't go yet." Rory stretched for her hand as he said it, but Linda slipped away from him.

"I'm sorry, I'm not up to doing it again. I like to think that I am in good form fitness-wise but it was like making love to two people at once, you've worn me out."

"It's funny, girls have said that before. One did say she was sure there was two blokes in her bed and that I sure 'ad enough f.....g energy for two. You know what's f.....g funny, though? When I was born there was *meant* to be two of me. What I mean is, I was a twin, but the other one died in me mum's womb. They couldn't tell if it was a boy or a girl, 'cos there wasn't anything down there."

Linda shuddered, considering Rory's utterance as strange and as if to reassure herself, confirmed Rory, "You do have the engine of two people but you are a super fit athlete, after all is said and done." She carried on towards the bathroom.

She quickly showered and dressed in something casual. When she came back Rory was sleeping like a baby, so she settled herself on the sofa in the lounge and did the same. She realised that she had not come any closer to learning the 'story' of this man, the man with whom she'd just enjoyed the most sensational sex she had ever experienced!

## 4

Lisa Stafford drove her Land Rover Discovery into the car park of the Kissingbourne Golf and Country Club and stopped in an empty space close to the clubhouse. She acknowledged Dee Hacker, her best friend and regular golf partner with a smile, a hug, and a kiss on the cheek. Today being Monday, they teed off early. It was the busiest day of their week.

After golf it would be lunch with the rest of the gang. Shopping followed lunch, followed by more shopping then a visit to the health club for the usual cosseting and a proper relaxed 'chin-wag'.

"Hello love, how was your weekend? Did you *do* the new Indian restaurant in Castertown? It's got a good name already and it's only been open a month! Did you go with David and Sue? Was it nice and clean? What were the waiters like, were they friendly? Was the service good? What was the food really like? People reckon that their Vindaloo is the hottest they've tasted. Was it hot? I don't like it too hot myself; spicy food gives me a 'dickie' tummy, anyway."

Dee waited for her friend to catch her breath, gave her a peck on the cheek and answered, "No, we didn't do the Indian after all, David doesn't 'do' Indian food apparently, so Jeff and I suggested that we all go to our village pub, they do Thai cuisine there. We've never had a bad meal yet and they didn't let us down either. David said he'd be telling his boss how good it was. Anyway, how are you? Has that phone stopped ringing yet?"

"No it hasn't, darlin', it's driving me mad. I don't know if I'm on foot or horseback! It wouldn't be so bad if His Lordship were there to pick it up sometimes. He just carries on like nothing had happened. He's got a thick skin, that husband of mine." Dee couldn't help thinking that wasn't the only thing 'thick' about him. Skull, was what came to mind.

They moved towards the changing room, put on their golf clothes and headed for the first tee. It was a pleasant day for golf, a slight breeze and no rain. They were accomplished golfers due to an unnecessarily excessive number of lessons with the handsome South African golf pro attached to their club, and the fact that they played at least twice a week throughout the year, weather permitting, of course.

They teed off and soon got into their stride. By the fifth hole they had caught up with the foursome playing in front of them. They marked their cards and stood a distance back from the tee so as not to disturb the other golfers, who carried on, indifferent to anything other than the game at hand.

"What did you score on that hole, five? The same as me? We're not doing badly so far. So what's happening with Rory, then? Is he having to lay low or what?" Dee enquired of her friend.

"Oh no, he's carrying on as normal. Like I said, only difference is he can't play or train with the first team squad. His manager has got him training with the youngsters. Thinks it will do him good and it keeps him out of the way of the media. Honest, Dee, the way Ror' talks and carries on you'd think he'd done the world a favour by putting that other f.....g feller in hospital. I'm sorry love, I know you don't like swearing, but it's really hard. I mean on telly they said Ror' might be charged with GBH, the Barcaster police are considering it. Or that other bloke might bring his own charges against him. Can he do that? Me mum says he could go to gaol. What'll happen to me and the kids if he goes inside?"

Lisa's voice got louder as the emotion came out and was almost at the point of hysteria, distracting the golfer at the tee and causing the others to turn round. Dee gestured an apology and bid them carry on; she put her arm round Lisa's shoulder and reassured her. "It hasn't come to that yet, dear, and I'm sure it won't go that far. Some of them think that, what's his name, Oscar, Oscar de la Scala, had it coming to him, anyway. Don't you upset yourself over it, I'm sure it will work itself out. Now let's concentrate on our golf, eh?"

This seemed to do the trick and Lisa was able to complete the round in comparative calm. They checked each other's card and agreed that it had been a decent score for both as they had each played close to their handicap. Happy with the result, they packed away their clubs and headed for the changing room arm in arm.

Dee studied Lisa as she undressed and made her

way to the shower; she followed close behind.

"You know, Lisa, you could easily go back to modelling. You've kept yourself in fantastic shape, to say that you've had two kids and you're still only in your twenties. You were very successful and everybody will remember you, no problem." She joined Lisa in the shower and soaped herself down. "Look at you, you're so firm." Dee gave an approving squeeze to Lisa's tight buttocks. "You've the figure of a teenager. Rory doesn't know how lucky he is; some men would kill to get into bed with you."

"Yeah, and don't think they haven't tried, love. My Ror' would kill them *and* me if he knew who had tried. Anyway, I'm only interested in one man. Even if I don't see that much of him these days, he keeps me satisfied."

*Yes, you and quite a few others if the stories are true,* Dee thought, her devotion to her friend not allowing her to say as much. Secretly Dee and their circle of friends were envious because they were well aware of Rory's sexual prowess. "It would be good for you to get back into work though, keep yourself occupied and earn your own money again. Why don't you think about it? It wouldn't do any harm."

"Rory wouldn't like that. Besides, I've got the kids to think about, and remember I married him for better and for worse."

"The only thing is, darling, that you, in your sweet way get better, and every day he seems to get worse! Put it another way... You're the fragrant one, he's the flagrant one! Sorry, I pinched that from one of my clients. What's more is that your Rory only made you quit modelling because he couldn't cope with your success. The kids are older now and besides, they've got Hilary, their minder. Sorry, I mean nanny; one can never be sure with that particular name. Quite daunting though, what with the S.A.S. training and all, but very good with Gavin and Fiona, I understand."

"Yeah, they absolutely love her."

"Does she live in?"

"Oh yeah, good thing too. She's company in the evenings when the kids go to bed and Ror's not around, which as I say is more often than not!"

"She is obviously a good cook, 'cos there's not an ounce of fat on either of the kids too. So you've nothing to worry about on that score. Anyway, think of yourself for a change, this might be just the time to do something about it if 'God forbid' the worst should happen."

They stepped out of the shower together and towelled off, before donning their street clothes and returning to their cars. Lisa had been deep in thought as they walked but suddenly turned to Dee and said, "I suppose I could try a bit of part-time work, love. Not too much travellin' though, y'know, 'cos I like to be there for the kids. I'm only thinkin', 'cos nobody knows how long Rory will play for. We don't know what he'll do when he stops playing. I am in good shape, as you say. Mind you, I work at it. Hilary helps, and she has a lovely soft touch to say how strong she is. She gives me the right sort of exercises to suit my shape, she says, and as you say, she does a lot of our cooking, and watching what we all eat. Talking of which, let's get going, the others'll think we're not coming. See you down at the 'caff', love."

The 'caff' is how the girls refer to the Brasserie, their favourite lunch-time meeting place. They jumped into their respective cars and headed off to the Arcade in the centre of Castertown, which housed the Brasserie *and* their favourite shops. Once they had parked in the multi-storey car park, they met the other girls who made up their circle of friends. The first to greet them was Sherry Porter, girlfriend of Michael Kelly, and Geraldine Grubbe, Ronnie's wife, known to her friends as 'Gee-Gee'. They spotted a table towards the rear of the restaurant, but a voice called out to them, from close to the window.

"Over here, girls!"

It was Stephanie Cousins, the wife of team captain, Dominic. "I thought we could keep an eye on things from here. Hi Dee, how are you?"

Dee Hacker thought, *Sit where you'll be noticed, more like. Typical of footballers' wives.* She followed up immediately. "Fine thanks, how are you? What do we all want? I believe it is my turn."

They all spoke at once, but Dee was quick to organise them, taking everybody's order and conveying it to the girl behind the counter. Once they had settled with a drink, the conversation turned towards the events of the weekend. They quickly moved on to the latest 'fad' in 'tops' now that the 'retro' shawl had seen its day. Which kind of boot was replacing the buckled ones? What was to be the most prominent colour this coming winter? Have pastels had their day? Does one go for stronger colours and is grey the new black? Before they knew it, their meal

– light as it was – had arrived, been consumed, and cleared away, and they were ready now for the real business of the day. Shopping!

For the assault on the shops they always split into two groups. Sherry and Stephanie went off together in the direction of the shoe store, whilst Geraldine, Dee, and Lisa made first for the clothes boutiques. They all agreed to meet up again at the health spa attached to the country club at three-thirty or thereabouts. The conversation was all quite light whilst they 'did' the shops, mostly concerning hairstyles, what goes with what, the occasional mention of their husbands and the more important issues of how their children are coping with school and life in general. Their tour of the boutiques took in the usual 'labels' such as Mango, Zara, Versace, Florence and Fred, and not least Per Una, although this was by no means the complete list. The two sets of girls bumped into each other on more than one occasion during their progression through the Arcade, fleetingly exchanging tips and advice as to where to obtain the shoes to match the dress or vice versa and just as importantly where to... ACCESSORISE.

Three-thirty came and went and at four-ten, Lisa, Dee, and Geraldine arrived in convoy at the health club and were followed by the other two at four-fifteen. They all met up in the steam room to 'chill out'.

"Now then, girls, take a good look at me and guess how much weight I've lost in the two weeks since I saw you last," Geraldine Grubbe demanded. "And don't spare my feelings; I'm a big girl, I can take it! I mean I'm a grown-up girl, I mean... I know I am a big girl... that's why I'm dieting."

Dee quickly reassured her. "It's alright, darling, we know what you mean. You have done well; you must have lost half a stone at least."

"Well, not quite, I've actually shed five and half pounds."

"That's fantastic, love, that means you've lost a whopping eleven f.....g pounds since you started. Oops, sorry ladies. Isn't she good though? She'll soon be in size fourteen again."

Lisa jumped up and down excitedly, and then she slipped and fell straight on to Dee's lap. Dee steadied herself, clutched hold of Lisa, pulled her close and whispered, "She's got a long way to go to compete with you, sweetheart."

Lisa allowed Dee a little peck on the cheek, then, hauled herself onto the bench beside her.

"How is Ronnie doing with his diet, Gee-Gee? Is he sticking to it or is he still finding it hard? It must be difficult; being in the catering business. I mean it can't help... he's serving food all day." Sherry did her best to encourage her friend, unable to avoid the fact that Geraldine was involved in the same way as Ronnie was at the pub.

"The girls are right, Gee-Gee. You have done brilliantly, we can really see the difference, and you deserve a great big pat on the back." Stephanie had been quiet up till now but felt compelled to join in the praise, even though she was struggling with her own weight problem. She gave Geraldine a warm hug and continued. "Thanks for showing me the way."

Dee Hacker picked up the theme, saying, "Would that we could all be as good as Lisa Stafford here, though. She's done marvellously to keep her figure, especially after having two children. I was saying earlier that she ought to consider going back to her old job. She would do well. The money is still good. I've still got the contacts and the 'ad' agencies are always on the lookout for gorgeous mums. After all, we don't know what's going to happen with Rory, in the near future, do we?"

"What are you saying, Dee? What has the silly sod done then?" Geraldine Grubbe asked concernedly. "How bad is it for him, Lisa?"

Stephanie chimed in with cutting voice. "Didn't you hear, Gee? Her other half has given up football and taken up boxing for a living."

Sherry also added, "He seems to make the headlines for all the wrong reasons these days, doesn't he? He actually broke that other guy's jaw, didn't he? Mikey is really upset because he idolises him."

At this Lisa broke in. "'Ere, hold on a minute, that's my Ror' you're running down. He might have 'is problems, but he's still my f.....g husband!"

"I know, darling, but you are my dearest friend and I don't like to think of you suffering on account of him doing something stupid," Gee-Gee said reassuringly. "What's the worst then, Dee?" she continued. "You're not suggesting Rory will go to prison, are you?"

Lisa burst into tears now and had to be consoled by Dee and Gee-Gee. The other two girls sat apart and nodded knowingly to each other. Stephanie had seen her friend like this so many times before, because of something Rory had *or* hadn't done. She was more cynical, having experienced Rory's 'prowess' and been abandoned like so many others, once he had sated himself. Neither of them could help Lisa see what a sad fool she was when she so innocently protected the 'animal' she called her husband. Sherry was unable to hold it in. "He doesn't seem worth it, Lis'. I've only known you a little while but it seems to me you are too good for him, you really should think of yourself sometimes. He seems to get it all his own way, just because he is the greatest footballer of his generation...Well, that's what my Mikey writes in the paper."

"Shel's right, Lis'. He thinks he can get away with anything, and treats everybody like sh..."

Lisa interrupted Stephanie's flow. "F...k off, you two! I ain't listening to any more of this s..t! You don't know my Ror' anyway! What's he ever done to you? Shut the f..k up, alright! Call yourself friends?!"

Lisa lunged towards Stephanie with fingers spread, ready to grab her round the throat, but Sherry threw herself across her path and for the second time Lisa found herself in a heap on the floor of the steam room, this time with the slippery body of Sherry on top of her.

Sherry gently stroked Lisa's thigh and pleaded. "Come on, sweetheart, you know we don't mean to hurt your feelings. We are just trying to be kind to you, that's all." She helped Lisa to her feet and cradling her head with her hands, pulled her closer. There they stood until Stephanie joined them and they huddled together, crying.

Dee eventually broke up the circle and said, "The girls are right, of course. It isn't fair on you and the children. They must feel it, too. Kids can be very sensitive at times. At other times they can be horrible little 'rat-bags', of course. I should know, I've have several of my own."

This broke the mood and they all laughed, knowing that she was childless. This was the same Dee Hacker, professional woman who successfully ran two marriages, one to long-suffering husband Jeff and the other to her job, Personal Manager to certain 'Celebrities'. She boasted that her clients were her 'family', and often referred to them as 'my boys' or 'my girls'. Lisa Stafford had always been her favourite 'girl', even though she was not now a working client. Their relationship went back to the time before Lisa met and married Rory. Dee continued. "You know what we should do? We should all enjoy a lovely 'all over' massage. I think we deserve it for the dedication to the cause that we have shown today. Are you with me, girls? Then follow me! Lisa, you go first!"

This worked a treat and the girls were in better spirits now as they trooped into the Alternative Therapies area of the spa. Just then, a mobile phone sounded. The girls looked around to see Dee pull a handset from under her towel.

"Bloody hell, Dee, where have you been keeping that all this time? On second thoughts don't bother. I'll use my imagination; of course it is one of those vibrating ones too, isn't it?" Sherry asked mischievously.

"What are you implying, young lady? Yes... I'm sorry, it is Dee Hacker speaking. No, Henry, I was not alluding to you being *gay,* when I said young lady... No, I wasn't talking to you. Hold on! What am I saying? You *are* gay and everybody knows it." Realising Henry was joking, Dee allowed herself a chuckle. "Sorry, I was a little slow there, Henry darling. I am 'chilling' in the health club with the girls... What...? Lesbian tendencies? That's very naughty of you, Henry; I'm not sure what Jeff would think of that suggestion. Anyway, to what do I owe the pleasure...? What, Oh God, Henry you can twist every little thing I say."

Dee continued her conversation with her client whilst she waited for her turn on the massage table. One by one they succumbed to the delights of the aroma from the 'essential' oils and the sheer luxury of having every part of their bodies gently but thoroughly 'pummelled'.

Geraldine made way for Dee, the last one on the table and declared, "This is the perfect way to end the day and it's not as if we've done anything to deserve it."

"Speak for yourself, darling," Dee said reproachfully. "I work very hard at what I do, thank you very much."

"Don't talk to me about hard work. You should try being married to Dominic Cousins. That's what *I* call hard work, Mr. Impeccable himself. 'Everything has a place and everything in its place,' he's always saying. It's like being in the flaming army with him. I even have to iron creases into his boxers. I don't enjoy the luxury of having a home help like you lot, y'know. Another thing he insists on."

"Yes, yes, I think I get your point. I was just saying... What's that, Stephanie, you actually put creases in his knickers? But where? Why? No, don't bother. Too much information and all that, but I'm sure you do a neat job of them."

"Here, you know when some folk make the excuse to stay in and sort out their sock drawer, Dom does it for real, doesn't he, Steph?" Sherry chipped in. "I bet he still tucks his shirt in his knickers too, doesn't he?"

"Actually, it's us girls who wear knickers, darlin'. Men wear pants!" was Lisa's contribution. "Or 'slips', as it says on the label, and of course, boxer shorts."

Geraldine followed up, saying, "As far as I'm concerned, men are the 'Pants'."

This caused a titter and the girls continued to enjoy the banter and relaxation in the soft chairs of the salon, but time was moving on, so when Dee had finished her session they all moved through to the showers. After showering they proceeded to the changing room and dressed, ready for a drink in the lounge at the clubhouse.

Their favourite treat was to have tea and chocolate muffins that were baked on the premises by the country club's own chef, Pauline. The muffins were so light and fluffy that the girls had convinced themselves they couldn't possibly contain any calories. Even so, they restricted themselves to one each, just to be sure.

They reflected on what a funny day it had been and they agreed that they were closer than ever for all their 'ups' and 'downs'. Lisa picked up on their earlier conversation.

"I know you all mean well when you 'ave a go about my Ror' and I know he can be trouble with a capital 'T', but let's face it, he's a 'one-off'. I've learnt to take the rough wiv' the smooth, 'cos I do really f.....g love him, pardon my French. It looks like I'm in for an even rougher ride in the future so I am counting on you lot, alright?"

Dee reiterated what she had said earlier. "You know very well that we are all here for you, to a man... woman, aren't we girls? But promise us that you will put the children and yourself first then, in future. Ok, pet?"

"It goes without saying, sweetheart, you can count on us all but listen to what Dee is saying," Geraldine emphasised.

Stephanie echoed Gee-Gee's words. "She's right; we're all here for you and the kids, right?"

Sherry nodded her agreement and they all gathered their things together, exchanged hugs and kisses, made arrangements for the next week then headed for the exit and home.

# 5

When Lisa arrived home, Hilary the nanny welcomed her.

"Hello Mrs. Stafford, did you have a successful day? The phone has been busy but it's quietened down some from what it was like last week. They seem to have let up a little bit. Gavin and Fiona have had something to eat and they are in their rooms doing their homework. I'm sure they would be pleased to see you."

"Thanks, love, I appreciate that." She pecked Hilary on the cheek and chided, "I wish you would call me Lisa, I've known you long enough. Mrs. Stafford is so stuffy, I mean you do live here, and we're friends, it's not a normal employer and employee relationship, it's way more than that."

Hilary was still a little nervous around Lisa and worked very hard to disguise the affection she had for her, keeping things fairly formal during the day and whilst the children were around. When evening came she often shared a glass of wine with her and was far more relaxed whilst they watched television or played card games together.

"I'm sorry but I think that it is right to address you more formally whilst I'm on duty, I suppose it harks back to my days in the regiment. Y'see, we used to mix socially with the officers 'off-duty' but always respected rank at work. It's just hard to change; besides, it makes our time together 'off-duty' all the more enjoyable."

"God, you do say some of the sweetest things, love. It's hard to believe what your life was before you came to us, but of course that's why we gave you the job 'ere in the first place. You've helped us out of a few scrapes whilst you've been with us, especially with those reporters and TV people crawling all over the place last week. I don't know what you told them but they haven't been back, except that Italian crew, they must have had problems with the language."

"Oh yes, the Italians. I managed to get the message through to them though, they won't be back."

"I won't ask how you did it as long we haven't any expensive cameras to pay for."

"All part of the service and no extra cost. Now then, when you've seen the little ones what would you like for supper? I thought I would do a vegetable lasagne, I got all fresh ingredients from the farmers' market today."

Lisa put her shopping down and slipping off her shoes, she said, "Sounds good to me, and I've got the usual lovely Chianti Classico to help wash it down a treat, one thing the Italians do well. Have you heard from His Lordship, by the way?" She padded across the hall towards the stairs and the children's rooms.

Hilary winced at the sound of Rory's name and

called back, "No, Mr. Stafford hasn't called; wine sounds good, should I prepare for three or what?"

"Or what, I guess; he usually gets something when he feels hungry. Honestly I don't know what keeps him going," Lisa called from the top of the stairs and disappeared into Gavin's room.

*I've got a pretty shrewd idea what keeps him going and it's not the free nibbles at the bookies.* Hilary kept this thought to herself, knowing she shared the same contempt for her employer's husband as most other people outside of football.

She picked up Lisa's shoes and took them through to the kitchen to clean them before she continued with supper for the two of them.

Lisa listened from outside Gavin's room for a moment then carried on in to be greeted by silence.

"How's my little hero, then? Give Mummy a big kiss. Did you have a good day at school?"

Gavin clung to her a little tighter and longer than normal. "Not particularly." He answered more sulkily than usual. "The other kids are giving me a hard time about Daddy, calling him an animal. They've completely changed, y'know. It was ok before he did what he did to that other man. They're always teasing me about him, they're saying he's gonna be a jail-bird, they say it's in the papers. He won't go to prison, will he Mummy? It's not fair, I don't see that much of him now, it's ages since he came to one of my games even."

"Don't you take any notice of the other kids, they should know better. I shall 'ave it out with that Principal tomorrow, you see if I don't! We're not paying all that money to send you to a 'posh' school for you to go through all that. Now dry your eyes and give me another hug. Have you finished your homework, 'cos it's nearly time for bed? Alright, darlin'? I'll just go and check on your sister, g'night."

Lisa tapped on Fiona's door and pushed it open. The room was tastefully decorated in Farrow and Ball's best pinks and creams with the odd 'pop' picture featuring 'tweeny' stars such as Zac Efron and Justin Bieber, over the bed. This was a huge contrast to her brother's room with its 'space' themed ceiling and rocket ship styled bed that covered half the room. Gavin kept one wall exclusively for his collection of football posters, many featuring his father.

"I hope you had a better day than your brother, sweetheart... I must say, you don't look too happy, what's wrong?"

Fiona burst into tears as Lisa kissed her and she pulled her mother closely to her as she said, "It is just not fair, Mummy. I haven't done anything wrong but they still pick on me. I can't go back to that school, they've been so nasty about Dad, and now they are telling me he may go to prison. That's not true is it, is it Mummy?"

"That's only what they've read in the newspapers, darlin', you know what *they* are like, don't take any notice. I am going to speak to the head tomorrow, those kids should know better, anyway."

Lisa stayed with Fiona long enough to settle her down, knowing that she was the more sensitive of her two children even though at eleven she was older by eighteen months than Gavin. Young Gavin had inherited more of his father's tendencies, like a thick skin and the ability to take things more for granted, so for him to take on like he did, she realised that things must be really bad at their school. She often remarked to friends that her Gavin was not one given to crying and even as a baby it would be a last resort only to get his own way. She resigned herself to speaking to the school Principal first thing in the morning; she knew that she would have to phone to make an appointment, that's how it was done these days. However, she was determined that he would see her whatever it took.

She made her way to her own sumptuous bedroom, to change out of her street clothes and into something more comfortable in which to spend the evening. One wall was completely covered with mirrors, behind which a walk-in wardrobe was large enough to be described as a dressing room for two; this boasted even more full-length mirrors. The mirrors were Rory's idea, naturally. Lisa had said an emphatic 'no' to the ceiling-mounted feature that he'd wanted when they moved in. Apart from the mirrors the bedroom was very tastefully decorated from the Colesta and Flockhart 'boudoir' range of wall coverings. She stripped off and stood naked for an instant in front of a mirror, eyeing herself critically and prodding here and there to test the firmness. She thought, Dee is right. *If push comes to shove, I can go back to the old studio work and earn a crust. That will hold it all together. I am certainly not gonna let my kids suffer, no f.....g way.* Then patting herself reassuringly on her bottom, she squeezed into bra and panties, gazing once more into the mirror to check all angles before slipping into a trendy cream-coloured jumpsuit with some comfortable trainer-style slip-ons to match. Once she had made the transformation from trendily dressed woman-about-town to comfortably, yet still stylishly dressed 'house mother', Lisa made her way downstairs towards the kitchen from which came the most delicious cooking smells.

"I see you've got the S.A.S. Survival Cook Book out again, I've never known worms and bugs taste so good as when you cook 'em; we ought to get you to educate the school dinner ladies. I'll phone that Jamie Oliver in the morning, after I've spoken to the kids' Principal. Seriously though, it smells fantastic. Are you sure it's not gonna be fattening? Don't look at me like that, love... I know... I'll get the wine!"

Lisa came back with a bottle and when she had opened it she put placemats and cutlery on the kitchen table, then pouring two glasses of the Chianti, handed one to Hilary and took a first approving gulp, then chinked her glass against Hilary's with a sigh and said, "Cheers!. I needed that. The kids are all 'uptight' because of the 'grief' they're getting over Rory's bit of trouble and even the girls have been 'aving a go at me about him being so selfish and that. I almost had a punch-up over it at the health club. It has just been one of those days."

"I thought the children were a bit withdrawn when they came in. I could hardly get a word out of them when I gave them their meal. That's not like them because they are normally so enthusiastic about school."

"That's right, and it takes a lot to get through to Gavin, bless him. That's where he takes after his dad."

Hilary bit her lip, not for the first time when Rory's name came up, and concealing what she felt, she commiserated with Lisa. "You've all got a lot on your plates, but Mr. Stafford seems to be able to let it wash all over him and carry on like nothing had happened. I don't know how he does it. He must have a really thick skin."

In her mind Hilary knew that he was just plain thick, 'no sense, no feelings' as the saying goes, but would not allow herself to say so, for fear of upsetting dear Lisa. Lisa, on the other hand, could not see this and still held her husband in the same regard as when she fell for him, almost to the point of idolatry. She answered Hilary in her usual innocent way. "Not you as well. It sounds like you're having a go at him now, that's not like you. You don't have a bad word for anyone, usually. Anyway, I thought we were special mates. Who can I rely on if you're not on my side?"

Hilary could see that Lisa was close to tears now, the last thing she had intended. She knew that neither she nor anyone else could drive a wedge between Lisa and her Ror'. *He must have something about him*, she thought. *All I know is that every time he looks at himself in the mirror he is transported to the Isle of You.* She chuckled inwardly. She stretched out a consoling arm and rested it on Lisa's shoulder, softly brushing a teardrop from her cheek with her other hand.

"Don't upset yourself, I was only remarking about his ability to rise above it all, that's all. He would have been great in the S.A.S., because nothing seems to rattle him."

"He has always been that way; I think it is down to his mum and dad spoiling him. You see he was one of twins, but the other one was stillborn and it seems that it was not completely formed, if you know what I mean. Tragic, really. I guess *they*, and nature, compensated by giving *him* everything. Anyway, that is why he is spoilt and so 'self-obsessed', I hope I got that right, I've heard it said often enough so I should do."

"That's awful, I didn't realise. That would explain a good deal. Anyway, this food is just about ready to eat, so let's get it eaten! I don't know about you but I'm ravenous, I haven't eaten since I came back from my run at 1200 hours, sorry, I mean midday. Are you ready?"

Lisa nodded and gave Hilary an encouraging smile whilst holding out two warm plates for her to serve up their pasta meal.

"It's ok, love. I am alright, besides, I always feel so much better when I'm back home pouring out my troubles to you. By the way, do you want salad with that?"

"It's alright, I've done it. *I'll* bring it over, you get started."

They enjoyed the lasagne, as they always did on a Monday, accompanied as it was by a glass or two of red wine. Their conversation concentrated mainly on what Lisa and the other girls had bought at the shops. Lisa had become more relaxed with the help of the wine as she told Hilary how she and the girls had gone from one shop after the other in their relentless pursuit of the latest fashions.

"Y'know, it's amazing what you can do with the help of a little piece of plastic! Clever little card. It's like magic! For instance... first you enter your favourite clothes shop, pick up a beautiful floral print dress that says £450 on the price tag, take it to a little girl at a desk, she smiles, she takes the bit of plastic, flashes it at a machine, asks you to sign a slip of paper or put a secret number into that same machine and the next thing y'know you are strolling out of same shop, with said dress, and on to the next one in search of the shoes to go with it! If that's not magic, love, then tell me what is? By the way, I want to see you try it on later to make sure it fits you, and the shoes, just in case." Hilary was taken aback and her face showed it. Before she could speak Lisa said, "Don't look so surprised, I thought I would treat you to something new, as a change from giving you all my old 'cast-offs'. It's just my way of saying thank you for being so good, especially with the kids; they are spoilt so rotten by their dad, though they would appreciate seeing a bit more of *him* and a bit less of his money." Then steering away from the subject of the absent Rory, she carried on. "So, when we've cleared away we'll have our own little fashion show, alright love?"

Hilary was touched and close to tears; she had been completely knocked off her feet by Lisa's largesse and after several moments more, she blurted out, "I don't know what to say, I'm so..."

Lisa stopped her in mid-sentence and said, "Well don't say anything until you've tried it all on, you may not like it."

"I'm sure I will. I always like your choice in clothes, it is so feminine, I always feel so good in it. People expect me to be 'butch' just because of what I am."

"Oh yeah, and what exactly are you? Have you got

a little secret? Is there something you haven't told us then?"

"You know what I mean. My job, being a minder to you and your offspring!"

"I'm just teasing, you know I am, love. Now if you're supposed to be looking out for me, do your job and pour us both a drop more of that red stuff."

"I'm not sure I should, you seem to have had enough, already."

"Here, I'll say when I've had enough and you'll really know when I've had enough because I'll be on the floor saying it to your feet."

At this they exploded into fits of laughter. Lisa got up from the table, shuffled across to one of the sofas and plonked herself down on it. Hilary, meanwhile, gave up trying to pour the wine and sank back onto her chair; in so doing she splashed some over her sweater and jeans.

"You do come out with some funny things at times but now look what you've made me do!"

"Never mind, there's more where that came from. I'll go and get some."

"I wasn't talking about spilling the wine; I was talking about me. Look, I'm soaked through!"

She looked across at Lisa to see her bury her face in her hands and her shoulders jerking up and down with laughter, then, realising she was joking, said, "Another one of your little jokes, at my expense. Well you wanna watch I don't come over there and sort you out, madam."

"Uh! Uh! Not in your state, misses, we'd better get

you upstairs and changed into something drier. In fact, now's a good time to try on the new stuff, so do as your mummy says and go and get out of those wet things. I'll come up after I've opened another bottle."

Hilary stared at her hard and long, feigning anger, then shrugged her shoulders and doing as she was told, went up to her room. Lisa gathered herself and went to the wine rack and selected another bottle. Once she had opened it and filled two fresh glasses, she balanced them precariously in one hand, went over to where she had left the shopping, picked up the bags and made her way up to Hilary's bedroom. This was at the opposite side of the stairs from the family's rooms, sharing the corridor with two guest bedrooms. She attempted a knock on the door but it was slightly ajar, so she walked in just as Hilary was taking off her wine-stained bra.

"I see it soaked all the way through then, ne'mind, I got you underwear too, love. Y'can try them on as well, while you're at it. God, you should be really proud of your figure, it's fabulous. I'll bet you drove the other 'squaddies' wild with those 'boys', didn't you? Talk about standing to attention, I bet they did an' all! Anyway, there you are, sort that lot out. Anything you don't like I'll have. Hey, what's the matter? Have I put my foot in it with my big gob, again?"

Lisa had dropped the bags onto Hilary's queen-sized bed but she noticed Hilary had turned away slightly.

"No, no, it just reminded me when you mentioned the army and boys. I was actually going to marry one of them, someone I met through the regiment. I didn't see a lot of him, 'cos he was always in and out of the country. He was involved in 'special ops' or something similar. We were very much in love and wanted to get married so we agreed that we'd resign and go into the private security business in a couple of years' time. Only thing is, he died in a top secret training exercise. It was all hushed up. I could not even go to the funeral. I only found out he was dead by asking after him through a fellow officer, when I hadn't heard from him for a while. The authorities were very 'jumpy' about it all."

Hilary started to cry but quickly resorted to type, reined herself in, took a large mouthful of wine, a deep breath, and then carried on as if nothing had happened.

"Anyway, thanks for the compliment, if it was a compliment, I can't really tell in your present mood." Hilary had been holding herself quite self-consciously up to this point but she was feeling more at ease now, perhaps sharing her little secret with Lisa had something to do with it, or maybe it was the wine. Whatever it was, she let her hands drop.

"Of course it was a compliment! I've never said it before but you really do have a fabulous body, love. Look at you. I *should* know, I was in the business, and if we could get you to smile a bit more you'd be very photogetic... er... photogelic. Oh, f..k it! You'd take a good picture! I might mention that to Dee Hacker sometime. Oh, and I'm really sorry about, y'know... your fiancé. You've never talked about him before, it's very sad. You nearly let yourself go then, too. Don't worry if you want to have a good cry, it's the natural thing to do, there's no-one else around. Hold on a minute, don't move, we need some more wine."

She gulped the dregs of her glass, quickly ran down stairs and returned almost as quickly with the wine bottle. When she got back Hilary was undoing the parcel that contained the bra and matching panties set. Lisa indicated for Hilary to drink some more wine and took up position on the bed with her own glass clutched in both hands.

"Ok, let the show begin. I think those are going to look great on you, the darker colours suit your skin tone best, and that's just the underwear we're talking about! Actually, that is almost a thong really, it's so small. Go on slip it on, I'll look away if you want." This, Lisa said whilst covering her eyes with the fingers of her right hand splayed open. "That's it, now the bra."

"I thought you were supposed to be looking away, lady."

"Sorry darlin', I can't help it. Jesus, Hilary, if I was a bloke I'd jump straight on your bones. That's what boys say, isn't it? I should know, I've heard Rory say it often enough. You are truly voluptuous; I can't wait to see the dress on you. It's in the Versace bag."

"Versace for me? You shouldn't have. All that money, I don't deserve this."

Hilary was shaking in anticipation and reached over for a mouthful of wine, and then she opened the bag, slowly taking out the expensive garment.

"It's beautiful, the colours are fabulous, oh, and I love it."

"Come on, try it on first. We're not gonna know whether we like it if you don't put it on, so get it on, my mouth is watering! And who said anything about money? I got it with my magic card. Remember?"

"Mouth watering! What is the matter with you, missus? Haven't you seen a woman naked before? I'm gonna have to watch you." Hilary slipped the Versace over her head and holding the bodice part up to her breasts, she asked Lisa, "Here, can you do the back up for me, please?"

Hilary's guard had dropped completely now, she was at ease standing half naked in front of her employer and enjoying the attention. Lisa put down her wine and took hold of Hilary's hand to get up off the bed, allowing herself to be gently projected towards her friend's rear, brushing her breasts playfully as she did so. Hilary halted Lisa's advance momentarily, allowing her to tweak her nipples, which were erect by now. Hilary gave her an encouraging smile. Lisa breathed in deeply, bit her bottom lip, kissed her between the shoulder blades then dutifully fastened the buttons on the back of the dress, slowly and gently smoothing out the skirt over Hilary's hips, saying more seriously now, "Why are men so different... from us girls?"

"What do you mean?"

"I mean, I'd only really had a couple of boyfriends before Rory came along, so he is the only man I've really experienced sexually. *He* is so physical with it, always in a rush and really rough, never... gentle. His mum said it seemed like he was living life for two always, one cup of tea was never enough, always had to have two. He has to have two servings of just about everything. Even when it comes to making love, once is never enough. I've had to draw the line though, could be why we only had two kids. What are you laughing at? No, I don't mean we only ever had sex twice, I mean I had to slow his gallop and I took the pill early on, otherwise God knows how many kids I'd have ended up with. Then, I'm never ready as quick as 'im to do it again. You know what I mean. Hey, you are getting really naughty, you are."

"I'm sorry; it's just the way it came out."

"What do you mean the way it came out? Have you been spying on me and my husband?"

They broke into greater fits of laughter, coming closer together and holding each other up.

"Seriously though, what's this all about, anyway?"

"Well, us girls are so much more gentle and well, different. I love all the soft, touchy-feely stuff and I've never seen you like this before, and I'm seeing you in a different light. I've only experienced your 'hard' image but you have a soft centre and can be just as vulnerable as the rest of us beneath it all, and certainly different from the men... Hold on a minute, something is missing. That one thing that sets the whole 'ensemble' off perfectly." Lisa reached for another bag from the bed and emptied the contents onto the floor in front of Hilary.

"The final piece, the 'piece of resistance'... the shoes!"

Hilary sat on the bed, pulling the dress above her knees, picked up the shoes, placed them on her feet and said with her best French accent, "I zink you'll find zat zat is the 'pièce de résistance', madam."

"And I think you'll find yourself out of a job if you come it with me, show us them shoes on and stuff your French where the monkey... Only joking, love. What do they feel like? Are they comfortable? They look great on you, fabulous long, sexy legs; by the way, they go all the way up to your elbows. I'm quite jealous, now, go on, and give us a twirl."

"How do I look, really?"

"Why not see for yourself? Have a look in the mirror." Lisa pulled her away from the bed and towards the full-length mirror on the inside of the wardrobe door. Hilary stared at her reflection and stepped back, she was overcome once again but covered up by studying her outfit from different angles, trying different poses, sashaying forward and back in the high-heeled shoes that she was not accustomed to wearing. As she was doing this Lisa took another drink of wine and muttered, "You can't prove imperfection... or is it you can't improve on perfection? I can never get it right, it means the same thing though, dunnit?"

She could see that Hilary was filling up again, so taking her hands she guided her around the bedroom in a clumsy but brave attempt at a waltz. Hilary pulled her within kissing distance and planted one on Lisa's cheek, saying, "Thank you for the beautiful outfit and for being the best employer in the world. It is only working for you that has helped me through my heartbreak, you couldn't have happened at a better time for me in that regard."

Lisa was touched and replied, "You're more than welcome, sweetheart. As I said, you've been a real rock for the kids and me too, it's just a token of my gratitude for all you've done, especially in this last week or so. Don't think any more about it, just enjoy it. Now give us a great big hug. Then we'll polish off the rest of this wine."

The girls clinched for a long time, enjoying the warmth of each other's bodies. It was Lisa who broke off, saying, "We mustn't do this." Then spotting the look of hurt on Hilary's face, she continued, "We'll crumple your lovely new dress. We don't want to ruin it before you get the chance to show it off to the world. Talking of which, we've got to arrange an occasion, a party or something to let everybody know what a beauty we've got 'ere. You can leave it to me, I'll think of something. Now take it off. 'Ere, I'll undo the back for you."

She spun Hilary round and helped her out of the Versace, placing it carefully over the back of the bedside chair. Then she placed her hands on Hilary's and directed them to her own cleavage and softly wove them around the curves, and reaching downwards to her hips she continued to caress her buttocks and inner thighs, and whispered into her friend's ear, "This is what us girls called 'workers' playtime'. We always did it on our glamour shoots so that we were at ease with one another, 'cos we often had to pose touching each other's 'parts' and look all suggestive for the camera. We'd carry on afterwards too, all soft and gentle like, nothing heavy or serious. It helped loosen inhibitions and make us feel relaxed. Especially with the ones we hadn't worked with before. Actually that is how I met my Ror'. I was on a calendar shoot with a couple of other girls and Rory walked in on us. He was doing a session for 'footy' boots in the studio next door; he got lost on the way back from the loo, so he said. You'd think all 'is

Christmases and birthdays had come on the same day by the look on his face. He said that it was most men's fantasies to see a couple of girls doing things to each other. What he actually said was, 'to see 'em touch each other's 'baps' and 'buns'.' Anyway, we were married within a year and the rest is history, as they say."

Hilary cringed inwardly at the thought but she did not let it spoil the moment, as she clung tighter to Lisa before starting to replicate the movements Lisa had shown her previously but this time using just the tips of her fingers of one hand and indulging herself with the other.

Lisa, who was enjoying the moment, continued. "In fact, he's always said he fancied watching me get it off with another girl. So we don't have to worry if he was to burst in on us now, do we?"

On hearing this, Hilary withdrew both hands and shoved Lisa away from her.

Lisa burst out laughing again and said, "Only joking love, you should see the look on your face. It's a picture!" As she was saying it she started to strip off her cat-suit. "Anyway, it's not fair. 'Ere you are half naked and 'ere's me fully clothed, where are my manners? That's better, now you can come over 'ere and you can give me one of your fabulous foot massages." Lisa was all but naked by now and pulling Hilary towards the bed, she added, "That will do for a start. Maybe we should lock your door though."

## 6

Meanwhile, back at Linda Morris's flat, Rory Stafford had woken up. He was totally disorientated and it took several moments before he realised where he was and what he had done. He fumbled in the dark for the bedside lamp and switched it on. He checked the time on the alarm clock; it was three minutes after midnight. He wandered around the flat in his semi-naked state and discovered Linda, who was still sound asleep on the sofa. Rory resisted the urge to touch her, realising that she was virtually fully clothed. He continued on into the kitchen and finding the light switch, turned it on. Then he checked out the fridge but was not tempted by anything in it, being mostly healthy, low-fat food, which did not appeal to him, so he closed the door and went back to the bedroom, collecting his scattered clothes as he did so. He quickly scrambled into his training kit, scribbled 'if you fance doin it agen eres me mobial no.' on the telephone pad; left the flat, not bothering to switch the lights off and closing the door noisily behind him. His immediate thought on leaving the car park of the apartment building was, *I wonder if Osman's Kebab Shop is open still?*

Rory pulled his car to a halt at the litter-strewn pavement in front of the dimly lit kebab shop. He could see movement inside so he got out and tried the door. A voice sounded from the back of the shop. "I soory mate, we closse now, no good knockin' dow' doors. I phones the pleece." The shop owner looked up from his cleaning and spotted Rory. "Oh! Mista Stamford, it iss you. Wai' a mini' I les you in."

Osman opened the door wide enough for Rory to slip through, and slip he very nearly did, on the greasy floor. Osman was delighted to see the star of his favourite football team in his shop again and accorded him the same friendly, gushing welcome that he did every time Rory favoured him with a visit, which as it happens was twice a week on average.

"Alrigh' my little Kiki Dee, ow is ev'ry think wid you? Hey, you trennin late thiss days, innit?"

Rory wasn't sure whether Osman had meant to say Chick-a-Dee and didn't really care because he had more pressing needs, so he let it pass, and ignoring the late training enquiry, asked Osman if he could have a double 'Donner' and chips. "If you waits I put samfin in the mecrawave for yo, 'cos ebry think he turn off, orright?"

Rory nodded and waited for Osman to sort out something edible and hot enough to eat. Whilst he was waiting Rory mused on the fact that he had visited this particular eatery for as long as he could remember, but despite this he was no nearer to knowing from which part of the planet Osman's accent actually came. He knew for sure that he wasn't a local lad. Osman could not have been happier at having a 'salavrity' in his establishment and spoke excitedly about the mid-week performance of the Rovers, ignorant of the fact that he was talking about the team from the other side of the town, the one that Rory *didn't* play for. Of course, this was totally lost on Rory, as he smiled and nodded in agreement, blissfully unaware.

He could hardly understand a word the other man uttered anyway. This would not have mattered to Rory as long as he thought that Osman was talking about his team and himself in particular. This one-way conversation carried on for several minutes as the 'mecrawave' worked its magic on the reconstituted goodies that Osman had gathered together for Rory's delectation and anticipated delight. In the meantime, Rory tried to sneak a look at himself in the greasy mirror above the now cooling barbecue grill at the back of the shop, but his view was obstructed by a poster advertising a concert in Castertown public park by 'Art and Sol'. Barcaster's own Jewish rhythm & blues duo. Rory thought to himself, *Hum. That's interesting... They've stuck a poster over the mirror there, and they didn't 'ave to use no sticky tape.*

The clunk of the antiquated microwave's door slamming rudely brought Rory out of his little muse and back to more serious matters. The food was shuffled off the microwave plate and onto a sheet of greaseproof paper that was being supported by several sheets of white wrapping paper. As Osman carried out this manoeuvre he said, "Hey Mr. Stamford, y'knose when I is in Germany I gos to de barbara's for gets me David Backham's 'aircuts, y'knose what the barbara 'is name iss? 'Is name iss called Herr Kutz." As usual Osman broke into fits of laughter and Rory did likewise, as he had every other time he'd heard it, still not understanding the joke, or perhaps that it *was* a joke, for that matter. However, as Osman had mentioned Germany, he told the only German story he knew, and when he had said the bit about his mate bursting in on his wife and the German footballer, Osman asked, "Blimey Mr. Stamford, what did your friend he say to this German, the footballer?"

To which Rory replied, "I don't know, but I think his name was Hans Hoffer!"

There was no reaction from Osman except a remark to the effect that you could not trust anybody these days. When the kebab shop owner turned round again he had the fully wrapped parcel of food in his hands.

Rory's eyes lit up at the sight of the package that Osman now thrust towards him and he gratefully accepted it saying, "Cheers Osman, can I pay ya later? I ain't got no money on me, 'cos I'm in me trainin' kit."

Osman nodded in confirmation that it would be ok, muttering something Rory understood to mean that 'he shouldn't try to leave town' and on seeing the kebab shop owner wink and laugh, joined in once again. Rory thanked him and shuffled carefully across the sticky floor towards the door. Osman overtook him and held the door open for his best customer and saw him safely off the premises. Rory thought to himself, *I still don't know how he does that; he must have special treads on them Jesus boots.*

He propped himself against his car and investigated the contents of Osman's package. It was hot and steaming and even to the trained eye it would have been difficult to detect the origin of any of the contents, but to Rory's it was 'Manna from Heaven', and he gorged himself, barely stopping for breath until every last morsel had been consumed. Once he had finished, he wiped his greasy hands on the wrapping, screwed it up and dumped it unceremoniously next to the waste bin at the edge of the pavement, farting loudly as he did so. Walking back to the car, he finished the cleaning job on his hands by rubbing them up and down on his shorts and track top. This complete, he climbed into the car, put the key in the ignition, turned the engine over and roared off.

# 7

The bell at the ambulance station rang harshly and very loudly, interrupting Keith Gardner's dream-filled slumber.

"Shit. Finally, I was going to get my wicked way with Madonna. I'd got rid of those poxy cones from her chest, and she was read... Hello, ambulance service. An accident... a sports car... Slow down... please... Tell me exactly where... How many people involved? You think only one... Right, we'll send an ambulance immediately... Have you phoned the police? No, that's ok I'll inform them straight away."

Keith summoned the on-duty paramedics and despatched them to the scene of the accident and then notified the Castertown Police of what had happened. After fulfilling his duty, he returned to his dream to try to pick up the pieces with Madonna.

Meanwhile, the paramedics had piled their equipment and themselves into the ambulance and were speeding towards the scene of the accident, lights flashing and siren filling the relatively still night air with its piercing sound.

The roads were fairly quiet so they arrived at the

spot where the vehicle had come off the road in pretty quick time. John Fulton pulled the ambulance to halt a few yards behind what looked like a green sports car and he and his fellow paramedic Doug Winter jumped out with their bags in hand. As they approached the car, Doug said, "No other vehicle involved then, from the look of it. Jeeez, look at the length of that skid mark and bugger me, look what he ran into!"

After a deep intake of breath, John answered Doug. "A pile of telegraph poles! God, look where that one landed and it's got a metal tip too, that *is* nasty. He was probably going too fast on the bend; it's not the first time that has happened at his spot. If you ask me though they got the gradient wrong when they built this road. That doesn't help. Lucky though, he hasn't gone through the windscreen. Thank God for airbags, eh?"

They were at the side of the car now and taking stock of the situation. The driver was as pale as a sheet, suggesting that he had lost a lot of blood and was slipping in and out of consciousness. The first thing they did was to try and stabilise his condition and then decide if he could be moved safely.

At this point the police arrived on the scene and started to talk to the young couple who had discovered the accident. The paramedics called to the two policemen to give them a hand. They looked over to see Doug and John attempting to pull a twenty-foot-long telegraph pole from the engine area of the car. Doug called out again. "It's gone all the way through to the driving seat, and it's the one thing that's stopping us from getting him out. I reckon if we all pull together we'll be able to haul it back far enough. It's between his legs. Ouch! All together now, one – two – three – heave! It's no good... I think we need a bit more help, call that couple over."

With everybody's cooperation they were able to shift the pole far enough to enable them to extricate the driver and get him onto a stretcher, but not before one of the policemen whispered to his colleague excitedly, "Here, look who it is. It's Rory Stafford and he's still got his shorts on, I bet he's been playing away from home again! Y'know he was in my team at school, don't you? I could have been a pro myself but I wanted to be a policeman more than anything else in the world."

The older policeman nodded enthusiastically and said, "Yeah, son, and if you keep at it you might make one, one day. Now give us a hand to get this trolley back up onto the road. Whoever it is, he's in a bad way and these lads have got to get him to A&E at C.G.H., A.S.A.P., ok?"

"Ye....ah, I think so, though I don't know what that last bit was all about."

"Never mind, son, you'll pick it up, give it a few more years on the force. By the way, I do know who he is. I've picked him up and dropped him home often enough, when he's been pickled. His wife is as good as gold, always makes us a cuppa. It's a shame 'cos he's a great footballer, been my favourite for as long as I can remember. We've kept quiet about his 'shenanigans' over the years, for her sake. She puts up with a lot from him and still worships the ground he plays on, or the ground he's got coming to him if we don't look lively."

Doug Winter drew an impatient breath, counted to three, and they hoisted the stretcher onto the trolley up on the road and safely into the ambulance. John Fulton got up behind the wheel of the ambulance whilst Doug tended Rory in the back. They sped off in the direction of Castertown General Hospital, leaving the policemen to their job of ringing off the accident area and taking measurements to assist in the task of establishing how the crash had happened.

John Fulton called on ahead to the accident and emergency department, to inform them of the condition and the identity of their passenger. When they arrived at the hospital there was quite a buzz about the place, more so than on a normal Monday night with its handful of casualties from the 'Oldies' night at the 'Golden Blades' ice rink. There was a small crowd awaiting them as they pulled up, none of which were medical staff. The whisper had obviously gone further than the A&E department because one or two autograph hunters were in evidence. Within a few seconds of the ambulance arriving a small team of doctors and nurses had burst through the crowd and were busy attending to the prostrate figure of Rory Stafford and assessing his injuries. Instructions were being issued even as he was being transferred to a hospital trolley and everybody went about their job in a very business-like manner. A rough voice from somewhere near the back of the crowd called out, "Any chance of an autograph, Rory?"

The crowd turned on the man, who was already in a wheelchair. Meanwhile the medical crew hurried on into the hospital proper.

# 8

Rory had been in the operating theatre for several hours already. During this time Lisa had called a taxi, dropped the children off at her mother's and taken Hilary to the hospital with her (on Hilary's insistence). The two of them were now standing in the reception of the A&E department waiting to hear what Rory's chances were. They both held mugs of hot coffee as they hovered near the desk. Neither was drinking. They stood there in silence, at first staring up the corridor then towards the desk, and then at each other. This continued for a while until the reception nurse said, "Why don't you take a seat and drink your coffees? You both look as though you need it, and don't worry, Mr. Stafford is in very good hands. Mr. Khan is the best surgeon there is."

She ushered them towards the waiting area and the girls responded, positioning themselves so that they would see if anyone were to come for them. Hilary gave Lisa a comforting smile and held her hand, encouraging her to drink her coffee.

"I don't know what I'll do if I lost my Ror', and the poor kids, what about them? They idolise him."

"Now why are you talking like that? It hasn't come

to that yet, they didn't say it was life threatening, they said he had to be operated on at the earliest. Don't think the worst, he is as strong as an ox, two oxes, or should that be oxen? You said as much yourself and he's a fighter, he'll be alright, I'm sure of it." There was an old couple sitting opposite them, the woman with her ankle strapped and her husband holding her skate blades next to his own.

"No good looking that way, dear," the old lady said. "They're the toilets."

Lisa realised that she had lost orientation when they had moved from the desk to sit down. She didn't want to get into conversation so she just acknowledged the woman with a smile and turned to face *up* the corridor once more. At this point, one of the double doors she was now looking at opened and a man who looked like he might be a doctor (You cannot tell these days because they don't all wear the white coats anymore...*ed.*) rushed through it. Lisa leapt to her feet and made towards him but when he skated right past her she realised that he was heading straight for the men's toilets.

Hilary reached out to Lisa and sat her down once again, resting her head on her shoulder for reassurance.

There was some activity going on behind the curtains in the A&E department, as people took it in turns to be seen. Lisa noticed that the old dear had been taken off and given the attention she had been waiting so patiently for.

It was a good four hours and several un-sipped coffees before Lisa and Hilary were to hear of Rory's condition. When the news came it came in a very bizarre way.

"Mike... Mike Conway, that is you, isn't it?" Hilary called out, recognising the doctor emerging from the room at the top of the corridor and now walking towards them. She jumped up and met him halfway, leaving Lisa asleep and slouched forward. "The last time I saw you were in Iraq. How are you?"

"Good God, Hilary... It's you! Here and in the flesh? That's right, Iraq, I was just arriving and you were leaving. It was pretty tough on all concerned out there. I mean we were well looked after and all that but it was terribly nerve-wracking. What with the water and electricity problems and not to mention the dire sanitation arrangements. How we didn't lose more than we saved, God only knows!"

"Yeah, I was very pleased to get away in one piece, I can tell you. Grateful for the fact that we were kept in reserve and got home without suffering the fate of some of our guys. Anyway, how are you? I must say you're looking in fine fettle."

"I am really fine, thank you. Been back here a couple of months now. Oh, by the way I was so sorry to hear about your fiancé. He was a great bloke. I mean I'm *really* sorry. So what are you doing now? Last I heard you were in private security."

"Yes thanks, everybody was so understanding when it happened, except the MOD. I'm fine, in good health, at least, but no, I can't really complain. I'm working for a real sweetheart, looking out for her and the two children. Her husband is a local football hero. By the way, what are you doing here this time of day, an emergency?"

"Oh my god yes, thanks for reminding me. I'm assisting Mr. Khan with a bit of a 'tricky' one, actually. I came out to look for the wife of the guy we're operating on. Hey, wait a minute; did you say a footballer's wife? Oh dear, it's not Rory Stafford, is it? It is, isn't it? And I've been standing here casually going over old times with you, for God's sake. I got quite carried away, but then I daresay you have that effect on most men. I must say it is a real pleasure to see you again, Hilary."

Hilary took Mike's hand and pulled him away from where Lisa was still dozing and asked, "How bad is it, Mike? Can you give me an idea so we can soften the blow, maybe?"

"I don't know, this is a tough one. Y'see, there's good news and there's bad news."

"Now come on, Mike, this is no time for the amputated legs and the slippers joke!"

"I am deadly serious, and I am frankly surprised that you could suggest that I would stoop so low as to joke about these things."

"I'm sorry; it's just that I'd had a particularly pleasant evening, coupled with the surprise of meeting you here. It's probably the wine talking. Please don't mind me."

"Well, that's ok. The good news is that he is going to live but there are certain complications."

"What sort of complications, Mike? Can you tell me? I could help you break it to her; she is very dear to me."

"I'm sorry, this is awfully difficult for me because

it's a very personal and sensitive issue; it is not a situation that I've experienced before. In fact, I think I can say without fear of contradiction that in my fifteen years as a surgeon, it is a unique case. I've cleaned up a few messed up bodies in my time but this is totally different. Mr. Khan has sent me out to prepare the ground because what he is going to want to know is that he has the full support of all, before he proceeds further."

"Mike, you are not making much sense. What is this entire support thing about? Please tell me more, I want to help."

"No, I have to speak to the lady herself. As I said, it is very sensitive and very personal, in fact a very intimate issue, something only the husband and the wife can resolve between them. The only problem is that only one of them is conscious and the other one is having to be kept unconscious long enough to be operated on in order to save his life. So which is the wife?"

"Here she is, I'll just rouse her. Mrs. Stafford, I mean Lisa. Wake up, the doctor wants to speak to you. He says everything is going to be alright but he wants to talk to you about Mr. Stafford. Do you feel up to it?"

Lisa pulled herself up as Mike Conway sat down on the seat next to her. He took her hand gently and said, "Mrs. Stafford, my name is Mike Conway. I've been assisting Mr. Khan. He has asked me to come and have a word with you as he thinks you are going to have to make a very big decision concerning your husband and yourself."

"What do you mean? You're not asking me whether you should turn off his life support machine or something, are you?"

"No, no. It's nothing like that. It's just that he's had a really nasty knock down below and..."

But before he could continue Lisa shouted out, "Oh no, not his legs! That alone will be enough to kill him, if you tell him he can't play football again."

"No it's higher up, it's his, how shall I put it? God, this is difficult and I haven't got to the hardest part yet. It's his private parts. I'm sorry, that wasn't meant as a pun, by the way. Oh God, what am I saying? I mean... ah, Mr. Khan!" Mike's voice amplified as Mr. Khan walked into the sitting area with some of his team in his sway.

"Mr. Conway, is this Mrs. Stafford?" He offered Hilary his hand, she shook it and as she did she introduced him to Lisa.

"Oh right, yes, Mrs. Stafford. I guess Mr. Conway has told you the hard facts about your husband's injury."

"No, but I get the feeling that he was just about to. What's this about my Ror's private bits?"

Mr. Khan gave Lisa his warmest smile and said, "Mrs. Stafford, I think we should sit down, we have a lot to talk about. In fact, I think it would be a good idea if we go into that office over there. It will be more private."

He led the group past the reception desk and into the room behind it. When they had all passed through, Mike Conway closed the door. Mr. Khan continued. "Your husband has had a very serious and unfortunate accident. He lost a considerable amount of blood at the scene of his crash but thanks to swift action by the paramedics and my staff we were able to save his life. However, that has created a more serious problem, not that there can be a much more serious one than saving a person's life. What I am trying to say is that during the course of our examination we found that you husband's manhood had been totally crushed and is now beyond any practical or functional repair."

Lisa and Hilary gasped in unison (Lisa had insisted her friend stay with her throughout, whatever was to be discussed). Lisa anxiously enquired, "What does that mean exactly? I know that when someone kicked him there a couple of years ago, it was a long while before he could use it properly but didn't he make up for it after?" Lisa coloured up slightly when she realised everyone was staring at her, aghast. She continued. "What are you saying? Does it mean that he won't be able to use it again for anything, not even peeing?"

"I think you are grasping the nub of what I am saying. It does mean that it has no further useful function and that if we leave it as it is, it will deteriorate and kill him. That part of it is far too difficult for me to explain for you to comprehend completely, I'm sorry. It means that we shall have to remove it completely. Now, Mr. Conway probably told you that there is some good news."

"Don't tell me, you can transplant another one onto him from a dead man. No! No! I can't even think about that, it would be like having a dead ma..."

"Mrs. Stafford, get a grip... control yourself. You are getting hysterical. Sadly, there is nothing like that that we can even dream of, ethical reasons, for starters. Even artificial ones are still on the drawing board, that is to say, still at the design stage. I am sorry to say that there is very little left that we can do other than to operate and create a kind of neutral organ that he could utilise to do the usual ablutions, so to speak. Now I am speaking with certain expertise in this field and can advise that this will guarantee a very good quality of life, as it will enable him to do all the other physical things that he enjoys doing normally, even getting back to playing his sport. Naturally, I shall need your permission to go ahead with this procedure, but I reiterate that not doing it will kill your husband anyway. If not right away, it will eventually. In my opinion we have no choice. However, I shall leave you to think about it and return in a short while." Mr. Khan and his entourage left the room, and Lisa and Hilary turned to each other and stared blankly. After a minute or so Hilary broke the silence.

"I'm not sure what I'd do. Having said that, I would not want to be responsible for condemning a person to an early death by letting them do nothing. So what is the answer? I think what I mean is there is only one answer. What do you think, Lisa? You've got to tell them what to do."

Lisa sat with her head in her hands as she agonised over what also seemed to her to be an obvious decision. She suddenly burst out, "F.....g hell, Hilary! What are the choices? I mean f.....g hell, I've got no choice. I ain't gonna say no and sit here and watch my

Ror' die, am I? What kind of person do they think I am? I want my husband back in one piece."

Hilary shook her head then nodded in quick succession as Lisa quickly added, "No, maybe not in one piece."

Hilary smiled and nodded again as Lisa continued. "Well yes, I mean in one piece. Alright, with one piece missing, but I still want him back! Whatever shape he's in. That's what I mean, for f..k's sake!"

Hilary gave up shaking and nodding and went over to Lisa and said, "That's it then, we'll get them back and tell them to stop wasting time and get on with the job of patching up Mr. Stafford. I'll tell the nurse to call them."

Lisa slumped back into her chair and called after Hilary, "Tell them to just get on with it, love. Say we've wasted enough time talking about it, let's see some action!"

Hilary contemplated the picture of the new Rory and Lisa and 'action', then scolded herself for her wickedness of thought.

Mr. Khan returned to the room and produced a form for Lisa to sign giving him and his team the authority to carry out whatever surgery was necessary to return Rory Stafford to as normal a life as possible, being fully aware of the circumstances and risks involved. He tried to reassure her that his team was the best there is, as she studied the form in front of her. Finally, Lisa sighed resignedly and signed the paper. Thus becoming the signatory who consigned the dignity of her Rory. (That's clever, I think...*ed.*)

Mr. Khan thanked her, saying, "This could be a

long night, what is left of it, for all of us."

At this point he took his leave of the girls with one last word of encouragement. "Try to relax, get some rest and... er... keep your pecker up. If only for your husband's sake, you must be strong for him."

This was too much for Lisa; her emotions were at bursting point and suddenly the floodgates opened and she was reduced to a sobbing wreck. Hilary did not know whether to laugh or cry at Mr. Khan's last remark, knowing that at the back of it there was a genuine and well-intentioned sentiment. She grabbed Lisa and wrapped her in her arms and softly patting her on the shoulder, made her as comfortable as possible on the waiting room couch, whilst snuggling up alongside her, both in the foetal position. Neither of them was too relaxed but Lisa had insisted on staying at the hospital so as to be on hand, should anything go wrong. Such was their state of exhaustion though, that they were both asleep within minutes, despite the discomfort.

# 9

In the operating theatre the routine preparations were well advanced and both Mr. Khan and Mike Conway were scrubbed up ready to go.

"Did you play any golf over the weekend, Mike? Or did you succumb to the weather and just watch the rugby on telly like me. It was a 'belter' of a game, shame either side had to lose. Still, the Aussies did and I think it sets England up quite well for the Six Nations in the New Year."

Mike answered, "As a matter of fact I did play, and managed a full round before the real rain set in. I'll bet it was a quagmire at Twickers, wasn't it? Would have suited our boys better, I guess."

"Yeah, it's funny though, because the England 'ladies' threw it around a lot better than their Aussie counterparts did. This is unusual for a Northern Hemisphere team."

"Do I detect a Southern Hemisphere bias here, old chap?"

"Perish the thought. Why, I have lived here so long I almost regard myself as an honorary Englishman. I have to make an exception when it comes to the rugby though."

"Yes, I guess it makes loyalties difficult being married to a Scot, too."

"Well it doesn't help but *they're* not exactly setting the rugby world on fire at the moment, so it's not so bad."

"What about the boys, who do they support?"

"Why, England of course, and that is where Moira and I are outnumbered, since there are the three of them. Anyway, what kind of golf are you playing these days? Has it improved since I took that £50 off you last month?"

"As a matter of fact I am playing the best golf of my life at the moment. I am nearly ready to win that money back." The two surgeons turned their focus towards the unconscious form in front of them and started procedure for removing the battlefield that was Rory Stafford's private parts. The anaesthetist gave them a friendly thumbs-up, and in turn they acknowledged him and the rest of the team.

Mr. Khan said, "Ok, let's see what we can do for this poor chap, shall we?" Then sounded his favourite battle cry, "Heads down and in we go."

There was no further chat for quite some time while they examined and re-examined the mess in front of them and started to cut away and remove the damaged, almost unrecognisable organ and accompanying parts. Taking their time and working in a very measured way, taking extra care over every little step. (I take it that that is a pun...*ed.*)

Mr. Khan sighed in dismay at the sight of Rory's

bereft nether regions. "I am afraid to say Mr. Stafford will not be singing bass in the future. In fact I'm not sure what voice he will be pitching in."

This introduced a bit of levity to an otherwise intense atmosphere within the operating theatre, and normally signalled to the others that the most difficult and intricate part of the proceedings was over, and that now would be time to commence the 'closing-up' process. However, they were only halfway through what could still be a pretty tricky situation which meant that they had to stay further focussed even though they had been working for several hours already.

Whilst he considered the next step, Mr. Khan asked Mike, "Do you really think your golf has improved that much that you can give me a run for my money? Sorry, I mean your money, of course. Could you rest your hand just there whilst I try to peel this back, so that we can see what we have to work with? I must warn you that I've hit a fresh vein of form myself recently. Sorry, no pun intended, now where have I heard that before? Seriously though, only last week over at Kissingbourne on that short hole, the one that takes you over the pond. I managed a Ho....leeeee Shit! What is that? Mike, David, take a closer look and tell me what you see! I do not believe my eyes!"

# 10

"Wake up, Mrs. Stafford. Mrs. Stafford, please wake up."

The voice came ever closer now as the alien floated down the ramp from the huge spacecraft. The signpost in the background indicated Roswell. Its long green fingers alighted on her shoulders and started to rock her backwards and forwards, at first gently but then with a measure of urgency as Lisa tried to resist, until finally...

"Ah, Mrs. Stafford, I am sorry but I had to wake you. Something has come... there has been a development."

The voice was coming from a light-skinned individual in total contrast to the luminescent green of the alien that had tried to abduct her *and* came as quite a shock to Lisa.

Seeing that Lisa was not fully with it, Mike Conway then tapped Hilary on the shoulder. At this Hilary sprang up and in a split second had him in an arm lock with his head pushed into the sofa in exactly the same spot she had occupied that split second before.

"Hilary, you can let go now, I'm not going to do

you any harm. It is me, Mike, Mike Conway. I would show you my face but you are very nearly sitting on it!"

Hilary slackened her hold on Mike but did not let go until she had looked around her and realised where they were. Then she helped him up, gently smoothed out his wrinkled shirt, picked up his fallen stethoscope and said, "I am so sorry, Mike. You caught me unawares. Old habits die hard, as they say. I wish there was something I could say to make it up to you."

"As a matter of fact there is. You can say you will have dinner with me sometime."

"This is rather sudden and something of a surprise."

"Well, 'tit for tat' I'd call it. Just say... yes." Whilst this was happening Lisa had gathered herself and was appraising the situation.

"Did I hear you right, Mr. Conway?" she enquired, rubbing her eyes as she did so.

"Yes, I just asked your friend out on a date. I hope that you will use your authority as her employer to persuade her to say yes."

Lisa registered fake disdain and then responded. "I was talking about my husband; you said something about a development, that sounds good. Come on, tell me the latest. By the way, I think you should go out with him, Hilary, he's obviously got a soft spot for you and he is quite a catch."

"Never mind that, I'll sort out Mr. Conway," Hilary chided with a smile.

"I reckon you've already sorted him out. I think he'll be seeking compensation now. Seriously Mr.

Conway, what is the latest on my Rory?"

Mike took a deep breath of resignation, exhaled and said, "Again, there is good news and bad news, I'm afraid." He hesitated whilst he chose the words to describe Rory's condition. "Remember that Mr. Khan said that we'd be able to repair Mr. Stafford to the point where his life would be normal except for his sexuality?" He hesitated again before saying, "Actually, would you give us another minute please?" He took Hilary out of the room and with both hands clutching hers, begged, "You've got to do your best to keep her calm when I tell her this."

From inside the room Lisa called out, "Hey, I hope you two are not discussing your love life again."

Mike answered, "No!" Then, more softly, "Not *our* love life, just give us a minute, I need to explain something to Hilary." Turning to Hilary again, he continued. "I don't know how the hell I can put it into words, so I'll use metaphor to explain to you and Mrs. Sta... what're you doing? Put your hands down! I said metaphor NOT semaphore! Look, when we removed the poor chap's parts we discovered a... a... a kind of orifice, you know, an opening, a hole to put it crudely. This meant that we didn't have to leave him in neutral. Yes, I can see you're interested now. It means he'll get his sex drive back. But he'll be driving a convertible. In fact, He should be riding horses side saddle from now on." Mike was so animated now that he was almost hysterical. "He'll be looking for sizes ten, twelve, or fourteen... not small, medium, or large! He'll be choosing between sensible shoes and high heels! It'll be all about B cups or double Ds! DO you hear what I am saying?"

"Mike, unless I miss my guess completely, what you are saying is-very-loud-and-very-clear... that there are now two Ms. Staffords. Lisa and her ex-husband... Aurora! You and Mr. Khan have turned Him into a... Her. A w-o-m-a-n!"

Mike nodded repeatedly and at that point Lisa burst out of the office, saying, "You two look all excited, have you fixed up that dinner date, or is it something more earth-shattering than that?"

Mike and Hilary shook their heads then nodded and grinned nervously in response. Hilary walked towards Lisa, took her arm and guided her back to her seat, ready to break the news.

She began. "Now I want you to stay calm. Apparently Mr. Stafford came through the surgery very well. Though things are a little different from what Mr. Khan expected, which is not altogether a bad thing. You see Mr. Stafford *will* be able to have sex again."

A huge smile appeared on Lisa's lips, but just as she was about to celebrate her good fortune, Hilary continued. "But not necessarily with you."

"What do you mean? He hasn't turned him into a queer, has he?"

Hilary shook her head. "No, not a queer, no."

Before she could continue Lisa burst out, "If he's not a queer, not a man like before, what the f.....g hell is he?"

"Well the truth is, He is now a... SHE!"

*

By the time Lisa regained consciousness Mr. Khan

was back in the room. At the sight of his face up close to hers she shouted at the top of her voice, "What have you done to my husband? First you tell me he won't be able to fulfil his normal male functions, as if that wasn't bad enough, now you are telling me he'll be carrying out effing female functions. Who's gonna wear the trousers in our relationship NOW?"

Hilary thought, *Well he always had trouble keeping his on anyway... so problem solved.*

Mr. Khan, struggling to keep his composure, replied, "Now, I know this is very difficult for you to digest and I realise it has been a long night for you, as it has been for all of us, but we must approach this with a reasoned attitude. I want you to consider your husband's position and indeed his condition; after all, it is *he* who has experienced the trauma of a lifesaving operation. We have to think how we can best help him through this change and prepare him for his... *her* new life. You see, the truth is that we had no real option when faced with what we discovered once we had removed the damaged parts. What was revealed to us was an almost completely formed female organ. All we had to do was to make a few little modifications, with a cut and a stitch here and there, then lo and behold. Now I know I make it sound quite simple, however, Ms. Stafford, as I shall refer to our patient, will need an enormous amount of care and attention. Hormones will change, breasts will develop..."

Before he could continue Lisa butted in. "That's good news, at least. He couldn't keep his effin' hands off mine."

Again, Hilary thought, *Yeah, and yours weren't the only ones, if truth be told.*

"He'll be able to play with his own from now on. Won't be so rough on mine."

"Yes, yes, I get the picture but I want you to understand, Mrs. Stafford. Your husband will have the feelings of a woman, the needs of a woman. Of course he... she, will need a lot of therapy to help to adjust to his, sorry, her new body and way of life."

"F.....g hell, so will I! And what about the children...? How do I tell them that their dad is not the man they think she is? This is all getting too much for me."

Hilary comforted her once more, saying, "Look, you mustn't get too carried away with all that has happened; things have a way of working out. The most important thing is that Mr. Stafford has come out of it alive and that you and the rest of us are there for him... er... her."

"You're right, darlin', I know. I should be grateful for that but it's all bin such a great big shock." Lisa turning to Mr. Khan now, asked, "When will I be able to see my Ror' anyway?"

Mr. Khan spoke in a soft and sympathetic tone. "I am afraid that it won't be for a while, the patient will be kept unconscious for approximately twenty-four hours and then kept under heavy sedation for a further period. Meanwhile we shall meet with other specialists and take a look at the case and decide what the next steps are going to be. I appreciate that it is going to be a stressful time and it will require a good deal of commitment from everyone, not least the patient. I recommend that you go home and try to lead your lives as normally as possible for now. I hope that this will allow you the chance to prepare the relatives, and more especially your children for what will be a very difficult time ahead." He drew a breath and continued. "I shall arrange for you to meet a colleague of mine; he is a psychiatrist. He'd be the best one to guide you and the patient through the next few weeks and months. His name is Ben Sidewell, Professor Ben Sidewell."

# 11

Linda Morris read the headline and reeled in shock as she recognised the face in the picture below it. She read the opening lines and registered even greater shock when she realised that the accident had happened shortly after Rory Stafford had been with her. Folding the newspaper under her arm she picked up her handbag, opened the door of her flat and set off hurriedly for the office.

The authorities at Castertown General Hospital had issued a statement to the effect that Rory Stafford had been admitted in a serious condition and thus set the engines of the country's media turning over at full pelt.

On arriving at the office Linda bumped into her best friend and workmate, Sally Farnham. Sally was excitedly waving and flapping the paper with the headline that Linda had already read.

"Linda, it's him, it's that horrible man from the pub, it's *him*, y'know, the one you had se..."

"Shut up, Sally, the others will hear you. Get in the office." Linda pushed Sally forcefully through the door to the office they shared. "Sally, I do not want everyone to know our secret. He is a married man, after all."

"I know all that, it didn't seem to bother you then. Anyway, that is not the BIG issue!"

"What do you mean not the BIG issue; there is no issue at all if you keep quiet about it. I don't want everyone knowing about my little tryst. After all, I'm not having an affair with him... it was a 'one-off', enjoyable as it was."

"I think you should, I think you could become a very rich girl off the back of this, or should I say, from being on your back with him?"

"What on earth are you talking about? I am not in the habit of blackmailing every individual I have sex with, whether they're married or not! Frankly I am disgusted that you could suggest it or even think that of me, that's an affront to my integrity!"

"What... blackmail? Who said anything about blackmail...? And where was your integrity when you let that foul-mouthed footballing yob get into your knickers! It is a whole lot more than that... For God's sake, Linda, have you read the story...? You are the last person to have done *it* with him, and..."

"Oh God, you're not saying that he's dead, are you? It just said seriously injured in my paper."

"NO! No! No! It is the nature of his injuries! Well, INJURY really, he suffered some cuts and bruises but they said the airbag prevented him from serious *upper* body problems."

"Oh no, not his legs, those gorgeous legs, and especially him being a footballer. He played for

England over fifty times y'know, if anyth..."

"No, Linda, it is not his legs, it is in his 'nether' regions. That is to say, it *is* his nether regions."

"That is terrible, what was the damage? Well, what I mean is will he recover? Not that I am thinking... it is only for his sake, it's a terrible thing to happen to any man, never mind someone as vir..."

"Shut up, shut up! You're babbling. What I'm trying to tell you, if you'll let me, is..." Sally took a deep breath and continued, "According to this newspaper, Linda Morris, you were the last person to have a heterosexual relationship with Mister Rory Stafford and I think..."

Linda interrupted her friend in mid-flow. "What? How did they know it was me? For God's sake, Sally, how did they know it was me? Did they follow us or something? Or did you tell them?"

"No, that is only what I am telling you, as you were with him the night that the accident happened it means you were the last girl to have normal sex with him. What the papers say is that to save his life they had to perform a very delicate and difficult operation to take away his 'manhood'. Surely you heard the radio this morning; they said his 'pipework' was damaged beyond repair and that it was a long old operation. It ended up with the surgeons turning *him*... into... well... *her*!"

Linda sat down at her desk and tried to take it all in. Meanwhile, Sally carried on. "You know what this means... it means that we can sell your story to the highest bidder from the tabloids or even television. Linda my dear, you won't have to work again if I play them one off against the other! We'll be worth a fortune, leave it to me."

Linda cut her friend short again, saying, "Sally, stop, stop. I don't believe you are saying this, how could you possibly think that I would do anything like that? The man..."

"Er... woman."

"Sally Farnham, stop it... stop it now! I am angry with you. It is upsetting enough to hear what has happened to the man... woman. It doesn't bear thinking about, what that poor being is going through laying alone in that hospital bed."

*There's a novelty then, alone in a bed, eh?* Sally mused then carried on with her attempt to convert Linda to her scheme.

"Look Lin, girl, don't you get it? Surely you've been in P.R. long enough to see the B-I-G picture, this is your opportunity to make some serious money, and as I said, handled right it could be *really* serious money! Think about it, we would be able to set up our own P.R. company. There is no problem of conscience here, we would only be taking money from the media and they spend millions every year digging up all that sensationalist dirt."

"Sally, I am not telling the press or anybody else for that matter, anything about what went on between that poor person and me, and I forbid you to say anything to them too! Now let's get down to some work. I would like to carry on as normal and try to distance myself from the whole thing. I want you to do the same, although it is difficult not to think of that poor individual and his... her family."

"If you say so, I suppose I should give you time to think about it as I guess that it must have come as quite a shock to you. I'm sorry, Linda. I got quite carried away I... nevertheless you must think of yourself too. Remember this is the individual that you had an extramarital relationship with, and is currently the most famous sporting icon this country has known for a very long time, it says here in my paper. The potential is mind-blowing; we could virtually name our own price. Now then, you were going to give me a hand with the Glowball Media presentation. It has to be finished by this afternoon."

# 12

Donnie Mclaren yawned as he answered the phone.

"No, I did not have time to read the paper this morning. I ordered the first team squad in for extra training after our poor performance in the last game, so I am in early myself to organise it. So tell me, what has the young fool done now? Don't tell me he's been caught with his trousers down again." He listened to the voice at the other end telling him the condition that his team's captain was now in, and holding the phone at arm's length, stared at it in disbelief then sat down heavily in the antique leather chair. Slowly he put the receiver back to his ear. "What...? Yes I'm still here, it took me by surprise, that's all. Are you sure you've got that right? This is not some kind of joke, is it? Or one of your usual 'cock and bull' stories? Oh God... I've just realised what I said. No, *that* was not meant to be *my* joke, what kind of person do you think I am? Are you sure you've got the facts right? I know just what you journalists are like. Don't let the truth get in the way of a good story... eh? Almost as bad as Hollywood in that regard."

Donnie listened intently as the journalist

continued. "They think that his last visit was to Osman's kebab shop as there were grease stains as well as brown ones on his shorts, well, that is what the paramedics told me."

"Och, spare me the sordid detail, I'm only interested in the lad's welfare. You said they saved his life by doing this operation but what about the long-term effects? What are the physical implications? Will he be able to play again soon? How long is it going to take?"

The voice at the other end of the line became heavy. "I don't think you quite understand what I'm saying here. The thing is that Rory Stafford is no more, the 'medics' are calling him Aurora already, so it's kind of official. Can you give me something from the club's angle?"

"Aurora...? What...? Oh yes, Rory, so Aurora, I see. Of course... ok... Aurora. Well, all I can say is that I shall have to find out for myself by speaking to someone at the hospital and getting confirmation of all of this, before I can comment further. All I will say is that he has been a good servant to this football club, I know we've had our 'ups' and 'downs' particularly in recent times, that is well documented, but the club will do the right thing by its player."

"Is that the official line? I can quote you on that, can I?"

"A quote? Well yes, that is it. The club will stand by its player and will offer support in any way possible and to the family too, that goes without saying. Now if you don't mind I must get in touch with the hospital, right away."

Donnie put the hand set down and looked up the number for Castertown General Hospital, then tapped out the six figures on the dialling pad. His call was answered by a very cold and officious-sounding pre-recorded voice, saying, "Castertown General Hospital, if you know the extension you require press the number now, for any other enquiry please hold the line for the operator to answer." He waited for what seemed like an eternity before a very formal voice asked him if she could help him.

"Yes please, I'm enquiring about Mr. Rory Stafford, he... he was brought in by ambulance... I'm sorry... what? I mean pardon. Yes I imagine you *have* had many calls, he's a very popular lad. I suppose I *am* lucky to get through, yes I did know... Actually it is over fifty times that he's played for England. Could I...? Yes, he is a good looking boy, he's also a fine footba... No, I did not know that, actually it is important that I spea... Yes I do... the wife... Lisa... Gavin and Fiona... are they? Do you think you could put me through to someone? I'd like to find out how he is doing... Sorry did you say *she*...? Yes, I'm sure but I'd like to find out the facts from someone dealing with his case... Ok, ok, yes, now *her* case. Please... oh don't bother, I shall just have to come down there myself."

He slammed the phone down more in frustration than in anger, thinking how he might act if he was the operator and had to cope with the sensational news that one of the country's favourite sporting *sons* probably *wasn't* anymore. However, he was no closer to official confirmation or clarification, even though the rest of the sports-loving population must have woken up to the headlines in the tabloids or seen the television news declaring that the boy he once called the 'son I never had' was now lying in a hospital bed coming to terms with the fact that he would never play football for England again, not as a man anyway. Donnie was determined to get the official line for himself and after leaving instructions on his desk for his assistants, set off for the hospital.

He could not park anywhere near the hospital grounds, so he parked up and walked several hundred yards to reach the main entrance, meaning that he could not avoid the crowds of newspapermen, television crews, fans, and just the usual band of 'rubber-neckers', all seeking to hear the very latest developments. Donnie now resigned himself to the fact that this was not an elaborate hoax and that any hope that things might have been exaggerated should be abandoned, so he pushed his way through the throng of journalists, cameramen, and presenters with their microphones, ignoring as he did, their calls for 'a statement or an interview'. His progress was very slow but eventually he made it to the steps up to the main door. A hospital official recognised Donnie as he reached the steps and called out, "Let Mr. Mclean through please, folks." And louder now, "If you don't mind, you people, allow Mr. Mclean through, that's it. This way Mr. Mclean, follow me."

A voice from the crowd called out, "Look, it's Donnie Mclaren, the United manager. Sorry to hear about the lad, Donnie. As if things weren't bad enough, eh?"

"Yeah thanks, what? But how do you mean? Oh yes, of course the ba..."

Before Donnie could finish another voice called to him.

"'Ere, Mr. Mclaren, any chance of an autograph?" There followed a clattering sound and through the corner of his eye Donnie thought he saw a man in a wheelchair careering precariously down the steps in the general direction of a large yellow skip.

The official led Donnie past the milling bodies at the top of the steps and on into the large reception area, whereupon Donnie enquired as to whether he could see Rory or speak to the person in charge of the case.

"I'm afraid Mr. Khan is not contactable at the moment but I could probably get his assistant to speak to you, I'll just page him. I'm sure Mr. Conway will be able to appraise you of the on-going situation and tell you if you'll be able to connect with the patient." The official was careful not to assign a name to the patient, thus being the first person Donnie Mclaren had spoken to who had not directly alluded to the change of 'circumstances' of Rory Stafford.

The official picked up the nearest phone and was answered almost immediately. "I have someone here at reception with an interest in the Stafford case... No, it is not the press, or the TV people, it is the football club manager Mr. Mclean. Ok, shall I bring him up to your office? I'll have to be there, as the hospital's chief executive, to see that we put the ticks in the right boxes. We'll be right up.

"I'm sorry, Mr. Mclean, I haven't introduced myself. My name is James Reece-Morton, I am the chief executive, the hospital manager."

"Yes, I guessed you were, and just for the record I am Donald Mclaren, not Mclean, and I am the manager of..."

The hospital manager took Donnie's hand and started shaking it furiously whilst apologising for his error and praising him for the magnificent job he was doing at the club, but at the same time confessing that he himself was a typical Manchester United fan, coming as he did from the Surrey side of the River Thames.

Donnie pulled his hand away after a while and said, "That's ok, easy mistake to make, I suppose. Mclean... Mclaren," wondering at the same time what hope there was if the chief executive of a major hospital was capable of mixing up the labels. He, being the *head* paper pusher!

Mike Conway greeted Donnie with a friendly if nervous smile, recognising immediately one of the most successful managers in the English Premiership.

"Hello Mr. Mclaren, honoured to meet you, although I would have preferred totally different circumstances from these I.. I..."

Donnie put him at his ease straightaway with a warm smile and a shake of his large hands.

"Mr. Conway, I believe we have you and your colleague to thank for saving the life of my star player. I hope you are able to bring me right up to date on his current condition."

The hospital administrator squirmed his way between the two men and offered Donnie a tea or coffee.

"No thank you, I would just like to hear how my boy is doing. How about it, Mr. Conway? What sort of state is he in? Is he going to be in hospital for long? Will he be able to play again and how soon?" Donnie was becoming more agitated with every moment that passed. "For God's sake, is he going to be alright? I appear to be the only one on the planet who doesn't know the score!"

"Please calm yourself, Mr. Mclaren. I'd like to think we're all professionals here, and please... take a seat. Are you sure you wouldn't like a coffee?"

"I am calm, I'm just anxious, and no, I would *not* like a coffee. I'd like to hear from this gentleman just what has happened to my football club's most valuable player. Just let him speak, please."

"I understand, I'll just sit over here. Carry on Mr. Conway... please."

Mike Conway nervously offered Donnie a seat across a table from himself and they both sat down.

"I don't know how much you know already but when Mr. Stafford arrived at A and E it was 'touch and go' whether we would be able to save him. As it turned out he was a very strong individual both mentally and physically, and by applying our skills we were able to bring him back from the brink, as it were. Regarding the necessity to perform the procedure that we did, we were very low on options. In fact, we had none. We had no alternative if we were to save Mr. Stafford's life."

"We did ascertain the permission of immediate family to carry..."

Donnie froze Reece-Morton in mid-sentence with

his most threatening look, and asked, "What procedure?"

Mike continued. "How much do you know already?"

"Well, very little. I understand that he took a nasty blow to his groin area and that's it, except that rumours are suggesting that his sex life has been affected in some way."

"Originally we established that there was so much damage down there, he'd already received a nasty knock in the groin area a couple of years back, damaging certain tissues, according to the records, whilst playing football," Donnie nodded in acknowledgement and Mike continued, "that it was obvious there was nothing more that we could do. In other words 'it' was inoperable, which meant we would have to remove 'it' completely."

Donnie gulped and said, "Hold on, are you saying that the poor lad has had his 'manhood' completely taken away?"

"In order to save his life," the administrator interjected.

"Yes, thank you, I was sure that is what Mr. Conway had said, just now. But where does that leave the lad, in respect of his future, with his... life... his... er... wife... his love... life?"

"That is what I was coming to. You see, during the operation to remove the shattered organ we discovered something quite amazing underneath," Mike anticipated Donnie's deeper anxiety and quickly continued, "which meant all was not such bad news."

Donnie's eyes lit up momentarily, in the hope of some good news for the first time today, but inevitably re-registered gloom with what Mike told him.

"What we found was something resembling a female womb. We had to perform some intricate surgery but luckily Mr. Khan is the best in the business, so the result was that we were able to give the patient a sex life, albeit the opposite to sex as he'd known it but... well, I am afraid that is the full story. We are now treating Mr. Stafford as... as... as... a... a woman."

Donnie had been sitting with his head in his hands listening to the last part of the story, sighing with despair and disbelief, his mind working overtime. He finally looked up, faced the others and blurted out, "Jeeesus! This is unbelievable. His life's not going to be worth living! Those 'comic cuts' that pass themselves off as newspapers will have a field day with this. Thinking up their next 'leery' jibes... like 'midfielder unable to dick-tate play as he did before'. I mean, that just came into *ma* head and they are past masters at it."

Donnie was interrupted by Mike Conway placing a hand on his shoulder.

"Mr. Mclaren, I think they will accord a little bit more sensitivity than that. After all, he is the country's favourite footballer. Anyway, it is important to remember that he is alive and... well... whilst not exactly... kicking. We'll have to wait and see on that one..."

Again the hospital administrator interjected. "Yes,

and with this hospital's help is going to recover and enjoy as normal a life as possible given the patient's changed circumstances. There will of course be individual counselling, specific therapies, specialised drugs and constant monitoring."

"Yeah, very reassuring I am sure. However, I wish I had been the first to know about this and not the last, it's already too late to think of damage limitation and I'm not referring to the operation. No, it's the press, it is a shame that they already know. They'll have an absolute feast on this one! Our man has already been getting a hammering because of his ban. Talk about kick him when he's down, he doesn't stand a chance. By the way, is there any possibility I can see the lad? Oh... ok, lass?" Donnie rolled his eyes in acknowledgement of the unavoidable truth.

# 13

"That Professor Sidewell is very good."

"Yes darlin', he's supposed to be the best in his field, but why are you talking in that high-pitched voice? You sound like an excited David Beckham."

"I am excited, it's because of 'im I'm discovering things I never knew existed... like my inner self... and sensisiv... senstivis... sensivist... oh, it's something like that! He's even put me in touch with my feminine side. I never thought I had one, but every bloke has... apparently."

"Well you already knew about all them other feminine parts, didn't you... don't you? What's that all about then?"

"He said he's getting me prepared for something big. I think I might be helping him with his research; it's all part of the treatment, so he says. We're taking it a little bit at a time. He said my body has experienced a very big shock."

*It's not alone, sweetheart, but at least your* body *is coming to terms with it. Wait until the rest of you finds out!* Lisa's smile hid what she was thinking and she clasped his hands to her to give them an extra squeeze. She was finding it difficult to hold it all in but Prof. Sidewell would only allow her to visit Ror' on the condition that she revealed nothing of the nature or the seriousness of his injuries for the time being. This applied to everyone else.

It was now three weeks into the recovery period and becoming ever more difficult not only for Lisa but everybody who came into contact with the patient. The hospital authorities had designated a private room so as to isolate Rory and make it easier to 'vet' everybody who was likely to have dealings with him. The professor insisted also that the patient was referred to as 'Rory or Mr. Stafford' until *he* said differently, insisting that to do otherwise at this stage would be catastrophic and could set back Rory's 'recovery' programme immeasurably.

"Professor Sidewell says that what I'd suffered in me privates was something traumatic, but I can't feel any pain down there. Come to think of it, I can't feel anything down there, even when I put my hand on me dressing."

"I expect that'll be the drugs," she lied, "they take away the feeling altogether?"

Luckily for Lisa, Rory was in a much chattier mood than she had seen him in previously, and was encouraged by it. "The food in here is very good y'know. All fresh, they say, and the cooking is of a pretty high standard too. Y'know what the nurse told me? She said Jamie Oliver visited the kitchens here early this year and he impressed them so much that straightaway things got better. Amazing, isn't it, what one visit can do?"

Lisa noted the first of many anticipated changes in Rory.

*That's funny, quality's not something he's ever noticed before, it's more the size of the portions, or the number of them, that mattered most.* She also spotted that everything on his dinner tray was tidy, with the knife and fork placed side by side on the plate and the serviette folded and tucked neatly under the cup and saucer. *So unlike the usual bomb-site.*

"One of the first things I am going to do when they say I can get up and start walking around, is go and visit that Di la Scala bloke, y'know, the one I elbowed. I want to see how he's getting on. I used to think he was the lowest scum and denominator but I'm seeing things a bit differently now. They said he won't be pressing charges, says he admires me too much and it wouldn't be fair after what's happened to me. *He's* in this hospital too, y'know, in the Green Wing! O'course I'll have to wait 'til he can talk again."

Lisa thought Rory sounded serious and a little excited at this prospect. In fact, she thought it a little bit scary as it was so out of character for her Ror'. Then as if to reassure her, Rory brought her back to earth with a jolt, saying, "How are the kids then, and when are ya gonna bring 'em in to see me? I bet they really miss their ol' man, don't they?"

*Not 'alf as much as you'll be missing your ol' man, darling, when you find out it's gone.* Lisa dug the stiletto heel of her right shoe hard into the flesh of her left foot, by way of punishment. She was sure she had drawn blood. Waters welled up in her eyes. *There'll certainly be a bruise there in the morning, my girl, and it serves you right.*

"They told me I can't bring them in yet, it would be too much excitement for you and too tiring." She quickly changed the subject. "Ah, I see you've finished your jigsaw puzzle already. I'm gonna have to get you a much harder one. I think I'll get you one with fifty pieces this time," she joked. "You're reading a lot more now, too. Shall I get you a book with less pictures? What d'ya think? What would you like?"

"Well I would like to get up to date with football; couldn't you sneak me in the 'footie' weekly? I'm not allowed radio or telly. I wanna check 'ow the boys are getting on without me, I wanna check on me mates, I wanna see how ol' Lenny Bolton's doing down at Millwall, too. I wanna find out how he's performing in the lower division this season. He's me ol' mucker, remember? 'Ere Lisa, y'know we call him 'strap-on', don't you?"

"No, why's that?"

"His name... Lenny Bolton... y'know... Bolt-on... so 'Strap-on'. Funny, ennit?"

"If you say so, darling. I don't get it... it must be a boy thing." Lisa could not help thinking, *Nothing changed there then.*

"Well anyway I really wanna get up to date with it all. I don't half miss it, Lisa."

"I know, darlin' but the professor said it's forbidden, it would get you all worked up too and we've got to avoid that like the plague."

"You'd think I had the plague, the way I'm being treated. 'Ere... I was talking about football not the oth..."

"I know, I know. Anyway, it is all for the best, and that's just how we all want to see you... back to ya best... Well, better." She could feel herself tripping over her own words, so again she tried a different tack. "My god, I'm going to have to organise a haircut for you m'lad, look how long it's got while you've bin in here. You were always so particular about keeping it trimmed. Paying all that money to that strange Marcel bloke every other week."

"I don't know about that, I'm getting to like it this long. It feels really good too, so soft and luxurious just like in the shampoo adverts, where the girl goes naked into a waterfall and comes out with a beautiful glossy sheen. Y'know... when she runs her hands through it and then tosses it back...Timothaay."

"Stop it, Ror', you sound strange, you're spooking me out. Besides, it was never her hair you were looking at before."

"Ok, only joking. Go on then, if you want to fix it make sure it's alright with the professor first, though. We don't want Marcel coming round 'ere getting me all excited, do we? But only a trim like, I only want a trim, alright."

"Your hair is more wavy now too, not just curly, but I suppose that's because it *is* much longer? Yes I know, I've got to check with the professor 'cos he has the say-so on everybody and everything that comes into contact with you."

"That's right, thanks darling."

Lisa was touched and almost reduced to tears. She could not remember the last time Rory had said a 'thank you' for anything.

# 14

Sally Farnham looked up from her desk and studied the face of her friend Linda Morris, who was sitting at the desk opposite hers. She had waited fully twelve months whilst the initial reactions to the news of Rory Stafford's accident and subsequent gender change, had died down, knowing that the novelty of the story would eventually wear off. It was pretty sensational stuff at the time after all is said and done. The whole world must know by now that the famous England international footballer had had to undergo a lifesaving operation and in the process had got himself a new life as a woman. It had been both ground breaking and ground shaking in its significance but in Britain now the Stafford story was not 'headlining' so much anymore. It was limited more to bulletins routinely printed within the first two pages of the 'tabloid' newspapers. Just to inform their readers of any changes, significant or not, in the progress or treatment the patient was receiving and generally just keeping the reader updated. As far as the readers knew, nothing much *had* changed in this time due to the strict control of any information by Professor Sidewell and his team. At the same time knowing that it was generally accepted 'no news was good news'. This made for pretty mundane reading, despite the best efforts of the more experienced 'hacks' to gain that little extra 'snippet' by fair means or foul, to dangle in front of their readers in their efforts to keep the story warm. Most serious editors held the view that it was too soon to speculate properly on the future of Castertown General Hospital's most famous in-patient and that they would just await developments.

The thing that the world was waiting to see, of course, was what the *new* Ror' Stafford looked like and how he, she, or it was coping with life. What kind of life would she return to? Would she play football again? Would she be eligible to play for England again? Countless other questions begged answers, guaranteeing that this would be the next BIG STORY! Sally knew that the best time to cash in on her story would be on the back of this. Thus, she had resigned herself to the wait.

Sally also knew that it would be the end of her friendship with Linda.

She had to patiently play along even though she was sitting on a 'red hot' story and was ever more anxious to cash in on it.

What convinced her of the need to be patient was that she had seen just how well it had worked so many times before, when certain 'celebrities' had strayed from the straight and narrow in one way or another, be it through drugs, drink, sex, or a combination of the three. The media always fell over themselves to be the first with the story, going as far as buying the rights to an 'exclusive' and parting with extraordinarily large amounts of cash in the process.

A picture of the 'compromised' individuals was even better and represented better value for money too, yielding so much more mileage.

Such is the state of play of modern journalism that nothing is better guaranteed to sell editors thousands more copies of their newspaper. This particular area had given birth to a new phrase, 'cheque book' journalism.

'Celebrity' has taken on a new meaning in recent years too, and Sally was well aware that it was possible to achieve celebrity by 'association' these days. Her work in advertising had served to inform her of its value to the point where one of the popular adages is 'any publicity is good publicity'. The knack was to milk it for all its worth. To this end she had put a lot of time into thinking through her strategy, knowing that she was unlikely to get any cooperation from Linda.

Linda had told her in no uncertain terms that she would not inflict further damage on the unfortunate Stafford family. The burden of guilt was weighing quite heavily on dear Linda's shoulders, despite Sally's best efforts to reassure her that if it hadn't been her it would have been someone else without doubt, and that she should console herself in the knowledge that she had given him a good 'send-off'. Of course, Linda had taken exception to this. She was ashamed of her weakness in the first place and she was haunted by the 'if only' element. She was certainly not willing to compound her own problems or those of the innocents of the piece, the poor children and the wife. Ignoring the appeals to her conscience, Sally contemplated on the time she would 'break' her story. To drop the 'bombshell', as it were.

*The art is choosing the optimum moment, in order to achieve the maximum impact. How much longer can I wait, though? Sex Romp Revelations of the Gender Change Soccer Star... Soccer Star Stafford's Last Fling as Rory... No need to bother my head with those details. They'll come up with the headlines that are their job, that's what they do so well.*

Linda broke into Sally's ponderings and asked, "A penny for them, Sal? You were miles away then, is it something I can help you with?"

"What? Oh no, that's ok, I was just thinking about holidays, haven't decided what to do for Christmas."

"You said it wasn't a problem last week, as you wouldn't be able to afford Christmas this year, what with your credit card overspend. What's happened to change all that?"

"What? Oh, nothing, no. I was daydreaming, really."

"Work not bothering you then."

"No, though it's pretty boring at the moment, don't you think?"

"What do you mean? It's pretty much the same as usual. Although, we've experienced a bit of a 'falling to Earth' after that Glowball presentation. That is our biggest account yet. Still, we are busy at least."

"That's true, I suppose. Hey, have you seen the time? We should be thinking of getting some lunch!"

"I'm with you there, girl. Let's go."

# 15

The television people and the representatives of every conceivable newspaper were arriving in their droves. The approach roads to the hospital were 'chock-a-block' with vehicles and people since it was leaked that Castertown General Hospital's most famous patient was being discharged that very morning, almost twelve months to the day after being admitted to the casualty department, the victim of a very serious road traffic accident.

James Reece-Morton, the hospital's chief executive, stood in his pomp at the top of the steps at the main entrance to the hospital building with a prepared statement in his hand.

"Allow me to introduce myself. My name is Reece-Morton, James Reece-Morton; I am the chief executive officer..."

A voice from the crowd called out, "The chief number cruncher!"

Reece-Morton, ignoring the interruption, continued. "..And on behalf of the doctors and staff of Castertown General Hospital I am pleased to announce the imminent discharge of our highest profile patient, Ms. Aurora Stafford. Now, as you will know she was brought to us as Mr. Rory Stafford in a condition that suggested that he would not survive the night, such were the terrible injuries he had sustained. However, we took this on board and due to the excellent standard of the primary care delivered at the roadside and..."

"You mean first aid!"

"...The unique and individual expertise of our surgical practitioners plus the application of Non-Negative Approach Systems."

"What the f..?"

The administrator cut across him without breaking his own flow.

"I am proud to say that with some Blue Sky Thinking we were able not only to save the patient's life but to guarantee a Quality Enhanced Existence in the future."

The objector let out an exasperated sigh and gave in.

"I would like to add that she has been a model patient and it has been a pleasure for our executive staff to interact with her. The patient responded very well to the initial surgery, and made great in-roads with the help of drugs, specialist therapies, and counselling. Of course certain elements of these treatments will continue and other issues will have to be addressed until all of the boxes are ticked and the final envelope pushed, but the experts consider the patient fit enough and well enough to return to her family unit. Going forward, the hospital team will keep an eye on developments and will be on hand

24/7 should anything unforeseen arise. I would like it to be flagged up that the Stafford family have made a generous donation to the Hospital Trust which will enable us to invest in many more Direct Drug Therapy Delivery Facilitators or, for the benefit of our friend over there, pain relief machines. Our sincere thanks to the Staffords for their overwhelming generosity. I know I speak for everybody when I say we wish you well in the future. Thank you. I am now happy to throw it open to the..."

He was cut short because just then a roar went up from the crowd and the hospital manager was swallowed up as bodies surged forward.

Ms. Aurora Stafford had appeared in the doorway surrounded by several bodyguards. She gingerly stepped forward in a smartly tailored, dark brown trouser suit with matching shoes to acknowledge the crowd. As she did so a wheelchair projected directly into her path; the man in it proffered an autograph book. Aurora accepted it, signed it, and smiling, returned it to the owner, who turned away, happy to be the proud possessor of the first autograph signed by 'Aurora' Stafford but at the same time regretting that he'd not achieved the full set.

This was to have been a quick 'photo call' but the bodyguards had difficulty holding off the combined thrust of fans, television crews, and pressmen so they immediately ushered Aurora back inside the building. The last the crowd saw of her was as she waved from the helicopter taking off from the heliport on the roof of Castertown General Hospital.

# 16

"Hello Ror', darlin', welcome home. I know it's *not* home but this place will be for as long as we need it to be. What do you think of it? It was nice of Mr. Mclaren to let us have it, wasn't it? He said we can stay here for as long as it takes for you to recuperate and it is far enough away from the glare of the media, and best of all no-one knows we are here. Hilary and me have explored every bit of it and it's really gorgeous, isn't it Hil? You won't believe the trouble *we* went through to get here, even 'ad to get a boat for the last bit. It was ok for you 'cos they laid on a helicopter for ya. I bet you got a great view of the island from up there didn't ya?"

"Hiya you two, are you a sight for sore eyes? Come and give us a hug. It's fantastic to be back with you outside hospital surroundings. I feel like I've been in a goldfish bowl all this time. It seemed like there was never any time I could really be alone, except when I was in the loo; even then there would be a nurse outside. I don't know what they thought I was gonna do in there. Hospital was too much like Big Brother. Bugger 'reality' TV, you can stuff that. God! They've got millions watching them. Do you know what? It was really draughty in that helicopter, I didn't take much notice of the view, to tell you the truth. I was too busy keeping myself warm, snuggling up to the security guard. I think he said his name was Arnie, or it might 'ave been Barney, I'm not sure."

Lisa was quite nervous and she sensed that Aurora was too, despite all the effort they had put in, preparing for this very moment, and although it was twelve months it had seemed an awful lot shorter, and now, this was the first time they had been together outside the hospital and away from the constant supervision of Professor Sidewell and his team. He'd spent an enormous amount of time and energy on training her and said that he had total faith in her and the family's ability to cope with the *new* Rory, and that they would all play a valuable part in helping Aurora's transition to something resembling normality in her new life and to make it as easy and as natural as possible. From now on *they* would be her crutch and succour in her efforts to overcome all the challenges that were bound to crop up as time goes on. He didn't say how awkward she would feel when it finally came to it. Nevertheless, the three shared a tentative hug until Lisa broke away, saying, "I tell you what, I'll just put the kettle on and make a nice cup of something, that'll warm you up, and we can sit down and you can tell us all about the flight and what happened this morning. Do y'know, I've never been in a helicopter."

Hilary moved in the direction of the kitchen, saying, "No, leave it to me, I'll do it. What do we all want?"

"Ok, I'll get Fiona and Gavin, tea for me please."

Before Lisa could move Aurora stepped forward and said, "Yeah, tea for me too, please. No, let me get the children, you help Hilary. Where are they, up here?"

"Alright then, darlin'. Well no, tell ya what, I'll come with you. We'll both get the kids."

This was the first time that Hilary had seen her boss's other half since the accident. *She's going to take some getting used to,* she thought. *I only remember an ill-mannered, mealy-mouthed, selfish, yobbish, male chauvinist pig. The new Ror' seems so sweet by comparison. It seems like another person entirely has taken over his body. It's amazing what counselling and some hormone treatment can do. Mustn't forget the part that the surgeon's knife performed, or should I say... the part it removed.* She smiled to herself.

Lisa reappeared in the doorway flanked by Fiona and Gavin, hand in hand with Aurora.

"You look pleased with yourself, darlin', what were you smiling at?"

"Oh, I was only thinking how nice it was going to be, seeing you all back together as a family. It has been an awful long time after all. Well, Fiona, Gavin, what do you want to drink? Are you ready for something to eat? You must be starving. Maybe I could rustle up a little something for all of us whilst I am at it." This suggestion was well received, so Hilary set about her task but she was completely taken aback when Aurora sauntered up to her and hugged her warmly whilst kissing her several times on each cheek.

"That is just to say thank you for all that you have done to hold things together here, for being such a rock and for supporting the family so fantastically.

Without you I know we would not have made it this far. Don't be so surprised. Lisa has told me all that you've done for her and the kids, so thank you again."

Hilary was overwhelmed, for apart from the sudden outflowing of affection and gratitude, *Rory* could never string a decent sentence together. Nevertheless, she was moved to tears by what seemed to be a genuine expression of thanks.

"Now then, now then, that's not the Hilary we're used to. Here, give us another hug!" Aurora gently wrapped her arms round her children's minder again and gestured with a finger to stay the flow of tears. Then she turned towards the children and jokingly said, "Well Gav, looks like you're the real man of the house now!"

"Oh, does that mean I've got to go out and get a job then? I was looking forward to a bit of a childhood and few more years at school first."

They all laughed and any remaining tension the occasion held just evaporated.

This atmosphere lasted throughout the meal. The first meal that they had all shared together that Lisa could remember. It seemed that everybody was more at ease with the new situation than she could have wished for, as they planned what they would do in the following days and weeks.

"At the hospital they said I could attempt a bit of light training. They said I was to 'feel' my way through it, not to rush it, y'know, just do a little bit at a time, see how things go. I did a bit in the hospital gym, as you know, so I've made a start. Besides, I've put on a bit of weight with all those drugs I've been taking, so I want to get back into shape and I can't wait to see how I get on with a ball at me feet. I want to get back to playing football as soon as I can."

"Yeah, as long as you don't overdo it. I know you of old."

"You've no worries there, Lisa, she's got us to keep an eye on her, don't forget. We've not to let her out of our sight – that was your promise to the professor, remember?"

"That's right, darlin', and we're gonna keep to it, aren't we kids?"

"You bet!" was all that Fiona could muster, as she sat on Aurora's lap and gazed into her eyes. She could not remember when she had last enjoyed a cuddle with her erstwhile *father*. Gavin nodded enthusiastically.

"Should be a doddle, that, 'cos it's only a small island, after all," Lisa concluded confidently.

Hilary said, "The countryside is absolutely gorgeous so there is no shortage of cross-country running routes or pleasant walks for the more 'laid back' approach."

"Here, you know there's a lawn out the back with a set of goal posts, so you can feel right at home straightaway," Gavin said excitedly. "And I can demonstrate my 'bendy' free kick, for you."

It was clear that everybody was getting along fine and the plans came thick and fast. The flow was only interrupted when Lisa had to get up to administer the appropriate drugs to Aurora then open a bottle of wine for she and Hilary to share. Their first evening together was going like a dream, much, much better than she anticipated.

When bedtime arrived the next hurdle presented itself.

For the first time for a very long time, together Lisa and Aurora saw the children off to their rooms and into bed. Aurora silently regretted missing, in her previous existence, the pleasure it brought. She vowed never to miss out again. She had lost time to make up. The children delighted in the fact that both parents were there and accepted the 'situation' without compromise. Meanwhile, downstairs Hilary contemplated the sleeping arrangements. She had dutifully kept Lisa 'company' in the early weeks of her separation from Rory and had continued to share her bed in the interim, only returning to her own when she was confident her mistress was sleeping peacefully.

Although she was seeing much more of Mike Conway these days, the number of times she had stayed over with him was restricted by the call on his services at the hospital, and *her* commitment to Lisa and the children. The upshot was that she was spending more time in bed with female company than was normal for a fully paid-up member of the 'hetero' club. Not that she did not enjoy the comfort of Lisa's firm body close to her but the female body is lacking in one particular area, as Aurora can now testify.

In the event the hurdle was straddled with relative ease and without any embarrassment to any of them.

With the children settled, the three of them relaxed on the sumptuous sofa in front of the log-fuelled open fire. The conversation flowed, along with the wine, although Aurora had to abstain due to, as she put it... having her very own 'cocktail', of drugs. This exacted the same effect as the drink, keeping her relaxed and ever so slightly 'spaced out'. They chatted on into the night just as old friends would.

The morning found the three of them in the same position, with Hilary and Lisa on either side of Aurora, arms and legs enfolded and clinging on to the warmth of each other's body. Hilary was the first to stir, feeling the 'nip' in the morning air. She immediately fetched a duvet to cover the other two, and then set about rekindling the remnants of the previous night's fire. Having done this she checked the clock, decided to forego her morning run and sought out a hot, refreshing shower and a subsequent change of clothes. She dutifully checked on the children and saw that they were still 'dead to the world', so taking care not to disturb them she carried on to the bathroom. Hilary luxuriated in the warmth and the softness of the shower water and indulged herself a little longer than usual. To finish off she turned the dial to cold but just then the bathroom door burst open and in walked Aurora. She was making for the toilet, but on seeing Hilary stopped dead in her tracks and let out a whoop of delight.

"I am sorry, I didn't mean to crash in on you like that and apologies for the reaction but I've never seen you out of your 'work' clothes, apart from when you turned up to our place that first time on your motorbike all decked out in your leather gear. I pictured you as a mass of muscles and it came as quite a shock, I mean surprise... an'... and... well, part of me was admiring your magnificent body, the other part was as jealous as hell." Hilary wasn't sure whether it was meant as a joke or not but she laughed, almost nervously, and reached for a towel. Aurora grabbed one from the rail and passed it to her and started to laugh with her.

"I *was* joking of course, about the second bit. Thank God I am able to, eh? Laugh, that is. When I say thank God I mean thank Professor Sidewell, of course. In fact I think I mean thank God for Professor Sidewell, or is it all getting a bit silly now? Shall I just shut up?"

They both laughed wholeheartedly then Hilary thanked her for the compliment whilst thinking. *Did I just have déjà vu?* She stepped out of the shower, wrapped herself in the towel and said, "You carry on, I've finished. I'll just go to my room and get dressed. By the way, did you sleep alright? Not too uncomfortable for you on the sofa? I thought as you're a little taller than the two of us."

Aurora replied, "Yes, thanks to you two, and the drugs I suppose. It was really cosy, I slept like a baby."

"Yes, you still had your thumb in your mouth this morning."

"Oh, was that me thumb?" she said, feigning disappointment. "I thought it was a nip..."

"No, it was your thumb alright." Hilary smiled as she said it and turned, leaving Aurora thinking about it. She met Lisa coming towards the bathroom.

Lisa stopped and asked, "Where's Ror? Is she in bed?"

"No, in the bathroom. None of us got as far as the bedroom, never mind bed. We three slept together on that incredibly comfortable sofa," Hilary replied.

"That's terrible, and on our first night too," Lisa said, affecting a wicked laugh. "What will the neighbours think?"

"Don't have to worry there. They never say much, they just stand around staring."

"Shame they've got nothing better to do."

"Well they are only sheep, after all!" Hilary said.

"Just as well, eh?"

"I think we can blame that wicked sofa. It seemed to seduce us, drawing us deeper and deeper into it as the night wore on."

"Might have had something to do with the wine."

"Um, maybe. All I know is that your other half went out like a light, and slept like a baby, so she said. And when I woke up this morning she was still in the same position, being sandwiched by the two of us! Look, I've showered already so I'll just get into some clothes and sort out some breakfast. I thought we should leave the children to sleep on a little, after the excitement of yesterday." Hilary continued in a whisper, "I thought they were terrific, given the circumstances."

"Yeah, let 'em sleep, very thoughtful. Yes, I agree, they were fantastic, it made me feel really proud to see how they coped. It was hard enough for us grownups, a hell of a lot harder for them, bless 'em. They're really looking forward to these next few weeks. It promises to be a great Christmas with the grandparents joining us with any luck. Anyway, I'll clean myself up and organise Ror' then we'll join you downstairs, ok darlin'."

# 17

The party was held at the Barcaster Conference Centre which was conveniently built into the New Stadium Complex right alongside the luxurious United Hotel. It promised to be an impressive affair with the Mayor and other city dignitaries, some representatives of the hospital staff, the Barcaster players, backroom staff and their families, plus several 'lucky' members of the Supporters' Club all invited for free.

The occasion was of a dual significance. Firstly, it was the annual Christmas get-together, that allowed the owners to mix with their 'assets', their families and followers and to celebrate their continued success.

Secondly, to welcome back to the fold their former favourite son and the most valuable player in the club's history. The place was beautifully decked out with glittering Christmas garlands, colourful decorations hanging from every wall and six huge trees positioned around the room. No expense had been spared to dress the place up appropriately for the occasion, the event being sponsored by the chairman, Sir Titus Aver.

This was as nothing compared with the adornments of the guests though. The Mayoral Chain came a poor second in the 'bling' stakes when compared with the precious metals and stones dripping and drooping from the necks and wrists of the footballers' wives and girlfriends (Yes, WAGS...*ed.*) and the footballers themselves, with notably few exceptions. A bouquet of expensive 'perfumes', pour homme et pour madam/mademoiselle, assailed the nostrils of one and all. But above all, there was an excited air of expectancy hanging over the place.

The bar was popular with all, predictably, as it was free, likewise the impressive-looking buffet, offering the chance for the ordinary fans to savour what the 'corporate brigade' experienced as a norm.

When Lisa arrived with Ror' (as everyone had been asked to call her – an attempt to avoid embarrassing faux-pas) accompanied by Hilary, Mike Conway, Fiona and Gavin, 'Eric and the Dominants', an eight-piece band from the University of Castertown; were already playing some terrific party music and the place was 'buzzing'.

Even with the gorgeous Lisa and the statuesque Hilary alongside, Ror' still stood out. At six feet two with those golden blonde locks cascading over bare tanned shoulders and a figure that now defined him as an attractive woman, Ror' brought the party to a standstill with a wholesale intake of breath.

This was the first occasion that the outside world had seen Ms. Aurora Stafford in the flesh, because apart from the few snapshots that were hastily taken before she was whipped away in the helicopter from the roof, on her release from hospital. None but Lisa,

Hilary, the children, and the wildlife population of Donnie's Scottish island had any idea what she looked like, let alone where she had been for the last fifteen months or so. Donnie Mclaren walked across to welcome them, awkwardly offering a hand to Ror' and being turned down in favour of an extended hug and a peck on each cheek.

"Thanks boss, you're a real friend. Thanks for everything you've done and most important, thanks for standing by us, and, I hope I haven't embarrassed you."

Lisa hugged Donnie in the same way and introduced Hilary and Mike to him and his wife, who had now joined them. Donnie acknowledged Hilary and said, "I know this gentleman, don't I? Mary, this is Mike Conway, he was one of the wonderful team that saved our Ror's life." He blushed when he realised how he'd introduced Ror'.

There then followed a 'melee' as the others jostled with one another in their eagerness to join in and soon Ror' was surrounded by team-mates, whilst Lisa and the rest of the Stafford entourage were being feted in the same way, by wives and girlfriends. Meanwhile, Fiona and Gavin had found friends and were excitedly relating their latest adventures on their beautiful island, being careful not to let on which.

Ror' was staggered and totally overwhelmed by the attention she was receiving. At first there were nervous remarks.

"Good to see you alive."

"Lucky to be alive."

"Have you tried driving yet?"

"What sort of state was the beast in?"

"Yeah, I *did* mean the car."

Moving on to, "What d'ya want to drink?"

"Why? You on the wagon?"

"Expect so after what... she-e's bin through."

"Mikey, get 'er a pint of Ole Griptite."

"Tonic water! Oh yeah, still on the drugs, of course."

And, 'Nice dress, it really suits your colouring and whoever did your hair? Was it that strange Marcel bloke?"

They turned as one and Michael Kelly continued. "Once upon a time, it was your superb athleticism and divine skills on the football field, but now I find myself admiring your 'femininity', your 'haute couture' and your taste in handbags. Thank God you are alive and seriously, I meant it, you look fantastic."

"Hey, stop it you, young man, I'm a married... person! Still, thanks for the compliments, now give us a big hug and before I forget, I wanna say sorry for all the hard times I've given you. When I think back, you were the last person to deserve what I dished out."

Michael was moved to the point of tears but with the eyes of very nearly the whole of the first team squad looking on, he controlled it, giving Ror' an extra hug to deflect their attention. "Mikey's right, Ror', you've turned into real 'Eye Candy', and incidentally who did you say did you hair?" Dominic Cousins carried on where Michael had left off, raising a laugh with his aside.

Professor Sidewell had warned that 'boys will be boys', whatever the circumstances, but despite the early nervousness Ror' felt she was able to engage fully with them and soon it was almost like she'd never been away. She could not help noticing that the boys seemed to be treating her with a new kind of respect, *respect* nonetheless.

Charlie Boyle remarked, "I always thought you were a good dancer, Ror', but seeing the way you move to the music now, it all makes sense."

"How do you mean, Charlie?"

"Never mind Lance-it, Ror', there are times when *he* doesn't know what he's on about and this is one of 'em, right Charlie?"

Charlie was trying hard to work out what Dominic meant, not sure whether he'd put his foot in it, or not.

"Yeah, that's right, Dom. As I say, it's so easy to 'go' with this music, 'ennit? Great band, great sound, 'Eric and the Dominants' really original na..."

"Shut up, Lance-it!" Dominic Cousins, eloquent as ever, curtailed Charlie's futile utterances and asked, "How are the kids, Ror', and Lisa, everything going along ok?"

"They're all fantastic, Dom; look at them, it's good to see them enjoy themselves. Their being around was by far the best therapy for me. I've got great family, great friends; in fact, I'm surrounded by some fabulous people. Without them I s'pose I wouldn't be here today. Thank you and the lads, and lasses, for all the get well messages, I really appreciated the support, cheered me up, and kept me going when things were hard. The kids have been great, Lisa has been, well...

Lisa, you know Lisa, everybody's favourite lady."

Dominic thought, *Moving little speech but this is the artist formerly known as Prince... of Darkness, the one and only Rory Stafford. Do my ears deceive me? Has not mentioned 'self' yet.*

"I must say you are looking pretty fit."

"Why thank you, you can 'ave the next dance after Mikey and Charlie."

"I did not mean it like that."

"Oh, now you've disappointed me, I was looking forward to our little dance."

"Ah, I see you've developed a sense of humour. No, but seriously, I hear you have been back in training and I was wondering, what your plans are for the future?"

"Wow! This is a bit sudden, isn't it? Oops, there I go again! I know, I'm sorry, I was just getting into the mood of things, I'm really enjoying myself with you and the lads, makes a change for me to be able to pull your leg though."

"As long as that's all you p..."

Dominic cut across Charlie, once again. "Oh, please Charlie for f..k's sake, zip it, alright? Sorry for the language, Aurora. Blimey, never thought I'd be apologising to you for my swearing."

Fortunately Charlie's remark did not register with Ror', who was getting more and more into the music, dancing and singing along to it.

Lisa strolled over and said hello to the boys one by one, giving them all a peck on the cheek.

"Is my Ror' giving you dancin' lessons, boys? Looks like she's getting' carried away. Still can't blame 'er, first time out and being back with you lot again." She took Ror' by the arm and said, "Don't go overdoing it, Ror'. C'mon now, we don't want you getting tired too quickly first time out, see you later boys." She led Aurora away from the boys and steered her back towards the others, who were standing around chatting and generally enjoying the mood and the music.

"Nothing's changed I see, Ror', leading from the front as usual," Donnie said.

"I don't know about that, Donnie, I think you may have missed something somewhere along the line."

"How do you mean? Oh yes, of course... change, I hope you don't think I intended it as a joke."

"Donnie, you are too much of a gentleman. I was the one making the joke."

"Aha, good on you, Ror'. I was a bit slow there."

"Don't worry about it; it's not easy under the circs'. Listen, I wanted to bend your ear about coming back to the club, now I am getting back to fitness. By the way, your island home is fantastic; it has been just the job for loads of reasons. Thanks again."

"You're more than welcome; I felt I owed it to you and the family. What do you mean back to the club? It is much too soon to think about anything like that, surely."

"What do you mean too soon? It has been about fifteen months. I can't think about anything else, and please, don't call me Shirley. My name is Aurora now."

"What d'ya...? Och, again with the joke, it is good to see you on such good form. I see I'll really have to up my game to stay with you."

Ror' put her hand on Donnie's sleeve and steered him towards a quieter corner of the room, behind one of the large Christmas trees. She continued, almost pleading. "Come on, come on, boss. You know what I mean. I'm serious. I've put a lot of fitness work in over the last couple of months I've been away and I'm feeling really good about myself. I'm looking forward to trying my hand alongside the others, actually playing again!" Donnie was clearly taken aback by Ror's outburst and was temporarily lost for words, so when he did reply he was careful with his choice.

"I did not mean to sound discouraging or disparaging, it is just that we have a slight dilemma, it is perplexing, to say the least."

"Donnie, don't blind me with your long words again, what's the problem?"

"Ladd... Lassie... can you not see what we're up against here? You are the problem – look at you! Whilst technically you're still registered as a player at Barcaster United, it is not as simple as saying yes, she's fit stick... *her*... back in the team. There are certain considerations, do you hear what I'm saying here?"

"I don't expect to go straight back in the team. I'm not that cocksure. What? Oh yeah... sorry, it wasn't a joke that time. Y'see, I forget myself sometimes, don't be embarrassed." Ror' attempted to reassure Donnie on seeing his blushes, then, continuing the theme she said, "I know I'll have to prove my fitness but I just want to join in training and see how I do. The doctors say I have made fantastic progress and they should know, they gave me a right going over earlier today. They've been great too, y'know, but they can't believe how well I've done, they say it's nothing short of a miracle. I reckon it's all down to the fresh, clean air on that island of yours and the mollycoddling from that gorgeous pair of ladies. They see to it that I eat proper food and rest plenty. Then there's Fiona and Gavin, they're out there eggin' me on like mad."

Donnie could not help thinking, *This is a different being from the old Ror', lavishing all the praise on others, heaping the credits in every direction but the usual one, totally unheard of before. What's more, there is a sense of humour there, where there wasn't before.*

"I have made such good progress that they say about the end of January when I don't have to rely on me drugs, I can think about proper training, not just the exercise, more of the heavy stuff. Y'know, the physical challenges, the sliding tackles, the powerful surges from mid-field and challenging in the air for a fifty-fifty ball."

The tone of Donnie's thought suddenly shifted. *That sounds more like the old Ror' but how far does it go? The clumsy tackles, the bad-mouthing of refs, the winding up of team-mates, and the casual disregard for the rules, the thoughtless indulgences, and the self-gratification.*

The problem for Donnie was not so much the 'When?' as the 'How?' to involve Ror'. For as far as he knew this was a 'first' for football and certainly his club. It was not something he could decide on without consulting *his* bosses. The board would have to be consulted, probably the F.A., U.E.F.A., and possibly even F.I.F.A...

"It wouldn't hurt just to let me join in on a trainin' sessions, and get involved in the kickabouts, would it now?" Ror' was really in his face and poor Donnie was uneasy at the closeness, to the extent that he thought Ror' was using her newly established sexuality to sway him. He was really at a loss to know what to do or say; he looked around him but he was cornered.

"I had not even considered the likelihood of you playing properly again because of the seriousness of your condition. Anyway, it's not just down to me alone, this is way out of my remit. I shall have to speak to the directors." Donnie felt himself caving in. "I don't suppose it would do any harm to join in the training sessions in the meantime, anything to help your progress. I promise to take it up with the people upstairs at the first opportunity. Meanwhile, I suggest we get back to the others before they start wondering what we are up to, eh?"

Ror' reached over and planted a huge kiss on Donnie's lips and said, "Thank you, Donnie, I knew I could count on you. Don't worry about the others; you are too much of a gentleman to give them anything untoward to think about."

They laughed together and started back towards the others. As they did, a voice boomed through the loud-speakers. "That song was dedicated to former Spice Girl, Victoria Beckham, who I am sad to say is suffering from M.D. at the moment, no doctor, not muscular dystrophy, Must-have-a Disc-for-me! I thought I heard a little titter go round the room.

Don't get nervous, darling, that was another joke. Seriously though, ladies and gentlemen, boys and girls, it's show time! It gives me great pleasure and it has done for as long as I can remember... (Yes, another joke... The look on your face, missus) to introduce to you this evening... yes... live... here on stage, all the way from the U.S. of A... Country and Western legend and star of the Grand Ole Oprey... the Pacific Label Recording Artist!! Everybody's favourite... Please give a great big Barcaster welcome to...oo the wonderful Mi...i...iss Ample... Cleavage!"

A tiny figure wearing a contour-hugging pink jumpsuit, reminiscent of a life-size Barbie doll, complete with oversized cowboy hat and bleach blonde pigtails, strolled onto the stage, guitar in hand.

"Ha-lo Bar-cesiter! Tha-ank yi-ew averbody a-and tha-ank yi-ew Pawol, ba the way, tha-at's A-amber, A-amber Cle-avitch, not A-umpul. Na-yu ma first nom-bur e-us ma lat-iest re-cud, it's a so-wong from the Dolly Partu-un Co-umpila-shi-un, Greati-est Hi-ets wun a-und tyo, e-ut goes sometha-ing la-ak the-us." She nodded to the musicians behind her and counted in. "They say the-at lurve is bli-ind, e-is the-at wha yi-ew je-ust walked straight pa-ast me la-ast night?"

Charlie Boyle's eyes popped as he said, "Never mind Dolly Parton's Greatest Tits, One and Two! That D.J. was right when he said... AMPLE CLEAVAGE, they defy, nay, challenge gravity!"

Dominic Cousins thought, *That's funny for Lance-it... must have heard it somewhere before though, couldn't be a Charlie Boyle original.*

Everybody was now looking towards the stage and

the room was transported by the twang of acoustic guitars, the throb of the double bass and the dexterity of the fiddle player, all in sympathetic accompaniment to the plaintive voice of Amber Cleavitch.

Amber was a regular visitor to Castertown since her first record charted over ten years ago. She always managed to fit in a visit to the city on her tour of the U.K., as she ranks the folks 'hereabouts' as some of her most ardent fans. She 'wowed' them every time, tonight was no different.

The night wore on; there was more dancing, a lot more eating and drinking and an overall feeling that all was well in the world that was Barcaster United Football Club.

# 18

Linda Morris had finished the crossword and the Sudoku puzzles and had started to read the 'news' content of the local journal, the *Castertown Mercury*, which was a clear sign that she was bored or had nothing more pressing to do. Early January in her office could be like this as not everyone was back from the Christmas break, this was significantly the case with the senior partners, who usually indulged their families with an extended winter break at one of the fashionable snow resorts in France, Austria, or Switzerland. This meant a more relaxed atmosphere about the place and the girls were not slow to take advantage of this.

"That's good to see, they are letting that footballer train again with the Barcaster club, after being away from it for all that time."

Sally Farnham had herself been reading, and looked up from the latest Danielle Steele novel.

"Which footballer's that?"

"Our footballer, the one who had the crash!"

"Our footballer? Don't you mean yours, Lin' dear?" Linda looked across at Sally and seeing a mischievous grin on her face, acknowledged it by feigning indignation then proceeded to read out loud. "It says the club have agreed to help her get back to full fitness while they look into the whole situation of her playing again, and in the meantime, Barcaster will continue to pay the player's wages. NOT an inconsiderable amount I dare say, some poor insurance company is taking a pounding, eh Sal? It goes on to say that she has made an incredible recovery from surgery and has adapted fantastically well to her new life, despite the traumatic changes that she has experienced, whilst remembering that she was very close to death as a result of a high-speed car crash. Friends and relatives have been quoted as saying; they've always said she had the constitution of two people...What a strange thing to say."

Linda shrugged, but thought to herself, *I'm sure I've heard that somewhere before though.*

Sally had kept half an ear to what Linda was saying but her mind was off on a different tack.

*There's obviously not much happening, if that is all they are writing, except of course, that bit about sorting out the playing thing, how long could that take? Probably involve lawyers, the various governing bodies. Would it have to go as far as parliament? The European Union? It could take forever! The more I think of it the more I am convinced that now would be a good time to drop my little bombshell since this has stirred the embers for me.*

"It also says that life in the Stafford household could not be better, as the family is together a whole lot more and the children have come to terms with having *two* doting mothers. There's a picture of them all together. Quite striking as a woman, who would have thought it? The mother looks good too." Linda carried on quoting extracts from the article and gave voice to her own thoughts. "If all is as normal as it says here, what kind of relationship must there be between our friend and the wife? They are *both* very attractive women."

"There you go again with *our* friend. It was you who slept with him, darling, remember?" Sally was slightly irritated by Linda's continued reference to the 'our friend' link but she was very much wrapped up in her own selfish thoughts.

*How do I go about this? No good speaking to the local rag. Got to think big, got to go big, start at the top. Hey, what am I talking about? I don't have to do this myself; all I do is get the biggest name in the P.R. business on the case, that way we Max-i-mise our return. Yes, I'll get in ol' Sam Sincere himself, H.R.H.'s former mouthpiece, the Right Horrible Sir Howard Eyeknow. Even allowing for his cut, it will surely be more than enough to get me away from this 'Godforsaken hole' and a return to civilisation, back to dear old London town, and I should be set up for life.*

Linda carried on. "Yes, but think about it. What are the practicalities? I mean for starters who would be the more dominant one? You've got to wonder, haven't you?" Linda carried on saucily. "Y'know, one was once a very demanding male, now confronting her newfound femininity, the other a very feminine female unexpectedly confronting her *husband's* femininity... eh...? And what do you think the sleeping arrangements are? Sally... Sal. What do you think, do you think they sleep together? It's a curious one, don't you think?"

"God, Linda, have you got nothing better to do

than to dwell on that? I would have thought that they'd be some sort of arrangement. It's obvious if they say that the family was living as normal. Now come on, get a grip! We are living in enlightened times. I mean same-sex couples are adopting; they're even getting married, for God's sake."

Linda was surprised by Sally's reaction and could not help thinking, *It's unusual for Sally to be so dismissive of the 'tittle-tattle'; she positively thrives on sharing her views on the minutiae of literally everything, from the extraordinary down to the very, very ordinary, exploring every angle until the subject was exhausted. No, this is not the Sally I know and love at all.*

"Are you alright, Sally? You seem to be preoccupied, is it something you can share?"

Sally shuffled uneasily in her chair, coughed, and lied. "No, I was just thinking how boring life is when we don't have a fresh account to work on, having something to get our teeth into, something to get the adrenaline flowing."

"You've changed then, darling. You're the one who is always complaining about the pressure of working here. Now come on, tell me the truth, what's on your mind? A few minutes ago you were blissfully whiling away the hours, reading the latest 'pulp fiction', and now you've gone all serious on me and secretive too."

"I don't know what you mean, secretive?"

"Was it something in the article? Is it about our... *the* footballer? Come on, what are you thinking?"

"Well if you really want to know, I was just dreaming about how nice it would be to get away from this place. In fact, I might just take advantage of the lull and 'pop' down to London and visit the folks, I'm sure Guy won't mind. Might even have a 'look-see' at the job situation down there." Sally was hoping that this was enough to fob off Linda.

"This is a bit sudden, isn't it?"

"No, in fact I've been thinking about it for quite a while now. I still don't think I'm quite over Robin. I know it was I who finished with him but that was because of coming up here with the job. I think I'll give him a call."

"I do not believe my ears! This is the first time you have mentioned Robin since we left London. Your affair with him was dying on its feet. Sally, you've been like a child let loose in a chocolate factory! You have had more men than I have had hot dinners up here. Once you'd mastered the language you have been going at it like..."

"Linda, I think you've made your point, thanks. Ok, I have enjoyed a healthy... er... lifestyle since we have been here but I'm sure a lot of that was the 'rebound' effect of splitting up with Robin."

"I think you mean the 'pinball' effect, sweetie. You haven't stopped... Then, who am I to talk? I have had my moments, I suppose."

"You're telling me, including your ever so secret one-night stand with a famous soccer star, a married famous soccer star at that!" Sally realised too late what she had said and quickly tried to cover up. "Not that you were to know. That Eric chap was sweet, though, I was quite jealous of you at the time. Shame he turned out to be gay, why is it always the best looking ones? Still, at least you know where to go for make-up tips and the like." She was relieved to see that Linda was laughing with her and carried on. "I realise now how shallow I have been and how much Robin meant to me. I am definitely going to call him and I'll probably go down this weekend."

"Good God, I think the girl is serious. I didn't realise you felt like that all this time and I've been sitting right opposite you! I feel bad about what I've said now. So to make amends I am going to take you out for a D-R-I-N-K to see you on your way. Is tonight ok?"

"Yeah, let's go to that horrible night club, the Piss Stop."

"You mean Pit Stop."

"I know exactly what I mean. Still, that won't stop us. We'll dance a bit, get drunk and generally let our hair down."

"Our usual sort of night then, let's do it!"

# 19

Dominic Cousins controlled the ball superbly and with his next touch sent it straight into the path of Aurora Stafford who deftly side-stepped a challenge from 'Lance-it' Boyle in mid-field, coasted past Michael Kelly, and without looking up played the perfect ball into the path of Paul Bastable to score an exquisite goal.

"Shame this is only the training pitch and not live on 'Match of the Day', that would have been top of Gary Lineker's list for 'Goal of the Month' and a hot contender for 'Goal of the Season'. Well done blues, especially you, Ror', you've still got some of the old touches!"

Donnie Mclaren stood and watched as his players carried on with their seven-a-side game that always concluded the daily training sessions. It was Michael Kelly who called back to the coach.

"It seems to me she's playing better than ever. She can outrun and outplay the rest of us and still have something left in the engine, she's unbelievable."

"Mikey's right, boss, she can run rings round the lot of us."

"Steady on, Dom, you'll make me blush. Here, that young Bastable lad has come on a bundle in the last year or so. A goal-scoring midfielder, eh?" She turned and shouted, "Nice finish, young Paul. God, it's seriously good to be back playing with you guys though, even if it is only a kick-about. I'm really enjoying it. D'ya think I'd make the current team, Donnie?"

"If only, eh lads?" Donnie replied with a rueful smile and more than a trace of regret in his voice. "Well, let's wrap this up and get a shower, you lot. I want to see you to discuss tactics for Saturday's game, so look lively... Ror', see you after the game on Saturday, alright?"

The players trotted off towards the changing rooms then Donnie walked over to Ror' and putting a hand on her shoulder, escorted her to her car, which was now an understated but very comfortable 'family' saloon.

"I meant what I said about your form, football-wise, that is," Donnie said with a twinkle in his eye. "It was like the old days, back to the time I first put you in the team."

"Thanks Donnie. As you say, if only, eh? What I'd do to play with the lads again. Still, see you on Saturday." Ror' sighed resignedly and climbed into the car.

The team talks always took place in the room next to Donnie's office. Dominic Cousins and Michael Kelly were the first to enter and made straight towards Donnie, who was propped on the edge of a metal table next to a white marker board. "Donnie, can we have a quick word? It's about Ror'. I can't believe that we now have an even better f.....g player on our hands, better than when she was *Rory* Stafford, and he was pretty special. She was incredible out there today and none of the old heavy stuff or the 'verbals', just great football, pure and simple."

"Dominic is so right, boss; it is a crime that she is not in the team."

"Well there you've said it, Michael, a crime... *She* is not in the team. What can I do? Don't think I haven't thought about it, it has been keeping me awake at night. It has even made it into the newspapers... the headlines! I've spoken to the managing director and he has promised to call an urgent extraordinary general meeting. That will take a week or two and will be like moving the earth, of course. They will probably consult lawyers and they'll do whatever they do. It's not as if it is a straightforward contract decision. This is a unique situation. If it was just a case of girls versus boys, we know the answer, but no, this is where a man... well, you know what I am saying."

Michael Kelly picked up where Donnie left off. "Yes boss, I guess we do. I do think that it is important to stress to the board that us players back you up 100% of the way, we should also talk to the supporters, let them know, get them behind us. That might motivate the board to move quicker, they should listen to the fans."

"Yes but they will probably still have to put it to the F.A., U.E.F.A., *then* F.I.F.A. It could take months. In the meantime, we've got a red hot performer going to waste and I can't do a thing about it, my hands are tied. It will be one long, drawn-out saga, I'm sure of it."

"Perhaps we could try 'player power'? I'm sure they would move pretty quickly if we all withheld our labour, don't you think?" Dom Cousins said hopefully.

"It would not matter what any of us did or said. They would still have to observe all the usual conventions, laddie. This is not your local amateur team; this is probably the highest profile team in football, before Man United. And Real Madrid, we are talking big business here and as such no matter how strongly everybody feels we are all bound by strict protocols. I would guess that they would have to keep the Stock Exchange abreast of the situation, 'cos it could affect the share value. We might as well resign ourselves to the fact that it is only a dream; because by the time things are sorted Aurora Stafford will probably be too old to play anyway! Apart from which, there would be a certain problem to address in the changing rooms." Donnie paused then said more earnestly, "Meanwhile, we have a match to win on Saturday and the rest of the lads are here now so let's press on."

"I'll write something about it in my piece this week... gets the pot boiling." This was Michael's parting shot. "Promise you won't give up though."

"Count on it, laddie! Now sit down and let's see about Barcaster United winning their next home game."

# *20*

**ORRITE?** Magazine emblazoned the cover of their February issue with a half-page picture of Linda Morris and headlines in bold print:- ENGLAND SOCCER STAR 'PLAYING AWAY' ON THE NIGHT OF NEAR FATAL CAR CRASH.

And carried on under the picture with:- ENGLAND'S TOP PLAYER HAD LAST ILLICIT ROMP BEFORE SEX-CHANGE ACCIDENT.

At the bottom of the page in slightly smaller print:- INSIDE WE REVEAL EXCLUSIVELY THE IDENTITY OF SUPERSTAR'S PARTNER IN SIGNIFICANT *LAST* ONE-NIGHT STAND.

The tabloids quickly fed off the 'scraps' from 'Orrite?' Magazine (who had paid Sir Howard Eyeknow for the exclusive rights to the story) and explored, or rather exploited, every nebulous angle in their efforts to create their own stories and give their take on the 'affair'.

The fact that Linda was not denying but not confirming did not stop them hounding her for her version of the events of that fateful evening (their words, not mine). With every part of the media circus offering her 'top dollar' for the exclusive rights to *her* story and a guarantee that it would be written with sensitivity and respect for her personal feelings (Yeah right! ...*ed.*). In response, she insisted that she would not surrender her integrity and 'spill the beans' over every sordid detail and she was ashamed and disgusted that her former friend and work colleague could sink so low as to go behind her back to sell the story and reveal her identity, for, as the papers said, a not inconsiderable but as yet unspecified amount of money. With no thought for the feelings of the soccer player's family or for Linda herself (Sally was definitely off Linda's Christmas card list). Besides, she had insisted that she was not proud of her weakness in giving in to the temptation of the flesh for the sake of a one-night stand, however good or bad it might have been.

In the meantime, Linda attempted to lead as normal a life as was possible under the glare of the media spotlight. She had spoken to Guy, the senior partner at the office, and reassured him that her work would not suffer, despite the departure of Sally. He did suggest that she might take some time off to allow the dust to settle, knowing full well that it was never going to be quick. He appreciated of course that the old adage 'any publicity is good publicity' applied to their situation, to the effect that every time Sally was quoted or whenever Linda was photographed in the press or on television, his company's name invariably got mentioned as former and current employer, respectively. More importantly it was... FREE!!

For that reason he did not mind fielding the odd question or two from the 'hacks' who had encamped almost permanently in the company's car park since the day the story first broke. After all, he was in the business of 'painting pictures' himself, so it was no hardship to pass on some worthless tittle-tattle, as long as he was not harming Linda or the company in any way. Guy came to enjoy his almost daily press conference, at which he would merely inform them of progress of the ad campaign on which the company were currently working, and most importantly, the extent of Linda's involvement.

Despite the incredible pressure exerted on her from all angles Linda did not give in once and after a while she too took delight in stringing the media types along, indulging them with their innumerable pictures, knowing full well that there was nothing new by way of a story. She even took extra care with her make-up so as not to be caught with her guard down (with her gorgeous looks and fabulous figure she need not have worried on that score). The photos were always well received.

After a while the press developed a grudging respect for her stoicism, to the point where their 'copy' started to reflect this and praised her unshakeable resolve to spare the feelings of the soccer player's family, etc., by not selling out to the 'big buck' as so many others had (and continued to so) in search of 'instant' celebrity, constantly courting the attention of anyone with a camera or a reporter's notebook.

Linda was gaining a huge reputation in the media for her sense of rightness and fairness and declared dislike for the 'sell and tell' brigade. She was quickly forgiven for her 'fling' with one of the country's most glamorous and popular sports stars and was regarded by most as being the innocent victim of the piece, since Mr. Stafford's reputation had 'gone on well ahead of him' and had come to be accepted by one and all as going with the territory. To most of the population Linda exuded a rare freshness and innocence that endeared her to them, man and woman alike. Elevated to the status of 'celebrity' in her own right for reintroducing some of the old values that have sadly been stripped away over recent decades, she became the model for an alternative form of fame, and was the subject of many a 'phone-in' programme and 'chat-show' interview. It was not long before Linda was offered her own advice 'slot' on a satellite channel lifestyle programme, as well as her own column in the newspaper with the Social Conscience. Guy was happy to accommodate the extra workload that this brought and he persuaded his fellow directors to promote her to 'junior' partner with an increased remuneration package, one of the 'perks' being the key to the executive 'loo'.

# 21

So far everything was going to plan for Sir Howard Eyeknow and his most recently acquired client, Sally Farnham. In fact, things were going better than even he could have anticipated.

"Never did care for those conceited, overpaid, overrated and overexposed, so-called superstars of sport. I've watched our target, sorry, subject and his antics over the years. I think he has been in the headlines as much for his performances off the football field as on it! And now I'd be quite happy to see him or her get his or her comeuppance. In fact I'm rather grateful that you chose to bring the story to me. If I can play any part in the downfall of this despicable individual, it would make me a very happy man. It could almost have been my 'raison d'être'. Y'know, we chose well with 'Orrite?' Magazine. They were drooling at the prospect of it! I just knew they would be the right choice. They have had him and his long-suffering wife in their pages as many times as that adorable David Beckham. Thank you again, Sally. Incidentally, I have employed the services of a private investigator to keep us up with current movements and to fish out anything else that we don't already know of the past that may be remotely 'interesting' about this horrible individual. Oh, and just so that you do not get the wrong impression of me, I have here a cheque for a very considerable amount and it is made out to you – this should be the first of many, if I know my business." Sally looked hard and long at the amount printed on the cheque, gazed up at Sir Howard's face and then back at the cheque, threw her arms around his neck, planted a huge kiss squarely on his lips and whooped with delight.

Sir Howard coloured up uncharacteristically and tried to cover his embarrassment with a quip, whilst wiping his lips with the red paisley patterned handkerchief swiftly produced from the breast pocket of his Laburnum yellow blazer. "No need for words, old thing, I can tell from your actions that you are pleased with the initial instalment of the yield from the fruits of our labour, so to speak."

He retreated behind the huge oak desk to the safety of his chair in anticipation of a repeat of the same frontal attack, the like of which he had not experienced before and certainly did not encourage, at least not from a member of the opposite sex.

Sally replied, "Sir Howard, you are wonderful. I knew I had done the right thing coming to you, thank you again." She reached across the desk but he anticipated her, holding a hand up directly in line with her face.

"No need, my dear; you've already thanked me enough! Now let us get down to the business at hand. What I must ask you to do is to give me as much information as you can about your friend's previous boyfriends and any significant peccadilloes that we may be able to 'mould' and feed to our colleagues at that dreadful 'rag', 'Orrite?' Magazine. You may omit any that may cause *you* embarrassment, naturally. It is so important that we keep the pot boiling as long as we can. Oh! It is times like these I really do love my job! Incidentally, let me have your C.V. when you next call in, I might have a position for you. I recognise in you some of the qualities that have stood me in such good stead all these years. Besides, the office could probably do with an extra feminine touch." He noticed that this last crack had not registered with Sally and he continued. "Just remember to keep your affections to yourself though, that's all!"

"I am sorry, Sir Howard, but the amount on the cheque took me by surprise. I mean I know you mentioned a very considerable amount but I just..."

He cut her short, saying, "I recommend you get yourself an accountant, and whilst you're at it a very good lawyer. I can put you in touch with people I know if you'd like. After all, that's the least I can do."

Sally wondered why she would need to consider engaging a solicitor as well as an accountant.

"A solicitor as well? Why's that?"

"Well my dear, just to cover your back, as it were. I'm not sure what your former best friend thinks of all this, but I think you had better have some professional help at hand, in case things get a little dirty. By the way, she seems to be doing alright for herself. She's in all the newspapers, doing lots of television, creating quite a fuss, a backlash to our story, in fact, refusing to indulge them with the sordid details of her little fling with our star. Saying all the right things. Apologising to the family and the whole world for her little transgression. How admirable; she has become such a pillar of our otherwise seedy society, but more importantly, she's so very good for our pension funds. This will run and run!"

Sally sat and smiled at Sir Howard wringing his hands, not fully understanding him.

"Now come on, let us get down to brass tacks. What little delicacies have you to lay before me, my girl? Shall we start with where you first met this Linda Morris? Or should it be... how? Was she a school friend? Was she bright at school? Was she a good girl? Did you go to church together? What happened at Girl Guides? Was she always attracted to the opposite sex or did she experiment? How did she lose her cherry? And to whom? C'mon, c'mon does she have any skeletons in her cupboard? You know what I am asking for here, don't you Sally? Just any little thing to get my creative juices flowing."

## 22

"I was given your number by Donnie Mclaren, the Barcaster manager. He suggested we talk about me having a try-out with your team. I'm desperate to get back to playing full-time."

There was no immediate response from the person at the other end of the phone, and then with a deep intake of breath in an attempt to cover up her excitement, she replied, "Did you say Aurora... Ror' Stafford? I don't understand. How is it that you could play for us?"

"Donnie said they would work it out so it would be a loan arrangement, to make it all legal and above board. I'm hoping to play for United again sometime but y'know how it is with governing bodies and the like, it could take forever. I need to get back to playing properly, y'know... competitively. I'm in good shape 'cos they've let me train with the lads."

"I know, I read all about it in the papers but what about all the other stuff they've said about you and that girl."

"Oh, that's nothing to worry about, I'm not saying any more and she's been as good as gold about it. It's just the 'tabloids' doing their usual thing, they won't let go, they milk it for all it's worth. So when can I start?"

"Well, I.. I.. I.. don't know, I guess... Let's see, I'm sorry, I don't know what to say. Training is on Monday and Wednesday evenings if you want to have a try-out."

"Ok, I'll be there tonight, today's Monday. What time and where?"

Kirsty Pye gave the details to Ror', replaced the phone and sat transfixed. It was several minutes before she was able to gather herself and properly take in the content of her phone conversation. She pinched herself to prove she had not dreamt it.

*Have I just been offered the services of one of the best players on the planet, to play for my team, the team currently residing at the bottom of the First Division North Ladies Football League, with two months or so of the season to go and the very slim prospect of progressing to the next round of the F.A. Cup!? My team, Barcaster Ladies XI! My team, the Barcaster Babes! Has Father Christmas come early to Barcaster this year, or what?!*

She jumped up and ran round the room, punching the air, then stopping abruptly, thought, *Hold on a minute now, how do we know what* she *plays like? Might have lost it completely now he's a lady, might have gone all soft. He did say she'd been training with the lads though. Let's just wait 'til tonight, eh? Don't go getting in front of yourself, girl.*

Kirsty put a call in to Donnie Mclaren to verify that it was not a hoax. He confirmed that everything was as it should be, wished her luck, suggested that she could be in for a very pleasant surprise and that she should keep him informed of Aurora and the team's progress. He appreciated that they had not had much luck recently what with injuries, etc., so she shouldn't hesitate to call him at any time if he could help in any way.

*What a nice man, a real gentleman. Nobody else before at the club has shown any real interest in the ladies' team at all and he seemed to know so much about us. I think I need to go and have a lie down.*

When Kirsty drew up outside the training ground the first person she noticed, she realised must be Aurora Stafford. She could tell she had a great figure even in the tracksuit and trainers. She was very nervous as she approached Aurora, especially as none of the regular girls were there yet. "You must be Aurora then."

"Yeah, but call me Ror'. I could never get used to Aurora despite all that goes with it, you know what I mean, don't you?" Kirsty was *not* sure what Ror' meant by it but nodded anyway whilst making a clumsy attempt to shake hands with her. They went into the changing room and got chatting. Kirsty found it quite easy to talk to Ror' even though she was in awe of her. After a while the others started arriving so Kirsty busied herself introducing their new team-mate and explaining the circumstances for those who could not guess.

The training went very well and there was no doubt that everybody was impressed with Aurora Stafford's contribution, introducing as she did, a more professionally honed approach to things. This encouraged the girls to push themselves that little bit harder than normal. All agreed that they'd got much more out of it as a consequence.

This was the best start possible as far as Kirsty was concerned and she knew that she had to include Aurora in the squad for Saturday's game. She took her to one side as the others trooped back to the changing room. They chatted for a while outside and agreed that Aurora would start on the bench and be introduced later in the game.

"Probably early in the second half but we'll see how we're doing, eh? We have a couple of girls back from injury."

"Sounds good to me. I don't want to upset anybody."

Kirsty was quick to reassure Ror'. "No worries there, 'cos we are a squad, we all pull together. No-one is bigger than the team. There's none of them spoilt brat superstar antics with this lot! Oh, I'm sorry... I didn't mean... I forgot that you... No, not that I meant you..."

Kirsty was digging herself into a deeper hole but noticed that Ror' was laughing and so she shut up and laughed along too. "There's no problem, Kirsty. I'm a changed man as you can see." Aurora laughed, arms akimbo. "I promise I'll be a better girl than I was a boy." Laughing even more, she gave Kirsty a reassuring hug and pulled her towards the changing room door. Once inside Kirsty explained the situation to the others and they talked at length about how they would make it work for the good of the team and the long-term good of Barcaster United in general.

*

Saturday came and Ror' drove herself to the

ground of Barcaster Ladies F.C. for her first competitive game as a girl. There was quite a struggle to find a parking space despite her early arrival.

No-one had specifically informed the newspapers of Ror' Stafford's return to competitive football but they were there 'en masse' anyway, along with representatives of TV and radio, guaranteeing that the occasion did not pass unnoticed. However, they were made to wait until fifteen minutes into the second half before a team change was made. Then, accompanied by a huge roar from a curious and massively increased crowd, that is, from the usual one man and his curious dog, Aurora Stafford ran out onto the pitch to be welcomed by an army of reporters and cameramen.

Slightly bewildered and taken aback by the reception she received, she purposefully but somewhat tearfully took up her position in the centre of mid-field, whilst the referee did her level best to assert her authority over the proceedings and clear the media types and all the well-wishers and non-playing individuals from the field of play.

This done, she signalled for the Barcaster right-back to take the throw-in and get the game going again.

The grass was longer than Ror' was used to, making it quite heavy-going and difficult for accurate passing but it was not long before she got into her stride and was able to make her mark on the game. Several well-timed tackles and some neat passing movements and it was like she had never been away.

The opposition, however, aware of the attention Aurora was receiving, did their utmost to spoil the party and steal a bit of her thunder, with some heavy challenges and over the top tackles, though with her experience at the highest level she was able to avoid any 'ugliness' with consummate ease. This all worked to the benefit of her team-mates because with all the attention the opposition were according Ror' they enjoyed a lot more space and as a result they hauled themselves back from two-nil down to win the game four-two.

"That was a valuable three points to win; it broke the 'hoodoo' of thirteen defeats by our 'bogy' team. Thanks to Aurora steadying the ship we all enjoyed a bit of extra time and space."

"I think it brought more out of us as individuals, Kirsty, made us play better as a team," Maureen Field said.

Centre-back Carole Servis concurred. "Yes, I think we were even playing a little better before Aurora came on though we were two down."

Ror' Stafford chipped in, "Donnie Mclaren always said football is as easy as you want to make it. He was always quoting Brian Clough's teams as his model. It is all about knowing when to give and when to hold on to the ball, caressing it and treating it with the utmost respect and most importantly, where possible, to make the ball do the work. Discipline and control were just as important. Mind you, that has let me down once or twice in the past but luckily I can see that now."

Everyone in the dressing room was listening intently as Aurora expanded on the football philosophy of Barcaster United's chief coach.

The discourse continued for several minutes until a loud thump on the door made them all jump and a voice called out, "Ms. Stafford, are you coming out? We want to interview you about your comeback!"

Ror' shouted back, "Yes, but you frightened the life out of us. Hold on, I'll be out in a few minutes."

She could hear the sound of several voices coming from outside the dressing room now and it appeared that there was jostling in the struggle to be the first in line to speak to her. Voices were being raised and a melee seemed inevitable. There was the occasional thud on the door and the outside wall of the changing room.

The girls inside were getting pretty nervous and not a little frightened.

"It sounds like things are getting out of hand out there. Don't worry girls, you carry on." Ror' attempted to reassure them. "I'll see if I can sort them out before someone gets hurt." She quickly donned her tracksuit and moved towards the door, at which goalkeeper Gabi Dean jumped up and opened it, positioning her giant frame in the gap she'd created. She quickly closed it again on seeing the unruly rabble that was pressing in on her and Aurora Stafford.

"She's not coming out until you move away from the door and start behaving like normal human beings, not like hooligans; someone is likely to get hurt. Here, Kirsty, phone the police and let them know the situation. We need a bit of crowd control out there... and ask 'em to make it quick; we don't want to be stuck in here all night."

Aurora offered Kirsty her mobile phone and she

called the Castertown police station.

The first squad car arrived at the ground after ten minutes but it took a whole hour and the help of several more police officers to gain control of the situation.

The senior officer, Inspector Nails, delivered a severe dressing down and warned the press people that some of them had come very close to arrest for their disgraceful behaviour. So it was that Ror' gave her first football-related interviews since the accident that changed *her* life and the world around her.

She told them that for the first time since that fateful day, she felt like she was back on familiar territory. The adrenaline had come at a real rush and she realised what she wanted more than anything now. That was, to make as big a name for herself as Aurora Stafford as she had as Rory Stafford, but this time it was to be different. She was not going to let it spoil what she shared with those around her, most importantly of all, her family. The lack of wages did not matter, there was money in the bank and investments that kept them comfortable and Lisa could work again, if necessary. Aurora Stafford had a point to prove and she wasn't going to miss the chance to do it. Whatever happened though, no-one but no-one was going to suffer, not this time. AND whilst she was at it she was determined to put a smile back on the face of football.

# 23

Some of the sentiment that Aurora had expressed to the media people actually made it into the newspapers and *was* reported on screen. This was treated with the usual scepticism that was reserved for stars wishing to wipe the slate clean and make a fresh start, questioning her ability to do so and reminding us of her all-too-chequered past, albeit as a man. 'Orrite?' Magazine devoted a lot of copy to doing just that, giving their readers several 'highlights'. Without having to pay a penny since they were already in the public domain, along with previously published pictures.

Sir Howard Eyeknow fed them fresh little snippets whenever he felt they had any mileage and value, thus keeping the 'pension fund' ticking over satisfactorily.

Football fans and the public in general were rather more forgiving and lived in expectancy of seeing their long-time favourite make the big-time once again. The biggest hope being that they would see her playing again at national level, for the men's side.

With the attention of the nation focussed on Aurora Stafford's progress, women's football had received a huge boost in popularity and was making it more often onto the sports pages *and* onto page three of a certain national newspaper, naturally. Therefore, it was impossible to avoid the fact that the Barcaster Babes had finished their season in the top three of their league and had walked away with the Ladies F.A. Cup.

Aurora Stafford's star was once again in the ascendancy! Kirsty Pye stepped down as manager to accommodate her as 'player-manager' but was delighted to stay on as assistant, in readiness for the new season. This made official what had been the arrangement since Kirsty realised the value of having a seasoned professional in her set-up.

Certain 'hacks' suggested that now might be a good time to bring Ror' back into the mainstream of the English game in some capacity. A trifle premature and somewhat unrealistic in most people's view.

No-one could have predicted the next sensational headline and it was not engineered by Sir Howard or his 'friends' at 'Orrite?' Magazine, nor was it anticipated by them. In fact, they were totally unprepared for it. The headline in one of the more respected broadsheets read:-

## 'Aurora Stafford Appointed English Ladies National Football Coach.'

The report went on to say that she would carry on in her new appointment as player-manager at Barcaster Ladies X1 next season, but will start immediately with England Ladies with the aim of taking them all the way to the Ladies World Cup Final, the competition being held in America, the following summer. The whole of football, the media and the soccer-loving English public had been totally taken by surprise at the news. Most people were happy. Some were sceptical. Some were even amused at the prospect.

There was a lot of speculation about who was responsible for the appointment, or more importantly, who had prompted the Women's F.A. to consider Ms. Stafford's elevation to such grand heights.

The more informed sources suggested that Donnie Mclaren was the likely one. After all, it was common knowledge that he had kept a regular eye on the progress of his former star playing with the ladies, in the hope that one day she would appear in *his* team's colours again, and, wasn't he the one who had introduced her to Barcaster Ladies in the first place? They knew that he was doing his utmost to keep Ror' Stafford's profile as high as possible and for as long as possible until the powers that be could no longer avoid the inevitable and would allow her to play alongside the male players.

The media as a whole were on board because it was very strongly a 'human interest' story and as such it helped to sell more newspapers, mimicking that popular daily 'tabloid' with its almost weekly reference to the Princess Diana Mystery (more power to their elbow too!).

# 24

Lisa popped the cork from the bottle of champagne she'd opened, in celebration of Aurora's appointment as coach of the England Ladies football team, soaking everybody in close proximity. They took it in good part as she was still everyone's favourite. Although now that she was in a lesbian relationship with the person who was formerly her husband and the country's most famous footballer, it brought a different slant to the term 'WAG'.

"To my Ror' and to success in her new job with the English Ladies Team! Come on everybody... Cheers... Just a couple of sips now, Ror', can't have you getting out of hand! You've got to stay out of trouble if you're going to play for 'em as well as coach 'em. No more little accidents, eh?"

"Alright darlin', just a drop to toast the girls and... may we do something the boys haven't done since 1966. Bring home the World Cup."

"What a fairy tale that would be," Kirsty Pye said.

"Ror's living a fairy tale now. How much further into the realms of fantasy can she travel?" Michael Kelly asked. "That would make a good title for your next newspaper article, Mikey, or better yet the latest, sorry, no, the first biography of the lady in question," Dominic Cousins suggested with a smile.

"Thanks for coming boys... and girls, of course." Lisa was talking to the male footballers and their wives or girlfriends then the members of the Barcaster Ladies football team and *their* opposite numbers, all of whom had been invited to the Stafford home in a gesture of thanks and appreciation of their success in finishing second in the league and winning the F.A. Cup, and for their part in her Ror's rehabilitation and what she had so far achieved. "You've all been great, sticking by us like you have and accepting the situation with me and Ror'. It's because of that we are closer than ever and I wouldn't change things now if I could and I know Ror' feels the same. One person who I think we should thank more than anybody though, is dear Donnie, for his encouragement and eagerness for Ror' to keep playing. It would all have fallen apart if it wasn't for 'im and the boys over there." Lisa walked in the direction she'd pointed, went straight up to Donnie, threw her arms round his neck and planted a kiss squarely on his lips. Donnie was taken aback but could not hide his pleasure at Lisa's action. The rest clapped and cheered encouragingly.

Donnie soon gathered himself and responded, "I did it for queen and country, well, for queen anyway. But more importantly, for football, so it would not be robbed early of its brightest star."

Not to be outdone by Lisa, Aurora strode up to Donnie and repeated what she had done, saying, "That's from me, anything she can do I can do bet...

almost as well." Everybody in the room laughed and from then on the party really took off.

Dee Hacker approached Lisa. "I see you are both on top form tonight, darling. Lovely party. It seems like an awful long time since we all got together like this, we shall have to do it more often. You promised we would get back to a regular game of golf too."

\*

Lisa kissed her best friend and gave her a reassuring hug. "Yeah well, now that our Ror's future seems set and she's going to be whole lot more involved with her football, I reckon I'll have more time on my hands to do things like that. I must say though, I am seeing so much more of my other 'alf than I ever did before the accident and I'm enjoying it, actually comes home after games. Ror's become much more lovin' and carin' too, not so selfish and much more attenta... atteniv."

"Attentive, that is the word you want. I know, I had noticed. Strikes me she's a different person altogether." Lisa fell backwards laughing into her hands.

"Oh gosh, I realise what I've just said; sorry, I did not... still, it made you laugh, so that's alright then."

"Dee, you say some funny things at times. I think that's why we all love ya so much."

"Thank you, darling. *You* say the sweetest things, enough for both of us in fact. Bless you."

"I promise we'll get back to our golf very soon. Now come and have some more champagne." Lisa snuggled into Dee's shoulder as they walked towards the drinks table in search of a fresh bottle.

Meanwhile, Dominic Cousins held court with some of his team-mates. "She's gonna have her hands full running and playing for two ladies teams, isn't she?"

For once Ronnie Grubbe was quickest off the mark.

"Hands full! Christ, I guess even *Rory* Stafford would have settled for that a couple of years ago... two teams of girls and the 'subs' too. Oh, I don't know though. With his appetite, I think he would still be looking for a bit on the side!"

This produced a good laugh all around, unusually for Ronnie.

"I'd settle for it right now! I'd settle for just one team of ladies, never mind two, or just the subs," Charlie Boyle offered in all seriousness.

"Lance-it, you'd settle for anything with two legs. Well, not necessarily *two* legs. Anything... with a pulse really. Not that *that* would matter to you either. And... knowing how quick you are, if you fell into a truck load of breasts you'd still come out with your hands in your pockets."

"Or sucking his thumb!" It was Ronnie Grubbe again offering his wisdom.

"That is unfair, Dominic Cousins, and you Foody; you seem to forget that I was married once."

Dominic was fastest off the mark again. "I think your missus forgot too!"

"Yeah, didn't she change the locks when you were out?" Ronnie reminded him.

"Yeah, she made sure I was out alright, out of the bleeding country! She didn't need to change the locks though. That was just being spiteful. She *had already* moved back to Thailand, for God's sake *and* I was only away for one night!"

"Maybe you should have gone home a bit more often, when she was there. Instead of resting your arse on one of my bar stools night after night. You might have had a clue as to what was going on then," Ronnie reasoned.

"I know she didn't match up to the picture she sent you, but you did marry her." Dominic picked up from Ronnie. "It must have cost you a packet though, what with buying, er, paying for her to come over here with her whole family and all, and then having to cough up again for the divorce settlement. I understand the restaurant is still doing good business under the new management. I guess that was that part of the divorce settlement too, eh?"

"Their Thai noodles were to die for," Ronnie submitted.

Michael Kelly chipped in. "Hold on a minute, fellers. These must be really painful memories for poor old Lance-it. What with losing his wife, his home, his restaurant, his money, and not to mention his marbles. Sorry, no, not the marbles, well not completely. Sorry Charlie... He still plays a mean game of football... never passes the ball! Seriously though, the important thing, though, after all is said and done... is... their spiced chicken took a lot of beating."

"That doesn't make me feel any better, thank you. Thank you for nothing, you lot. Especially you,

Mikey! I thought you were more sensitive than them. Still, I guess you all managed a good laugh at my expense."

"Why not? Your Thai bride and her family certainly did, but at least we are still here with you, more than can be said for them." Dom Cousins affected concern and gave Charlie an encouraging wink.

"I can't help thinking a firing squad would have been a lot kinder to me."

"It's not too late!" This time it was Ronnie's turn.

Dom quickly jumped in. "Honest, Charlie mate, you know we don't mean it. Except for the Thai food bit; that, we were deadly serious about! Eh, Mikey?"

"There you go again. Don't know when to stop, do you?"

"Don't take it so hard, it's only a bit of fun, not worth getting upset about. How about another drink everybody? Let's have us a beer this time. Alright by you, Charlie?" Michael put his arm around Charlie's shoulders and led him away, humouring him as they went.

Meanwhile, in another part of the room Mike Conway approached Lisa, saying, "Thanks again for inviting me; it is very kind of you."

Lisa hugged Mike, gave him a special kiss on both cheeks and answered warmly, "What are you talking about? You're almost part of the family. It wouldn't be right without you, and Hilary. It is lovely to see both of you here, and together. You are usually too busy to make it. By the way, 'ow is your boss, Mr. Khan? Still saving lives with 'is carving knife?"

Before Mike could answer, Hilary slipped between him and Lisa, pulling both towards her, and cuddling and kissing them indulgently.

"My god, missus, you are hot tonight. What 'ave you been doing to her, Mike? She's on fire! Don't blush, I'm only joking... you should know me by now."

"I'm sorry, it's just that it's such a lovely party and I'm in an extra specially good mood tonight."

"Why's that, sweetheart? Have you come into a fortune?"

"It's better than that, much better!"

"C'mon then, do tell. What? Tell us, what? What is it?!"

Hilary held a handkerchief to her nose, blew it, then exploded into tears. "Mike has asked me to marry him and I have said YES! We are engaged. I am so happy!"

Lisa hugged Hilary and burst into tears herself, spluttering, "Me too! I am so happy for you both. I've prayed for this since I first saw the two of you together." She pulled them towards her and embraced them separately, then together. "Congratulations, both of you. Just when I think things couldn't get any better, they effing well do! I have got to tell everybody! This calls for more champagne! God, I am so excited, a wedding in the family! This is turning out to be the best party ever! Listen everybody, I've got even more good news."

Hilary chased after Lisa, trying to stop her broadcasting it to the world but to no avail.

## 25

"I am very pleased for all of them. It has certainly put ladies' football well and truly on the radar. They've even got me watching it but please don't tell my family, they are all rugby mad! I have to say, though, it seems to me that certain women's sports have not been taken seriously enough. They've been treated almost as side shows. Remember too, they do not get the huge amounts of money that is splashed around in the men's game and I am sure that they give just as much entertainment value, if not more. Is it still a male-dominated world? I must say, though, it speaks reams for the character of an individual that after all she has gone through Aurora Stafford could pull herself up again almost to the very pinnacle of her sport in such a short time. Who knows yet how far she is capable of taking it? In any case, good luck to her and her teams, the Barcaster Babes *and* the England Girls."

"Thank you Linda, thank you for your thoughts. Ladies and gentlemen that was popular presenter Ms. Linda Morris talking about our England Ladies' football team and their celebrated Player-Coach Aurora Stafford who as Linda alluded to... good word that Lawro... will be taking them to the World Cup Finals in America next year following her incredible success with the Barcaster Babes team. As you know the England Girls qualified second in their group to Germany which means that both teams will be going to the States. Germany, of course, are the current holders. Aurora just has a few friendly games to acquaint herself... another good word, you should be writing these down... with the new set-up. Good luck girls, I say, and I'm sure I speak for the other lads here with me in the studio! And sadly, that's all from Match of the Day for this week so join us again next week meanwhile from Alan Hansen, Mark Lawrensen... put the pad down now, Lawro... and me, Gary Lineker, it's good night, good night!"

Back in the hospitality suite at the B.B.C. Linda thanked Gary for sparing her blushes.

"How is that then?"

"It is just that whenever I do a chat show or interview away from my own programme some of them think it is fair game to prod me about the Rory Stafford 'affair' – their word, not mine. Last week one of those fresh-faced DJs had the temerity to suggest that I had done well out of knowing Rory. I told him that I had done well *despite* knowing Rory Stafford and I had to remind him that I was vilified by the press and just about everyone else, until I'd convinced them that there were two of us there, it takes two to tango, etc., and that it *was* only one night. He persisted and asked why else would I sleep with a famous footballer? He could not, or rather, would not accept that it was a moment of weakness on my part. It was difficult to convince him otherwise. I even explained to him about 'animal attraction'. He laboured the 'famous footballer' theme, despite my insistence that up to that point I knew absolutely nothing about football and even less about footballers, although I know now that they are overpaid, overrated, and overexposed spoilt brats who gang up to brow-beat the poor referee just about every time he blows his whistle! They could learn a lot about discipline and respect from rugby! Perhaps even a bit about giving value for money. As I said on your programme I come from a rugby-mad family. Football was almost a swear word in our household, so forgive me for being more than a little biased."

Gary answered, "I'm sure he was out to impress his audience by being controversial. That might be his appeal. What were you doing on his programme anyway? Don't tell me you've got a record to plug on top everything else you've done recently?"

"No, not exactly. I was publicising a new programme that we're doing about changing standards in society in general, but with an emphasis on the effect on the young in particular."

"So you were appealing to his listeners and him I suppose, to... to tune in."

"Yes, and it was just his kind of behaviour and rudeness that we'll be discussing in the programme."

"Well I'm happy to say that when my producer heard you were in the studio next to ours he couldn't resist asking you in to comment on the news about the ladies and their new boss, nothing more sinister than that."

"That's very reassuring, Gary, and thank you. It

was a pleasure to meet you and the others. It has helped me believe that there are some really decent people in football. Now I guess I should get back to work. Perhaps we could return the favour and have you on our show. I shall have a word with Sebastian the producer. I believe he is a really big fan of yours anyway, bye-bye for now."

Gary waved off Linda and turned to rejoin his colleagues. As he did, Mark Lawrenson remarked, with a sideways wink, to Alan Hansen, "I think you made an impression there, Gal, you should look out for that Sebastian though, he's more than a fan, mate. The make-up girls say he carries a picture of you everywhere with him. According to them he never puts it down. Well, he can't... it's a tattoo! They wouldn't let on which part it covers; actually they didn't say it was on a part but... well never mind the details, just be careful around him, that's all."

"Yeah thanks, I get the picture. Oops... well hopefully not! Cor, listen to me! Never know when to take you seriously, Lawro, even after all these years. Still, thanks for the warning, now perhaps you could get us a drink. It's your turn and don't try to impress by getting your wallet out, everybody knows they're free, even Hansen, though he's never actually been to the bar to find out. Just my little joke, Alan."

Hansen replied dryly, "What was? I must have missed it!"

Gary and Alan engaged in general conversation whilst Lawro went to the bar but soon came back to the topic that had occupied them so much during the show. Gary started off, saying, "What a fantastic story, eh? This Rory Stafford one. Real Boy's Own stuff."

"Girl's Own, mate." Lawro was on his way back with the drinks and couldn't resist correcting Gary.

"Rory of the Rovers even, or should that be Aurora of the Rovers," Hansen suggested, allowing himself a wry smile.

"Seriously though, it would make a great 'Before and After' tale. It would be difficult to find a more original subject for a film. Think of the fun Hollywood would have with it. It would be a blockbuster!"

Lawro couldn't resist. "Or should that be a ball-buster or even bra-buster?"

"God, I didn't think even you could sink that low, Lawro," Hansen said.

Gary Lineker remarked, "Oh, he can go a lot lower than that but let's not go there for now. I do love the Hollywood idea, though. Of course, they'd insist on one of their own actors to play our hero. Sly Stallone has *played* a bit of footie, remember 'Escape to Victory'?"

"No, before my time," Lawro said, "but I just about remember Ian McShane having good footballing legs. Wouldn't stop a pig in a passage but couldn't half kick a ball! I think it was him, could have been a body double I suppose. No... not with those legs. Unless they found a stunt man who'd had *his* badly reset after a stunt went wrong. Anything's possible these days but Sylvester Stallone playing football? Naaaa! Apart from anything else, he's not tall enough."

Gary allowed Lawro to finish, then continued. "Can you imagine an American doing Rory or

Aurora? Well, as you said, anything was possible, after all Kevin Costner did play Robin Hood. Did they mistake the Prince of Thieves for the Prince of Bel-Air? It wouldn't surprise me. He'd have no trouble doing Aurora's voice though, would he?"

Lawro, like Gary, was warming to the theme. "They'd really go over the top with the surgery bit. They'd employ a well-known actress to milk the drama from the 'sweat on the forehead bits'. Perhaps even Hugh Laurie as 'House' to be the argumentative and 'know-it-all' consultant with Denzil Washington, his agonising and empathising assistant who did all the serious work, anyway."

Gary's imaginative juices were really flowing now. "And Barbara Windsor to play the nurse with the instruments and the surgeon's... tools. Plenty of 'double entendres' to grind some laughs out of an otherwise deadly serious situation."

"No, no Madeline Khan. She would be so much drier and sardonic. There's a word for you, Gary – write it down. And she lives local to Hollywood."

Alan Hansen, was happy to let the other two indulge in their flight of fancy but nevertheless chipped in. "Why not Jo Brand?" He continued, "At least she's had some nursing experience, she'd bring a bit of authenticity to the proceedings... and professional know-how."

"Are you saying Babs Windsor hasn't had nursing experience? She's only the most famous film nurse ever! Besides, Jo's is the wrong kind of experience," replied Lawro in all seriousness. "She was a psychiatric nurse!"

Hansen insisted, "Precisely, I would say that's exactly what you need! I rest my case."

Gary and Lawro looked askance at each other, shrugged shoulders and turned to their drinks.

# 26

Sir Howard Eyeknow put the newspaper down and ruminated on the latest story.

"They are suggesting that an Arab Potentate, Sheikh Mafustatit, was showing an interest in investing in English football in some way. In some way? In some way? Why don't they just say it? He's going to buy a Premiership club for pity's sake! What else would he be doing? It's the kind of thing his sort does now for a hobby... What else does it mean?"

Sally Farnham, who was now employed as Sir Howard's assistant and sharing his office, replied, "Actually, nowadays it seems there are certain financial institutions who own an individual player's contract and somehow have a 'rental' arrangement for their 'asset' with the highest bidder. They negotiate the best terms and conditions, as I see it they pocket an up-front fee and a nice percentage of the player's wages... and you know that he won't go short, then everybody is happy! As long as he does the job on the field, of course. So your Arab Potentate could actually be doing that with his money, I suppose, instead of getting involved in the ownership of a club. Another way for an equities company to make money."

"That's a good point, Sally. Come to think of it, I believe I remember reading about an Iranian-born business man organising a consortium, something along those lines to do just that." He paused for thought. "It means less risk. Because if the team was not performing too well and got themselves relegated, they could always move *their* asset, the player, to a club that was doing better, using the expression 'to further his career', whether it be in this country or abroad and of course within the transfer 'windows'. Hold on one second, how do you know so much about these things all of a sudden?"

"Well, since we have a special interest in the lives of Aurora Stafford and all around her, in my pursuit of further education I have cultivated the friendship of one of the media's star sports correspondents, Jacques Boutes. He specialises in digging the dirt and serving up as many heads on plates as possible in his entirely commendable quest to keep the Beautiful Game as clean as possible!"

"How clever of you and how devious!"

"Steady on there, Sir Howard. You are speaking of the man I love. Well, perhaps love is putting it a little strongly but he is quite cute and he's tall, handsome, has a terrific body, a slight French accent and coincidentally happens to be very good in bed and I do not mean at sleeping. Most important of all, though, he is a veritable fountain of knowledge on the subject of the workings of football and sport in general."

"God, he sounds perfect. You've even got my juices going, damn it! Come, come, come now, control yourself, Howard. Take deep breaths and show a little decorum in front of the lady. That's better, now where was I? Ah yes, we were talking ownership of clubs and players and such... I just remember that when I was a youngster it was normal for the successful business man, the builder or the book shop owner, to shore up his local team purely for the love of the club that he had grown up watching. I suppose it was kind of a hobby to him too. He wanted success for them, naturally, and he would do what he could afford to help them. Of course, the bigger his company the bigger the team would be, that is to say, the higher the league in which they played... Inevitably, the time came when some of the biggest teams got to be limited companies and their shares were quoted on the Stock Market, turning it into much more of a business than a sport. It then became important to make a profit and give a return to the shareholders, even to the point of selling off your best players, than deliver entertainment to the poor long-suffering but faithful supporters. I mean to say, look at poor old West Ham!

"*Now* it's got to the point where large American corporations and even multi-national companies are involved in the purchase of some of our clubs. In fact, didn't I hear that a Far Eastern government had made an offer for a Premiership club recently? Nothing surprises me about football anymore. It really is big business! Colossal, even! I can't remember at which point sponsorship crept into the game, I only know that it is absolutely impossible to avoid now. As far as I was concerned there was no harm in local firms advertising on pitch-side hoardings but now it's names and corporate logos on the shirts, waring the balls, 'scuse me, balling the wares of international companies to the world through the medium of television? Yes, and it doesn't stop there. I mean to say, it's the J.J.B. Stadium now, thank you very much, not so much your Boleyn Roads or White Hart Lanes, no, it's the Emirates Stadium, and yes, the Reebok Stadium if you don't mind, and, and Pride Park. That ought to be Mother's Pride Park? The Bakers missed a trick there didn't they? I shudder to think what they have dreamt up for the new Wembley Stadium. I am sure that it will be something bizarre with absolutely nothing to do with football! God forefend it became the Budweiser Stadium!"

Sally smiled and shuddered at the Mother's Pride and Wembley reference respectively and whilst Sir Howard took a breath, pitched in, "What about the Coca-Cola Cup? What an insult to the oldest knockout competition in the world! It is the F.A. Cup for God's sake! It's a highly treasured and hugely respected trophy and after the 'victors' have paraded it around proudly for their adoring fans it is filled with champagne for them to celebrate with, NOT blooming... Coca-Cola!"

"I did not realise you felt as strongly as that, too, Sally. How about Nike then? For years I thought that tick of theirs was to do with 'quality control'. Never dreamt it was anything else!"

"That's very funny, Sir Howard. I don't know how you think of them, though I suppo..."

Sir Howard cut her short, saying, "I wasn't joking. I was being serious."

Sally apologised and returned to what she had been doing.

"That's alright, Sally. I've got hundreds more of them up here!" he said, tapping the side of his head and smiling.

Sally mischievously ventured one of her own. "Well as a matter of fact, I was always a little confused with the printing on T-shirts and such. So being a little anorexic, I always read it as Russell Arthritic until someone pointed out that it says Russell Athletic."

"No, Sally. That would be dyslexic, not anorexic."

Sally quickly replied, "Y'see, I said I was a little amnesic, didn't I?"

"Touché, Sally, touché. Now where was I? Oh yes, football! Y'know, with all the big money floating around in the game today from the television rights and the like, and yes, plus our special friends... sponsorship and advertising. It is a travesty the amount what they charge the ordinary fans to see the game. *Not* the people who sit in corporate boxes stuffing their faces with designer chef sandwiches and toasting each other with expensive-sounding champagne *but* the ones who queue up come rain or shine, Saturday or Sunday, Monday or Wednesday or Thursday or Friday or sometimes even Monday or Tuesday, depending on whether it is in one of the Domestic Cups or one of the European Competitions; I hope you are keeping up with this 'cos I'll be asking questions later; or a Domestic League game or a replay or second leg of one or other of the above, or both, and depending on whether it is being shown live on television or not."

He stopped for breath and continued.

"The ones who have to check with every game for the kick-off time for all the same reasons as mentioned above." Sir Howard took a further deep breath and carried on. "Yes, those poor individuals who pay a membership charge at the beginning of the season and are still expected to part with anything from between £20 and £50 per game as compared with less than £10 at German and other top continental clubs. I ask you, Sally. Why, with all that money coming in from so many other sources, do they have to charge the faithful fans so much? It is scandalous! The price of a programme too, do you know some of them charge as much as five pounds? I would much rather put the rest to it and buy a good book! Get a few more hours of enjoyment out of that." Sally had sat nodding agreement and respectfully waited for Sir Howard to finish before responding.

"Still, you'll be going to watch Spurs again next season, won't you?"

"Ooh yes, I have already sent off the application for my season ticket. One of my little indulgences, y'know!"

"Have their charges gone up again?"

"Yes, but that's different, you're talking about *my* team. They did finish fifth last season and I'm not an ordinary fan." Sally bit her lip to prevent herself from saying what she was thinking.

"Still, it's good to see our friend doing so well in the world of female soccer. I wonder what sensations await her in her ever expanding world?" Sally asked, whilst checking her lip for blood.

"Sally, what an inspiration you are! Here was I sitting wondering where we go next with our Aurora Stafford story... and you've got it! It's obvious! More and more females are getting interested in football as a result of our friend's success. We'll ask *them* what next? We must create a regular feature for 'Orrite?' Magazine where they invite their 'girlie' readers to send in their aspirations, hopes, or even their predictions for Aurora Stafford's future as the 'Figurehead' or new 'Icon', your choice, of ladies' football in this country. Do you hear where I am going with this? I am talking... fashion, make-up, hairstyles, the occasional vague reference to football... We could have a catchy heading, such as... SOCCER SLUTS. No, no, no... SOCCER BELLES or FOOTIE BABES HAVE YOUR SAY! I am sure that with the right words we can paint the picture and make it sound heavyweight... By that I mean lightweight enough to get our 'Teenage' and 'Tweenage' gals on board. Now that is where you'd be a little closer to them than I. So I shall rely on you to create it in 'Orrite?' language, the better for them to understand, bless them. I think I can feel another injection into the pension fund coming."

Sally was encouraged by her boss's remarks so she made another suggestion. "Yes, we could run an online message board for them, or even a chat room, let them feel involved. It might be fun to see inside the minds of these youngsters, it would help us to keep it cooking."

"Yes! Yes! Yes! We'll use one of those new-fangled website thingies like Facelook, Tweeter, or whatever they are called, so that it comes straight here to this office, to you. I could probably get 'Orrite?' to subsidise it, especially if I make it sound like it was their idea."

# 27

The England Ladies training ground was situated just inside the M25 Motorway in rural Hertfordshire, which meant that Aurora Stafford had to make the journey down from Barcaster by car with her assistant, Kirsty Pye. They were put up at the hotel where the England men's team stay when they play at Wembley. So after checking into the room they were to share and freshening up, Ror' and Kirsty headed for the Hospitality Suite where a 'meet and greet' reception, including a buffet and 'soft' drinks had been arranged by the F.A. There were some very strong personalities in the existing international squad, including a couple who had been round the block a few times and regarded themselves as 'hardcases'. This made the challenge of integrating into the world of international female football even more daunting for Aurora, and she was understandably filled with trepidation as she approached the Hospitality Suite. Kirsty Pie sensed her friend's nerves and put a reassuring hand on her shoulder, saying, "This is nothing you can't handle. Remember... you are a seasoned international yourself, so they've never been anywhere that you haven't been a thousand times or more!"

"I know but this is a bit different. This is my first time with the English Ladies' squad and if we're going to live up to all the 'hype', they're expecting us to win the World Cup in about nine months' time and I haven't even met them yet!"

Kirsty opened the door and said, "Don't worry about it, it will be alright. Besides, you know the girls from our club, that's a start."

The girls walked into the room and were greeted with hand-clapping and cheers from every corner, even the officials from the F.A. joined in. Aurora and Kirsty were taken by surprise and totally overwhelmed by the welcome.

Carole Servis jumped up, hugged them both, then set about introducing them to the rest of the squad and the officials including Ror's predecessor, who was now Director of Footballing Affairs or something similar. By this time Aurora and Kirsty felt more relaxed, so after being introduced to everybody in the set-up, Ror' respectfully asked them to sit down and listen whilst she explained the circumstances surrounding her appointment to the job of England Ladies coach, in case there was any lingering resentment from some of the more established members of the squad.

"Girls, I guess you'll all know by now that I came into ladies' football by accident, *an* accident in fact. It was like I caught something on the fence when I tried to jump it. Enough said, I think."

Everybody reacted by laughing and applauded Ror' for making light of what was a traumatic and life changing... (Well you know the rest...*ed.*)

"I cannot thank Kirsty enough for what she has done for me in pushing me to actually coach as well as play for the 'Belles'. It is mainly down to her and the encouragement of my old manager Donnie Mclaren that I've ended up here in such a short time as part of the England set-up. That and a bit of dedication and hard work from me, I suppose! I appreciate the chance I've been given and just to say thank you, I am going to America next summer with the intention of bringing back the World Cup! And I hope you girls are all with me."

The girls, to a man, jumped up to cheer and applaud Aurora as she held Kirsty's hand aloft then she in return acknowledged all of them, moving amongst them, one by one.

"A great start, Aurora. You seem to have their respect, but a word of caution. Do watch your back and keep your wits about you because there are one or two individuals who like to show that they are graduates of the 'School of Hard Knocks'. Kirsty knows the ones I mean, so make the most of her experience. Meanwhile, on behalf of the English Ladies Football Association may I say officially, welcome and the very best of luck to you and the girls in your quest to bring back the biggest prize of all! I bet you can't wait to get started. Well, you can relax a little for the rest of today and start with a vengeance tomorrow." Dame Judy Dishes delivered one of her broadest smiles and spoke most encouragingly as she held Aurora's hand in hers. "I can't think of anyone better equipped to do the job than you. I am quite optimistic having experienced it for myself and coming so close last time, all the best." She gave Ror' a peck on both cheeks and moved off to speak to others in the room.

Ror', not sure how to take 'the better equipped' remark, turned and caught up with Kirsty who was handing out timetables for the next day's training, bringing the players' attention to the whereabouts of the coach and time that it would be leaving, also reminding them of the fines for latecomers. There had always been a strict regime in the ladies' camp and Kirsty was anxious not to allow it to slacken under their new set-up. To be fair to the girls, their discipline was generally pretty good, so previous coaches had experienced very few problems except for a few 'high spirited pranks', as they were described to the media. The seriousness of most incidents had been carefully kept under wraps. However, certain information regarding some had found their way into the hands of one of the more 'creative' reporters and as a result had caused a significant 'stir'.

With this in mind and taking on board what former head coach Judy Dishes had told her, Ror' resolved to find out from Kirsty who the most likely culprits were and who she would need to keep keenest eye on and who to rein in. So at the earliest opportunity Ror' took Kirsty to one side and said, "Kirsty, we have to have a chat about what Dame Judy said. Did you hear what she said? Despite the fantastic reception the girls gave us she still told me to watch my back."

"I did hear but don't worry about it now, we'll talk about it back in the room. You'll send out the wrong signals if you start out looking worried now. You've gotta be positive, ok? Let's get ourselves a cuppa, my throat's dry from all this chatting! I hope we haven't got too long to wait for dinner 'cos these sandwiches aren't doing much for me, makes me feel hungry just looking at 'em."

Later that night back in their room Aurora and Kirsty were getting ready for bed. Kirsty was the first to speak.

"Y'know, I always fancied you when you were Rory Stafford, along with the thousands of others. Now it seems I'm gonna be forever jealous of you, 'cos you seem to have gone from being the man who had everything, to being the woman who has everything. It is like living two successful lives in one."

Ror' came over to Kirsty, clinched her tightly and kissed her full on the lips, saying, "That was one from Rory and now this one is from Aurora."

She held Kirsty tight to her for several moments before her friend gently, slowly, and almost reluctantly pulled herself away.

"God, that was enough to send anybody the other way, I thought it was Rory I fancied; now I'm not so sure. Don't tell my old man, whatever you do! Oh, I don't know though, maybe it would be good to let him know. Keep 'im on his toes!"

Aurora laughed and stroked Kirsty's face reassuringly then in a serious tone said, "Thanks for the compliments, Kirsty. Remember we are best friends... right? What success I have had so far as a woman you have been a big, big part of it. We are the female Cloughie and Taylor. Without you there I couldn't have achieved half, and don't you forget that! You were especially good in there today. Now give us another big hug and let's turn in, gotta get a good night's sleep 'cos tomorrow a new chapter begins!"

\*

The next morning at the training ground everybody appeared full of high spirits and fired up, ready to go. Kirsty was the first to speak. "Now we know that you come from various teams and are used to the different training methods of your clubs. Most of you here have trained with England before but... this is going to be different again. I appreciate that this is a pre-season get-together and some of you might have indulged a little in your holidays so we shall start off gently but please remember this... I intend us to be the fittest outfit at the World Cup next summer! Whatever we do here we want you all to promise that you'll keep it up during the season even when you feel you are doing far more than your club-mates. I'll let Ror' fill you in further."

"As Kirsty said, we shall be aiming for absolute peak fitness from you all. You can have the best ball skills in the world but they will count for nothing if you are off the pace and get caught out. WE aim to get that extra yard of pace out of you ALL before you leave here. So where you might have put in an hour on sprinting before, we shall make it two. One hour on stamina will become two; instead of one lap of the track we'll be doing two. The good news is... when you've done all that, where it used to be one shower... you can have two!" Ror' paused for the laugh but received groans and cat calling, so she carried on. "When we're happy with everybody's fitness, we'll maybe spend some time doing something with a football. If there are any of you who don't think they're up to it they should pack their bags now, if you *are* up for it and want to give it a go... then you're mad. Only joking. C'mon, let's get started!" This was greeted with a chuckle from the majority.

Aurora and Kirsty were really pleased at the way the girls applied themselves and couldn't fault them for attitude. Although there were one or two who struggled at first, even *they* came to enjoy pushing themselves to the absolute limit, on occasion being reassured by their coach that it was going to make all the difference when the time came.

Every one of them was advised to pay special attention to the importance of 'warming up' and 'warming down', as well as all the other disciplines imposed on them each time they trained. Needless to say the physios were kept very busy but *they* were impressed with the girls' application and discipline, bearing in mind that some had reacted badly to the appointment of their new player-coach.

By keeping the girls hard at it all the time the coaches had succeeded in creating a great spirit throughout the squad and it left little opportunity for personal 'niggles' and differences of opinion to occur. This was just as well since Kirsty had not had the time to name the 'likely candidates' on the first evening of the training camp. Overall though, they had imbued in them the same 'passion' that Rory Stafford brought to every international game he had played in.

# 28

The great spirit in the camp bode quite well for the future of the ladies' game in England and after seeing them win handsomely a couple of friendly games against top-notch opposition, everybody considered that they would do well in America and even stood a good chance of bringing back the World Cup.

In certain newspapers the interest in Aurora Stafford and her involvement in ladies' football, both with Barcaster Belles and the England girls, often rivalled and sometimes overshadowed the coverage of the men's game. This was due, in part, to the regular promptings of the likes of Sir Howard Eyeknow and his 'cronies' at 'Orrite?' Magazine in their quest to keep Ror's profile as large as possible for as long as it served their purpose.

To this end any little 'incident' would be turned into a sensational event with the twist of a few words and the accompaniment of a questionably 'compromising' photograph. These stories were often followed by apologies from the newspapers and phrases such as... 'taken out of context'... 'alleged involvement'... were quite commonplace, though not everybody would spot an apology as it was invariably placed several pages deep into the paper and in a none too noticeable position on the page. In complete contrast to the prominence of the original item which was often headlines or invitingly 'trailed' on the front page with the 'full story' to be found inside.

There was no end to what the media would go to get a story, even alluding to the prospect of Aurora doing a photo shoot for a 'nudey' magazine. One of the tabloids took it one step further with the suggestion that she might pose with her marriage partner, Lisa Stafford. After all *she* had done it before. (No doubt it would be shot in the best possible taste! ...*ed.*)

The relevant newspaperman supported the suggestion by saying, "Think what it would do for Ror's profile."

'Yes... it would expose it... fully!' would be the obvious reply.

Meanwhile, Ror' was back at the Barcaster club engineering the latest sweep of trophies with her ladies and by the end of the season they had the League Title, the F.A. Cup, the Coach of the Season and the Outstanding Player of the Season award secured and in the trophy cabinet.

Whilst all of this was happening another season had come and gone for Barcaster United men's team and all they had to show for it was the League Cup and a position just outside the places in the Premiership Table to qualify for a place in any of the European competitions the following season. The League Cup *was* an improvement on previous seasons which had yielded *no* trophies.

Since he'd lost the services of Rory Stafford, Donnie Mclaren had tried different patterns of play with youngsters from the Academy and brought in several new faces, including a few foreign imports and the Welsh 'wing wizard', Dai Dare, who was more 'prima donna' than 'Maradona'. So despite all, he had not been able to replace him successfully.

All thoughts she might have of playing again at the highest level in the men's game seemed to have been forgotten, though it was impossible for the board at Barcaster United not to notice that Aurora Stafford was effectively sweeping everyone and everything before her and seemed to be making the ladies' game bigger and some would say better than the men's game. Her Belles team had certainly achieved more success than their male counterparts in the last two seasons. With Donnie McLaren's persistent prompting the board had canvassed the relevant bodies regularly with regard to making it possible for Aurora to play her football back in the Premiership.

However, despite all their efforts the only development to show was that F.I.F.A. or U.E.F.A. had issued a statement to say they would be 'considering' whether eleven-year-old girls and upwards should be allowed to play in mixed games. So, no hope for the foreseeable future then.

On the home front, Ror' and Lisa were enjoying a happy, loving relationship which was appreciated by the children, who were much more settled and now both were doing very well at school.

Hilary had married Mike Conway and they were living in Mike's house, although she still looked after the Staffords in much the same way as before, staying over when Mike was doing the 'twilight' watch. Mike was still putting in as many hours as before at the hospital, which meant Hilary probably saw more of the Staffords than she did of her new husband. She enjoyed an 'all girls together' working relationship with them now.

Hilary still had her hands full protecting them from the 'paparazzi' but it was a duty that she coped with quite well. The press guys got to know just how far they could go with her. This did not stop certain photographers from overstepping the mark and having to be physically removed from the grounds whilst trying to get some 'hot' pictures from the house that contained not one, not two, but three physically attractive women. Which editor is going to miss out on a shot showing all three women together, however innocent it might seem.

There would always be a story to go with it... that is the easiest bit!

The amount of cash to be made from just a couple of pictures is enormous, so it was nothing for Hilary to have to climb up into one of the trees standing within the grounds of the Stafford home to 'assist' the opportunistic 'snapper' on his way down... and out! Often with disastrous results, accidents with cameras were inevitable and quite common, as you would expect.

No good complaining though, 'cos it was always awkward explaining oneself to the police when the words 'private property' and 'trespass' enter the conversation.

At times Hilary had to stand back in admiration at

their ingenuity in managing to dodge the C.C.T.V. cameras *and* avoid doing themselves serious harm as they negotiated the defences. She could not help thinking what a credit some would be to the S.A.S.

Because of the likely financial rewards some would go to the extreme of employing the latest technology in their efforts to capture an 'exclusive'. In one instance, a couple actually drove up in a cherry picker, all dressed and tooled up. One of them actually proceeded to pollard a huge tree. When a photo opportunity presented itself, he produced his camera and started snapping away. Upon being challenged he alerted his partner and they made their getaway with him stuck in the cage of the cherry picker. The police were called and their description and the direction in which they were travelling given. Despite their slow progress they managed to throw the police off their trail but eventually they were apprehended at the plant hire yard in the process of getting their deposit back. You have to admire their cheek *and* dedication to their money!

Still, it did the Staffords a favour, saved them the expense of getting the tree surgeons in to sort out the ugly low branches on that particular tree.

Apart from this, life could not have been much better for all of them. Aurora was as popular and successful as she *had* been as Rory Stafford.

## 29

"Germany is the current holder of the Ladies Soccer World Cup and you can bet your bottom dollar, or should that be Deutsche Mark?"

"Euro, that should be your bottom euro."

"Whatever it is, we all know they'll be doing their darndest to hang on to that cup! They are always very professional and prepare so meticulously in everything they do but ah cain't see anybody beating those beautiful ladies from the U.S. of A. this time round. Remember, they're playing at home so I'm sure we can count on them to bring home the corn."

"I don't know, Randy. I think the English team could surprise a lot of people. Could be the dark horses of this competition, they look pretty sharp to me. Well, pretty and sharp, actually. Sorry about that."

"Nothing to apologise for."

"What? Oh I see... yes... But seriously they did get as far as the semi-finals last time round, just missing out in the penalty shoot-out, usual story. Back home everyone has been talking about their performances under the new player-coach. Football performances, I mean, naturally. Big news over there of course, what with the sex change and all. I guess you know all about that though."

Randy Forelock replied, "What do ya mean? I resent that implication! I know absolutely nothing about sex changes. The only operation I've undergone is an enhancement one. Yeah, I know what y're thinking. Well as a matter of fact it was not an operation at all, just therapy, a massage, to enhance my... ego! Anyway, that's enough about me. Folks, let me introduce you to my distinguished guest Mr. Trad Britt, the star of the biggest grossing sex comedy of all time, both sides of the pond, 'Love Eventually' aka 'Willing but Unable' and a few other 'biggies', and I use that word advisedly – too many to mention right now. He has a special interest being here today people, not necessarily sporting, eh?" he said with a nod and a wink a la Monty Python.

"Yes, 'cos y'see folks, Mr. Britt is dating the U.S. team's Star Offensive player, Ms. Sally Fifth, isn't that so, Trad?"

"That is correct, Randy. But we call them strikers back home; 'offensive' paints quite a different picture for us."

"Hey, cultural differences already folks. Well thanks for pointing that out for us, Trad, but we wanna hear more about you."

"Well, 'er, I came over from London late last night, especially for the competition. I am a keen football supporter and I play a bit, in fact I represented my prep school as a child."

"I'm impressed. Did you hear that, folks? Mr. Britt went to a prep school back home in England Land."

"By the way, that should be romantic comedy, not sex comedy!"

"Oh sure, that's right. I'm sorry, I must have gotten hold of the wrong end of the dick, er, stick. Oops, there I go again. It's just you naughty English are so famous for your stiff... upper... lip. Nearly had ya going there folks, nudge, nudge, wink, wink. Say no more. So how long have you been dating the sexy Sally?"

"Big Python fan, are we? Actually we have been seeing each other some six months now. We were introduced at a Hollywood party."

"So you've seen a lot of our Sally then over the last six months. All there is to see, eh, eh? Know what I mean?"

"No, I don't, frankly. Could we just carry on...?" Randy cut across Trad again, this time affecting a woman's voice and waving a make-believe fan in front of his face.

"Carry on indeed... I'm sure I don't know what you mean Mr. D'Arcy. You would do well to remember that I am a married woman for I am betrothed to his grace, Lord Habuff. Still, what had you in mind?"

Seeing that he was uncomfortable with this, Randy apologised to Trad. "I'm sorry but normally my guests from over the water join in, knowing how much we all love the Pythons here in the States and there's no bigger fan than me of British humour. The guys on the other side of the glass should have warned you. So where did we get to? Oh yeah, let's get back to soccer and the gorgeous Sally Fifth. You gotta admit they are funny though!" Randy launched into a pretty credible impression of Eric Idle singing 'Always Look on the Bright Side of Life', and calling out, "Join in if you know the words."

He saw no reaction from Trad so he stopped singing and gestured for him to speak.

"I have to say that Monty Python was a little before my time. I know of their work, of course, who doesn't? But I am more in touch with contemporary humour as you kindly alluded to in your introduction. Still, since you've brought them up I really will have to get hold of the DVD and watch it, when I am not so busy."

Randy faced the people in the control box with a look that said, 'Which planet is this guy from?' Then returning to Trad, continued. "Trad, don't worry, I'll have one of my guys rustle you up a box-set with my compliments. There's about ten years' worth altogether – enjoy! Meantime, tell us more about you and America's top scorer."

Trad was not sure how to take this and hesitated, so to fill the hiatus Randy carried on, "You did know that Sally has scored and had more 'assists' than any other international player in ladies' soccer."

"Yes, I'm sorry; I was expecting a 'double entendre' bearing in mind what has gone before in our interview."

"Oh sure... No, I could see I was wasting your time. Maybe we could talk about your take on what's funny a little later. Meantime, tell us more about Sally and you. I'm sure the viewers are fascinated." This time he looked towards the control room, with eyebrows raised.

"As a matter of fact, I am fully aware of Sally's prowess." Randy's ears pricked in anticipation. "On the football pitch." Randy's jaw dropped.

"Wow, for a minute there... No, I guess not! Everybody agrees that she does have a good head as well as a great pair of... feet. That's what we are talking about. It wouldn't take much to turn that one round though, now would it?"

"I'm sorry, I'm not with you."

"That's fine, what we are saying is when it comes to finishing them off, Sally's as good with her head as she is with her... feet."

The guys in the control box were in hysterics but Randy kept a straight face throughout.

"I do know that, yes, she gave me a DVD of her best shots."

"Her best shots? Oh yeah... shots... I get it... As in goals, not... photo... shots. So you have to agree with the rest of us... she's the best 'finisher' in the business and I guess us Americans hope that she will... keep it up... throughout this World Cup competition. So who will you be shouting for Trad?" Randy took a breath and allowed himself a quick glance in the direction of the control box again, to avoid laughing out loud, only to see that the guys behind the glass were now in apoplexy.

"Well, it's very difficult for me, being a red-blooded Englishman and at the same time being very much in love with America's finest footballer. Female, that is."

"Hey folks, you heard it here first! Forget what you've read in those 'glossy' magazines. This guy is very much in lu-urv with the gorgeous Sally. So tell me, Trad, does the beautiful lady feel the same way about the handsome gentleman and is that the sound of wedding bells I can hear in the background?"

"Well, yes to the former, I think... I hope, and an emphatic 'no' to the latter. I'm not about to rush into another situation where, when it goes 'belly-up' things get very messy and certain people become very nasty, then expensive lawyers get very much richer in taking an inordinately long time to sort out a settlement to suit 'all parties', particularly, as we all know... themselves!" Trad spoke with obvious rancour and Randy picked up on it instantly.

"Still bitter about the divorce from that other well known... actor from Tinsel Town? I won't dwell on it... to spare your feelings... Must have cost you dearly, I'm guessing, 'cos *she* insisted that she'd given up her own successful acting career for you."

Trad was visibly irritated and rose to the bait Randy had thrown him.

"I thought you were going to *spare* my feelings, and how was it she'd given up a *successful* career for me? Her last three films had bombed! They sank like lead weights! They were lost without trace! The producers were down by millions of dollars! The studio had to close and they didn't even make it onto DVD! It was her good fortune that I was around at the time. Everybody knows that!"

"Well I wasn't going to say..." Trad cut Randy short.

"Whereas *all* of my movies have been outstanding box office successes. Even *her* lawyers could see that much, surely!"

"Apparently not. Whatever they did or did not see, and I am not playing Devil's Advocate here, but they must have seen something 'cos they argued a pretty darned strong case. Oh, and please don't call me Shirley."

"What, what are you talking about?"

"Sorry Trad... Leslie Neilson, Naked Gun, or was it Airplane? Another great comedy actor, much the same as yourself 'cept he's Canadian." Once again Randy raised an eyebrow in the direction of the boys behind the glass, sighed resignedly then carried on. "So what you're saying is that you're not about to rush into another 'high-profile' show-biz style wedding."

"Certainly not."

"In case our Sally becomes another Suzanne."

"Suzanne?"

"Yeah, Suzanne, Suzanne Getsall! That was the name me and the guys came up with for your wife at the time... and... er... others like her... Y'know what..." Trad cut him off mid-sentence.

"Ex-wife. Oh yes, and whilst you were at it did you find one for the likes of me? F.N. Sucker perhaps?"

"As a matter of fact, no, but hey, that is very funny. Do you mind if we use it next time?"

"Be my guest, please. What do you mean, next time?"

Randy spoke directly into the camera. "Thanks, the best we could manage was Willie B. Shafted and I did not necessarily mean *your* next time. Divorce is a common thing in Tinsel Town. Well I wanna thank you for coming on and talking to us Trad. Friends... that was the wonderfully talented comedy actor Mister... Trad... Britt! Good luck with the latest film. Good luck to the beautiful Sally Fifth, the U.S. Ladies and whichever team you'll be shouting for, Trad, and thanks for giving up your valuable time. It was much appreciated, I'm sure."

He rolled his eyes before he turned to shake Trad's hand and gesture him towards the exit. He looked towards the control booth and as the adverts came on screen he called out, "Can you guys get us the low-down on this sex change guy who's in charge of England's ladies? Sounds like we might have gotten ourselves a bit of a 'human interest' story there... know what I mean...? Let's get hold of him and get us an interview with the guy. Gotta be more interesting than Billy Brown Eyes there! Hey, and while you're about it, try to get Sally on, for her angle on our friend. Can she see how far up his own ass he is? Or could it be I'm being a Trad, sorry, a 'tad' judgemental?" Randy could see that the others were cringing at this last bit. "Hey, help me out here, guys. Gimme a break. I'm doin' my best, alright?"

## *30*

Meanwhile, over at the Los Angeles Galactics Soccer Stadium, Carrie Whaite, team physio, was at the changing room door ready to assess the injuries to the English players after a bruising encounter with the Uruguayan team.

The first to appear was the team's tall centre-back, Carol Servis, and her fellow defender Valerie Crow, who was limping quite badly.

"I've never played against such an uncompromisingly dirty and devious set of players as that lot of..."

"You can say that again, Val. I had to change my top at half-time, it was soaked through."

"Me too, but God it *was* hot out there though?"

"I'm not talking sweat! It was covered in spit from that bloody striker of theirs! I mean it's not healthy, is it? I showed it to the ref but she just nodded, pointed to the sun and mopped her brow in sympathy, silly cow. Still, she did award us a penalty, just one out of a possible hatful; even then the assistant kept her flag down... again. How is that leg of yours? I reckon you're lucky you can still walk on it. She could easily have broken it for you with that tackle. I'm not saying it was late but the rest of us had already started walking towards the changing room."

"The old ones, always the best ones, eh? If you're trying to cheer me up, Carol, you're doing a lousy job of it! Oh! Ms. Whaite, will you take another look at this leg for me? It seems to have swollen a whole lot more."

"Yes, I'm sure it has. I still think it was a mistake to carry on playing on it, though I admire you for doing so, but for the time being go and get out of that kit, clean yourself up, then come and let me take a really close look at it."

Kirsty Pye, assistant coach, turned to Aurora Stafford, approaching the tunnel to the changing room and said excitedly, "Didn't the girls perform well out there today? It must have been hard for them to keep their heads with all that provocation and nastiness. It gets even harder from now on though, so we could well do without the injuries to key players, especially you. Those South Americans don't take any prisoners, do they? Is your ankle gonna be alright, Ror'?"

"Well they stopped the blood ok, could be quite a gash, we'll see when I get the sock off. Lucky we've got the best part of a week to sort it out. C'mon, let's check on the others."

Despite the battering they had taken and the cuts and bruises sustained, the English girls' spirits were very high and the atmosphere in the changing room was pretty lively, in complete contrast to that of the Uruguayans, because despite their overly physical approach to the game and their attempts to run rough-shod over the rules and the officials, they had lost two-one. They were out of the competition and contemplating the journey home *and* the reception they would face when they arrived there.

"Give yourselves a big hand, girls. You can be really proud of yourselves out there today – you kept your heads despite the provocation, you had discipline, and most impressively of all you played the better football. I am really proud of you, every one of you."

Aurora Stafford carried on where Kirsty Pye left off.

"That goes for me too, double. I am proud of the way we held it together as a team, though *I* nearly let you down when that number six tried to separate my foot from my ankle. Anyway, we are the ones in the quarter finals, only two games away from the final. Nothing's gonna stop us now, eh girls?"

*

When the draw was made for the last eight of the competition, the German ladies were to play the United States, thus denying the possibility of a re-run of the previous final. The England team would play another South American side, the very skilful but equally competitive Brazilians. The other fixtures were Italy v Spain and Poland against rank outsiders Morocco.

There had been some very entertaining games in the previous round but none more so than the one that saw Morocco knock out the second seeded Holland. On the evidence of their performance many people, especially the neutrals, were encouraged to think that the Moroccans could go all the way and possibly win the final.

*

The day came for their match with the Brazilians and although they were shored up by Val Crow's recovery from injury, the England girls were understandably nervous, especially Aurora Stafford, who had undergone treatment on her ankle right up to the last training session and was worried that *she* might not be one hundred per cent fit. What weighed on her mind and the others in the England set-up was that they had successfully kept the seriousness of the injury secret right up to that last workout, then, somehow the press and TV people got to know. This meant that the opposition would know too and Aurora anticipated being the target for special treatment by the Brazilian ladies, but not of the medical kind.

In the event the English girls dominated the game and managed to shield Aurora to the point where she almost had free reign in the mid-field and was able to impose herself going forward on every possible occasion, ably assisted by the newfound 'star' of the team in the diminutive form of Mai Wei, whose dad owns a Chinese restaurant in Outer Wedlock, a small town near Chester.

The Brazilians had no answer to the foraging runs and incredible footwork as she worked her magic from out on the left wing. She was so fast and adept at avoiding the clumsy challenges that it was rare for her to be caught, but when she was it was inside the opposition's penalty box, resulting in a spot kick for her side which Aurora Stafford despatched with clinical efficiency to the top right-hand corner of the Brazilian goalkeeper's net.

Despite England's superiority, that was the only score and although the English girls went close on many occasions, the Brazilians defended stubbornly and held out to the final whistle without conceding another goal.

England were in the semi-finals and one game away from the ultimate prize.

The match between Italy and Spain kicked off at the same time as the England-Brazil game and the girls were greeted as they left the pitch with the news that the Spanish ladies had beaten their European counterparts one-nil in another hotly contested, ill-tempered, but nevertheless dull game, where the defences were on top for most of the time and where both teams packed five players into mid-field. With a lone striker on both sides, the attacking options were cut to a bare minimum, and entertainment value was almost zero. Significantly, this was symptomatic of all that was currently wrong with the **men's** game.

The U.S. ladies versus Germany contest was a total contrast, with both sides playing open and enterprising football, which is what we had come to expect from them. However, despite several 'strikes' on and many more 'off-target', from both sets of players, at the end there was only one that counted, settling it in favour of the Home side, scored by... yes, you've guessed it! None other than Ms. Sally Fifth!

Morocco turned in another 'spirited' performance and entertained the crowd with their enterprise and audacity, showing slick skills and impressive ball control, and despite some heavy-handed tactics from the Poles, carried the day with three goals to two.

There was a large amount of money paid out by the 'bookies' on this result. They had given 'odds' of 250-1 against the Moroccans reaching the semi-finals and they were now hastily cutting them back even further, from the original 500-1 to reach the World Cup Final.

## 31

"What would be your 'dream final', Lawro? England-Morocco, England-U.S., or all European England-Spain? Any one would be a mouth-watering prospect. Well, perhaps not so much your England-Spain."

"To be absolutely honest with you, Gary, I *would* take Spain, 'cos our girls are more used to the European approach and I think they would fare better. Whereas Morocco, they are definitely the 'dark horses' of this competition. I'd take them to give any of the surviving teams a good run for their money. The U.S. has got the best striker in the cup by a country mile in Sally Fifth. Carole Servis would have her hands full with her, if you ask me. She's good on the ground and good with her head – look at that goal she scored against Germany. I reckon the most attractive tie has to be England-Morocco though."

"Where would you put your money, Alan?"

"Well, as a neutral I would like to see U.S.-Morocco then England-Morocco, then U.S.-England if I was looking at it purely for entertainment value."

"We are only speculating, of course, whilst we wait

for the draw for the semi-finals of the Ladies' World Cup to be made but I have to say, with the quality of the football in the games that we have seen so far, whichever way it turns out, it promises to be very interesting. Ah! Right! A little man in my ear has just told me that we can now go live to America."

"Yes, hello England, you've joined us just in time for the Governor of New York, Kent Belleavit, to pull out the name of the first semi-finalist, and it is... Morocco... to play... England. That means that the good old U. S. of A. will be playing Spain in the other semi. The first semi-final will be played in San Francisco and the other in Los Angeles. Was that what you were hoping to hear over there in London, Gary? A game against the 'minnows', as you English quaintly put it?"

"Randy, I don't think the Moroccan ladies are anybody's fools. They didn't get this far by luck, and they've played some excellent football and impressed everybody with their skills and the quality of their game generally. How do you fancy your girls' chances, are they gonna go all the way? They have looked very good in every game so far and I feel sure that they've played well within themselves up 'til now, just can't see Spain turning them over somehow."

Randy Forelock hesitated before answering Gary Lineker in the London studio.

"Gary, I understood and agreed with everything you said until that last bit about 'in themselves' and 'turning over'. Was that anything to do with that famous Maggie Thatcher speech about 'ladies not for turning'? Jees, that was some woman. I would put my money on any team she was on! By the way, what was that about our girls going 'all the way'? You're still talking soccer, right?"

"Sorry Randy, footballing terms, we use them a lot over here. We all agree that the U.S. ladies look like they will be in the final and we hope that it is gonna be our girls who meet them there. Meanwhile, I'm afraid it is time for us to say a big thank you and goodbye until we hook up with you again for the next couple of all-important 'soccer' games."

"Yeah Gary, look forward to experiencing some more of that good old fashioned 'football' wisdom when we next speak. Adios, muchacho!"

Gary Lineker affected an exaggerated bow towards Randy on his monitor and turned towards the people in the studio.

"Can you see Spain upsetting the applecart, Alan?"

"No, and I'm glad you didn't ask Randy that, he seemed confused enough. For me though, the U.S. have got too much in their armoury to lose that one."

"You're still talking soccer now, right?"

There was no reaction from Alan Hansen so Gary continued. "Yes, I tend to agree, they have looked formidable and I can't see them slipping up at this late stage. I'm sure they'll make it to the final. How about you, Lawro?"

Mark Lawrenson nodded in agreement. "My money would be on a U.S. v England final and I reckon with the form, and I am speaking football form, which both teams have shown in this competition so far, it will be a showpiece occasion and as I alluded to earlier, remember that word, Gary?

If Carol Servis can keep Sally Fifth quiet and Gabby Dean, the English goalie, plays out of her skin like she has in previous rounds, then England could very well run out winners."

"Let's hope you are right. I know that there really is great interest over here but we've got to play the semi-finals first and don't forget you will see both, and the final itself, on this very channel. Meanwhile, we have to say goodbye to you for now but in case you've just tuned in, the semi-finals of the Ladies' World Cup will be between England and Morocco and the U.S. against Spain. To be played one week from tonight in San Francisco and Los Angeles. So from Alan Hansen, Mark Lawrenson, and myself, goodnight until next week. Goodnight."

## 32

"Hello darlin', only the semi to play against Morocco and you're there, eh? Everybody's going mad here, people are driving round in their cars with flags flyin' and tootin' their horns, it's a mad 'ouse! No, not in our lounge ya silly sausage! Our Gavin and Fiona are 'over the moon'. Was your leg alright? Only two more games to play. Well, hopefully two, then you can rest it. We had everybody round here tonight for the game and they're drinking us dry – even Hilary, despite her condition. What do ya mean? Didn't I tell you? She's pregnant. You're right, I know, but he managed to get the time for that alright, didn't he? Isn't it great? Hold on, Gavin wants to have a word."

"Hello Da... Ror'. Brilliant result, can't wait for the final... I know but Morocco's no problem... Really proud... of you... and the other girls. Here... Fiona's pulling at my arm... Alright, Fiona, alright... Here she is."

"Hi... it's incredible, I can't believe it, suddenly everybody is supporting the England Ladies' football team and they're all being so nice to Gav and me now! What will it be like if you win the World Cup?

Sorry, *when* you win it, *phurp*! Yes, I did just burp, pardon me. Mu... Lisa gave me a little glass of champagne to try. Here she is, I'll give her back. Love you."

"Hallo again, darlin'. 'Ere, Hilary just said that if her baby's a girl they'll name it after everybody in the team when you win the Cup. She also said that 'er and Mike are now praying like mad for a boy! They are actually on their knees as we speak, only joking. What are you going to do now... celebrate wiv' an early night? I thought you'd say that. Ok, speak to you again soon, bye darlin'. Luv you!"

Lisa replaced the phone and turned to rejoin the celebrations; she motioned to Hilary. Hilary came towards her, they kissed and gently and lovingly squeezed Hilary's swollen stomach between them.

"Something has come between us."

"Oh don't say that. I couldn't stand it."

"I'm talking about the baby, darlin'. What did you think I meant? I was joking about your lump. Look at you getting all serious on me, again. Where's that husband of yours? He should be taking care of you, especially in your state... I mean... being pregnant... not necessarily the drink... I do know that this is a special occasion and you'll not be getting sozzled whilst you are with child... but what will you be like if they go all the way and win the World Cup?!"

"Are you telling me off? Are you lecturing me? You think I'm a little tipsy, don't you? Well, what was it you told me? 'You'll know when I'm drunk 'cos I'll be on the floor, but me with this bump, I won't be talking to your feet, and I'll be chatting to your knees.'

I thought that was really funny when you told it the first time but I think it is even funnier now." Hilary pulled Lisa to her in another hug and they laughed together for several moments. The others gathered round them, curious to know what was so funny.

# 33

"What a beautiful day, and I am not talking about the weather. The world is a wonderful place to be right now, the world that gave us its wonderful Ladies' World Football... Football Ladies' World... Ladies' Football World... CUP!! Sally, your idea with the chat line and the online website thingy was a master stroke. Do you realise we make money every time one of those young things gets in touch? And the continued involvement of our dear Ror' Stafford and the England girls in the Ladies' Football World Cup guarantees that we are making much, much more even when we are at home tucked up in our little beds. The girls are struggling to answer the phones though they are working in 'shifts', and I am not speaking of their 'attire' at this point. Forgive me; I will have my little joke. NO, but our pension fund is increasing 24/7, excuse the ugly expression. Not pension fund, nothing ugly about that... the 24/7 reference... horrible abbreviations. By the way, what does our dear friend, I mean, *your* dear friend, Jacques Boutes, think of the chances of our girls going all the way? Oh God, did I just say what I think I said? I have to stop watching these cheap television programmes. I mean to say does Jacques think that the girls will..."

"Pull it off and actually get into the final." There was no reaction from Sir Howard so Sally carried on. "Well, there is only one more game to play before we find out and he says he wouldn't be at all surprised if they went on to win the Cup. After all, they have played very well to get this far and if they can get their heads round it they should do it." Sally thought she saw a slight twitch of an eyebrow this time. "He says that it will be down to the more senior members of the squad to help the others to negotiate what will be for some of them... uncharted waters."

Sir Howard seemed to be considering each word of the sentences that Sally had delivered and hesitated before replying.

"Yes, I value his input and I tend to agree. They have done exceptionally well for themselves but more especially for us, bless them! By the way, when is their next game? They seem to have longer between games than the boys, or is it because there are less, sorry, fewer games to play and so they are spread out more? Or is it simply that I am getting carried away with the excitement of it all and do not know what I am talking about?" Sally recognised that Sir Howard Eyeknow's excitement was ever so slightly misplaced, as his only previous interest in the game of football was strictly limited to the support of his beloved Tottenham Hotspur. Even then, she was not altogether sure that the interest lay solely with the play as much as with the *players* of the 'beautiful game'. However, this she was prepared to overlook as she was on a decent percentage for bringing what was for him a 'whole new ball game' and had turned out to be 'a nice little earner' for herself too.

"The semi-finals take place next Saturday afternoon in the U.S. but it will be evening over here, of course."

"In that case, Sally, why don't you bring the magnificent Jacques round to my place and we shall watch it with a few 'special' friends, together with some of our 'favoured' clients?"

"Thank you, Sir Howard, that would be rather nice, but what can I do to help with the arrangements?"

"Well, if I do a hand written list you could send a little invite to everyone on it. Thank you. The rest you can leave to me!"

# 34

"If you have only just joined us and you've missed the start – the news is not good. After thirteen minutes of play the Moroccans have scored. England are already one-nil down. They were caught on the break after having the best of the early exchanges. It is not looking good for the English ladies. The Moroccans have got their tails up and they are looking to add to their early success. The ladies in the English defence have been shaken up and are playing quite nervously. The Moroccans have the upper hand and are forcing our girls into elementary mistakes. Someone has got to get a grip on this situation or it looks very much like there could be more goals. I don't know what you think, Dame Judy. For the benefit of the folks back home we have Dame Judy Dishes, the former England ladies' coach, with us in the commentary box. Something has to be done; they are in total disarray down there!"

"I couldn't agree more, John. There's no co-ordination, they've been rocked by that early goal but at this stage of the game there is no need to panic. There's plenty of time on the clock but they just seem to be in shock, they're not challenging for the ball.

"Or at best it's half-hearted."

Tony Cottee chipped in. "Yeah, and when they do get hold of it the distribution is woeful. It is time for someone to step up to the plate and take this game by the scruff of the neck."

"I agree, and surely that someone is Aurora Stafford. With all her experience, she should be the one to pull them together and wake them out of their stupor."

"John, this was tailor-made for someone like the old Ror' Stafford, but has Mark 2 got the same inner resolve and strength of character that could always be called upon in situations like these in the past? She's performed very well so far in this competition but the heat is really on here. Oh no! I do not believe it! That's number two! An own goal. That was Maureen Field's fault; the central midfielder tried to play herself out of trouble and held on to the ball too long. I'm sorry John, for hogging the commentary."

"No problem, Tony. There are plenty of problems for this England team now, though. That was a silly back pass that caught the goalie completely unprepared; it looked easier just to clear it into touch! How can they come back from this, Dame Judy? It's a total disaster!"

"Well, John, if they can hold out until half-time and get back into that dressing room, Aurora and her assistant, Kirsty Pye, can sit them down, knock their heads together and basically pull them out of this state of shock and then tell 'em, I hope, what they're doing wrong, 'cos they're playing like novices. Some of them are treating the ball like it's a hot potato at times, it's just unbelievable at the moment. They're all over the place." John Motson carried on. "They've now got three minutes and whatever stoppage time in this first half to play. There you are, the fourth official has just signalled an extra three minutes, so six minutes left to hold out. Can they do it? Can they avoid giving away another goal?"

They did hold out, rather nervously but without conceding any more goals and from the studio back in London, Gary Lineker, stunned, stutteringly thanked John Motson for his first half commentary and Dame Judy Dishes and Tony Cottee for their comments.

"Lawro, can they come back from this? Or is it asking for too much?"

"Look, Gary, there's a lot of experience in that dressing room and they've got possibly the best in the business when it comes to motivation in Aurora Stafford. Having said that, it is a big ask to expect them to recover and score the three goals they need to win. The Moroccan ladies are well on top at this stage, they've got the wind in their sails. One thing I thought of, Gary, is, do they have the staying power or will they run out of... wind? They did play the game at a very fast pace in that first half."

"Well, maybe that gives us something to cling on to! Are we clutching at straws? What do you think, Alan?"

"Why clutching at straws?" Alan Hansen coughed, and then continued, "There's only half the game gone and they can't possibly play as badly as they did in that first half. Look how well they've done to get this far. It's down to them to get back on track. I can imagine the scene in the England ladies' dressing room at this moment in time though!"

Mark Lawrenson continued the theme. "I know Kirsty Pie can breathe fire at times like these but I think it will be down to Ror' Stafford to stamp her authority on the game and inspire the others in the second half; she seemed a little off the pace. I don't know whether it is anything to do with her earlier injury but I will be looking for her to put her mark on this game otherwise I can see it slipping even further away from them."

"Thanks for that Alan, Mark...I agree with you both. I can't remember any team representing England, ladies or otherwise, performing quite so badly. I think they have got to go out there and play with pride in the shirt, especially for the thousands of fans who've made the trip all the way over here to support them. I am sure *they'll* be feeling let down by what they have seen so far in this game. If they work really hard and get those same fans behind them early on in the second half they are going to stand a chance of advancing to the final of what has been for them, so far, a fantastic competition. In this situation, with a huge crowd cheering them on, it would be as good as having that extra man – sorry... I mean... player – in the side."

Gary Lineker looked sheepishly into the camera then quickly announced, "Ah, I see the players are beginning to emerge from the tunnel, so I shall hand you back to John Motson for commentary on what looks to be a crucial second half of football for this English ladies' team."

"Thanks to Gary and co. Yes, it is set up to be at

the very least an interesting forty-five minutes or so, Judy. By the way, viewers, I have been told by Dame Judy to dispense with the 'dame' tag, so here goes again. What do you expect from these ladies now, Judy?"

"Well, John, I can imagine that they received the sharp edge of Kirsty's tongue and that for a while the air would have been quite blue in that dressing room, but then Aurora would remind them to return to the disciplines and values that the two of them had inspired them with on taking over. I.e. patience, control, intelligent movement off the ball, etcetera, etcetera..."

Motson turned to Cottee and asked, "Tony, you heard Da... er... Judy."

"Yes John, I think she has hit the nail on the head. They'd lost it and the break did not come quick enough. I can't wait, though. I hope the English girls had a little something in their half-time drinks to help settle their nerves. I did, but still I'm shakin' like a jelly! It might have something to do with those screaming falsetto voices, or do I mean soprano? Whatever, I ain't 'alf glad I'm not out there! I do think, though, that there's enough experience in the side to still get somethin' out of this game."

"Can't make out any changes to either team, no subs, so we could be in for more of the same in this second half of action that will decide who is going to the final of the Ladies' Football World Cup. I think you'll find it's a mix of falsetto and soprano, with a little bit of contralto thrown in for good measure."

"You've lost me now. As I say, John, the English

girls need an early strike to settle them down a bit and get 'em back on track but It ain't gonna be easy."

"They've got to look a lot sharper than they did in that first half, that's for sure. Here we go then, the ref has blown her whistle and the ball goes back to the Moroccan central mid-fielder... and would you believe it, she's taken the most audacious of punts towards Gabby Dean's goal... from just inside her own half. It was right on target too! Dean has gathered it into those huge arms of hers and thrown it out to Maureen Field to get England going forward."

Judy Dishes remarked, "Our goalkeeper was way off her line but to be fair to Gabby, she recovered very quickly. She covered the ground very fast for someone so large."

"Judy, Tony, it looks to me like the Moroccans are keeping everyone behind the ball now. A change of tactics, it seems. They look as though they are set up to shut out England, hold on to what they have and close the game down. Is this a sensible approach or could it backfire on them?"

Tony Cottee jumped in and said, "Well I guess I can see now what they were doing with that first shot. A third goal would have wrapped it up for 'em nicely. I think you're right, John; the Moroccan forwards have not set foot outside their half of the pitch yet. I think they could be showing a bit of tiredness by packing it in mid-field, possibly try to save their legs and maybe catch the England girls on the break as *they* go looking for the goals. It is a risky strategy if you ask me."

Play followed this pattern for several minutes, with England passing the ball around and generally keeping possession, which was made a little easier as they were not being pressed or challenged for the ball as much as in the first half. The Moroccan girls were content to let their opponents force the play. This was not a ploy that they had resorted to in their previous games, as they were keen to show their skills with the ball at their feet. Playing on the back foot seemed a little alien to them and it would be obvious to the keen-eyed spectator that their best form of defence was attack! Aurora Stafford was enjoying more time on the ball and suddenly Mai Wei was creating chances with her sprints down the left touch line. The English girls started threading the ball through to her at every opportunity and it was taking two defenders to try to shut her down. Ominously for the Moroccans, holes began to appear in their defence where their attention was centring on Mai Wei. It seemed like only a matter of time before the English girls would cash in.

"We are watching a different ball game now, Judy. England must score soon surely."

Dame Judy answered, "They've only got to get someone on the end of one of Mai Wei's crosses and they're back in it. The two strikers were a bit lacklustre in that first half and did nothing, just like the rest of them."

"Tony, what do you say?"

"I was gonna say, nobody actually shone, to be fair, but at least they are looking more lively now and they are seeing more of the ball!"

"Thanks Judy, Tony. Hallo, Mai Wei has been fouled just as she was about to dance between two defenders. No suggestion of a dive there, you two? It was just outside the box in any case, but it would be a good opportunity for Aurora Stafford to conjure up something here. Carole Servis is coming up for it. Davinia Lapp, England's gangly number nine is being jostled quite manfully inside that penalty area, as is her strike, or should that be *striking*, partner, Ophelia Munney. I have to say she *is* quite striking for a five-footer!"

"Back to what you do best, John, describing football. Must say though, you've got a good eye."

"She could probably earn a living as a glamour model outside of football." Tony Cottee this time. "Mind you, there are quite a few 'lookers' in that England team, know what I mean? Maybe they could do a calendar, raise some money for Children in Need or something similar. There'd be no shortage of takers."

"Meanwhile, back on the pitch, Tony. Stafford is standing over the ball as the referee does her best to keep the two sets of players apart and get the Moroccans back ten yards which means their own goal-line, in effect. I think they're ready, she blows. Stafford looks set to blast it but she has fooled everybody, including me, as the Moroccans stepped forward she has chipped it beautifully into the far corner of the net. It's a goal and England are back in this game!"

Dame Judy, standing up and clapping appreciatively, said, "It was a clever free kick, John. She anticipated the charge down, kept her cool and 'dinked' it sweetly into the far corner. Took some nerve to do it and that's just what was needed to get this England team back on track."

"It was inspirational. I see Tony nodding, just what the English girls needed."

Tony Cottee added, "Exactly, plus two more to go with it of course!"

Despite being imbued with a renewed vigour that the goal had given them, the English ladies were foiled by the staunch efforts of the opposition to deny them further success in raid after raid on the Moroccans' goal area.

However, as the half wore on the English girls' persistence began to wear their rivals down.

"There are some tired legs out there now, John, mostly on the Moroccan side. They've done well, they've kept England out so far but they've not launched a single counter-attack."

"They have fifteen minutes to go to keep this up, Tony. These England ladies are super fit and have had all the play since the goal but have not been able to take advantage. The Moroccan coach is very animated in the Technical Area. She's trying to attract the attention of the match officials."

"She's wanting to make some substitutions I believe, John."

"Judy's right, John. She's got three or is it four running up and down as we speak? The ball has gone out for a throw-in and the referee has signalled for the changeover. She has sent on four, no, five. It's five replacements, including the goalie! That is all of the substitutes used in one go. I can't remember seeing anything like this at any level of football.

Wholesale changes! Surely it could affect the balance of the team and what if someone gets injured?"

John Motson concurred. "I'll tell you what it will do, too; it'll run down the clock and eat away at those precious minutes unless the ref takes note. Also, of course it breaks the flow of play and gives the others a breather. What are your thoughts, Judy?"

"It is quite cynical, they are taking their time and there is a lot of unnecessary to-ing and fro-ing going on! The referee has signalled her displeasure and is speaking to the Moroccan coach who, incidentally, is an Italian, Signor Bagnioni."

"I notice that Aurora Stafford has kept her girls moving whilst this is going on and chatted to Kirsty Pye, but there are no changes to the England line-up as far as I can see, John. Keeping faith with her first-choice eleven."

"I think you are right, Tony. It would have made sense to have done it whilst all this was going on, wouldn't it? Finally though, play is getting under way again with that throw-in. Stafford moved the ball swiftly into the path of fellow mid-fielder Maureen Field, she sweeps it out to little Mai Wei on the left who hits it first-time towards the head of Davinia Lapp and she nods down to the right boot of Ophelia Munney, who calmly strokes the ball past the outstretched arm of the replacement Moroccan goalkeeper, it is two all! That was one of the sweetest passages of play that I can ever recall describing. It was so clinical in its execution, Judy."

Dame Judy was ecstatic. "It was poetry. The Moroccans were just caught out by the sheer speed of it! The substitutes hardly had time to take up position. They are stunned."

"Fantastic stuff, I couldn't agree more, John." Cottee continued. "Absolutely beautiful, the Moroccans have been made to pay for their antics. The English girls knew exactly what they were doing; cut a swathe clean through them before they had time to take a breath. If ever there was a case of instant justice, that was it. It was poetic justice, even! The Moroccans have been made to pay for their shenanigans."

"Can you spell that last word, Tony? Don't worry, I won't ask you to do it on air. Meanwhile, there is a real buzz around this stadium now. This crowd has just witnessed something very special and there is an air of expectancy from the English contingent now. Is there more of the same to come? Let's hope so!"

"I tell you what, John; they'd be hard pushed to witness anything as good as that if they sat here 'til Doomsday."

"Too right, Tony. Back down on the pitch the Moroccans are lining up for the restart. Remember, they can't afford to sustain any injuries, they've used up their quota of substitutes. The ball is played backwards, surely not another snap-shot from inside their own half. No, they are playing it round a bit, sensible stuff, letting the newcomers get a feel of it. The English girls are not holding back, though, they are getting stuck right in. The clock is ticking down and they desperately need another goal to avoid going to extra time. You get the feeling, Tony, that the Moroccan girls would settle for extra time but having used all of their subs it is precarious to say the least."

"Surely they're not, John. Don't forget England have not brought on any replacements. They'll have five fresh pairs of legs to call on. However, I expect the Moroccans and their Italian coach have still got a trick or two up their sleeves."

"It is true to say that our girls have to do a little more defending than before but now they are more assured. Did I speak too soon? One of the Moroccan strikers has gone to ground a touch too theatrically for my liking. What has the referee given? No, a free kick, again, just outside the area. What were you saying about tricks and sleeves, Tony?"

Dame Judy was off her seat at this and exclaimed, "John, that was a diabolical decision! The ref was totally fooled. It was obvious they were looking for a penalty and not only that... it was their first time over the halfway line!"

Tony Cottee agreed, angrily shouting, "It was so obvious... This is unbelievable! What was she thinking, giving a free kick for that...? It deserved an Oscar! I'm gonna have to close my eyes now."

"I'll be your eyes for you then, Tony. The referee is holding up her whistle to indicate when the kick can be taken. Let's hope they weren't watching too closely when Ms. Stafford took her free kick. The Moroccan captain floats her kick around the England wall and the ball ends up nestling in the huge all-enveloping arms of the mighty Gabby Dean, England's ever-dependable goalie. A mighty roar goes up from the England fans and the ball is safely shifted upfield."

Dame Judy returned to her seat. "I'd say more of a mighty shriek, John, but whatever it was; it was the sound of relief. Hello, what have we got now?"

"There's an English girl on the floor, it looks to be Aurora Stafford. This could be serious, she is not moving. I did not see what happened there; maybe the replay will show us. The ball has been kicked into touch and the medical staff has been called on. The replay shows an off-the-ball incident where the English player turned out of the tackle after winning the ball cleanly to be pole-axed by a mighty blow to the head from the elbow of her Moroccan opposite number."

Cottee was quite animated now. "In no way can you say that was accidental, it was a blatant block right after she was tackled."

Motson carried on his commentary. "The ref is talking to the Moroccan girl who in turn is reaching down to the prostrate figure of Aurora Stafford. Ms. Stafford is not reacting because she is out cold. This is not looking good for Ms. Stafford or England."

"It looks like the ref is just calming the Moroccan player as if to say, 'It's alright, it was an accident.' She's not reaching for a card or anything. That is diabolical."

"I think you may be right, Tony, it looks like she may have got away with it. Meanwhile, England have a player, their main inspiration and arguably their most influential player, about to be stretchered off! The good news is that she is coming round as we speak after what seemed like a long time, but she will definitely not be able to take any further part in this game – she was out cold. Well, if you were looking for drama we've got it aplenty in this game."

Dame Judy responded, "Never a truer word spoken, John, but it is a relief to see Ms. Stafford coming round, because that was one almighty whack she took. It would have put Mike Tyson away, that would, and I can't believe that the Moroccan player got away with it Scot free though."

"Well of course, they can take delayed disciplinary action were they to check the video replay, but that won't help them in their current crisis. What to do, Tony?"

"John, they've got to call on all their reserves now. Well, no, sorry, what I mean is they have got to dig deep and use their experience. I think Carole Servis will step up to the plate, have a strong word about how they've got to keep on going for Aurora Stafford's sake. Mustn't let her down, she's guided us this far, stuff like that, and make sure that they don't just go to pieces like in the first half!"

"Sounds to me like you ought to be down there doing it for her, Tony."

"Hang on then, I'll be back in a mo'. Seriously though, the sub is just coming on. I recognise her – she is very experienced and another girl that has been there and done it before at the highest level."

At this point there was a chuckle in the background and John Motson quickly came in. "Yes, if I am not very much mistaken, Tony, it is Cindy Damage, who is in footballing terms a seasoned old pro." There was a louder chuckle but he carried on. "It was Cindy who more or less took a back seat when Aurora Stafford came on the scene." More chuckles. "What on earth is going on back there?"

"I think one of the backroom lads just caught his funny bone, John," Cottee replied.

"Well thank goodness for that, I thought it was something we'd said. Meanwhile, back on the pitch the game is ready to get going again. No action has been taken against the Moroccan girl. They are going to carry on with the throw-in; still, at least the Moroccan is playing it back to the English goalie."

"John, I think the English girls are set up to play five across mid-field with Cindy making the extra man... er... player. Good plan – press 'em, get 'old of the ball and keep feeding it out to Mai Wei to supply the crosses for the front two."

"Thanks for that insight, Judy, and of course you know very well the 'attributes' of the substitute for Aurora Stafford." He continued, "Cindy Damage has a massive presence, reminds me a little of Dave Mackay the Spurs right-half (as they used to be known then) if you can remember that far back, Tony."

"No, John, but I have seen the 'black and white' films of him. Only joking. The opposition quite often just seemed to bounce off him, didn't they?"

"I'm sure that'll be the case with our Cindy if they come too close! She's on the ball now, that was a sweet enough pass to Maureen Field and she has found Mai Wei, who swept past the right mid-fielder like she wasn't there. Her cross found Ophelia Munney and her shot was parried away for a corner kick. This is interesting, Tony. Carole Servis is staying back, she has sent Cindy up to challenge at the corner."

"That is good thinking, John, 'cos they've dealt with Carole quite well. Cindy is an unknown quantity, she's got two people marking her at present and she's making a real nuisance of herself, stepping up then stepping back; she's a real handful but they are all over her like a rash, jostling her and tugging at her shirt."

"The cross is played into the near post and Davinia Lapp has thrown herself full-length to meet it about waste high, which would be at about everybody else's shoulder height, and project it into the back of the net. It's a goal! It was arguably a free header but it was most definitely a goal! England Ladies are a goal to the good and look to be on their way to the final."

"All credit to little Mai Wei there, John. She saw what was happening around Cindy and waited 'til just the right moment, as Cindy pulled away from goal again with her markers and put the ball into exactly the right spot to bring out a fantastic header from Davinia, absolutely brilliant! Peter Crouch at his best! Almost as good as England's equaliser."

"You are absolutely right, Tony, I can see with the benefit of the replay. All credit to Mai Wei for hitting the right spot at the right time and Davinia for timing her run so well."

"Let's not forget Carole Servis, I think she might have inspired that one."

"I agree, Judy. It was inspirational sending Cindy up to make her more than considerable presence felt in the box."

Play continued with England dictating possession, controlling the game and generally outplaying and outclassing their opposition. Although there were to be no more goals, they successfully managed to close the game down. So it was that the English ladies won a controversial semi-final game to find themselves in the final of the Ladies' Football World Cup competition.

# 35

Meanwhile, back at the sumptuous Mayfair flat of Sir Howard Eyeknow, the party was in full swing.

"Oh, what a thoroughly pleasant evening. Not without its drama, I grant you, but the outcome totally welcome. I think I shall have to have another large brandy to celebrate, as well as to calm my nerves. By the way, Sally, will the final be at the same time next week? Because if it is, I say let's do this all over again. What do you say, everybody? Same time, same place next week? Of course!"

Jacques Boutes, Sally Farnham's French sports journalist boyfriend, approached him.

"Sir 'oward Eyeknow, if I did not know you better I would say that you 'ave actually got a taste for the ladies and their football. But will it be enough to supplant the interest that you 'ave in the 'boys' at your beloved Tottenham 'otspur? I suspect not, but I can see that you are genuinely affected by the performance of the ladies."

"Purely business, my dear Jacques, it is purely business. I am not absolutely sure to what you are alluding when you say 'affected' by the 'performance of the ladies' but I can assure you that my proclivity towards the boys and the boys' game, especially those noble 'Gladiators' who perform at the 'Coliseum' known as White Hart Line, certainly has not wavered... Now tell me, Inspector Clueso, do you consider that we girls, I mean *the* girls, have any chance of beating... Sally, Sally, who did you say had won the other game?"

Jacques answered for Sally. "It will be the United States; it just came through on the television. I think that it will be another interesting contest but I 'ope that the English ladies do not show the same faults as just now, because the American girls are a very different proposition. They are a very professional outfit, like a well-oiled machine from top to bottom." Sir Howard was not sure whether Jacques was being serious or playing with him, not that it mattered because when he spoke Sir Howard hung on his every word.

Sally slid in between them, linking arms with both.

"Now then, we're not getting into heavy discussion about the merits of the girls' versus the boys' game, are we, because I think I know where you both stand on that one!"

"No, Sally, this gorgeous hunk of French manhood was giving me the top and bottom of the game as played by the girls from the other side of the 'pond' and comparing them with the shortcomings of our own delightful girls, I think."

"I know it smacks of corn but I think our blog should lead off with – 'All the way with Aurora?'"

"Sally, I could not have put it better myself! Corn

it is, but corn it shall be! After all, it is in America! Let it run! Now come on, we deserve another drink before we put this little soiree to bed."

"Do you not think it a little callous and mercenary to carry on like this, bearing in mind the unfortunate condition of Ms. Stafford? Because there is a distinct possibility that she may not be able to play in the final."

"Jacques, she took a blow to her head, that's all," Sally said.

"She was unconscious for several minutes and we do not know what damage might 'ave been done. There will 'ave to be x-rays and tests before anyone will know."

"Jacques is right of course, Sally. I had forgotten, I got quite carried away with the mood of the moment, I am sorry. We shall have to wait and see what happens. Meanwhile, I shall pour another little one and we can drink to her speedy recovery."

# 36

"I want to speak to Kirsty, Kirsty Pye. She's the team coach... alright... assistant team coach. I want to know how Aurora Stafford is, she was knocked out during the game and no-one seems to be able to tell me how she is doing. I am not the 'media', I am her partner! This is the third effing time I have been transferred. Hello, hello? Oh no, it's gone dead. F... Eh? What? Hello? Who is that? Thank Gawd, someone who speaks proper English! Oh, it is you Kirsty? Well thank fu... sorry darlin'. How's my Ror'? Is she gonna be alright? Has she broken anything? What are the doctors saying? Is she goin' to be ok? Yeah, yeah alright, but tell me she's ok!"

"It is ok, they've taken her to hospital just for overnight observation, and they do that in all cases of concussion. She seemed to know what was going on and she was smiling when we told her that we were in the final. They've made her comfortable. I'll tell you what, I'll try to call you from the hospital tomorrow and see if you can get to chat to her, ok? The girls send their best, bye-bye."

"Alright darlin', thanks. Tell them we are all really proud of 'em, they've done fantastic."

Fiona approached her mother, still dabbing a tissue at her swollen, tear-stained eyes. "What did they say? Is she alright, she is going to be ok, isn't she Mummy?"

"Well, Kirsty said she smiled when they told her they were in the final, so that's a good sign, innit? We'll know more in the morning though, she says, 'cos they keep 'em in overnight for observation."

It was Dee Hacker's turn to ask the question as she put a comforting arm around her best friend's shoulder. "I guess they will take x-rays and give her a thorough check-up all over. The Americans are good like that. She's in very good hands and I'm sure there is nothing to worry about. So come and have a nice strong G and T, it will buck you up."

Dee gave Lisa a hug and a reassuring kiss on the cheek, and she pulled Fiona to her and did the same to her. Gavin stepped out of the way so as to avoid getting similar treatment. The rest of their friends who had been watching the game with them started to say their 'goodbyes' and 'thanks'. Hilary Conway (as she was now, of course) sidled up to Lisa so as not to collide with her pregnant bump and said, "I am going to stay the night and take care of you, as I always do on occasions like this!"

"I'd like that but are you sure, darlin'? What about Mike?"

"Mike's working, so he's not a problem, and anyway it would be nice. We haven't done it for a while."

Dee Hacker was just in earshot and asked, "Not done what for a while, you two?"

"Eh, what Dee? Oh yeah, Hilary is going to stay over to keep an eye on me and the kids, just for tonight."

"Good, good, that's a good idea; bless you Hilary, that is very thoughtful of you. She'll be in capable hands. Jeff, come on darling, time to go. I'll call you in the morning, sweetheart. Bye Fiona, bye Gavin, see you soon. Have you got a kiss for your auntie Dee?"

When Dee and Jeff had left, Hilary instructed Lisa to put the children to bed whilst she made a start on the clearing up. Lisa reappeared after about half an hour having settled the youngsters down and seeing them both off to sleep. She was now dressed in her black silk night-dress and dressing gown. Hilary came from the kitchen and ordered Lisa to sit down on the large sofa and walked behind it. She undid Lisa's dressing gown to reveal her naked shoulders and proceeded to gently and slowly massage them.

"That is wonderful; you haven't lost your magic touch, have you?"

"I am only pregnant, you know, not paralysed. I've still got the use of my hands and most, if not all, of my other functions and digits."

"Don't I know it though, but please, don't stop; I was just beginning to get into it."

Lisa reached up and took Hilary's hands and placed them over her breasts. Hilary withdrew them slightly, saying, "Steady on there, missus. I was working on the tension in your shoulders and neck. I'm not sure I detected any just there."

"Right now I'm tensing up all over, for Gawd's sake get on with it!"

"Patience, my girl."

Hilary deliberately went back to Lisa's shoulders, concentrating her fingers and thumbs around the neck and also applying Indian head massage to her skull until she could feel Lisa was so relaxed she was barely able to move. "Wha' 'ave you du' to be?" Lisa was slurring her words too. "Thi' I' thur mos' relas' I've ev' fel'. Do-o' sto'!"

Hilary did not stop. With slow, gently accentuated finger movements, she gradually worked her way down to Lisa's breasts and diaphragm, then her stomach, her navel, on to her thighs, her knees, her calves, her ankles, and finally her feet and toes, which she kissed and tickled, yielding no physical reaction from Lisa at all. Though each movement elicited soft murmurs of ecstasy from Lisa, it was the ecstasy of being totally relaxed, from head to toe. It had been more sensual than sexual, which it had always seemed to be previously. She could neither move *nor* speak now. This was a journey she had never taken before and it took several minutes before she was able to frame a word properly, and it would be quite a while before she could actually move.

Hilary was well aware of this, of course, and Lisa could barely feel the weight of Hilary's enlarged abdomen on her own flat and toned stomach as she leant over and placed a long, lingering kiss full on her lips.

"Ar' yu-u ta-in' avantae o' mee? No' tha' I mi-i'."

"Perish the thought, madam, just rendering an essential service, as requested or rather, ordered, I believe. I trust it has had the desired effect. Now in a while we may attempt to put you, and me, to bed and then maybe we can enjoy a proper cuddle. For old time's sake!"

# 37

The day of the final of the Ladies' Football World Cup arrived and with it a huge interest from a totally new audience. Whereas it had been mainly the preserve of a predominantly female fan-base previously, the success of the English Ladies' team had captured the attention and imagination of an increasing number of male 'aficionados' of the 'beautiful game'. It has to be said that there would be a large element of curiosity involved in bringing such significant numbers of male spectators to bear. This curiosity would be due in large part to the continued advancement of the game's most famous former *male* soccer idol, Rory, now known as Aurora Stafford. It would have nothing to do with the fact that the six-foot-tall blond Adonis that was Rory Stafford had been transformed by some improvised but creative surgery into the vivacious, curvaceous, blonde Amazon that was now Aurora Stafford!

Just for the record, in Great Britain as a whole the viewing figures for the semi-final of the Ladies' Football World Cup had virtually doubled those recorded at the same stage of the men's competition. This is a testament to the effectiveness of the Stafford brand. The figures for the rest of the world are still coming in.

The teams had been announced and the good news for the English ladies was that this same Aurora Stafford, inspirational coach and key mid-field player, had been cleared to play, although they decided that she would start on the bench, erring on the side of caution, so Cindy Damage could carry on where she left off in the semi-final. With no other changes, England were fielding as close as they could get to their strongest team.

The Americans represented a formidable challenge as they had played impressively throughout the whole competition and did not seem to have a weakness in any position. They were also the most experienced side, having gone all the way to the previous final with the same set of players, only to be narrowly defeated by the Germans, of course.

Needless to say, all of these facts had been noted, taken on board and studied in the English camp. In fact, Aurora Stafford and her assistant Kirsty Pye had drawn up a game plan to cope with the U.S. girls' 'open' style of play. The main objective would be to cut off the supply of balls to their prolific 'goal-scorer', Sally Fifth, who, as well as being a fantastic footballer was every bit as glamorous and high profile as the English *former* Male Footballer of the Year (for almost a decade), Aurora herself. Not surprisingly the popularity of 'soccer' in the States had been given an encouraging boost. Especially since English heart-throb Trad Britt, star of two of the biggest ever grossing films (Or should that be just 'Gross'? ...*ed.*) 'Love Eventually' and 'Willing but Unable', was still 'canoodling' with the aforementioned Sally. Thus bringing intense focus to two of the largest 'popular' cultures on the planet.

The atmosphere inside the enormous 120,000-seater Los Angeles stadium was amazing. The English supporters were outnumbered by about five to one and there were very few 'neutrals'. It has to be said that the English support sang far more lustily than their opponents' fans but then there was a far greater tradition for that sort of thing on the other side of the Atlantic. As kick-off approached the pre-match entertainment built to an exciting crescendo with The Boss, aka Bruce Springsteen, performing 'Girls in Their Summer Clothes' hotly followed by 'Born to Run'. The whole stadium seemed to move in time to the beat, as the crowd responded by clapping along with the 'star' and joining in on the lyrics. The international football governing body, F.I.F.A., dissuaded him from singing 'Born in the U.S.A.'.

The kick-off was delayed whilst Springsteen took three encores, leaving both sets of supporters on a real 'high' but when the two teams were led out to be presented to the U.S. President's wife, Michelle Obama, the whole place erupted once again. When the national anthems were played all sang along lustily, though rather hoarsely, leaving very little in the voice boxes to cheer on their respective teams in the game that was to follow. However, when it did get under way, more than half an hour after it was due to, no-one seemed to mind.

Over in the commentary box, high above the pitch, John Motson, Dame Judy Dishes, and Tony Cottee were enjoying a 'high' of a different kind.

honestly say that I have never been so far from the pitch and still been able to see what's what and who's who. I still do not feel too comfortable with it. Do you, Judy... Tony?"

Dame Judy seemed awestruck but replied, "I love it; it's almost as impressive as looking down the Grand Canyon. They are using a special glass that brings us closer to the action even though we are as high as the clouds!"

Tony Cottee cut across Dame Judy. "You have to forget about your legs dangling over the pitch. What about that Bruce Springsteen though? What a performer. Wasn't he fantastic? I've always liked him!"

Motson picked up on the two of them. "I suppose we ought to concentrate on the football, as that is supposed to be the main event. What an act to follow though, as you say! The referee has looked at her watch; it must be a hundred times or so. I think we are about to kick off. The English have won the toss and are going to get the first touch of the ball, in *this,* the biggest game of their lives. Here goes, the whistle blows and Davinia Lapp plays it to Ophelia Munney and it goes back to Cindy Damage."

"Nice sensible play, not being rushed, playing it into feet, denying the opposition a touch, waiting for the moment to press forward, I like this. Everyone is on their toes and covering back, nipping into the spaces, creating space for each other."

"All very workmanlike, as it should be. This is a big game, the American girls are no mugs. They know what it is all about, they have been this far before."

"Shouldn't that be workwomanlike, John?"

"Probably, Tony, but at this point I think I should bring in our special guest, to throw a light on it for you and the benefit of our worldwide audience. Dame Judy Dishes, the former chief coach of our English Ladies' team. What are your thoughts?"

Dame Judy quickly remarked, "I would settle for 'businesslike'. Seriously though, they have approached the first few minutes very intelligently. In fact, I am rather impressed with the start they've made bearing in mind that the U.S. girls have far more experience of the big occasion."

"This is just what we were saying beforehand, wasn't it Tony?"

"Yes John, it's like most things in life, experience accounts for a lot, more especially in these high profile occasions. The secret is *not* to be overawed by it all. I'm sure that Aurora and Kirsty will have spent ages drumming this into the girls. Bearing in mind the amount of experience those two also have. They will have told them they've got the ability and they've just got to believe in themselves."

"I could not agree more. As a coach myself, the hardest job of all was to convince the girls that they had it within their gift to deliver, and with a little more belief I think we might just have pulled it off last time round. Then of course, I would say that, wouldn't I?"

"I think you are probably right, although I did not see all of last time's campaign. On the strength of what I did see, your girls had a very good chance of winning. In case you are wondering why all the chat from us three. One of the U.S. ladies is receiving attention. I don't think it is anything serious, she is standing."

"I think she may have broken fingernail. Only joking – sorry, I couldn't help myself."

"Tony, if you are not going to take this seriously I'm gonna have to ask you to leave."

"Typical male chauvinistic remark. Actually, I was just about to say the same 'cos I did not see any contact. Hold on, though, as a matter of fact it was *all* about contact, a contact lens. She's lost a contact lens."

"That was very good, Dame Judy. Well spotted, and funny too." John Motson shifted nervously in his seat, gave Tony Cottee a coy wink, and then carried on his commentary. The game progressed with both sets of players giving each other respect but not too much room to manoeuvre. The passing was impressive from both sides but defences were generally on top, neither goalkeeper having to do anything that was memorable, save clear their lines on the odd occasion that the ball was passed back to them. So it was until Austrian referee blew the whistle to signal half-time.

"Well that was an interesting if unexciting first half, Dame Judy. Enjoyable if you are a football purist, I suppose."

"True, I do think that both sides gave each other too much respect, not wanting to take any risks. Do you know I cannot remember a single foul? Just a couple of offsides maybe? What an example to the rest of football."

Tony Cottee agreed. "I was really impressed,

except for the lack of goalmouth incident; I thought it was a pleasure to watch. There was no diving, no play acting, no arguing with the ref and no heavy handed tactics. Of course, it can't carry on like that in the second half."

"I'm sure you are right, I for one can't wait to find out. Meanwhile, thanks for that, Dame Judy, Tony. Now I'm going to hand you over to the guys in the studio back there in London, what did you think, Gary?"

"We all agree, exhibition football, hardly a foot wrong or stray pass, a hair out of place... Apologies to Dame Judy and the girls, I couldn't resist that after I saw Cottee get away with it! Anyway, yes, the first half. What did you think, Alan?"

Alan Hansen sat forward in his seat, affected a half smile and said, "I would like to have seen a bit more action, a bit of 'cut and thrust', a few risks taken. For me it was like watching a game of chess... and you know how exciting that is. It is now a question of who breaks first, who will take a risk, who is bold enough to break the deadlock."

"Lawro, how was it for you?"

"Well, I'm not reaching for that cigarette yet, we're only halfway there. I'm looking for a little more action in the second half. A few risks taken, as Alan said. I think they could throw away one level of protection er... defence, and commit more going forward and..."

Gary stopped him mid-sentence to say, "I'm not sure where you're coming from or going to with that but *we* are going over to the guys in the American half of the U.S. studio to pick up on the thoughts of

Randy Forelock! Hello Randy, how are we today and what did you make of your ladies' performance in the first forty-five minutes?"

"Hey Gary, we are fine today and how are we?"

"Everyone is fine here too, thanks."

"Hey, was that forty-five minutes? That has to be the longest forty-five minutes I've ever had! That's me with women, though! I'm sorry... did I speak out of turn...? My producer just burnt my ear! Gary, good to hook up with you again to, as my producer reminds me, talk soccer. Hey, that was soccer, wasn't it? So what happened to G-O-A-L-S? Have they become unfashionable? These crazy women, eh?"

"Randy, in England we have a saying − 'both teams kept it tight at the back'. That means that they were very good at closing each other down and not giving too much away."

"Gary, can we just talk soccer here? My producer has got me on a tight rein, I'm not sure what I've done or said in the past but if it's all the same to you I'll just talk about what is going to happen in the second period of the game. After all, this is the biggest game of the year for these ladies."

"That's right, Randy; I think we are speaking the same language there at least. I would say that it is the biggest game of their lives for some of them. Mark and Alan both think that the girls should throw caution to the wind, just a little bit, in order to get a result. Whilst at the same time not conceding too much."

"I would go for that, as long we can have a few goals in this period and yeah, a little more action!

What are they afraid of – ruining their make-up? Sorry Gary... got to go... apparently!"

"Sure, thanks Randy. Bye for now! Surprising how he was affected by the lack of goals, Mark."

"Not really, Gary. These are the people who gave us 'Escape to Victory', after all, where you break someone's arm to get into the action, and other such fairy tales. Remember their version of the penalty shoot-out? When Rodney Marsh, playing for Tampa Bay Rowdies, I think it was, had to dribble the ball past the oncoming goalkeeper and score. Only ever gonna be one winner there. It would make the game a whole lot more exciting, though, and I can see it happening because to keep up this level of concentration for another forty-five minutes is virtually impossible. I am prepared to be proved wrong though." Gary Lineker nodded to Alan Hansen.

"The game needs a goal. We've seen some good football so far but I would hate to see it go to extra time or even a penalty shoot-out. It will be down to who is prepared to take that extra touch, that extra risk, to stretch the opposition. I'm looking forward to a more open game. Like both sides have shown they are capable of, so far in this competition."

"I have to say it would be a shame to see either side lose. Naturally though, I would love to see our girls pull it off in fine style. Well, all will be revealed soon as we place you back in the capable hands of John Motson, Tony Cottee, and Dame Judy Dishes. John, over to you for what promises to be a very interesting and probably nerve-wracking forty-five minutes of football."

"Thanks once again, Gary. Yes, let us hope that the English ladies can keep their heads and concentration. They are only forty-five minutes from what could be the most momentous occasion of their lives, the World Cup Final. These could be the longest forty-five minutes of their young lives too!"

"They acquitted themselves superbly in the first half. I just want to see them push on a little bit more this half, without stretching themselves. We all know they are capable."

"Don't let's forget who they are up against, Judy. As I say, these American ladies have been here before; they've got the patience, they have the nous to just sit in and wait for the little error, the odd little slip. England have to be cautious, play themselves back into it after the break and then probe."

"I agree with Tony. I wouldn't like to see them throw caution to the wind. It hasn't been mentioned yet but they do have an ace up their sleeve in Aurora Stafford. Passed fit and on the bench. At what point should they bring her on, Dame Judy?"

"Do you know, John? She had slipped right out of my thoughts. Of course, well now then, I think I would give it about ten, maybe fifteen minutes, no longer than that, and if there's no change in the score line I would bring her on for Cindy Damage."

"Tony?"

"I reckon the same, if anyone can change a game it is our Aurora Stafford. I'm not sure how badly she was affected by her knock but they said she trained very hard in the final session, so I guess she must be up to it. Let's hope so."

"I've had a look and I cannot see any changes and no-one has indicated any, so we are kicking off this second half with exactly the same personnel as the first. The referee has checked with her assistants and blows the whistle. The U.S. girls get the first touch of course and it has been passed all the way back to the keeper. Very negative start, Tony."

"You can say that again, John. Maybe it is all part of their game plan for this second half, make sure everybody gets a touch. Have to say, they are all pretty comfortable on the ball."

Dame Judy Dishes remarked, "I think they are being quite clever here, I'm sure they are trying to draw the English girls out a bit, *they've* got to be careful not to get drawn too far upfield so as not to get caught on the break. This is quite shrewd of the U.S. coach. Feeding from the fact that the English girls just do not have the same amount of experience as hers. This will be a good test for our girls in holding their nerve and more importantly, holding their formation."

"I'm with you there, Dame Judy; it will be a real test for them. It only takes for one of them, perhaps, just to commit too far forward. The ball is again with Tara Carport, the U.S. goalie. She rolls it to Cheryl Rook, her centre-back. She plays it to Siobhan Smith at left back, who returns the ball to Rook, now out to Wilhelmina Sixtrees, her right-back, and so it goes on. They are inviting the opposition to come and get it."

This was the pattern of play for the next ten minutes or so with the Americans very happy playing 'keep-ball', expertly passing it around amongst them, teasing and testing the nerve of the English girls.

Tony Cottee moved agitatedly in his seat and said anxiously, "John, I hate to say this but just about all of them are in the U.S. half of the field. The back four are on the halfway line. Only Gabby Dean, the goalkeeper, is actually in the English half. I can see Kirsty Pye and Aurora Stafford doing their pieces in the coaching area and they are actually being asked to sit down. Well, one of them is!"

Dame Judy sighed deeply and said, "This is suicide, they are going to get caught out. The front pairing of Ophelia Munney and Davinia Lapp are doing their bit by challenging and harassing as much as they can, and Mai Wei also is weighing in with her efforts to get hold of the ball. They should just wait for a mistake. A little slip, a misplaced pass or something. There is still plenty of time on the clock, after all."

"I agree, this is extraordinary, the coaches must get the message over to them. Kirsty Pye is doing her best but the noise down there in the stadium must be very oppressive and overbearing."

"Meanwhile, the Americans are still coolly passing it around among themselves. This is a real test for my nerves, never mind the players. Here we go! There is a break on here! I'm sorry for shouting but Delphinia Plant just received a quick ball straight from the goalie and has threaded a beautiful pass beyond the English back-four, for the tall and speedy Sally Fifth to run on to. It caught them square and flat-footed and there'll be no catching the centre-forward now. With only the goalie to beat, my money is on the competition's top-scorer so far. Gabby has come out as far as she can to minimise the options but the American goal machine coolly 'chips' her from just around the penalty spot. I don't think we'll see a classier finish than that at any level wherever football is played. That was worth the admission money alone."

"You're right, John, that was pure class and I'd have merrily paid money to see it too!"

"I am sorry to say, we saw it coming but that does not detract from what was sheer poetry as was the way you described it too John! It was an absolute 'peach' of a goal. That could be it for the English girls. It is going to be quite a big ask to pick themselves up from this now that the Americans have their noses in front."

Dame Judy spoke almost resignedly now but John Motson suddenly sat up with a start from his commentary position and he described the scene unfolding in front of them.

"The referee has placed the ball back on the centre spot ready for the restart, but waits a minute. What's happening? He's looking over towards the touchline. There is going to be a substitution, England are going to make a change. Is it who we expect it to be, or rather, want it to be? Yes it is! It is the tall blonde figure of Aurora Stafford; she is making her way towards where the action is. You hope they haven't left it too late for her to make an impression on this game."

"I'll tell you what, Motty; she's already making an impression. She seems to be reading the 'riot act' to her whole team, going from one to another to get her message over!"

"I believe she's cleaned up her act quite a lot now that she is Aurora Stafford, because if it was Rory down there the air would be really blue!"

Tony Cottee replied, laughing, "You are so right, John. Even embarrassed me at times and I'm no prude! Had bin known to make grown men cry."

"Actually, a few old fashioned expletives might be just what these girls need right now," said Dame Judy Dishes, and the commentary went dead for a moment or so as the two men looked incredulously at each other.

John Motson, gathering his wits the quickest, responded to Dame Judy. "I am so glad that it was you who said that but I am sure that you put into words what everyone here and at home was thinking. Meanwhile, the tongue-lashing is over and the action has recommenced on the field with the English defence taking up less advanced positions and mainly in their own half of the field. Aurora Stafford, as you would expect is directing operations from her position in mid-field. The Americans have managed to retake possession of the ball after the kick-off though and are moving forward menacingly. What are your thoughts now, Tony?"

"I think the U.S. are going looking for another goal just to nail this one. Their noses are in front and by pushing on, they think they can get another."

"Tony's right you know, John. They have the confidence and the belief to go on and finish the job whatever the changes."

"It is going to be fascinating to watch how this develops. That particular attack has broken down with a clearance up field from Gabby Dean finding Aurora Stafford for her first touch of the ball. That was a clever pass, Mai Wei took it in her stride went past Sixtrees like she wasn't there, but it was the cleverly flighted ball from Ms. Stafford that made it possible. In fact, the move was so slick that it caught out little Ophelia Munney and she was unable to latch onto Mai's pass inside. Still, that is encouraging, Dame Judy."

"Absolutely, John. If it caught her out it certainly caught out the defence, though the goalie *was* able to gather it up in 'no man's land' – as it were."

"Could not have put it better. Hey, I think there might be a job for you in commentating, should you give up your Director of Football's job?"

"Thank you; is it your job I'll be getting?"

"Hold on a minute, I'm not thinking of retiring yet awhile but I shall bear you in mind when the time comes and should they ask me to name my replacement. Meanwhile, back to the action on the pitch. Well, nothing to report really because the American girls have just been caught offside, going forward again. Do y'know I can't remember another offside being given in the whole of this game so far."

"You're right there, John." Dame Judy hesitated before continuing. "No... no... I think I remember commenting that there were just two in the first half. This is the first in this half and Aurora is organising the troops as she prepares to take the free kick herself."

"No, she's not taking it. Carole Servis is lining up to take it whilst Aurora moves over the halfway line with a couple of opposition players in her wake. This is a good tactic, because already she has effectively moved all of the opposition except the goal scorer back into their own half and with two markers on her she has made more room for the likes of Mai Wei. Now then, who is Carole going to play this to? Mai Wei has come short to receive it, she turns with the ball at her feet, feints to go inside then calmly runs around Sixtrees, the right-back, Cheryl Rook at centre-back advances to close her down, this time Mai feints to run outside the huge defender and darts inside her. There is only the goalie to beat but no, she's pulled it sideways right into the path of the diminutive Ophelia Munney, it's a goal! That's the equaliser! She only had to touch it in, she did and she is away celebrating with her team-mates whilst the Americans are asking about an offside. They may ask as much as they like, the ball was pulled back and as you can see on the replay they had bodies there. There was nothing they could do and unlike before, Ophelia was *not* caught out. She timed her run to perfection and if there was any doubt her tall strike partner, Davinia Lapp, was right behind her. How about that for a finish, Dame Judy?"

"I think the whole move was sensational, with Ms. Stafford very cleverly making her presence felt off the ball and the brilliance of Mai Wei on it. Finishing became a formality once Mai had done her bit and as you say Davinia was right behind her for insurance. A really good team effort."

"Tony?"

"John, we have seen two of the best goals in the whole of the tournament this afternoon and I am looking forward to more, what else can I say?"

"You feel that there are more goals in this game then, both of you?"

Tony Cottee answered first. "If they are of the same high quality, bring 'em on, I say."

Dame Judy was a little more restrained. "I would settle for one more as long as it is the winner for the English girls, naturally. I can see a bit of 'cat and mouse' coming back into this game with each side treating the other with more respect. I do think that our girls can afford to be more adventurous now that they have Aurora right at the heart of things, encouraging them and bringing to bear her vast experience of the big occasion. I know it has been said before."

"I've got to say, the American girls don't seem to be so confident on the ball as before the equaliser but they're bound to be more cautious now that they've been caught out once. Even so, the English players can't afford to get cocky or careless 'cos that's where the American girls as a team have the edge, their greater experience. Sorry to harp on, they have *all* been here before."

"Wise words all round there, viewers. Dame Judy encouraging our girls to believe they have the backbone in Aurora Stafford – who incidentally does not show any signs of the effect of her nasty knock thus far – to go on and win this game. Tony Cottee advocating caution in deferring to the greater experience of this American line-up. From a 'neutral' point of view it would be a shame to see either side lose. Unfortunately, that is not how it works and if after full-time and half an hour of extra time there is no result, this game will go to penalties. For the time being though, a promising move from the English girls has just fizzled out and the ball is back with the

Americans. They are pressing forward with menace; left-back Siobhan Smith has dribbled out of defence and over the halfway line, this is looking really dangerous. She moves it infield to Delphinia Plant and goes on the overlap but the ball did not reach her, it was brilliantly intercepted by Aurora Stafford. Now she can set up an attack herself with the defender out of position. Delphinia Plant is doing her best to get back to cover her team-mate's position but this is really promising for the English, because Davinia Lapp has dropped off her defender and picked up the ball from Aurora, done a quick one-two with Ophelia Munney and there it is, in the back of the net. It's a goal! What, what went on there I am not sure myself. It happened so quickly. I did not see how the ball ended up in the back of the net. I am going to have to watch the replay. It matters not how I saw it, though, the fact is that the referee has signalled a goal. Crucially, England are a goal up. How did that happen? Did either of you see, Dame Judy, Tony?"

"I think Davinia cleverly back-heeled it to Aurora for her to put it away."

"You've got better eyes than me if you saw that. Is he right, Dame Judy?"

"To be honest, it was too quick for me too. However, as Tony said, Aurora was very close at the finish, it is definitely a goal to the English girls and they are swarming round Aurora. Davinia and Ophelia are in there somewhere too! It was a great move and very swiftly executed. Like us, the American girls did not know what had hit them."

John Motson studied the monitor and summarised

the action as he saw it.

"Ah yes, I see. On the replay it looks to me as if Davinia just dummied no back-heel. With the benefit of slow motion we can see that she must have got the call to leave it from Aurora, who was following up at full throttle. That was a master stroke and the English girls take the lead for the first time in this match."

"A great footballing brain at work there, John. Not yours, Ms. Stafford's."

"I agree with Tony, you cannot argue with that. It was down to her experience and sheer brilliant opportunism, purely and simply put."

"Thanks for that, you two. As you say, sheer brilliance. She started the move and finished it in fine style! Sometimes words are not enough, that was one of those occasions." John Motson cleared his throat away from the microphone and continued. "This is turning into a *very* interesting contest, because for the first time in this competition and as far back as the U.S. girls can probably remember, but certainly as far as I can remember, they are behind in a game."

"They will have to up their game now, John, have to find another gear. Don't you think, Judy?"

"Tony's right, John, this really is unfamiliar territory for the Americans but having said that, they've not got to this and the two previous finals by luck. They have all worked very hard and I can't see them letting this get away from them without a fight."

"Dame Judy is absolutely right, they had their backs to the wall against the German ladies in the last final and still came through with flying colours, or should that be with the 'Stars and Stripes' flying high?

Whichever it is, the atmosphere down there in the stadium is 'electric' and I can't help thinking that the goal might have turned a few 'neutrals' the way of these English girls, who after all were regarded as the underdogs before the start of this game."

Dame Judy responded, "I couldn't agree more, John. With twenty minutes to go, I have a feeling that it's going to be a real 'humdinger' of a finish!"

"What do you think, Tony? Is it in the bag for Aurora and the girls? Dare they go out and wrap it up with another goal or tighten it up to protect their lead?"

"Well the old Rory Stafford would be out there going for more goals and trying to rub their noses in it but wearing two hats now, she obviously has to think more selflessly, but I'm confident that they have enough about them as a team not to throw this one away, in any case."

"As Dame Judy said there are fully twenty, well, eighteen minutes now, to go to the final whistle. The U.S. team seem to be playing the ball around cautiously at the back as if to get a 'feel' of it again. They've got the English front two, Davinia and Ophelia, almost chasing shadows, though they are not diving in or committing themselves unnecessarily, a good sign. They can let the Americans play it about in their own half because it's their time they are wasting."

Tony Cottee nodded in agreement and said, "It will suit Aurora and her girls to sit back a little bit and I can see Kirsty Pye signalling to her back line not to venture too far forward just as I'm saying it."

"Tony is right, in fact, Kirsty is looking quite

animated, her body language is very clear for all to see and I hope that the players have taken it on board, John."

"I am sure you are both right. Caution is the order of the day now for this England team but as they say, a minute is a long time in football, or 'soccer' as our American friends prefer to call it, and an awful lot hangs on this next fifteen."

Dame Judy Dishes agreed with John Motson, saying, "Could be the longest fifteen... er, fourteen and a half... they have collectively experienced."

"The American central defender has launched a long ball from inside her own half and it looks like it is meant for their Striker, Sally Fifth. She brings it down with her head but before she can do anything with it, the ball is whipped off her feet by that other tall and equally statuesque blonde, Aurora Stafford, who has stabbed it forward herself and dropped it perfectly into the stride of the shortest girl on the pitch, Mae Wei. Now will she go on one of her dazzling runs? No, she in turn plays it back to Aurora who now has her whole strike force bearing down on the Americans' goal. This is promising but they must make the most of it, as any mistake and it could be curtains. Ophelia Munney has run wide, taking her marker with her, and Davinia Lapp has done a similar run with her marker tight on her, meanwhile little Mai Wei is running straight down on goal, she should hold back a little to avoid being caught off-side but she's stopped, looked around, run short of her marker whilst with perfect timing and precision Aurora has placed the ball onto Mai's left foot. Now facing the goal and with no back-lift she pulls the trigger and the ball has exploded into the back of the net. It's a goal!! The England girls are three to one up and two goals in the lead!" Motson paused, looked to either side and carried on. "I'm sorry for shouting, viewers, and I apologise if I am deafening my colleagues here in the commentary box too. I got carried away with the moment. Another beautifully worked move, resulting in another sensational strike. It just doesn't come any better than this, surely?"

"We can only hope it does but I doubt it!"

At this point Dame Judy said, "Well don't hold your breath, Tony, because I think our girls have got the bit between their teeth and anything is possible, as long as they just keep the Americans out! I think they are even 'upping' the tempo as I speak. It is a delight to watch them."

Dame Judy was only too right; the English team started to turn the screw on their opposition who looked like they were suffering from shell-shock. They were still competing for every ball but it seemed like the English girls were quicker off the mark and were really playing with confidence and a total lack of nerves.

It was almost 'exhibition' stuff and the crowd were highlighting every pass that England made with a familiar 'olé' borrowed from those bullfighting 'aficionados'.

After playing just over the ninety minutes the referee finally blew her whistle and brought one of the most exciting, exhilarating, and memorable football tournaments to an end. The huge screens at either end of the ground declared 'The **Winners** of the Ladies' Football World Cup for 2009 – **ENGLAND**' accompanied by the Union Flag fluttering proudly, albeit digitally, alongside.

The England girls commiserated very sportingly with the Americans and exchanged hugs and kisses all around the field, to a man (I know! ...*ed*.).

The scenes that followed were incredible, unique, and memorable. It seemed that the spectators wanted to get in on the act, for despite the best efforts of the stewards, the pitch was soon awash with bodies – mostly ladies, it has to be said, and they had reached the area where the English team and coaching staff were located. Whereupon every one of them was hoisted onto shoulders and unceremoniously paraded around the ground. In the centre of them all Aurora Stafford was shouting and pointing and within a few short moments the fans had encircled the American players and before long they had done the same to them and were now carrying both sets of players and officials shoulder high. In fact they were being passed around in much the same way as happens to the singers at rock concerts, only more gently, maybe. A very noble gesture by England's player-coach there, acknowledging as it does the very fine contribution that these home-based girls made to an 'epic' final.

It was all good natured, friendly fun and the U.S. girls, although beaten, delighted in being treated the same as their conquerors.

The atmosphere was reminiscent of the famous 'White Horse' FA Cup final at Wembley all those years ago. Back then, there were several thousand more people in the stadium than the one hundred thousand capacity of Wembley, with the overflow completely covering the green of the pitch. However, despite the huge number of bodies, probably all male, it took only a single policeman on a white horse to clear them for the game to go ahead. With no trouble at all. During the game, those 'extra' supporters were sitting right up to the edge of the pitch, just about allowing the 'linesmen' to do the job of policing the activity on it. Very civilised and peaceful.

Here in Los Angeles it was slightly different in as much as the game had finished and then the spectators had taken over the playing area. It was time for the Award Ceremony to take place but what to do?

The answer came in the form of a 'loudspeaker' announcement.

"Ladies and gentlemen, especially you ladies. I would like to say how much we at the governing body appreciate this wonderful outpouring of love towards the two teams involved in this afternoon's final. Could I ask you to put them down now please?" There was laughter all around. The voice continued. "Preferably close to where you picked them up from." More laughter. "That is, in the area next to the tunnel. Then if you would all return to your seats, well, *a* seat, at least."

A little more laughter as the crowd eased away from the grass.

"That way we may move on to the Award Ceremony. Just to remind you, wherever you are in the stadium, you will see it all on our stadium screens. Finally, thank you all and give yourselves a big hand."

The applause lasted for fully two minutes. Then the crowd fell silent and still, until that is, the figure of

Bruce Springsteen appeared on the screens, at the table bearing the medallions and the Ladies' Football World Cup trophy, with a microphone in his hand. There was uproar. The decibel count soared with the sound of thousands of somewhat croaky female voices filling the stadium again.

The Boss spoke. "Los Angeles... it has been a privilege... a real privilege! To witness what I have just seen and to feel part of it, but I'm sorry to have to tell you that the First Lady of America, Michelle Obama, has had to head off to honour another commitment, so now the people back here have asked me to present the Soccer World Cup to the winning ladies. Don't you wish you were me, guys? I get to kiss 'em all! Don't worry, girls, that's not an obligation!"

After the subsequent hubbub had died down the Award Ceremony took place, with Springsteen true to his word, kissing the whole of the U.S. girls' line-up. When it came to the English girls' turn everybody was expecting Ms. Stafford to lead her ladies up but she resisted the calls and instead pushed forward Cindy Damage, the player she had replaced in the second half, and although Cindy refused at first, on Aurora's insistence she carried on. Another wonderful, heart-warming gesture on the part of Ms. Stafford. Needless to say, every one of the English girls lined up for a kiss from the 'Boss' with Cindy Damage trying her luck for a second one!

# 38

"Listen to me, Sally Farnham, I insist! Take another day off! I can take care of things hereabouts; you snuggle up to that gorgeous French Adonis of yours! Give him an extra hug for me! I am working on a piece about our heroine... Ms. Stafford for Prime Minister! Can she really walk on water? You know, the usual idiotic stuff that we serve up to our gullible, moronic... what do we call them now? What is that new word... bloggers? Besides, you deserve extra special thanks for making the party – what turned out to be our celebration party – go so well. You and dear Aurora and her beautiful girls. Those girls really came through for us. I could kiss every single one of them! They are so wholesome and so strong, in every sense of the word. I almost envy that Springsteen character. Oh dear, I'm beginning to come over all 'hetero'. Heaven forefend!"

At the other end of the line, Sally Farnham sighed inwardly and looked up at the ceiling. She had not left her home for the two days since the English ladies had lifted the World Cup *and* with it, the spirit of a whole nation. However, it was 'spirit' of a different kind that had laid her low for so long and she had phoned Sir Howard Eyeknow to apologise for her absence from work. Bearing in mind that this particular spirit had come from *his* collection of bottles and more specifically the double malt, one that he had insisted on her trying more than once; *not* that she showed 'heroic' resistance, which was responsible for her current state.

"Did *notre brave* Jacques Boutes get you home unbruised and fully clothed? I must say, that was a memorable cameo performance, my other guests and dear friends were very impressed with your dance, especially the men."

Sally hesitated, and then stuttered, "Da...ance...? I...danced, but who with?"

Sir Howard replied, "With whom? No-one. You danced alone and very entertaining it was, erotic almost, but don't worry. Jacques did not let you reveal too much, bless him. Such a gentleman, you are a very lucky girl!"

"I don't remember anything; I must have drunk far too much. Did I upset anyone? Did I insult any of your friends?"

"I think only Jacques was a trifle upset but as I said, everybody else enjoyed it, immensely."

"I have not seen Jacques since then and he has not called me and he does not answer his phone. Now I guess I know why."

"Don't worry, I shall give him a call and say that it was my entire fault. I feel wholly responsible. Meanwhile, if you are up to it come into the office tomorrow. We can pick up the pieces and get you back into the swing of things."

"Thank you, Sir Howard, you are a saint."

"Steady on, old thing, I have a reputation to uphold. If anyone should hear you describing me thus I would be ruined. Bye for now."

\*

When Sally arrived at the office the next day she was surprised to be met at the door by Sir Howard, who shuffled her into a side room before whispering, "I was not expecting you quite so soon. I have the lovely Jacques in the office now and I am in the middle of explaining things to him so he must not see you yet. He seems very angry still. Sit quietly in here for a few more minutes. He must not know you are here." Only when he had finished speaking did he remove the hand that was covering her mouth.

After what seemed like an age to Sally, she heard the door to Sir Howard's office open and *he* excitedly declared, "There, it's done! It's agreed! Everything is in place, all you have to do is to turn up! Now don't let me down, will you?"

On hearing the street door open and then close after the two men had said their 'goodbyes', Sally burst out of the side room and asked with more than a hint of suspicion, "What has been agreed? What have you got him to do? Where has he got to go for you?"

"Why, Sally? What do you think we have agreed? Where do you think? Oh I see, you suspect me of doing something underhand with our... your Jacques. Well, the truth is that I have done something underhand, though not with Jacques, and I hope you can forgive me for it. Because what I have done *is*, I have told a little white lie to procure a table for you at Dino's, *everyone's* favourite Italian restaurant. I told Lorenzo that you and the handsome Jacques want to celebrate a special occasion."

"And what is this special occasion we will be celebrating?"

"Your engagement!"

"Our engagement! I should think that that is the last thing *our* Jacques will want to be doing!"

"It was the best I could manage. Lorenzo told me they are full for tonight."

"Tonight?!"

"Yes, tonight. He had already turned away Madonna and for the rest of the week he said something about royalty or Jordan, I'm not sure, same thing in *her* eyes, taking the place over. I was lucky; he owed me quite a large favour."

Sally wondered what sort of service Sir Howard could have performed to or for Lorenzo, to warrant such a huge favour. She thought it best not to ask; instead, she responded, "So, tonight I am going to Dino's to try to patch it up with my boyfriend and at the same time I have to pretend that we have just become engaged. That would be a hard one to pull off, even for as experienced an actress as Dame Judy Dench!"

"It is on me. I'm paying the bill. Consider it another overdue bonus. Order the best food and the best wine. Oh, and I told Lorenzo... Definitely no spirits! What, why are you looking at me like you have a bad taste in your mouth? Sorry, how thoughtless of me. You probably have."

"Are you poking fun at me? You are, aren't you?"

"I would not dream of it. After all, you did introduce me to Monsieur Jacques Boutes and I will be forever in your debt for that."

"What do you mean? You haven't had your wicked way with him, have you?"

"Come now, how could you think such a thing? I know that in the past I may have alluded to the... possibilities... A man can dream but I am sure that you know better than anyone that he is most definitely a 'ladies' man. No, during our little chat – that I organised, may I remind you – in order to save your relationship with the divine Jacques, we got into discussion about our heroine, Aurora Stafford vis-à-vis – 'What next for the Woman of the Hour, the Month, the Year, the Decade and Possibly... the Century?' No, now that would be taking things too far, but we shall see. Do you know what he said? He said that there was no limit to what she could achieve now. Walking on water, healing sick children, running for parliament, the American Presidency, converting Iran to Christianity is of nothing compared with what he said, in all seriousness, and that was – managing the English *Men's* football team! So I said, 'You are being serious, aren't you?' and he said, 'You would have her at your beloved Tottenham after all she has achieved, would you not?' I'm sorry I cannot do 'zat hendearing Fraanch haccent of 'is."

At this point Sally felt the need to interrupt him. "Yes, but where are you going with this?"

"He was evidently quite serious and well, the man

is a genius. He got me thinking and suddenly I realised that it was staring me right in the face."

"What was?"

"Where I, that is... *we*, are going with this!"

"And that is?"

"It is obvious. We start a campaign to have her installed as the England Men's coach, manager, or whatever the job description is now."

"How do we go about doing that?"

"We start off with the girls and of course the boys 'blogging' or whatever it is they do, and when we have thousands of signatures to make waves with, we go with 'Orrite?' Magazine to drum up a bigger storm, get the tabloids on board and before you know it, Ms. Stafford will be in Germany leading our brave boys to victory in the real World Cup!"

"You seem to have it all mapped out. Let us hope that things are as smooth and easy for me with Jacques this evening."

"You have nothing to worry your pretty blonde head about, it's in the bag! Believe me." Then he added mischievously, "Just tell him that you performed the dance especially for him. No, on second thoughts best not to mention the dance."

# 39

"I have never seen so many cards and flowers, well, not since Princess Diana's funeral. Do you believe this? The messages are lovely. There are even some from men too, though some of 'em might be a bit naughty. I think the whole population of the country must have been watchin' on Saturday. That's two days ago and they're still comin'! I reckon this is the best thing to 'appen to my Ror' ever. He won everything else but he never won the World Cup with the men!"

Lisa Stafford was talking to Hilary Conway, who was helping her employer to sort through the mountain of congratulatory letters and cards that had arrived at the house since the weekend. Despite being heavily pregnant, she had stayed with Lisa and the children for most of the time that Aurora had been in America for the World Cup, keeping an eye on their security and acting as companion to Lisa during the evenings. Her condition did not allow her to be too physically involved should their safety be threatened but Lisa insisted on having her around. In any case, the police kept a regular watch on them, with patrol cars on 'around the clock' vigil.

"There's still a chance she could, though. She has really enhanced her profile these last couple of weeks. In the newspapers it is always, 'Ms. Stafford's team this, Aurora's Girls that', hardly a mention of any of the other girls. Although she is always very gracious in interviews, she always talks of what her girls have achieved but it is only *she* who is interviewed. I think offers will come in from all over the place to manage abroad and at some of the biggest clubs in this country."

"I suppose you're right, I didn't think of all that. Still, I can't wait to see 'er and I know the kids are really excited 'cos this time maybe they'll get to share in it all with her. I 'ope so, 'cos before when the team won anything she... *he* would go missing for a few days, even a whole week once! Gawd knows what he got up to."

Hilary thought to herself, *I've got a pretty shrewd idea but let's hope that it is different with Ms. Aurora Stafford.*

Lisa carried on, oblivious to the look on Hilary's face. "How about I make us a nice cup of tea, or would you prefer coffee?"

"Let me do it, I'll do us..."

Lisa cut her short, saying, "No! You sit there, I'm already up and you've bin on yer feet all morning. Can't have you overdoing it in your state."

"My state? And what do you mean by that, misses?" This was what Hilary always called her boss when she was in playful mood.

"I mean you're a big fat lump, that's what I mean!" Lisa walked over to where Hilary sat and leant over her, then supporting her weight she gently lowered herself onto Hilary's pregnant bulge and said, "See? I can't even get close enough to snog you anymore!"

"You've never called it that before! And that's never been a problem before; you've always found a way up to now. Have you gone off me all of a sudden?" Hilary affected a look of hurt.

"Don't be silly, I wouldn't let a little thing like that come between us."

"Well make up your mind, woman. One minute I'm a big fat lump, the next it's a *little* thing come between us. Actually, that would be more of a challenge."

"What would?"

"A little thing between us!"

"Hark at you being saucy; what would *Mister* Conway say hearing you talk like that?"

"Not much. In case he thought I was referring to him!" Hilary laughed and gently pushed Lisa away, saying, "How about that cup of tea? Then I won't feel so bad about myself, or Mike, or you for that matter!"

"Ok darlin'. Come to think of it, I'll have to get used to not having you around in the future when 'sprog' comes along, and I reckon my Ror' is going be away even more too, after all her success with the girls."

Hilary considered the passage 'all her success with the girls' and it triggered a thought that buzzed around in her head for a while, until she dismissed it with shrug of her shoulders. She looked across at Lisa and seeing that her friend was staring at her, she asked, "Now don't get all heavy on me. Didn't you say something about going back to your modelling work? You said before that you would have a go at that, to get you out of the house a little. Dee was very keen for you to do it. The children are not a problem, anymore; they are much more grown up now. It would be good to branch out a little yourself. And don't worry, I'll visit you still, with 'sprog'. I'm sure my Mike will still be doing the hours all the same, 'sprog' or no 'sprog'. Actually, you could help me with the washing of the dirty nappies; there'll be no 'disposables' for the Conway child!"

"That's right; I'll hire myself out to you as a nanny. I'm not sure about doing without disposables though, they're too convenient. Seriously though, whatever happens, don't forget, as you were there for me, I'll always be here for you."

"That's lovely, you really are very special."

At this Hilary hauled herself up from the chair, wrapped her arms around Lisa, kissed her and hugged her for several moments. After which she declared, "I'll put the kettle on, or at this rate we'll never get that cup of tea!"

Just as she was reaching for the kettle the phone rang. Lisa answered it.

"Stafford 'ousehold, who's speaking? Oh, hello darling. What airport? What time? Yeah, tomorrow, alright. Me and the kids'll be in that special lounge. Can't wait to see ya, and the kids are over the moon wiv' it all. They just can't believe it, well none of us can! What do ya mean make the most of tomorrow? Just passing through... goin' to London? What for? What's lined up? A whole week! Just interviews... For the F.A., I'll F.A. 'em, F somethin' or other...

Couldn't it wait for a couple of days or so? The poor kids... we're only gonna see you a couple of hours! ...Guess so. Alright then, bye then."

Lisa put down the phone and stared at the floor dejectedly.

"What's wrong?"

"It's started already. She's only comin' to our airport for a couple of 'ours before she gets a connectin' flight to London, she says. Then we gotta wait another whole week 'til she comes 'ome properly. I know I promised not to swear any more but I think I'm gonna f.....g get started again!"

Hilary put her arms around Lisa again and commiserated, "I guess we could have expected this, but like everything before, nothing properly prepares you for it. Maybe when the fuss has died down a little you could think about taking a break as a family, away together. Especially as there will be media people outside the house when they know that Ms. Stafford is back home here, look what it has been like these last couple of days without her here."

"Yeah, you're right, I s'pose I should have expected somethin' like this. It's the kids though."

"I think they will be alright. After all, Ms. Stafford has been away for almost a month already, another week shouldn't make too much difference to them."

"That's if it is just a week!"

"What do you mean?"

"Well you know how these things go on, she said a week or so but once the TV and the papers get 'old of ya they think they own ya. You quickly become public property, again. They really put you about when they get their 'ooks into ya. Besides, she's a woman now and Gawd knows what they'll expect her to do! Remember that magazine wantin' all three of us to pose for them that time!"

"Yes I do. Well, there's one consolation."

"What's that?"

"They won't be asking me to pose, looking like this!"

"Don't you be too sure! Anything goes these days! All done 'in the best possible taste', that's what they said, wasn't it?"

Hilary started to chuckle and then they both fell about laughing. When they had recovered enough they enjoyed a cup of tea and chatted on endlessly about all that they had experienced, individually and together, both good times and bad – mostly the good.

They were still talking away and in the same good spirit when Fiona and Gavin arrived home from school. This helped when it came to making light of the prospect of Aurora's further absence from the family.

# 40

Gary Lineker wore his trademark cheeky, almost self-satisfied grin, as he sat waiting to introduce the England Ladies Football World Cup winning player-coach, as well he might, because it was something of a 'coup' getting an interview with her on television, the **first** back on home soil. He pecked her on both cheeks and eased her onto the couch next to him.

"Welcome back, Aurora, and let me say how much of a pleasure it is to see you here tonight. I notice that you have brought the trophy with you. It is much bigger than the Jules Rimet Trophy. *Not* that I ever got to see it close-up. *You* can stop laughing, Hansen. At least we got closer than just a photo of it! Anyway, enough of what might have been. We are here to celebrate the present and the fact that we *do* have a World Cup winning football team from these very shores."

"Almost got poetical there, Gary, almost."

"Mark Lawrenson there folks, another one with a photo of the Jules Rimet! All joking apart though, let's not take anything away from the magnificence of the achievement of our wonderful girls, out there in America! What do you say, Alan?"

"A fantastic achievement under the circumstances. They were underdogs, up against vastly more experienced teams, like the U.S. and the Germans and they suffered setbacks and injuries in 'key' positions, but under the leadership of the lady sitting opposite they showed true character and came through brilliantly – marvellous."

"Can't argue with that, Mark."

"Teamwork was key, Gary, and it's thanks to Aurora and her assistant Kirsty Pye, for pulling them together at the time when it was most needed. That and making the crucial substitution in the final."

"I don't think anyone at home will argue with any of that but let's hear from the lady herself. Aurora Stafford, what have you got to say for yourself?"

"That makes me sound like a naughty school kid after doing something wrong, takes me back. It's alright; I know you didn't mean it like that, Gary. The first thing to say is that my feet have hardly touched the ground since we won the trophy but I would not trade this moment for anything."

"How much does this mean to you in the light of what you achieved as a... when you were... before you... back in the days when... you played for your only other team, Barcaster United. Oh, and England, of course."

"You mean when I was a bloke, Gary! Thanks for trying to spare my blushes. It's ok, I've had counselling and everything and I am very much at home in this body. You could say 'I've settled in quite well' and I am quite a different person from the one you've interviewed in the past. I promise you."

Gary was reassured by this and began again more confidently. "I appreciate you putting me at ease. Normally it is down to me to do that for the guests on the show. Anyway, I am really pleased to be able to congratulate you and the girls, on behalf of our viewers and the rest of the sporting world, for what is a fantastic achievement. The next thing to ask is, what now?"

"Well, what I am dying to do is to get back home and spend some quality time with my family. I know I have been away before for long periods at a time but this seems to have dragged on forever. Not that I haven't enjoyed it. It is just that I have never been so close to my family as I have in the last couple of years, since my accident. They mean the world to me now and I can't stand to be away from them. This is the longest time since my accident, of course. In a way I'm making up for the time I wasted before."

Gary was touched by Aurora's outpouring and thought he detected tears welling up in her eyes, so allowing her time to recover, he pointed towards the Ladies' World Cup trophy and said, "Why don't we take a closer look at the fabulous trophy Aurora was kind enough to bring with her?"

He signalled to the producer in the same way as he had to Bobby Robson in the 1990 World Cup semi-final when Paul Gascoigne realised that because of his yellow card, he would not be playing in the final itself were England to make it, which of course they didn't, they went out to W. Germany on penalties but you knew that anyway. (I think the whole world knew! ...*ed.*)

"It looks quite heavy," Gary continued.

Aurora drew in a heavy breath and lifting her head back towards the camera, said cheerily, "Ah but it's not, because it is made out of a brand new metal which is very, very light. Why not try it? I'm sure you will look good with it."

Gary caught the little wink that Aurora flashed him and almost, *almost* coloured up thinking that she might be flirting with him.

At this point Mark Lawrenson remarked, "That's it Gary, you can fulfil your ambition of lifting the World Cup for England, you can tell your grandkids that you did and you wouldn't be telling 'porky-pies'. Isn't that right, Alan?"

Hansen shifted in his seat and said, "I'm not commenting. Enough to say I'm impressed with the size of it just like the rest of you... Magnificent. Titanium... that's what it is made of, isn't it? Much lighter and stronger and wouldn't show the dog's teeth marks."

Here he was referring to March 1966 when the Men's World Cup, the Jules Rimet Trophy was stolen from the Methodist Central Hall in Westminster whilst it was in the care of the English Football Association.

Following a bungled ransom attempt involving the Metropolitan Police it was eventually found, wrapped up in newspaper, by Pickles the dog, who was out for his usual Sunday evening stroll. This was three months prior to England actually winning the trophy, of course.

Mark Lawrenson corrected Alan Hansen. "I think you will find that titanium trophies are something to do with PlayStation games and *their* levels of achievement. Ask Gary, he'll know."

Gary was quick to pick up the gauntlet. "Yeah thanks, Lawro, but at least I can beat my kids at it, unlike some people I know! Right then Aurora, thanks again for bringing this impressive trophy in for us to see. I feel quite humbled by it all and I'm sure the others do too. Now, coming back to you. It is not long before a new season starts, only about six weeks or so."

Aurora took a laboured breath and with strained expression on her face, responded, "That is why it is so important to get back to my lovely family and make the most before the job takes over again. I am determined to spend some time with them even if it means slipping away on the quiet for a while to do it."

"I can appreciate what it means to you and I'm pretty sure you *will* have to get away from it all. Secrecy, anonymity though? Gonna be very difficult now that your face is known in just about every corner of the planet."

"You're right, it's gonna be hard, especially as I can't even grow a beard these days."

Aurora laughed gustily at her own joke. The men joined in instantly though a little nervously. Then once again it was down to Gary Lineker to take a rein on the proceedings.

"Good luck to you and the family, Aurora. Do hope you manage to pack a holiday in successfully. Heaven knows you deserve it. After the heights you and your girls have scaled recently I'm sure that getting back to normal will be a bit of an anti-climax, but what are your plans for the future in the game? I've no doubt you have already been inundated with job offers inside and outside of football too!"

"Well I was hoping that I could go to the World Cup in Germany next year with the boys. Only joking, Lisa, honest! Outside of football I have *already* been offered a lot of money to do a photo shoot... all very tasteful of course, they say... again."

Alan Hansen quickly picked up on this theme. "It just shows the ends these people will go to! Not content to just celebrate an individual's sporting achievement, they have to indulge in smut. That is just crass!"

"Thanks Alan, I think that also sums up how the rest of us feel about that kind of offer. However, I guess you've had many more *decent* offers. Any that you can tell us about? We realise that you were joking about going with the boys, of course. Did you mean as a player or coach or both?"

"Gary I *was* joking, really I was."

"Yes, so was I." He allowed himself a broad smile and continued. "So you will be going back to your job at Barcaster United Ladies and hopefully repeating the successes of last season whilst keeping an eye on the England Ladies, eh?"

"That is the situation at the moment. I have no reason to think otherwise as yet. Though the officials did say something about increasing my salary with the England Ladies just after the tournament. Which would be nice, I suppose."

Gary, not wishing to appear too interrogative, brought Mark Lawrenson in.

"Mark Lawrenson suggested beforehand that there would be other international teams willing to pay 'top-dollar' to buy in your services and expertise and not exclusively *ladies'* teams. What exactly did you say, Mark?"

"You repeated almost word for word what I actually said, Gary, though I did also say that I thought it would be very difficult for someone like Aurora to pull away from the club that meant so much to her and to whom she owed such an enormous debt of gratitude because of the way they stood by her, especially the magnificent Mr. Donnie Mclaren."

"You also alluded to certain other offers that might come Aurora's way, like a book deal, which would be the second biography, of course. We've read 'the Before'; this would be 'the After'. Alan suggested that a film of Aurora's life would be a box-office smash."

Alan Hansen responded to Gary's prompting. "I merely said that if they made a film of Aurora Stafford's life I would be at the front of the queue at the box office."

Mark Lawrenson felt compelled to add his comments. "There would be absolutely no need for a 'Hollywood-style' embellishment of the story; there is no way that *they* could make it more interesting or rather, 'far-fetched', as they normally do."

"Good point there, Lawro, it is already an incredible 'fairy tale'. Would you sell your story to Hollywood, Aurora?"

"No way, not if I wanted to keep its credibility.

Until you mentioned it I hadn't even thought about it."

"So are you telling us that it hasn't even been mentioned?"

"Gary, I have been told to keep quiet about my future in that respect, especially to you media types for just the reasons you lot have been suggesting."

"Is this the F.A. laying the law down?"

"I'm not saying, all I will say is – watch this space."

Gary shifted in his seat, checked the others' faces and adopting his 'serious' face, declared to the world, "You heard it here first folks – absolutely nothing! So what you are saying is that there may be a statement or a formal announcement in the future. Can't you give us a clue, just a hint of what it is?"

"All that I am allowed to say is that from now on the most famous P.R. man in the business, Sir Howard Eyeknow, is handling my affairs in this regard and all announcements about my future away from the football pitch will be dealt with by him."

"Ah so, Sir Howard himself, as you say the biggest in the business. Well he sure knows his business, and he is looking after you." Gary was a little lost for words, aware as he was of Sir Howard's reputation. However, he carried on with a smile. "Glad to see you're in the hands of someone at the top of their game too, as it were, and I'm sure he will do his best to keep you at the top of yours. Good luck to you anyway." He did not know how convincing he had sounded or whether he had sounded at all sincere but Gary had to wind up the interview and thank Aurora for coming in, and Alan Hansen and Mark Lawrenson for their contributions. At the same time hoping that he had not given away what he genuinely thought of Sir Howard.

# 41

Sir Howard Eyeknow had a self-satisfied look on his face as he bounded into his office late morning and engaged his assistant Sally Farnham in enthusiastic conversation.

"I am so glad that we employed the direct approach to our hero/heroine. Because it paid off! It is true to say that he/she had never had representation of any kind before, never needed an agent because he/she was never going to play for any club other than the one that *he* joined from school. Always got a pay increase because his/her club did not ever want to lose his/her services to other big spenders. Always stayed faithful to the manufacturers who made his/her favourite boots and did their advertising as a matter of course and for a few shillings only. Had no need of representation! But now having in mind the commitment to the security of her family's future, she needed the advice and good services of experts in the field of public relations to achieve the best possible return in negotiating contracts for such things as books and possible eventual film rights! *We* offered it and *she* was willing to take it! You know what this means... it has put us in the position we are now in to recommend her for and direct her towards the ultimate achievement in the world of football and fulfilling *our* aim for *her,* naturally... that of managing the England Men's World Cup team. It is all coming together so well!"

Sally Farnham was finding Sir Howard Eyeknow's repetition of the 'he/she' little joke (Emphasis on little ...*ed.*) and his 'triumphalism' quite tiresome but since she was wholeheartedly behind everything he did and quite often the inspiration for much of it, she indulged him by greeting every sentence enthusiastically.

"Actually, I was going to speak to you about that. Because maybe now is the time take our plan to the next level. 'Orrite?' Magazine has exceeded all expectations with their campaign and they say they are selling as many copies to male readers as female. Though I think they're being a little economical with the truth there. However, our arrangement with them to get the rest of the media on board is set to kick off, forgive the pun."

"What pun? Only joking. Well, I am before you there. Everyone agrees that she is the brightest star in the galaxy at the moment so we must make the most of the current momentum and strike whilst the proverbial iron is still red hot!"

Sally was pleased to note that no mention was made of the pension pot this time.

For several days after the initiation of the campaign the telephones at Sir Howard's office did not stop ringing and Sally and he had devised a system whereby they were able to select between the high-profile callers and the not so important ones, by switching to a third receiver in another room, supposedly for the other one to answer, with obvious results. Simple, really.

"You know what, Sally? I can honestly say that I have developed a genuine liking for our heroine. She comes over so sweet, self-effacing, generous, kind and sincere in all of the interviews and press receptions that we have engineered on her behalf and in general since her success with the ladies' team. In total contrast to the conceited, hedonistic, opinionated, selfish... in fact, I could swear that it is a different person altogether living in that female body... And what is more, she is so much more mature in every way. She articulates well too! Do you know, Sally, I cannot believe I am saying this but it is true nonetheless, every word of it. The whole thing is that we can trust her on her own without having to worry about her saying the wrong thing or putting her foot in it. Unlike some of our other 'Pupils'. How many of them could we safely leave to their own devices in interview, etcetera? I shudder to think of the consequences with most of them, eh? What do you say?"

Sally was having difficulty understanding her boss, who always made it a rule never to become fond of or get close to any of his clients. Never before had he been so 'gushing' about any of them, certainly none that she had met. He always maintained a 'business-like' relationship with everyone, even though he did fall for The Opera Singer who had won *that* Television Talent Show. It had been a very difficult time for him and he almost weakened but he realised that it was not to be, bearing in mind the forty-year difference in their ages and not to forget that the boy in question was very positively 'straight'. The lad was saved from a fate worse than death in Sally's view. In a way Sally might have helped to save him, but that is another story and not one to be repeated in front of Jacques Boutes.

Could this be the melting of the hardest and most ruthless heart in the whole of the P.R. business, or is it all part of a wicked, devious plan? Was *he* now going to become 'Mister Nice-guy'? Sir Howard continued. "Already she has tugged at the ladies' heart strings and even made grown men cry. BUT, *we* are going to make her *so* beloved, *so* adored, *so* idolised that she will 'knock into a cocked hat' the late Princess Diana's popularity!"

Sally was a little perturbed by this last reference and generally the way in which Sir Howard had delivered this last speech. He had employed such vigour and energy. It was delivered with such passion that a result of which he was quite red in the face after it. It was all so out of character for him that it seemed so unbelievable and unreal.

"Are you sure you are not getting too close to your subject here? It is not like you to show this kind of emotion with any of our clients. You are normally so detached and cold-hearted towards them, when they are not in the room, of course. The only other time you show that sort of feeling is when you are speaking of your beloved Tottenham Hotspurs."

"Do not worry on that score, Sally; I still have *them* closest to my heart, well, second closest since my encounter with that divine new waiter at the Toupee and Crayon Club last Monday! Still, it is good of you to keep a 'weather-eye' out for me. Incidentally, that would be Tottenham Hotspur not Tottenham Hotspurs. By the way, have you confirmed a table for next week? Monday again, naturally?"

"Why of course, I did it as soon as you asked me to. A table for one as close to the Servery as possible."

"You are a saint, Sally Farnham!"

"You are too kind, Sir Howard, though I fear my halo may have slipped on the odd occasion."

"Oh really, anything you can share? Nothing too lurid one hopes, nothing worse than your exotic dance of celebration on that special evening."

"No, nothing I would care to share with you. I was very young. I am a lot older now and more mature. So what is *our* next move?"

"Ah yes, back to the business at hand, though I shall remind you every so often of your untold story. I am fascinated."

"I am afraid you may have to wait quite a while, like all the others in fact, and read my autobiography."

"Ok, with bated breath I'll join the queue. Meanwhile, I think we may have to consider purchasing an extra copy or two of all of this weekend's newspapers because we'll both be busy reading every word and taking in all that is said about our 'goddess', because there are bound to be 'doubters' and 'knockers' amongst some of those 'Hacks' out there, even though her record speaks for itself and the argument for 'exceptional circumstances' is out there too."

"I think I understand." Sally paused momentarily,

and then continued. "Do I take it that you and our friends at 'Orrite?' have already pitched the campaign at the tabloids?"

"Not only the tabloids but the broadsheets too! This is the biggest 'human interest' story ever... surely! We agreed that I release the details in time for going to print for Saturday's *and* Sunday's issue."

"Who am I to argue? For now is definitely the right time, of that there can be no doubt. Have you informed Aurora of what is happening?"

"Well actually that was going to be my next action, that is... to speak to her. We shall need her to come into the office; we should organise a press reception here in order for her to give her reaction. No, actually we shall have to hire a sizeable room in a popular hotel. The office would be much too small! What we must do is to get our client in beforehand and gently 'brief' her of our actions."

"Have you forgotten that our client is at home with her family in the very North of England? Well, no... actually they are all having a break away somewhere... secret... that is even further north from here."

Sir Howard's face took on a look of sheer horror. He staggered backwards; reaching for the armrest of his luxurious leather-bound chair, he steadied himself and just managed to avoid ending up in a heap on the floor.

"How could I forget that? We cannot stop the press now; it is all going to happen this weekend. We have to get her back here quickly, or, or maybe we could do it up in Barcaster or a large hotel in one of those big northern cities. We can drive up there. Sally, get her on the phone now and then organise a hotel."

"What phone? Ah! Ah... yes, the mobile phone that we issued her with, solely for the purpose of keeping in touch with us. What is the number, do you have it?"

"Why are you asking me? Sally, surely you have that number, please tell me that you do!"

"Don't you remember? We gave it to *her* with the strict instruction that *she* keep in touch with *us* by phoning at the same time every day. Which she has done religiously so far but that time is 10am. So we have to wait until tomorrow morning to speak to her again."

"But it is Saturday tomorrow! How are we going to organise things in just a day?"

"Why do we have to organise for her to be here? It might be better for her to be out of sight whilst we register the reactions from the people in the sport and the common folk first – that is what we are good at. After all, that is our job, which is what she, pays us for. It is bound to be high on the agenda with the TV and radio people. When she phones we should tell her to stay put and keep her ignorant of what we have done. Let her read it for herself, if they have newspapers wherever she is, at the back of beyond. In any case London is the obvious place to face the press because it is the main hub as all of the foreign papers have their representatives here too."

"Sally Farnham, you are a genius. Keep ticking, oh heart of mine! Of course... you are right... let us just hold her back from the press and the rest of the media. That way we create the greater need, their desire becomes even greater and we keep them dangling! It's obvious she is the first person they will want to speak to when it hits the streets but they won't be able to, and then it is up to us. I mean to say it's not as if she doesn't know what our intentions are for her, our agreement was explicit on that very point, bearing in mind our emphasis on the 'securing the future of the family' requirement. It is all down to us, this is where we earn our money. Can we be sure that no-one knows of her whereabouts?"

Sally replied firmly, "We do not know where she is ourselves, how would anyone else know?"

"You are right again. No need to worry on that score then, is there? Still, I think I need a drink."

# 42

Aurora Stafford stood by the large picture window taking in the beautiful view of the countryside surrounding Donnie Mclaren's cottage, situated as it was on one of the multitude of tiny islands at the northernmost tip of Scotland.

They had just finished unpacking the people carrier that had been hired in Hilary Conway's name at the mainland airport, and had been ferried across to the island with them and all of their suitcases and provisions in it, for the few days' stay.

"Here we all are again, and about time too! I've had a hankering to come back here again after our lovely original stay, even more so with what has been going on of late. I've been longing for a bit of peace and quiet since I got back from the States; to enjoy time with the ones I love the most. The ones who mean the most to me. So here we all are. You, Gavin, Fiona, and Hilary plus her lump. Shame Mike could not make it, though; it would have made a nice break for him too."

Lisa Stafford walked over to Aurora and sliding her hand into hers, replied, "I'm with you there, darling. It's been horrible you bein' away so long.

Yeah, pity about Mike too, he was looking quite tired when he saw us off. Anyway, let's make the most of it 'cos it ain't for long – let's get unpacked. Tell you what, we'll get the bags upstairs, you put the kettle on, Hilary, and we'll have a cuppa. C'mon you lot, gimme a hand with these cases."

\*

The unpacking done and cases away, everyone enjoyed a welcome cup of tea.

Lisa collected up the empty tea mugs and as she rinsed them out said, "No telly here so I say we go for a walk and build up a decent appetite for a 'scrummy' dinner me and Hilary planned earlier."

"Marvellous what you can 'Boil in a Bag' these days!" Fiona said excitedly.

"Yes, let's, and we can check on those beautiful Highland cattle, the ones with the long coats and the funny horns. We'll see if they've had any more babies."

Gavin chipped in, "Not too far though, it's going to get dark soon."

"Ooh is my 'ickle brother scared of the dark then?" Fiona teased.

"No! I just don't want to get lost, that's all!"

"Well there's not much chance of that, old son, this island isn't so big," Aurora said laughingly. "You only have to whistle and we'll all know where you are straight away."

"Well let's get going anyway, let's get a load of this good, clean, fresh air while we can, 'cos there's even a chance it might rain later. You know what it is like up here," Lisa suggested.

"I'll stay here if you don't mind. I can make a start on dinner," Hilary said.

"We understand, what with all the travelling and you in your condition an' all, you must be worn out. I know how you feel. I've had two of 'em myself!" Lisa smiled at the children and continued. "Not that it wasn't worth all the pain and the sufferin' but I wouldn't wanna go through it again."

She put a reassuring hand on Hilary's bulge and waved the others towards the outside door of the cottage, and they left, chattering excitedly as they walked into a fresh north-easterly wind. "I'm glad it's no later in the year otherwise this wind would feel really cold and we would all be in danger of catching a chill, dressed like this. C'mon, let's run for a bit, that'll help." Aurora encouraged them as she broke into a steady trot.

\*

A wonderful smell of cooking greeted them when they returned to the cottage and as she opened the door and held it for the others to step through, Aurora said, "Those 'boil in bag' meals have improved since I last had one."

"You can say that again, darlin'. You bin working your magic with the spatula again?" Lisa asked.

"I've added a few ingredients of my own and few fresh bits and pieces, to spice things up a little," Hilary replied.

"Anythin' I can do to help, sweetheart?"

"No, it's virtually done but if you want to freshen up for dinner it will be ready as soon as you are. I'll have a shower after dinner."

"Fiona, Gavin, go and clean yourselves up whilst I set the table. You too, Ror'. I'll be up in a minute."

\*

Dinner was consumed with relish by all. Then by way of 'thank you' the Stafford family cleared away and washed the dishes, insisting that Hilary take her time having a shower, whilst they did so.

This done, they all settled down to an evening of games and chat.

However, it was not long before the subject came round to what Aurora was going to do next, with Fiona asking if she was going to be spending even more time away now that she and her England 'ladies' were so successful.

Aurora paused for a while before answering, then taking a deep breath and letting it out almost in exasperation, said, "I hope not, but then it is not easy to say 'cos I think they want me to stay in charge of the Barcaster girls... as well as keeping on with England. They don't play so many games and the next big competition is in two years, but with Barcaster I'll be around most of the time, I guess, I hope."

Fiona's face lit up and looking across at her brother and mother she smiled broadly. She crossed to where Aurora was sitting and threw herself on her lap and hugged her tightly.

Lisa said, "That sounds good to me, almost too good to be true but you won't hear me complainin'. What do you think, Hilary?"

"I think it would be marvellous for you all-round.

Especially as I shall not be around so much to keep an eye on you. Pretty soon I shall have my hands full looking after my own 'extended' family." Hilary said this with a wink and a mock superior face.

Gavin frowned on hearing this and said, "This doesn't mean you are looking to me to do so much more, I *am* still at school, you know."

His mother laughed and replied, "Don't you worry, darlin', we won't expect you to look out for us... not just yet, anyway! Now let's play another game of charades. It's *your* turn, Gav, and do something we can all guess this time, not just you and Fiona. Give the grown-ups a chance."

# 43

The time was a few minutes after ten the next morning when Aurora phoned the office of Sir Howard Eyeknow, and it was a very anxious Sir Howard who answered her. "I was beginning to think that you had forgotten all about us in that holiday hideaway of yours, thought you were relaxing too much with that lovely family of yours, but thank God you called now. Firstly, tell me you are in possession of today's newspaper."

Aurora let out a hearty laugh and replied, "There is not even a food store here, let alone a newsagent's... Why?"

"That's good. Secondly, does anyone know of your whereabouts?"

"Not unless Donnie Mclaren himself told them because he is the only other person who knows besides the people with me. Not even the rest of our family know. Why? What is the problem? We were very careful not to let anyone else know. We even had Hilary mock-up a baker's van and sneak us and our luggage out of the house. We checked in at the airport in two groups. I think our disguises worked well, us girls did rather overdo it with the makeup but we seemed to have got away with it at the check-in desk. We only have the birds, a herd of Highland cattle and the usual wildlife for neighbours. The farmer wouldn't know us from Adam. Why do you ask about papers?"

"No reason... not for you to bother with, anyway. Sally and I can handle things."

"What things? What's happened? What are they saying now?"

"Well, it's nothing really. It's just that there has been a campaign in one of those fashionable magazines to have you made manager or coach... whatever it is these days... to put you in charge of the full England Men's football team... and now of course every newspaper in the country has jumped on the 'bandwagon', taken up the mantle and run with it in today's issue. The common theme being... 'Her Record Speaks for Itself'. We concur wholeheartedly, naturally... What do you think...? I mean... what are your feelings? Sally says that it would be a good way of furthering the Female Cause in the Grand Scheme of Things."

Sally Farnham cringed a little at this particular reference of Sir Howard's being attributed to her.

The phone fell silent for a few moments, then Sir Howard spoke with a hint of panic. "Hello, are you still there? Have we been cut off?"

Aurora Stafford put the receiver back to her ear and asked, "What did you mean when you said 'no reason' and 'it's nothing really'? I would have thought there was every reason to be bothered about it. This is *me* you are talking about and *mine* and *my* family's future, as you are always at pains to remind me. What am I supposed to think? I come away for a little peace and quiet and a little time with my family and then you drop this bombshell!"

"I did not mean to upset you. I merely wished to let you know that we have it all in hand and that you should not worry yourself or the family."

"But our lives will be even more exposed than ever and I would never have thought *that* possible. Until now, that is."

"That is why it was important to know that no-one can get to you there. We can handle the media but we need to know what your reaction would be to the suggestion that you be put in charge of the England men's team, because it is obvious that a lot of people would be behind it. What is your response to the question that must be on everybody's lips? Those who have read today's newspapers or seen the TV news, that is, and there can't be many that haven't! Would you accept the job if it were to be offered to you?"

"Look, give me a chance to think about this. I have got the family to think of. I'm not sure I would have the enthusiasm after my recent experiences. It is all very nice being so well thought of but I do have commitments. I am involved with some wonderful people at the moment and it could affect the way they think of me if I was to say 'never mind them' and just go for it. Remember, they were the ones that have worked with me to achieve the success we enjoyed. I would want everybody to know this."

Sir Howard interrupted Aurora. "I understand

everything you are saying and I apologise for interrupting you, but this is the importance of speaking to you now. Because when we communicate with the press and TV these are the things that we shall express on your behalf – your sensitivities, and your exact feelings. I think that we know enough of your personality now to be able to couch those thoughts and reactions in a way you would find acceptable. Sally will bear me out on this because we have spent hours agonising very deeply on what would be right for you as our client, taking into account your commitment and loyalty to those around you. Your devotion to them is admirable and we applaud you for it. Is that not so, Sally?"

Sally Farnham put a hand in front of her face to cover a wince as her boss nodded in her direction.

Sir Howard continued. "Sally is nodding very animatedly here. So we'll proceed with the suggestion that you would be willing to consider taking on the men's job should it be offered to you. Without your provisional 'OK' I could not possibly contemplate going further with this."

Sally was sure that Sir Howard had his fingers crossed on the hand that was not holding the phone.

Aurora replied hesitantly, "I don't know... no-one in their right mind would turn down the biggest job in football... but like I said... I have so much to think about... Leave it..."

Sir Howard interrupted Aurora once again, saying, "That is good enough for us. We shall tell the media exactly that! That it would be difficult for anyone to turn their back on the England job and that you would have to consider it very seriously. That is excellent, we could not have put it better ourselves, eh Sally? She is nodding agreement here. Well, good, leave it all to us now then. You get back to that lovely family of yours and give them our regards. Oh, and don't forget to call us tomorrow at the usual time. Goodbye, Ms. Stafford, goodbye."

Sir Howard put down the phone rather hastily in order to forestall any further reaction from Aurora Stafford. He rubbed his hands together as if it was a 'fait accompli'.

Sally thought for a while before speaking. "You know, I think we may have to use Kid Gloves whilst dealing with our client over this one. She has highly developed sensitivities as a result of her experiences with the media in the past and her more recent involvement."

"Well yes, but that is where she will benefit from the accumulated knowledge and expertise of the two of us."

Sally pulled up a chair and sat opposite Sir Howard at his grand antique desk and continued. "What I am saying, though, is that it is probably relatively uncharted territory even for someone as knowledgeable as yourself. This is a person who has gone where no-one has gone before. You know what I mean by that, don't you? All that success as a man with men, and not to forget with the opposite sex, then all the other success as a... a... woman with the women... in a working capacity of course! Now the expectancy that she would be equally successful as a man, sorry a... a... woman doing it with the men, I mean playing with men, I mean of course... working with men! She is very much family orientated now and has seen the error of her ways in the past."

"Sally, do not worry your pretty blonde head about it! I have been working on a strategy, not only to make sure that the whole of the world of sport wants her to take on the role of coaching the men's team but also to guarantee that she actually takes the job!"

"And how are you going to achieve all that?"

"Psychology, Sally girl, psychology. We are going to work on her mind in a way that will make it impossible for her to turn down, as it has been said so many times before... the biggest job in world football."

Although it was a 'given', Sally could not have anticipated her employer, himself, actually employing the phrase 'the biggest job in world football'. *That*, he would normally leave to the 'hacks' and 'pundits' of the media. More normally, his remit was to create the image for them to work on and not resort to employing their language.

"You see, that is why I love to have our little 'tête-a-têtes' because once again you have inspired me, dear Sally! It is that all-important word... achievement!"

Sally paused, and thought back. *What did I say to inspire him? I simply asked how he was going to* achieve *all that.*

Sir Howard continued. "Not present the job as a poisoned chalice, as some might see it, but as the ultimate challenge to someone who has achieved the ultimate, the seemingly *impossible,* already. I know, judging by recent performances, it seems unlikely that anyone, anywhere, be they from Sweden, Italy, even Scotland or any of the other far-flung corners of the globe, would be able to bring together a bunch of overrated, overpaid, overindulged, overexposed, overfed, actually I'm not sure about that one, maybe it is more the Drink Thing. Anyway, where was I? Oh yes... and most evidently of all... oversexed!! That bunch of underperforming, underachieving, Under the Blankets, Under my Skin... I see you are laughing but I am deadly serious! That is to say, how anyone could draw together a decent squad of male footballers from these shores and **proudly** call them the England team, is beyond me!"

"Well now that you have put it like that, I can't see our client turning it down for one minute. Not a 'poisoned chalice', then, but what are we going to offer her?"

"An opportunity, my dear Sally, and inspiration in a challenge that no-one could possibly turn down."

"I am not any the wiser, you will have to hallucinate – sorry, I mean elucidate for me."

Sir Howard hesitated, then with a smile, said, "I see what you did there, Sally. Funny, very good, I like that. Now to get serious for a moment, I will make sense of what I said and how we shall proceed to convince our Ms. Stafford that this job is tailor-made for her."

Sally thought, *If you can convince me first. Give him a chance then, girl. This is gonna be good. It had better be! It has got to be!* She drew herself up in the chair and placed her face squarely in front of Sir Howard's.

Sir Howard drew back slightly and carried on. "Well I see I have got your full attention, so here goes... We have to remind her of exactly what she has experienced in her short life on this earth. Going back to her... his school days and playing England schoolboys' football, then his first game for Mr. Mclaren's team and breaking into the full England squad at nineteen years of age, not to mention surviving a near-fatal car crash and the traumas that followed that. There were plenty of those. For instance, he had to come to terms with the fact that she was not him anymore. (Been 'milked', that one ...*ed.*) We have to build on the fact that she had probably become even more successful than she was as a man. After all, her Barcaster team won the league title and the ladies' equivalent of the F.A. Cup. Then her England ladies actually won the World Cup! How could it get any bigger...? How...? How...? Eh...? I'll tell you how!" At this point he took in a deep breath and putting his face right up to Sally's, shouted, "By winning the World Cup! The real World Cup! The Men's World Cup... the Jude Rimet Trophy, that's how!"

"I think you will find that it is the *Jules* Rimet Trophy."

"That's the one, yes."

"By the way, did you have garlic with your meal last night?"

"No, it was the night before!"

Sally pulled her face out of the 'firing line' that was Sir Howard's breath and took in a deep one of her own.

He continued. "By now we have convinced her and the rest of the sporting world that – She Truly Is The Only One For The Job! The Holy One For The

Job .Sorry, that is going too far now, even for me! Do you agree? Sally, do you agree?"

"What, about going too far? Well, yes. No, I mean, I am finding it difficult... not to... not to agree."

"We shall use plenty of emphasis and exaggerations to construct the case **for**. I am sure that between us we can dream up plenty more stuff to help paint the picture and thereby add more colour to it."

Sally allowed herself another silent thought. *Nothing new there then. Still, that is our stock in trade... and I do so love this business!*

\*

When the phone rang in Sir Howard's office the next morning it was Sally Farnham who answered it. "Oh, hello Aurora, how are you all today? Still enjoying good weather? We were just getting up to date with the papers. It is all very good news. The reaction to the call for you to be made England men's coach has been overwhelming and overwhelmingly, I think that is a word, positive. One second, I'll put Sir Howard on." She passed the handset to her boss.

"Ah! Ms. Stafford... Aurora. Let me start by congratulating you on being the most popular person on the planet, or so it would seem from the headlines in the newspapers today!"

Sally stiffened up in anticipation of what was to come; she was not to be disappointed as Sir Howard carried on gushing. "From what *I* am reading they have you walking on water and sitting on the right hand of God. Something I personally have not seen the like of since the days of the 'sainted' Brian

Clough. Though I have to say that all of your successes to date seem to erode the total of his achievements, with the exception perhaps, of the European Cup, but what is that compared with the World Cup and the possibility, I mean, *probability* of two World Cups? The *ladies'* and the *gents'* competitions. Naturally, I have said only that 'you are considering the prospect and would not contemplate anything beyond that without an official approach from the Football Association themselves.' Everybody but everybody, from what I can see, really believes that you are the only one who is capable of bringing success to our boys. They think that the sooner the better, too! They've suffered disappointment for far too long! I am sorry, what were you trying to say? I am afraid that some of the enthusiasm and excitement at the prospect of you taking over 'the biggest job in world football' is rubbing off on me too! I'm like an overgrown schoolboy at times. Yes, you were saying. Oh indeed, no, nothing has changed, it is just the groundswell of opinion. It is just that everybody, without exception is pushing for their most popular individual, that is you, to be made chief coach of England's senior footballing side. Ok, same time tomorrow. Good... yes... thank you for calling." He put down the phone, took a deep breath and asked Sally, "Not too much, was it?"

She replied, "I'm not sure. Is it too soon to try to sway her. After all, the F.A. are not 'on board' yet... are they?"

"Sally, it can only be a matter of a short time before they see the light and react to what must be the biggest ever response to what was a mere 'suggestion' on our part. There have been waves upon waves of letters and calls and e-mails and texts coming in from all over the world! It has stirred up such a response that it would be impossible for the people at the Football Association to even consider anyone else. Do you think it would be possible for our client to resist when she hears about all this? I do not think so! Our job is being made so much easier for us by the day, do you not agree?"

Sally thought for a moment before responding.

"One thing worries me, I mean, *really* worries me, and that is the F.A. themselves. History tells us that they can be immovable. Take for instance the Brian Clough case. Now he too had the backing of every single English football fan, as well as the whole of the media plus the vast majority of the managers, coaches *and* players within the English game. Remember the quote that everyone uses, 'The Greatest Football Manager That England Never Had', something like that. Yet they still gave the job to someone else, whose name I cannot remember. That's how good *he* was. I was only a child at the time but I can remember my father going on about it for a long time afterwards!"

Sir Howard sighed. "Yes, yes... I think it was Don Revie. It took him years to achieve anything with Leeds, and it was not good football to watch! Whereas the worshipful Clough did it within a matter of a couple of seasons, if that, at both Derby and Nottingham Forest, with both of his teams playing very attractive football. I think his right-hand man Peter Taylor should take some of the credit for actually finding some of the key players. Still, enough of 'what wasn't to be'. Let us concentrate our attention on 'what is going to be for sure', so help me God!"

This latest expression of emotion was so out of character for Sir Howard Eyeknow that it was all that Sally could do to stay on her chair; such was her reaction to it. However, she quickly recovered her poise and replied, "We have to rise to the challenge that we appear to have set ourselves. I am not meaning to sound negative about it. It is just that we do not have history on our side, do we?"

"Well thank you for the negativity anyway, Sally dear. Maybe we should call it a day now then, eh? No, 'onwards and ever upwards' as my father would often say to my mother... I could not help eavesdropping on them, those occasions when they went to their bedroom earlier than was normal for them. Sunday afternoon, three o'clock, to be precise, you could set your clock by them, and on a full stomach too."

Sally was not sure whether or not this was her boss's little joke again so she affected a catch in her throat by way of acknowledgement.

Sir Howard continued. "We do have something up our sleeves, however. A secret weapon, even. Because our dear friends at 'Orrite?' Magazine have been running a little campaign to canvass support from the fans, etcetera, and with the cooperation of all of the major newspapers they have amassed an amazing four and a half million names through texts, e-mails, telephone messages, and letters. Is that not incredible?"

Sally looked at Sir Howard with eyes popping in disbelief.

"How many? Wow! That is absolutely unbelievable! They won't be able to ignore that... or will they?"

Sir Howard quickly answered her. "Sally Farnham! I will not countenance doubt here. This is the most powerful weapon in the armoury. We will be hitting the F.A. with the confidence that a confidence trickster has when he is playing a card trick on a blindfolded three-year-old child. That is how confident I am and that is how confident everybody should be!"

"I like your little analogy. Very funny but seriously, I am sure that your confidence is well founded. I am sorry for throwing any doubt on it now."

"Alright old girl, not your fault. Now let us make a few telephone calls. I have a list here of all of the football managers and coaches who have signed up to our little 'campaign'. I would like you to call them and get a quote from every single one of them, please. Meanwhile, I shall start turning the 'screw' individually on some of the men at the very top of English football; the people who run the Premier League and the Football Association. I may have to hit the 'Expense Account' a trifle hard but I am sure it is going to be worth it. The same goes for you, old thing. If you have to spend a little, feel free but do not forget to keep the receipts!"

Sally smiled to herself as she mimicked the latter part of Sir Howard's delivery. She knew her boss so well. Here was the reason she had refused a company credit card and opted for just dealing with her 'out of pocket expenses', so much more straightforward and easier to account for. Fewer questions asked.

# *44*

The banner headlines on the front page of the World's Most Popular Newspaper (Their words, not ours...*ed.*) declared 'SURPRISE MOVE BY THE F.A. – see inside for full story, pages 5, 6 and 7.'

The *Daily Chronicle* had indeed obtained a 'world exclusive' on the Football Association's announcement of their intended approach to Aurora Stafford, offering her the job of coach to the full England men's team, through the scheming and machinations of the Right Horrible Sir Howard Eyeknow.

Such was the reaction to their announcement that the F.A.'s switchboard was jammed for twenty-four hours and their computer 'went down' almost immediately. (Yeah, one computer, that's what I thought...*ed.*)

Sally and Sir Howard had to decamp to a temporary office as they were also under siege at their normal place of work, 223b Baker Street, as well as being inundated with calls. Next they hired a fashionable hotel close to the centre of London in which to hold a press conference. Where it was hoped that Aurora Stafford would announce her decision to accept the position of Senior Coach to the England

Football Squad. Sally harboured misgivings about this event, as she thought that her boss was jumping the gun a little, since he had not received confirmation from the lady herself.

However, she realised that it was Sir Howard's way of manipulating the situation and putting pressure on Aurora to do the only acceptable thing, in *his* eyes, naturally.

Sir Howard could only justify this action by reminding Sally 'of how many millions of ordinary people whose hopes had been raised to expect that at last someone eminently capable was going to take over the reins of the 'sick dog' that English *men's* football had become and would almost certainly guarantee that they could look forward to better times and actually see them playing good football and possibly bring home a few trophies'. This was rather a large mouthful even by his standards! Sally had to agree that the disappointment would, of course, be absolutely immeasurable.

*

When the time came for the press conference, a helicopter was hired to fly Aurora Stafford in from Heathrow Airport. Another reason for choosing this particular hotel. It had a helipad.

Sir Howard and Sally had very little time to prepare Aurora before meeting the press as her flight was hampered by bad weather and the pilot had to divert from his planned route. So with the world's press and the media present they entered what was the largest of all the London hotels' exhibition halls. Even so, there were still hundreds left out on the street, for which the hotel fairly quickly 'rigged up' a public address system, through which they could relay the interviews to them.

The green and white striped helicopter landed gently on the roof of the magnificent Mayfair Court Hotel. It was agreed that this was the only way possible to transport Aurora Stafford from the main airport to meet the press and not get crushed by the throng waiting down in the street, where there must have been fifty or more police officers in attendance.

Inside the large hall Sally was feeling tense, nervous, and not a little apprehensive, understandably, since neither she nor anyone else knew what Aurora's answer to the big question of the hour was going to be.

Meanwhile, Sir Howard was busily priming the gathered host that was the media, for the 'Biggest News Item of the Year or for Many Years, Come to That', 'The Most Significant Decision Since Maggie Thatcher Resigned', 'The Most Important Announcement In Recent History'.

At this point, Sally thought that her boss was starting to lose it and was bordering on the hysterical, so she put a hand on his elbow in an attempt to rein him in but just as she did so a door in the corner of the huge room burst open and in swept a flustered-looking Aurora Stafford accompanied by four large security guards.

Sir Howard resisted the attempt at a kiss on the cheek from Aurora and shook her warmly by the hand instead, with both hands, it has to be noted. Sally considered the attempted kiss a good sign since all previous intercourse between the two of them was conducted strictly at arm's length or with his huge desk dividing them. Sally, who received a peck on both cheeks from Aurora, hugged her, then taking her hand showed her to a seat behind a large table strewn with microphones and cables. Sir Howard in the meantime, speaking into a microphone, introduced Aurora Stafford as someone 'who needs no introduction'!

The reporter from the *Daily Chronicle*, predictably and rather creepily, was the first to ask, "Have you enjoyed the break away with your family, Ms. Stafford? And have you made what, as Sir Howard stated, 'The Most Significant Decision Since Margaret Thatcher Resigned'." (She did not actually resign, she was 'ushered' out...*ed.*)

Another voice from the middle of the enormous room called out, "Yes, put us out of our misery! Are you taking the job or not?"

Several other voices joined in, creating an immense cacophony of sound that just reverberated around the place. By this time, flash lights were going off in huge numbers and more and more calls were coming from the hall.

Sir Howard stepped up to a mike and said, "Gentlemen, ladies, let us have a little decorum, please. Give Ms. Stafford time to catch her breath and then I am sure that she would be happy to speak to you. She has just experienced a harrowing helicopter flight and she needs to rel..." Sir Howard halted abruptly, Sally Farnham tugging at his elbow. There was movement from the chair between them.

Aurora leaned forward to be closer to the microphones.

"I'm sorry everybody."

There was instant silence in the hall and Sir Howard took an anxious breath and looked over at Aurora in horror.

She continued. "Yes, I'm really sorry."

Sir Howard let out an anguished sigh this time but Aurora continued. "I had to take the time to gather my thoughts, and really think hard about it and consider how to say what I have to say."

Sir Howard was beside himself with anticipation at the decision from his client being in the 'negative'. He eased himself down on to the nearest chair.

Aurora stood up and leaned into the mikes and said, "It has not been an easy decision to make; in fact, it has been the hardest decision I've ever had in my life. There's my lovely family to think of. I've maybe not been the best parent in the world, I have improved though, you see. There are the wonderful people I work with and those that I work for. I have had to take everything and everybody in my life into consideration."

The room was in respectful silence and hanging on every word. Sir Howard, on the other hand, was having difficulty holding it in and was breathing quite heavily now.

Aurora continued. "Football has been my whole life for so long and it has brought fantastic times and great successes, fame and fortune. I really don't need to work again. There are also incredible pressures involved in doing certain jobs. I got to the point where I think, 'do I need all the extra pressure that being in charge of the England football team of whom so much is always expected?' Do I... seriously... do I?"

Sir Howard seem totally resigned to the fact that their client was preparing the gathered assembly and most importantly, Sir Howard himself, for the *worst* and had his face buried deep in his hands.

Sally looked across at her boss and wondered whether she should console him or let him 'stew in his own juices'. After all, he should have been prepared for this possibility.

Aurora Stafford leaned over and reached down into her bag and pulled out a scarf, held it aloft and shouted at the top of her voice, "OF COURSE I DO! BRING IT ON! BRING IT ON! COME ON ENGLAND!" It was an England supporter's scarf, naturally!

There was uproar; journalists were vying for position to ask the important questions but Sir Howard, anticipating the melee, signalled for the security guards to shepherd the new England F.A. senior coach to safety.

*

The next morning every newspaper in the land and very many abroad ran with the headline of **'The Woman Who Will Lead the England Men to the World Cup Competition in Germany.'**

In an unidentified television studio the next morning, an interview was taking place and being broadcast live. This was a little arrangement made by

Sir Howard Eyeknow to guarantee that the organisation he trusted implicitly would broadcast the good news to the world and conduct a civil interview without fear and favour.

"Aurora, congratulations on your new post at the F.A. All the very best and I am sure everybody joins me in wishing you every success in the future."

"Thank you very much, Gary. Thank you."

"So now that you have the job of looking after the boys, I have to ask you, who will be taking your place in charge of the girls?"

Aurora Stafford sat forward in her seat and looking straight at the camera replied, "I'm not sure I know what you mean when you say 'looking after the boys', Gary... Only joking of course! Seriously though, I had no hesitation in recommending Kirsty Pye, my assistant, for the position. I know that she is more than capable, she has the experience and will do an excellent job."

Garry Lineker responded, "You obviously have a lot of faith in her and I am sure she will do alright, bearing in mind the knowledge she has gained from being with you."

"Gary, she is the best qualified by a long way, she is the *most* experienced of the candidates, and she has a fantastic rapport with the girls too."

"Well I cannot argue with that and I am sure that knowing you have confidence in her will really encourage her in going about the job. Thank you for coming and talking to us, and again, we wish you all the luck in the world with your new job!"

# 45

The F.A.'s decision to appoint Aurora Stafford to the senior England post was very well received by the general public, supporters, the media, and more importantly the England players themselves. It was common knowledge throughout English football that a fresh face and approach was needed and had been long overdue. We have fallen badly behind most of the other footballing nations and not got further than the quarter-finals of the major competitions and won nothing since 1966.

Other countries had long since set up football academies whilst so many years on from when it was first muted, the English are about to move into theirs. The whole set-up was in need of a 'shake-up' with a radical 'root and branch' reorganisation too.

The majority of people considered that Ms. Aurora Stafford was just the one to achieve it.

She lost no time in telling the top brass at the F.A. that she intended to apply methods personal to her, although she fell short of using the abrasive approach to them that Brian Clough had employed when he applied for the job.

On and off the training ground she demonstrated that she was in charge and that her word was 'final'. Whilst not all of the professionals in her charge agreed with her approach, they all said that she was firm but fair.

Her earliest 'trial' was to be quite the sternest test, with a 'friendly' game against the current European and World Cup holders, Spain. It was a game of 'two halves' (I wondered when that would rear its ugly head, so predictable! ...ed.). In the first half, Aurora sent out the team that she had inherited from her predecessor, asking them to play to style that was new to them.

Her instructions were:-

Do not give the ball away. Move into space when you do not have the ball. Short, sharp passes making sure you find your team-mate. Track back and make a challenge if you do lose the ball. No long 'hopeful' balls into an empty penalty area. Remember, it is called football for a reason.

No cheating. No swearing at or harassing the referee or his assistants.

And above all, remember – **To Play For Each Other and the Team. No-one Is Bigger Than the Team!** (Now where have I heard all of that before? ...ed.)

\*

The team that took to the field in the first half was made up of her most experienced professionals, with the exception of a couple of injured players.

Sadly, they were exposed to a Spanish side that

were well established, very comfortable on the ball (and still it goes on! ...*ed.*) and had swept away all before them, including a well-drilled German side, a week before.

Needless to say *they* were also swept aside and left the field at half-time three goals down, and it could have been worse were it not for the heroics of goalkeeper, Seph Handys. Veteran centre-back Dominic Cousins apologised to his coach as he entered the England changing room. "We were naïve out there, they had us chasing shadows."

Aurora replied, "We were still giving the ball away cheaply and it is always difficult to get it back from a team as good as this lot. Well done, Seph... some fantastic saves. As for the rest of you, I'm going to stick with you for the first ten or so minutes in the second half but Paul, you and Michael have got to press on when they have the ball, deny them their space as much as possible." She was speaking to Michael Kelly and Paul Bastable, both established members of the England side now and former team-mates at her club side before her life-changing accident. "Terry... Terry Bull on the left wing there, you've forgotten about tracking back. Mark Thyme, you are our sharpest striker at the moment, don't let them intimidate you, keep calm, you are *the* most instinctive goal scorer I know. Play your normal game; you've had the chances, make sure you convert them in this second half. Right, the rest of you, you're all playing to hold on to your places. Let's see you do it in the next forty-five minutes or I bring in the new boys. Remember, there are some really talented lads sitting on the bench and they are hungry. Let's go!

C'mon, let's get these goals back."

The second half proved a lot better than the first. English managed to limit the strikes on their own goal but were unable to make a mark at the other end.

After enduring a virtual stalemate for the best part of twenty minutes Aurora decided it was time to change things and maybe 'experiment' with the new faces. The first change was to bring on Ulysses Grant, the tricky nineteen-year-old right winger. Taking off veteran Charlie Hunt, who it has to be said was carrying a little extra weight these days.

This change was encouraging. Grant's movement proved to be more than a handful for the Spanish defence and on a dash inside from his wing position he left the full-back on his backside, then, attempting to swerve past the centre-back he was clumsily upended and gained a penalty. Paul Bastable arrogantly pushed aside his team-mates who were vying to take the spot-kick. Bastable teed-up the ball and stepped back two paces, the referee blew his whistle and with the smallest of back lifts he blasted the ball into the bottom right hand corner of the net. He then followed it into the net retrieved the ball and carried it all the way back to the centre spot for the restart. Three-one to Spain. Aurora was encouraged by this and signalled to the officials that she wished to make another change before the referee could blow again.

This time the change was to be in defence. Firstly, Leydon Lowe, another bright youngster at twenty-one, an attacking right full-back who was used to linking up with right winger Ulysses Grant for their home club. Along with twenty-one year old, six feet, four inches tall centre-back, Colin Dett, who replaced Dominic Cousins.

The effect on the Spanish seemed to prove that the changes were working. They had difficulty containing the creative Ulysses Grant as he combined beautifully with Leydon Lowe down the right. The supply to front man Thyme increased markedly (Markedly... get it...? What? ...*ed.*) and it wasn't long before his patience paid off with a goal that he merely had to tap in. Three-two Spain. Football never looked so simple!

The game now seemed to be edging England's way; they were enjoying the biggest share of possession, although the score line remained the same. That is, until ten minutes before full-time, when Colin Dett the lanky centre-back set off his winger, Terry Bull, down the left-hand side. On receipt of the ball he deftly turned inside and sent an inch-perfect pass to the feet of Ulysses Grant, who was on a diagonal run from his wing on the right down on goal. One touch to put the ball past the full-back and another to beat the goalie and the score was three-all!

The Spanish response was to attack immediately from the restart with some brilliant short, sharp passing moves that ended with a shot that brought out a spectacular save from Seph Handys. He quickly ran to the edge of his area and with a superb long throw managed to find Mark Thyme. Thyme was slightly taken aback by the speed of the goalie's action but did not need a second bidding, and finding himself on-side – just – with most of the Spanish committed to attack, he fended off the pushing and pulling of the lone defender who probably deserved a yellow card, drew the goalie and slotted the ball narrowly wide! Still three-three but it was so close to the winner.

Aurora Stafford was off her feet quickly and signalling to her team to keep it tight and not to get too carried away. With just minutes left until the final whistle, she did not want them to undo all the good work with a silly little slip. In training she had taken every opportunity to drill into the whole squad the importance of discipline. We have to remember that most of them are young and relatively inexperienced playing at this level.

In the event they kept it together until the final whistle, even though they had to endure an extra four minutes' play, for what... no-one could fathom! But they survived anyway. Ms. Stafford told the media that it was a 'highly satisfactory' result for the team and she looked forward to building on it with a view to making a credible attempt at bringing the World Cup back to these shores.

*

Needless to say the media, next day, had her 'walking on water' and 'replacing Brian Clough at the right hand of God' but she kept reminding them that although it was a fine performance and a good result for her England team, it was still only a draw and was merely a friendly warm-up game for the real contest later in the year, the World Cup. At the same time Ms. Stafford assured them that her players would not let it affect their attitude or approach or their focus on the business ahead. (It doesn't stop! ...*ed.*)

It was encouraging though, because the Spanish

players and the Spanish media alike spoke of the re-emergence of English football like the 'phoenix from the ashes'. They all agreed that this England team would be 'a force to reckon with' at the up-coming World Cup Finals. Their next fixture was against the German national side.

The exalted German football team paid them the utmost respect by putting out a full-strength team. Despite this, the relatively younger-looking England team turned them over four-two on their own turf. (Sounding even more like an old-fashioned 'Hack'...*ed*.)

This was the last full-blown game before the World Cup knockout competition over in Germany itself. So the result had sent a message that would 'rock' the German Football Federation to its foundation (not to mention the rest of the footballing world).

English football was well and truly back on track!

# 46

Gary Lineker was about to introduce the pundits with whom he would share the studio for the duration of the World Cup competition now taking place in Germany. "The weather is good and from what I have seen of them, the pitches are in immaculate condition and we wouldn't expect anything less than perfection from our German hosts, would we? I will get straight down to it and introduce you to the team. As well as our regulars, Alan Hansen and Mark Lawrenson, I am very pleased to be able to introduce you to an ex-German international and more importantly, of course, one of Tottenham Hotspur's top goal scorers... Mr. Jurgen Klinsmann... Welcome, Jurgen, please make yourself comfortable. It's good to see you. You've met Lawro and Hansen, for *sure*."

The German leant over to shake the hands of the other two pundits, but realising what Lineker had finished off his introduction with, he hesitated and broke into laughter, pretended to take a swipe at the host then carried on shaking hands.

As he took his seat he said, "You still have your sense of humour, I see, for *sure*."

Gary replied, "I'm glad you have kept yours, *for sure.*"

Hansen butted in. "Would this be the sense of humour you needed to be able to play for Tottenham Hotspur?"

Lineker answered, "That's very good, Alan. I see you're developing one too! What about you, Lawro, wanna put in your two-penneth?"

"As a matter of fact, yes, but I can't be *sure for* what."

"Perhaps we should leave it there, then. Anyway, folks, maybe we should concentrate on the feast that has been set before us."

Mark Lawrenson could not resist a little aside. "You're not referring to the German sausages again, are you Gary? That was all you could talk about on the way over here."

"No, Lawro, I am not talking about the buffet or 'Schnell Imbiss' as you keep referring to it, since you saw it on that takeaway food outlet van! I am speaking of the possibility of a 'Footballing Feast'. What with the Germans suffering defeat at the hands of a young England team and current holders Spain only managing a draw with them, and then only by the seat of their pants. Maybe we can expect a few surprises and some more upsets leading up to the World Cup Final itself. Jurgen, how do you view the prospects of this resurgent English team?"

"Gary, I have a problem with that word... resurgent."

"Oh, I see, you think it might be a flash in the pan."

"No! No! I don't know what it means, I have never heard it before and what is a flash in a pain?"

"That is a flash in the pan, pan... it means a one-off, now don't tell me you don't know what that means."

"You know, I normally get compliments for my English. I know people do not like my American accent but they can usually understand me and I them, *for sure*."

"Well what I'm asking is, do you think that this English team can go all the way and win the World Cup?"

Jurgen Klinsmann hesitated before answering. "I think they have a very good chance besides two or three other outstanding European and South American countries. It is a hard one to call, *for sure*. Still, you have not told me what is the meaning of this word... tre-surg-eon."

Lawrenson and Hansen were trying to hold it together but with difficulty. They could not be sure whether Klinsmann was joking or being serious now.

"That's very good, Jurgen. I'm guessing that you are joking this time." Lineker hesitated, and then continued. "What I am saying is that our England teams have not been at the races for a long, long time but this might just be their moment if their manager *stroke* coach can keep them focused. What do you say, Alan?"

Alan Hansen answered, "That is a very important point, Gary. We have seen English players in the past lose the plot. With so many outside influences to divert their attention, their weaknesses have been exposed and that's not all they've exposed. No, seriously though, they are playing a much better quality of football under Aurora Stafford. It is more akin to the continental style now. With more emphasis on keeping the ball and less of the 'hurried passes' game. I know that Ms. Stafford is very much a Brian Clough fan and is always reminding her players that it is called **foot...**ball for a reason, just as Cloughie regularly did, whichever club he was at the time."

Mark Lawrenson picked up on what Hansen said. "Gary, I could not agree more. It is all about respecting the ball, keeping possession, making the opposition work to get it off you, creating space, creating opportunities for the front men, and generally not giving the ball away cheaply as they have done so often in the past."

"Well I think we can all agree there then, and Jurgen you have seen them in the warm-up games. Do you see these qualities in this new England team?"

"For sure."

Gary Lineker hesitated, expecting more from his German guest, but that was it, apparently.

However, Alan Hansen came in with an observation that covered the void left by Klinsmann's abrupt answer. "I don't think we have seen the best from this England side, but then life is full of surprises."

"Pearls of wisdom indeed. Thank you both of you, and you too, Lawro. Meanwhile, the first game we have been honoured to watch is the opener between the hosts Germany and the current holders of the trophy, Spain. I'll come to you last, Jurgen, as I ask our other experts... who's gonna win this one? Alan."

"I can see this being a tight game, neither side wanting to lose, Germany still smarting from losing to England and Spain wanting to re-establish their credentials after their lucky draw with them. I could see it being a draw and a low scoring one at that. I think that the defences will be key tonight. Mid-fields packed and only one man up front."

"Well, thanks for that, Alan. Anything to add to that, Mark?"

"You know, Gary, I don't think I have. As Alan says, defences will be on top and the result decided by a goal on the break but more likely a goalless draw."

Gary Lineker gave a wry smile and said, "Looks like we are in for dull night then. Do you agree with the boys, Jurgen?"

Klinsmann sat up in his seat, smiled and answered, "Y'know, it takes two to tango. Someone told that to me on my way here tonight. I don't know what that has to do with football but I thought I would say it anyway."

"Well the tango is a Spanish dance so whoever said it was possibly suggesting that the Spanish were going to dance around their German opponents and waltz off with a win."

Mark Lawrenson grimaced at this and said, "That is pretty bad, Gary, even for you!"

"Yes, apologies to the viewers for that. I hope to raise the bar a little bit as the tournament progresses."

Alan Hansen chipped in. "Otherwise you best stay

*in* the bar for the whole competition."

"Time to get serious, because the teams are lining up ready to be introduced to Angela Merkel, the German Chancellor. Jurgen, I believe you have met the Chancellor. Does she have a sense of humour? I notice she smiles quite a bit, so did Gordon Brown but he frightened little children... and quite a few grown-ups too!"

"She is pleasant enough to talk to. She is a big German soccer fan but I think did boxing back in school!" He laughed loudly at his own joke.

Gary Lineker replied with a straight face. "Oh, you were joking, and here I was thinking you were being serious, her being from the old East Germany. It's more likely she was into weightlifting or something even more physical."

Hansen and Lawrenson looked blankly straight ahead to what was unfolding on the pitch.

*

The opening game was a very boring affair and was played out to a nil-nil draw with neither the home side or the Spanish willing to commit numbers into their opponent's half, both sides waiting for the break that never came. The goalkeepers had nothing more threatening to deal with than the odd nervous back pass from one of their own players.

Gary Lineker started with, "Well if you have just joined welcome to what..."

At this point Alan Hansen interjected with, "You haven't missed much!"

"Yes, I was going to say something along those

lines but perhaps not quite as blunt as that, Alan. Do you agree, Lawro, or would you express it another way?"

"Well, to be honest you could learn a lot about what 'possession' football is by running and re-running the recording of this game but as a spectacle... zero."

Lineker turned to Jurgen Klinsmann and asked, "Can you make a case for your countrymen playing like this, Jurgen?"

The German replied, "If I could make a case big enough, I would pack all twenty-two players in it and put it on a ship to, how do you say it, 'the back of beyond'? With a one-way ticket! For sure."

When the laughter had died down Gary Lineker responded. "So you did not enjoy it either. Anything more to add, Alan?"

"Well, to make it more enjoyable and interesting it would have been better to have given both sides a ball and let them play amongst themselves."

More laughter, then adapting a serious face, Gary continued. "So we all agree, worst game of the competition so far." Yet more laughter. "And on that note it is time to return you to the studio in London. Many thanks to our pundits and special guest Jurgen Klinsmann. From me, Gary Lineker, good night and hopefully we shall see you tomorrow night for the next game which will be between Greece and England."

*

"This Greek team are a lot more physical than we've seen them before, that is the third challenge from behind on the striker Mark Thyme by the *same* player each time, yet the referee has not even spoken to him. I think a yellow card at the very least is due." Mark Lawrenson was almost off his seat with anger. There was a stoppage in the play whilst the English player got some attention from the 'medic' so in the studio the pundits were registering their thoughts.

Gary Lineker answered, "I've got to agree with Mark there. We've only been playing ten minutes and as he said this is the third time by the same player, *on* the same player to boot, no pun intended."

Alan Hansen added, "This fellow has played his football in Italy for the last three years, you would have thought he'd learnt how to disguise his 'misdemeanours' by now, they're as plain as day. Still, he's got away with it so far. I canna' see it lasting, though."

Mark Lawrenson also added, "Yeah, in Italy he has been playing alongside Oscar di la Scala and we all know what he's capable of! This Theodorakis lad could learn a lot from him, he's the past master at 'dishing it out' and getting away with it. By the way, I see that he's been called up to the Italian squad to replace the injured Marco Solo."

Gary Lineker thanked Lawrenson for his observation and handed back to the match commentator, Des Kryber. He in turn thanked Lineker and continued with his commentary. "Michael Kelly is lining up the free-kick and six-foot, four-inch centre-back Colin Dett is jostling with his marker. The ball is floated in and Dett gets a glancing header in on the Greek goal. The goalie gets a hand to it, enough to deflect it away from goal but young number nine Mark Thyme sticks out a foot and sends the ball into the corner of the net. England is one-nil up. The goalkeeper did well to deflect it but Mark Thyme was like lightning."

Back in the studio Mark Lawrenson remarked, "Justice has been done."

The Greek team played almost the whole of the rest of the game with ten men behind the ball and just a lone striker. As a contest it was over from the minute the goal went in. There was no further score, as hard as the English boys tried. They had almost all of the possession and suffered some horrific tackles and yet only two yellow cards were handed out to the opposition. Theodorakis, the player who gave away the free kick from which the goal came, was not one of them, despite continuing to 'dish it out'.

The after-game discussion was mainly about how lenient the officials were when it came to dealing with the Greek side's 'misdemeanours'.

Alan Hansen kicked off. "I cannot believe that there was not one red card shown out there today. Some of the fouls were shocking. I am sure there will be at least seven of the England players on the treatment table as we speak."

Before Gary Lineker could speak, Mark Lawrenson took up the cudgels. "F.I.F.A. has got to have a word, because I could not see how they could let this referee and his 'assistants' handle another game. It is scandalous!"

"Well, there you have it. The thoughts of our experts in the studio. They were not impressed. How do you at home feel? Maybe we'll be able to read your thoughts in some of your texts or e-mails a little later on. My own opinion is that it was another disaster, sadly lacking in entertainment. As the boys say, there were too many fouls, making for scrappy play and all in all a really bad advert for the 'beautiful game'. Especially when you consider that this is the top level, the World Cup. The result was a one-nil win for a badly battered young England side. I've just been handed a few of your texts and e-mails. They contain an awful lot of 'expletives' and I'll call it 'colourful' language. Therefore, I think I can say that you seem to be in agreement with the lads in the studio. I won't embarrass them by asking them to read out any! Theodorakis has a new nickname which I am unable to reveal to you. Suffice to say that it is not particularly flattering, yet very descriptive. Yes, and even... colourful! I think at this point we have to say goodbye and thank you for watching. Please join us for the next big game, Russia versus Croatia. For now, goodbye from Alan Hansen, Mark Lawrenson, and myself. Goodbye."

# 47

Meanwhile, back in the North-West of England, the town of Barcaster to be precise, at the home of the England team coach Aurora Stafford, there was quite a gathering of family and friends to watch her team's first outing in the World Cup competition. The atmosphere was not exactly full of 'ecstasy'. (Not talking drugs here are we? ...*ed.*)

*

Lisa Stafford was the first to speak and said, "Well not much to write home about but at least they're successfully over the first obstic... obstoc... hurdle."

Her friend Dee Hacker agreed. "You are right, darling, it could not get much worse than that. How did that Greek team ever qualify to play at such an important tournament? I thought that only the *best* teams in the world were the ones to be playing there. They were disgraceful and that is based on what little I know about football. It was more like wrestling, the way some of them carried on. Anyway, well done to dear Aurora and her boys."

"Hear, hear, and so say all of us. They kept their heads and did us proud!" echoed Hilary, the family's general factotum. (I think they know that by now...*ed.*)

Fiona and Gavin were just excited at the fact that Aurora and her team were still in the competition and chatted excitedly among themselves and a couple of their friends.

Lisa carried on. "Who's for a cuppa tea, coffee, or something stronger?"

They all settled for tea except the kids – they asked for fizzy drinks.

When she was alone with Hilary in the kitchen she touched her friend's arm and in a low voice said, "Y'know, since all this happened with our 'Ror I have never felt happier. I feel more loved now than ever I felt before 'the big change' and everything about our relationship is so much more meaningful. Makes me feel so much more 'feminine'."

At this point Hilary pulled her towards her and hugged her warmly, saying, "No-one could ever be more feminine than you, I can assure you of that much, and don't worry, I know that you are speaking of your relationship with Aurora. I agree with you, and whatever, we are much closer too." At this she squeezed Lisa closer and kissed the nape of her neck then reached over for the kettle, filled it and put it on the hob to boil.

Lisa smiled warmly back and with a wink said, "I'll see you later. You are staying over, ain't ya, darlin'?"

"Yes, as long as there's room for little Julian too in that huge, huge bedroom."

"There's no problem there, darlin', we could lose him in that bed anyway."

"That's ok. I have his carry-cot, that way we'll know exactly where he is at all times."

"That lovely man of yours must miss the two of you desperately with that job of his. How long is he away this time and where is it? Afghanistan again?"

"Yes it is, and it will be another month or so before he comes home. That's the trouble with being a reservist and such a good surgeon. Kettle has boiled, who's having what milk and sugar?"

"Oh, just bring milk and sugar with you. 'Ere, I'll take that for ya."

Later on that night, after friends had been seen off, her children had been put to bed and settled, Lisa went into the kitchen and selected a bottle of wine and turning to Hilary, insisted, "I'm counting on you to help me make an impression on this bottle of our favourite tipple. It's not a celebration, it's to drink the toast of our 'lads' and their gorgeous coach and to wish 'em well in their next game. This is just the start, trust me, I'm sure they'll do really well. Ooh and a special toast to that lovely husband of yours. Hope *he's* keeping safe and well. Now don't 'ang about, come and get comfortable, or do I mean 'up close and personal'?"

Hilary responded, "Let's try up comfortably close, shall we?"

"Here y'are then, get that down your gullet."

Both girls gulped down the first glass fairly quickly and sighed deeply in appreciation. In her attempt at a refill Lisa spilt wine down Hilary's dress.

"Oops, sorry darlin', I meant it for your 'froat', not

your front."

The two of them laughed and clinked glasses once Lisa had successfully recharged Hilary's.

"You might want to take that frock off and put it in to soak, 'cos it's sure to stain. Ain't nobody around to see you, except me of course and I ain't gonna do ya no 'arm."

"Yeah, I wouldn't bet on that, the mood you are in already. However, I will do as you say and maybe borrow a robe from your bedroom. I can check on Julian whilst I am at it." When she returned Hilary noticed that her glass had been topped up again.

"You are a bad influence on me, madam, but I think you know that. I didn't drink before you came into my life, well not so much at least. I have to act like a responsible parent with my young son around. He is sleeping very soundly, mind you." Lisa gave her great big smile and signalled for her to snuggle up to her again.

Having finished off the bottle between them they decided to 'hit the sack' – as Lisa put it.

They took a shower together and touched each other's 'parts' playfully, giggling softly so as not to wake the children. Afterwards they dried each other down with huge, luxurious towels. Lisa helped her friend on with one of her own nightdresses and slipped into one herself.

Once inside the enormous bed they came together in the middle and Lisa started where she had left off in the shower, only this time caressing gently and sensually Hilary's more private 'parts'. Hilary took Lisa's chin in her hands and kissed her very warmly on the lips.

"Gawd, this is just as good as the real thing. Cor, what am I saying? This is the *real* thing, or as I know it now!"

Hilary pulled back from their embrace.

"I'm sorry darling, I didn't mean... Well this *is* the real thing as far as me and you goes, but you've got Mike and I've got my 'Ror, that's what I mean. I mean we've got each other to comfort when our 'loves' are away. Sorry darlin', I didn't mean... gissa another one of those smackers."

Lisa grabbed Hilary closer to her and planted a 'smacker' of her own, holding it there for several moments.

Hilary responded by hugging her more tightly and moving her legs so that they enveloped Lisa's lower body. Lisa moved her hands slowly over Hilary's body, gently moulding and probing more intimately now. Hilary's breathing became slightly heavier as she responded to the expert touches of her friend and employer.

"You've got me all wet now!"

"That's the whole idea, darlin'."

Lisa took Hilary's hands and placed them between her own thighs.

"Well maybe you can return the favour; maybe you can pull the trigger for me, darlin'. That's right, you 'ave a way about ya too. Don't stop, you've got *me* goin' now!"

"We've never gone this far before."

"It's not for the want of tryin', believe me."

"What do you mean? We've always respected boundaries before."

"Oh, is that what it was? I guess you're right but remember what I told you about 'worker's playtime' with the girls on our fashion and glamour shoots?"

"Yes, of course."

"Well, this is what it was all about...-this is what it was like, this is what we did."

"I didn't realise you went that far."

"I couldn't tell you then 'cos I did not know ya as well as I do now. That's where I learnt the skills. Anyway, where were we?"

Once again Lisa took hold of Hilary's hands and guided them between her thighs. She sighed contentedly as Hilary's fingers penetrated deeper inside with the help of a little pressure from herself.

Hilary responded with a 'whoop' of delight as Lisa forced her legs apart and expertly worked her magic and eventually brought her to a climax.

Hilary was caught up in the moment and felt warm sensations coursing all through her body and then she remembered where she had *her* hands and she quickly applied herself to duplicating the experience for her friend.

At this point Lisa reached under the pillow behind Hilary's head and produced a plastic 'sex aid'. (Very delicate there...*ed.*)

"Here, try this... it's what Ror' and me use now."

Hilary was taken aback not only at the sight of it

but also the size and weight of it. Nevertheless, with Lisa's encouragement and guiding hands it wasn't long before Hilary had affected a similar result to her own.

Then wrapping themselves together, they rolled around the bed soaking up the warmth of each other's body whilst bathing in perspiration.

At the end of this they were both totally exhausted and soon fell into deep sleep.

Their slumber was only interrupted by the cries of baby Julian wanting a night-time feed. This Hilary attended to as quickly as possible, so as not to wake up the rest of the household. Lisa asked her if she would let her feed the baby and was delighted when Hilary handed him over.

After a few minutes feeding and fussing little Julian, Lisa turned to Hilary and said, "He's such a little darlin' and he loves his food, don't he? Ooh, that's a big burp. A wonder it didn't wake Fiona and Gavin! By the smell of things he may need changing. 'Ere, I'll let you do that."

"Thanks, I thought you might."

# 48

Gary Lineker's voice was tinged with excitement as he began his introduction. "It has been a much more interesting tournament after a rather dull and at times very 'scrappy' first few ties. We've seen some of the 'hot' favourites, such as Spain and Brazil, exit during the knockout stages. We've seen some great performances and good football from the Croatians and the Danes. We saw a very, very disciplined and able, some would say predictable progression by the German side and here we are at the semi-final stage of the World Cup and what do you know...? Yes... England is still in it!"

"Do I detect a note of disbelief, Gary? Shall I pinch you to convince you you're not dreaming it?" Mark Lawrenson teased his friend.

Alan Hansen added his two-penneth. "C'mon, Lineker, wake up. You're only dreamin', man!! Honestly though, they are truly here on merit. This England team have played some of the best football I have seen for a very long time and as a Scot it hurts me to say it!"

"Well you heard **that** here first, folks! Thank you, gentlemen, and now to the business at hand. Before us we have the first of the semi-finals which is between the Danes and the Croats. These two teams have provided us with some of the most entertaining play. I for one think that they too, deserve to be here at this stage of the World Cup competition and I'm sure our 'experts' will agree. What do you think, Mark?"

"Gary, I agree with everything you said. Both of these teams have entertained us with some attractive, expansive football throughout their involvement in this competition. Good word for you there, Gary... expansive."

"Oh, I thought you were gonna say involvement! Alan, do you see either side changing tactics or style of play?"

"Well no, why would they? They only got this far by doing what they do best and that's playing good attacking football. It's gonnae be interesting to see which team comes out on top though, because they play a very similar style to each other."

Mark Lawrenson interjected. "I agree, a very difficult one to predict. Should be an interesting tie. I have to say though that from what I've seen so far, the Croats can get a little bit rough when things don't go entirely their way. I'll keep an open mind though."

Gary Lineker agreed. "I know what you mean, some of their challenges have been, let's say, a little 'heavy handed'. What about you, Alan, anything to add?"

"Well, I think their stuff has been a little tame compared with some of the stuff that we saw in the knockout rounds. I'm beginning to see now why they are called the 'knockout' rounds!"

"Very good, Alan, and I'm sure a lot of people would agree with you. I personally cannot remember covering a competition quite so 'dirty' as this one was in the earlier stages. Just as Alan Hansen says, folks. Well I think they are ready for us over in the commentary box so I'll leave you in the very capable hands of your commentator for this evening's game, Des Kryber. Over to you, Des."

"Thank you Gary and thanks too to Mark Lawrenson and Alan Hansen. The experts there with their views on this World Cup competition so far, and speculation on today's match. No predictions though. You join me here this evening in Cologne for the first semi-final between Croatia and Denmark. The teams are lining up for the anthems and we are very close to kick-off. The atmosphere inside the stadium is building. It is quite a warm evening but the temperature is down from the mid-day high of twenty-five degrees. I have Tony Cottee in the box beside me and we are looking forward to another veritable feast of football. What say you, Tony?"

"Des, you've summed up what we are all feeling, I think. Two good footballing sides with the 'prize' of a place in the final of this World Cup competition. By the way, again the pitch is in fantastic condition."

"Thanks Tony, now the ref is just about to put the whistle to his lips to get us underway, with the Danes getting the first touch."

*

The Croats played a cautious first twenty minutes, hardly crossing the halfway line and successfully containing the Danes in mid-field, challenging for the ball and not allowing them to settle into a pattern or rhythm of play.

In fact, it was not until Theo Rasmussen intercepted a pass from his opposite number, midfielder Luka Modric, and played it into the feet of Brian Larsen, did the game come alive. Because on receipt of Rasmussen's pass Larsen went on a jinking run that left Sucha Suker on his backside and called for a desperate tackle from Igor Tudor. So desperate in fact that the referee awarded a penalty to the Danes.

Des Kryber commented, "A harsh decision, Tony?"

"I don't know, Des. It looked like he took his leg as well as the ball. On seeing the replay I'd say it was because the tackle was ever so slightly from behind as well. After all, he was chasing back."

"Well the referee's decision is final and despite their remonstrations the Croatians now have to rely on the goalie to keep it out. I think the ref has gone to his pocket; yes, he has taken out a yellow card and waved in the faces of at least three Croatian players. We'll perhaps find out later who the recipients were. Meanwhile, Brian Larsen is poised ready to take the spot kick. I think he has an almost perfect scoring record of penalties."

Tony Cottee answered, "He's a very cool character, nothing seems to faze him. Look, he's just standing there with his hands on his hips, as if to say 'when you're ready'. The goalie on the other hand is looking positively nervous, unless of course all that movement is his attempt to unsettle Larsen."

"No, I think you are on the money there, Tony.

Larsen is coolly looking round the stadium waiting for the referee to restore order and blow his whistle."

"Nerves of steel," said Cottee.

"The referee has turned his focus towards the spot kick, told the goalie to get back on his line, looked at Brian Larsen and pointed to his whistle. Larsen steps back, the goalie is just as animated, the whistle sounds and the ball is in the back of the net!"

Tony Cottee commented, "Y'see, I have a problem with that. I do not think that the penalty taker should be allowed to stop or hesitate in his approach. It should be a straightforward walk-up or run-up and then kick it."

"I know what you are saying, Tony, but I'm not sure I agree. I don't think there is anything in the rules governing the approach to the kick."

"Well if there is, like a lot of other questionable actions, they still do it and get away with it."

"Well, the fact is that the Danes have broken the stalemate and are celebrating going a goal up with just a few minutes to go to half-time."

The rest of the half was smattered with several little 'incidents' and a good deal livelier and quite physical football action.

Tony Cottee remarked, "The referee has to keep a tight rein on this game now otherwise it could 'boil over' into something quite ugly. Which would be a shame because both teams are capable of great football, as we have seen before in this competition."

"I agree. I hope that when they get back to their respective dressing rooms the two coaches will calm them down and tell them to get back to what they do best, which is as you say, Tony, to play attractive, entertaining football. It would be a shame to spoil it at this stage of the competition bearing in mind what we saw in earlier games. I'll now hand you over to the boys back in the studio. Over to you, Gary."

"Thanks, Des. The lads here have been nodding their heads in agreement to all that you two have said. I think I agree with Tony about the 'staggered' penalty kick, but it seems to be accepted at all levels of the game. Lawro, you think the same way as I do too. Alan, it doesn't bother you at all?"

"I think the issue of the penalty, the tackle from behind and an incident like that, has put a completely different complexion on what was an absorbing game of attractive football. It is true to say that up 'til that point the game was absorbing and entertaining, quite thrilling even. Let's hope that the coaches do as our commentary team suggests and cool the atmosphere and convince them to play the game they were playing before the incident that resulted in the penalty goal."

Mark Lawrenson commented, "Sadly this is a result of players letting the heart rule their heads and generally having a disregard for the rule of law. Referees should be encouraged to take a firmer grip on games too, and not let some of the 'little things' go, because if a player sees he can get away with stuff he will push it further. As you say, the coaches should 'reign them in' and I sincerely hope that this is what is happening in both dressing rooms right now as we speak, and that they can all play the second half with the discipline that they showed before the penalty was given. After all, this is biggest stage for them to show off their footballing talent that they will experience in their lifetimes!"

"Thank you, Lawro, I'll just give you time to get your breath back. Seriously though, Mark Lawrenson is so right and I'm sure we all go along with what he is thinking, in hoping that the second half does deliver some of the same fare as we enjoyed in the first half, as he said, before the incident that brought about the goal. Now at this point and without much further ado, I'll hand you back to our commentary team Des Kryber and of course... Tony Cottee."

"Thanks Gary... lads. Lawro... rather eloquent there I thought. Yes, and he does speak for us all... 'Play up and play the game' so read the notice over the entrance to the changing rooms at my old school. I'm sure you don't need me to explain what that means. Oh you do, maybe a bit later then. Meanwhile, I can see the Danes running out onto the field of play followed rather more slowly by the Croatians. If they don't move a little quicker I think the referee might start the second half without them."

"That'll shake 'em, Des," Cottee replied. "Can't afford to go another goal behind, at least not before they've had a touch of the ball."

"All present and correct. The ref puts the whistle to his lips and blows. We're off! For the second half of this World Cup first semi-final between Croatia and Denmark. It's the Danes that are attacking first, Larsen has beaten two men and swept it out to the right wing where he finds Rasmussen, who has lost it to the diminutive form that is Luka Modric and he is now advancing over the halfway line towards the Danish goal. He's seen off two challenges as he reaches the edge of his opponents' penalty area. He turns one way then to the other; he dips his shoulder and sends a low shot into the corner of the Danish goal. What a sensational goal! The goalkeeper had no chance!"

Tony Cottee echoed his colleague's words. "Absolutely no chance! I don't think he even saw it! If he did, he reacted too slow! Wow, what a fantastic way to draw level. That's gonna make it interesting. Game on, Des."

"Indeed, Tony. We won't see a better goal than that one, I am sure of it. That has really set it up, especially coming so soon after the break. We have a game on our hands now, for sure (Echoes of Jurgen Klinsmann again there...*ed.*). It has certainly lifted the heads of the Croatian players."

"And the crowd too. They've suddenly found their voices again. It's like the place is full of Croats singing now."

Des Kryber picked up where Tony Cottee left off. "This is the most noise that we have heard throughout this competition, I think. It has certainly gone up by quite a few decibels! Meanwhile, back to the action on the pitch. The Danes must look for a pretty quick response to dampen the ardour of the Croatian fans. The Danes have the ball through Larsen; Larsen has lost it but he wins it back. They are knocking the ball around quite comfortably, not affected by the atmosphere it would appear, Tony."

"It's good 'end to end' stuff, Des, and I'm enjoying it. The tackles are coming in fair and square, not too many errors being made. It's an interesting game of football. You get the feeling it might just be down to who makes the first real mistake."

"Well said there, Tony, I cannot argue with that. This game is on a knife-edge."

The match continued like this for the best part of the second half and looked very much like it was going to be played out to a draw. As the game went on both teams seemed to become more defensive and less adventurous in their play.

The mood of the crowd seemed to change too. Boos now accompanied just about every back pass or negative action. Des Kryber commented, "It is looking very much like we'll be going to penalties at this rate. After all the wonderful football that we have witnessed from these two teams it is rather disappointing to see it come to this. What say you, Tony?"

Tony Cottee sustained a fake yawn and replied, "Des, it is a crime that this game should be ending like this with neither team looking for the deciding goal. It is the semi-final of the biggest footballing competition of 'em all... the World Cup, after all!"

"I couldn't agree more. Now what is this? The referee has awarded a free kick to the Croatians quite close to the Danish box. Very kickable, don't you think, Tony? I'm betting back in the studio the boys are on the edge of their seats at this. Could there be an upset here? A real sting in the tail!"

"Well Des, he's signalled that it's a *direct* free kick so I'm sure they'll be going for it. Luka Modric is standing over the ball as we speak."

"We have seen what this little fellow is capable of,

Tony. I wonder whether goalkeeper Nils Lofgren knows that he has a hundred per cent record for penalties. This is a little different though, at least he has a defensive line to help him."

"The ref has his foam marker out and spraying around the boots of that defensive line now."

"Yes, and the ref has shown his whistle to Modric."

Tony Cottee cut in jokingly. "Yes, I think he was admiring it a little earlier, Des. Maybe he'd like to get his hands on it."

"You will have your little joke, Mr. Cottee, with emphasis on the 'little'. Seriously though, the ref has it out in front of him now for *all* to see and we are waiting for him to blow it." Cottee sniggered in the background.

Des Kryber continued. "He blows it; Modric strolls up to the ball and curls his shot around the wall, sending it towards the far corner of the Danish goal. The goalie dives with outstretched arms and manages to deflect it on to the post. It is immediately cleared by his right-back, and it falls to the feet of Brian Larsen, the only outfield player from either side not in the Danish penalty area. He has no-one to beat but the goalie and so he puts his head down and races towards his opponents' goal. The Croatian defence is desperately trying to track back but there is an awful lot of green between them and Larsen. He closes on the Croatian box; as I said, he only has the goalie to beat. Slobavic comes off his line to close the options but Larsen anticipates and loops a clever kick over the advancing keeper's head and into the open goal."

Des Kryber pauses to take a breath then carries on.

"Two-one to the Danes! Larsen is buried under a pile of bodies as he and his team-mates celebrate. Meanwhile, the Croat goalkeeper is berating his players for deserting him, whilst they in turn are having heated exchanges, some quite physical in nature! The referee and his assistants are doing their level best to bring order to bear. Tony, this is extraordinary. Who would have thought it?"

"Des, I'm amazed. The referee has got to sort it out or it might get really ugly. I see the Croatian bench are getting involved and doing *their* best to break it up!"

"Yes, thankfully it seems to be working. There can only be a matter of three minutes and whatever added time, if any, to play. The players have got back to their positions for the restart. The heart must have gone out of the Croatian team and their spirit drained. So close to clinching it at one end with the free-kick; only for the ball to end up, just seconds later, in the back of their own net."

"Des, it doesn't help now that they lost it with each other. More than anything they need to stand together and you'd expect that the coach and the rest of the Croatian bench tried to get that over to 'em."

"A clarion call, that is what was required, Tony. A clarion call."

"I'm sure you are right, Des, but isn't that one of those fancy throws that a baseball pitcher uses."

"That would be a 'curl' of some sort, Tony, not that I'm any kind of expert on that topic. I said call, a clarion call. It's a call to war... a rousing sound or... call! Hereabouts play has commenced and the losing side are passing the ball around quite brightly. Shows they are true professionals I suppose, despite the nastiness of a few moments ago. As you might expect the Danes are getting back and defending, mostly inside their own half. There are eighty seconds left to play plus three minutes added time. Does not give the Croats much time but they seem to be applying themselves. Sucha Suker plays it out of defence to the little mid-field general Luka Modric, he's encouraging his players to move forward and guides a deft little pass to Bogovic. He in turn finds Stoikovic who is down on the Danish goal, he is challenged and goes to ground, too easily in my opinion but the Croats are calling for a penalty. The referee is having none of it. He checked with his assistant who shook his head and carried his flag pointing downwards. The referee went to his pocket and produced a yellow card, presumably for Bogovic diving. Tony?"

"Des, that was a perfectly good tackle and Bogovic was obviously looking for a penalty, couldn't be more blatant about it than that. He needs to watch it, he's right in the face of the official with his protests and not many of his team-mates are joining in with him."

"It is also wasting time; he should get on with it. I can't see the referee adding extra time for this. I make it only one minute to go. Brian Larsen is dwelling on the ball, killing time, denying the Croats possession. It is a matter of seconds now. You can hear the Danish fans counting them down... three... two... one; the referee allows play to continue, though, but now his whistle goes to his mouth and it is all over, the Danes are in the World Cup Final and the Croats are on their way home!!"

"Well that was an entertaining game, Des. It had everything, didn't it?"

"Everything but the kitchen sink, Tony, and if it had gone on any longer who knows maybe that could have been thrown in too? To summarise though... for variety you could not match it. There was excellent quality football and some negative play from both sides plus three very different goals. We also saw the 'ugly' side of the game towards the end, Tony."

"I thought the match officials handled the whole thing pretty well by letting the game flow throughout and not getting intimidated towards the end there."

"I am with you there, Tony, and thank you for your company today. Now, I wonder what our experts back in the studio make of it all? Over to you, Gary."

"Thanks Des, for the excellent commentary, and Tony for your informed input, and now for the views of our pundits here in the studio. You've got to admit, gents, that we were thoroughly entertained tonight. As Tony Cottee said, Alan, this game had everything... good flowing football... great goals... terrific individual performances... incidents... bookings... and yes... controversy! Anything to add?"

Alan Hansen sat up in his chair, gave a wry smile, and spoke. "No, I agree, we've seen all sides of what's known as the 'beautiful' game here tonight. Fortunately, most was the prettier side of the game but sadly the thing that will stick in the memory is the reaction of the Croats to the award of the penalty given against them, and that awful attempt to get a penalty kick of their own in the second half. The 'pug-ugly' side of football. The memory of two excellent goals and a clinically executed penalty will be shaded by those awful incidents and what went on afterwards."

Gary Lineker signalled to Mark Lawrenson to come in at this point.

"Gary, I thought overall that it was a good game to watch but I can't help but agree with Alan and the others, 'cos it's the ugly bits that the papers will pick up on, and who can blame 'em really?"

Gary Lineker attempted to promote the good points of the game, saying, "The positives are that we saw a lovely contest in mid-field between two masters of the game – Theo Rasmussen, but especially from the little 'maestro' himself, Luka Modric. It's a shame we won't be seeing more of him. Some excellent finishing and when both sides played their football it was a delight to watch. However, we now know that the Danes will be in the final, but we have to wait until later today to find out who they'll be meeting on the big day. So from Alan Hansen, Mark Lawrenson, and myself, goodbye from Cologne. See you back here in two hours' time for Germany versus England in the other semi-final."

\*

The second semi-final of the World Cup competition is being played at the F.C. Hamburg ground, and although there are still two hours to kick-off, the stadium, which holds nearly 57,000 spectators, is just about full already. There is a good percentage of English fans here to cheer on their team and the already bristling atmosphere is building even more in anticipation of another historical game of football between these two protagonists.

(Heavy stuff there, my *author* friend...*ed.*)

It was getting close to the time for the television companies to start their coverage of the game so the story picks up where it left off, with Gary Lineker in the studio re-introducing his pundit friends and the studio guest.

"Hello again and welcome back to the studio with our regular team of Alan Hansen, Mark Lawrenson, and me, Gary Lineker, for what promises to be an outstanding game of football – the second semi-final of this World Cup competition. Let me tell you that we are joined by a special guest and old friend of ours, the Tottenham Hotspur and German striker Mr. Jurgen Klinsmann. Welcome back, Jurgen, and let me start off by asking how you, as a 'local', see the way this game is going to go."

"Hello Gary... guys, and thanks for inviting me back. I think that you have thrown me into the deep end asking me that question first up. Yes, but I have seen both team sheets so I think I am able to state an opinion. As you are aware this German team are a very experienced lot, for sure, and have been in this position on a few occasions. They have selected what appears to be the strongest... line-up, I learnt that word today. So I think it will be hard for this young English side to compete. Even so, they are very talented. It should be an interesting game, for sure."

Gary Lineker thanked him and asked Mark

Lawrenson's opinion.

"Gary, can't help thinking that Jurgen's right. Talented but inexperienced; at this level it could all be too much for them. Having said that, look what they have achieved so far. Face it, they have beaten some powerful line-ups with good, creative, flowing play but could they just run out of steam?"

"Good point there, Mark, but as a 'neutral', Alan, which way do you see it going?"

"Well I see it as a 'make or break' situation for this developing English side. I guess my money is on the much more experienced Germans."

Lineker remarked, "I personally think there's hope for the English lads but Jurgen, these guys seem to be in agreement with you. So I'll just reserve judgement in the hope of an unlikely surprise result."

Alan Hansen responded, "Only time will tell who's right but I'm looking forward to it being the best game of the tournament so far, because that is what it's shaping up to be."

Mark Lawrenson interjected. "Gary, could I just add that these young English lads will have nothing to be ashamed of if it is their last game in this particular World Cup, because I am sure they will be there or thereabouts in the next big competition. So good luck to 'em!"

"A good positive note there, bearing in mind that England did not make the knockout stages at the last time of asking! I see that it is time now for the teams to be introduced and the anthems to be performed so I'll just hand you over to our relatively new and young commentator in Hamburg... Mr. Colm Nelson. Good evening, Colm, and how are things with you there in the commentary box?"

Colm Nelson took a steadying breath and answered Lineker nervously. "Hi Gary, hi guys! I'm a little bit nervous, Gary. Talk about being pushed in at the deep end, Jurgen. This is my very first 'big' game commentary on the 'Beeb'. I've only done local Norfolk Radio before but I've done quite a lot of that so I'll be leaning on that experience to pull me through. This is a real honour and a pleasure for me to be chatting to you guys, such esteemed company and for what it's worth I was a fully paid-up member of the Tottenham Hotspur Fan Club, so you and Jurgen are two of my absolute idols. I'm sure Lawro and Hansen won't mind me getting that in. I..."

At this point Lineker cut in, saying, "Colm, that's great and *I'm* flattered and I'm sure Jurgen is too, but I couldn't help noticing that the teams are lined up ready for the national anthems."

"Oh... Yes... that's right, Gary, my producer has just mentioned it. He's a fan of yours too by the way! Ok, everybody we are just gonna listen to 'God Save the Queen' then the 'Deutschland, Deutschland Uber Alles'. There is total silence throughout the stadium as everyone respects the anthems."

Back in the studio Gary Lineker sustained a slight chuckle as he registered the look of disbelief on the faces of the others. Then with the anthems over, Colm Nelson continued. "It is now my pleasure to introduce you to the gentleman who will be sharing the box with me throughout this game. Someone who doesn't really need any introduction but here I go anyway... Here it is... here *he* is, former England right-back... Jonny..."

A voice 'off-mic' quickly called out, "Left-back! And I bet they don't share a box in cricket. Just my little joke, Colm."

"Sorry... *Left*-back... Jonny Egar. Welcome Jonny and thanks for correcting me. What's that about a cricket joke? I don't get it."

"That's ok, bit of a dodgy start really. I'm just as nervous as you so I thought I'd try a light-hearted approach. This is the biggest game I've been involved in since I stopped playing for England two years ago. 'Cos like you, I've been doing local radio but up in the north of England."

"Alright then. We'll hold each other's hands, ok?"

"I don't think we need to go that far, Colm. Oh look, the referee is about to blow his whistle to start the game – phew!"

"Yes, here we go. Well spotted, Jonny, and it is England to kick off. I see. It's Mark Thyme with his foot on the ball and the ref gets the game under way. Mark Thyme plays it out to the right wing where Ulysses Grant, the nineteen-year-old, tries to get straight into his stride with a run right at the German left-back, but unfortunately lands on his backside. He got a free kick for his troubles though; I'm not sure what that was for. It looked a perfectly good challenge to me. What do you say, Jonny?"

There was a pregnant pause and then Egar answered, "Sorry, Colm, what was the question? Only I dropped me 'crib sheet' on the floor, y'know the paper with all the names, etcetera, on it. Anyway, what was you sayin'?"

"I know what a 'crib sheet' is! It doesn't matter; they've taken the free kick already. Grant launched it deep into the German box but too close to the goal and the German keeper Hans Eidel gathered it safely and cleared it upfield, and now the Germans have launched *their* first attack. This comes to nothing because the right winger Kurt Reiplie overran it and England get the first throw-in of the match."

The game continued for most of the half with neither side threatening the other's goal. As a contest it was full of good, exciting football but it had to be said that the defences seemed to be on top and seemed impenetrable, but then it happened. Back to Colm Nelson's commentary.

"Terry Bull has been brought down just inside the German penalty area. No doubt about that, Jonny."

"No doubt at all, 'e 'ad done 'im for speed and the German just stuck a foot out!"

"Can't tell who is gonna take it. It looks like there's a bit of a squabble between three or four of the England boys about who will take it."

Jonny Egar chipped in. "Don't tell me they 'aven't sorted out who's the penalty taker. I bet they've practised long enough for a penalty shootout, it being the Germans they're against! 'Ere y'know he's got a twin brother don't ya?"

"Who has?"

"Terry... Terry Bull and *his* name is Eddie, d'ya get it? Eddie Bull!"

(*Terrible* and **edible** – by way of explanation...*ed.*)

(**Not** necessary...*me.*)

"No, but that's a good point about the penalty, Jonny. Colin Dett the giant centre-back is signalling animatedly to the bench with all manner of gestures coming back at him. Finally it looks as if Paul Bastable (Remember him from the first page? ...*ed.*) the dependable mid-fielder is gonna take on the responsibility."

"Paul has a steadying influence on the England boys, 'e 'as matured into a very classy Premiership and international player. I fancy 'im to convert this spot kick."

"Thanks Jonny, and I think you've said what we all think. Bastable stands over the ball waiting for the ref's whistle, *he* has had to tell German goalie to get back on his line, no need for the white foam stuff. He goes back but he's moving about like a mad man. The ref now puts the whistle to his lips; he blows it. Bastable steps back a yard then forward and with a minimal back lift strikes the ball to the bottom right-hand corner of the goal. The German goalie got only the slightest of touches on it but it was just enough to guide it wide of the post. No goal."

Jonny Egar was out of his seat but quickly spoke up. "He had no right to get to that. That was an unbelievable save! I was just about to do a lap of the box to cebral... celbrel... ate... You know what I mean. I thought it was goin' in the bottom corner! What an incredible save!"

Colm Nelson calmed the situation, saying, "We get the picture, Jonny, but meanwhile the Germans have successfully defended the resultant corner and are breaking out with short, sharp passes that see them bearing down on the English goal. Goalie Seph

Handys has snatched a cross from the Germans' right wing straight off the head of giant centre-back Colin Dett, and Michael Kelly is now on the ball. Kelly passes it to Terry Bull out on his side's left-wing. He takes it to the bye-line and pulls it back into the path of Mark Thyme whose first time shot was saved, once again, by the penalty stop hero, Hans Eidel. Another good save, Jonny."

"Got to admit it, this guy is on fire! He can't put a foot wrong. I guess that should be *'and* wrong, really. I know you'll probably kick me for saying this but this is real end-to-end stuff."

"No, to be honest I was thinking the very same because we've had it all in this first forty-five minutes. Time seems to have flown by. I don't know about you, Jonny?"

"Yeah, same 'ere. It has been good entertainment. Oh look, the ref has blown for 'alf-time."

"Well thanks for spotting that, J. E. We'll now go back to the studio and see what *they* all think. Back to you, Gary."

"Thanks Colm and welcome back, viewers. I'm with Mark Lawrenson, Alan Hansen, and special guest Jurgen Klinsmann. Well what a great game this has been so far. I'll ask Jurgen for his thoughts first, Jurgen?"

"I have enjoyed the game and I want it to carry on like this, but you know I am thinking that possibly the younger English players may just find this pressure harder as the game goes on. It is where experience kicks in at this type of game."

Gary Lineker thanked him and signalled to Alan

Hansen. "Alan?"

"I am inclined to agree although I think they've coped very well so far. In fact they probably had the better of that first half and with that in mind it may spur them on to greater heights."

Lineker, a little taken aback by Hansen's words, turned to Lawrenson. "Is Alan alright...? Sorry... I mean *right* there, Lawro?"

Lawrenson smiled knowingly at Lineker and replied, "Gary, I think he is spot on 'cos the lads have got their heads up and are going for it in a big way. I think it would only be psychological pressure that came to bear but they seem to be enjoying it as much as we are so perhaps that will see them through the second half ok. I certainly hope so."

Lineker nodded in Jurgen Klinsmann's direction, saying, "Jurgen, I know you said you are happy at the way it has gone so far but you have to bear in mind that the Germans could have been a goal down at this point."

Klinsmann pulled himself up in his chair, clicked his heels together and answered (Of course he didn't!! ...Ridiculous!! ...Uhm!! ...*ed.*), "As Alan and Mark said, the English players are enjoying themselves for sure and their coach Aurora Stafford will be in that dressing room and saying to keep it up. Boys, why are you laughing?"

Gary Lineker quickly jumped in, saying, "Just a private joke they shared. I'm sure it can't be repeated on air. Carry on with what you were saying, please."

"Well, I think still that the German boys will call up their experience in this second half of the game to win through in the end."

"Thank you, Jurgen, and Alan and Mark too. It is now time to hand you back to Colm Nelson and Jonny Egar for that second half. I wonder what surprises are in store for us."

"Thanks Gary, it promises to be an interesting forty-five minutes that's for sure."

(Oh-um, can't resist can you? ...*ed.*)

(No, no, that was unintentional, honest...*me.*)

Jonny Egar chimed in. "I look at it this way, youthful enthusiasm versus experienced professionalism."

"I wondered what you were going to say there for a minute, Jonny, but well put. I have to say that is what it looks like to me too and if it is as interesting and enjoyable as the first half then the next forty-five minutes will fly by just as quickly."

Jonny Egar observed, "It looks to me as though the Germans are lining up in a more defensive formation. Think they might be 'appy to soak up early pressure and try to 'it the English lads on the break. I've seen that work so many times before but you gotta think that the younger squad 'as prob'ly got the better energy levels. I don' know. It's gonna be a good one, I know that."

"A little insight from Jonny Egar there, now let's see whether he is right. It'll be the Germans to get this second half under way in the shape of tall blond striker Gustav Vindt, and he strokes the ball straight back to his centre-back Hans Bach, who in turn plays it to right-back Willi Heff. Now repeat that after a couple of steins of the local lager!"

Jonny Egar corrected Nelson. "That would be steins of beer, Colm. Deutsche Bier, they don't call it lager over 'ere. I don't think they do. That's what I was told, anyway."

"Thanks again, J.E. I stand corrected. What a wonderful gift this education thing is! Meanwhile, Willi Heff has resisted the attentions of Paul Bastable and played a lovely long looping ball into the path of Gustav Vindt, who instinctively launches a first-time shot goalwards, which Seph Handys spectacularly snatches out of the air and hugs to his chest."

Jonny Egar is quick to exclaim, "Another sensational save, Colm, and this time it's the England goalie that's made it!"

"True, Jonny, and I think the Germans were probably luring us and the English players into a false sense of security with that move from the kick-off as with two negative passes and one very positive one, an accurate shot on goal in fact, which brought out a fine save."

"I'm sure they've practised that on the training ground, probably the idea was to get an early goal and then go on the defensive like I said, Colm."

"Quite astute with your observations then, J.E."

Jonny Egar affected his 'plumiest' accent and replied, "One does one's best, don't ya know."

Colm Nelson adopted a similar accent. "I am so glad and I am sure that our watching audience are very much appreciative of same. Meanwhile, back on the pitch it is all happening. Actually what is going on is an awful lot of sideways or backwards passing and this by the English players."

"Yeah, they're playing keep ball now and they're very good at it too."

"True, Jonny, they're acquitting themselves quite well. So long as they don't lose it. But no, they're passing in neat little triangles."

"Trouble is, it's bogging it down in mid-field."

"They're playing the patience game but now the ball goes from Paul Bastable to Michael Kelly and with a clever sidestep he goes past Kurt Rieplie, draws right-back Willi Heff, and plays a lovely ball to the feet of Terry Bull who then picks out Grant on the right wing. He in turn sends a low ball across the back of the German defence for centre-forward Mark Thyme to run it past Hans Eidel into the net. A wonderful team goal. England are one up on the Germans!"

"That was a great team goal, a great example of 'one-touch' football. That was pretty sensational stuff, I gotta say."

Colm Nelson wiped his forehead with the back of his hand and said, "One of the best passages of play I've seen for many a year."

"I 'ope we can see a few more where that came from, Colm, that had class written all over it. Wow!"

Colm Nelson continued his commentary. "Play has restarted with the Germans moving the ball around with cool efficiency. They are being closed down very quickly by the English players and not being allowed time on the ball."

"That is a good tactic for these boys to use, Colm, 'cos they're keeping the Germans in their own 'alf. They're pressing 'em 'igh upfield, great stuff."

"Yes, 'cos while they're out there, there's no threat on their own goal. Good thinking."

"Well, somehow the ball has been stolen by Leydon Lowe, the twenty-one year old attacking English full-back, and passed to Ulysses Grant on the right wing. He's motoring along the touchline at a rate of knots. He looks up, sees no English player is in the box, gets his head down again and carries on past the German left-back. Upon reaching the goal-line he looks up again, still no-one there, so in one move he turns and beats central defender Hans Bach, then shoots at goal only to see Hans Eidel pull off another great save. This time he did not hold it and Mark Thyme was there to send it into the bottom right-hand corner of the German net. England are two-nil up! Would you believe it?"

Jonny Egar was out of his chair in excitement, again spilling his 'crib sheets'. "That was somethin' special! Grant could see none of 'is own players were with 'im so realised 'e 'ad to go it alone. I remember me dad telling me about Jimmy Greaves when 'e was playing for Spurs. 'Ow 'e received the ball on the 'alfway line and 'e thought, well I better not say wot 'e thought, not exactly 'is words. Well, one in particular. He realised that 'e was expected to score so 'e dribbled past about four defenders and the goalie and *did*. Simple as that!"

"Thanks for sharing that with us, Jonny, but what a performance from these young English lads. They are really doing us proud!"

"Is that a tear I see, Colm? Ya getting all emotional. That's not like you, mate!"

"No." Colm Nelson takes a deep breath and continues. "I must remain neutral at all times, after all I am just here to deliver an unbiased, helpful, and informative narrative to what is happening in front of us on the pitch. Having said that, it is pretty sensational and moving stuff for a red-blooded Englishman... Sorry, back to the action. Very quickly from the restart the Germans are pressing. I did notice a little bit of finger-pointing and animated reaction by them to the goal but I have to say that you could not blame any one of them. It was very much an incredible individual effort. Mark Thyme just finished it off for Ulysses Grant but Grant should take the plaudits for 99.9% of that goal. As I said, the Germans are pressing, in fact, Paul Bastable has just brought down Kurt Reiplie as he tried to cut inside from his right wing. It is even distance between halfway and the goal."

Jonny Egar cut in. "This could be a chance for the Germans 'cos they're pretty good at set-pieces. Looks like Willi 'Eff's coming from the back an' Gustav Vindt is in there, an' 'e's the tallest bloke on the field!"

"You're right there, J. E., this will really test the English defence, for sure. (?? ...*ed*.) They are aware of the aerial power of the Germans; they've got two men on Vindt. Kurt Reiplie is standing over the ball as the referee gets his foam out to mark the spot for the English lads. Whistle to mouth, a loud blast and Kurt Reiplie sends in an accurate kick towards the blond head of Gustav Vindt who'll make contact now, or *would* were it not for the hands of Seph Handys, the England goalkeeper, who takes it out of the air just at the point of contact! Another crucial save by the England goalie! Wonderful stuff! What say you, Jonny?"

"Brilliant! Looked really close but Seph pulled it off!"

"England's turn to press now. Seph Handys has found Terry Bull on the left and he has found Bastable, always a steadying influence in the centre of mid-field. He sends it back to Bull who has gone past Heff at right-back. Bull looks like he fancies his chances but selflessly he has played it into the path of Mark Thyme and he shoots for the far corner of the goal, and once again the enormous hands of Hans Eidel come to the rescue of the German defence."

Jonny Egar jumped in very quickly. "This game 'as seen some fantastic football, not leash... leashed..."

Colm Nelson cut in helpfully. "Least."

"Yeah, not least for the brilliant and cruc... important saves."

"You're not wrong there, Jonny. Amazing game all round, I'd say, with a special mention of the part that the goalkeepers have played in it. I'd go so far as to say I personally don't want to see it end."

Jonny Egar added, "I'm wiv' ya there, Colm. 'Ello, what's happening down there?"

"Looks like the Germans have a throw-in and are taking the opportunity to make a couple of substitutions. Yes, not just one but two! Let's see who is off and who's on. Gustav Vindt is walking towards the touchline so the tall striker is being replaced and I can see warming up and stripping for action, it will be the much shorter but nippier Orstin Tayshus, the Werner Bremen striker."

"He was very effective in front of goal, Colm, 'elpin' 'is team win the League and Cup Double last season, wasn't 'e?"

"That's right, Jonny. Quite a handful, though I've not seen him in action this year as he's just come back from injury. In fact, it surprised a lot of people when he was brought into the squad for the World Cup."

"So it's Tayshus on for Vindt. Who's coming on for 'Ans Eidel, he seems to be 'oldin' 'is left wrist. 'E's carryin' an injury, I reckon."

Colm Nelson seized the moment. "Yes, with his other hand! Sorry, just my little joke! Y'know 'carrying an injury... with his... his other hand', no?" Colm Nelson shrugged his shoulders at the blank look he got from Jonny Egar. "Seriously though, I'm guessing that it will be Mustapha Sheikh, their substitute goalie of Turkish origin coming on for Hans Eidel, as Jonny said. A very able replacement too! Sure enough, it is he."

Once the changes had been made the referee signalled and whistled for the throw-in to be taken.

Colm Nelson took up the commentary. "Right-winger Kurt Reiplie found Willi Heff, his right-back. He takes the return ball on his chest and flicks it past Michael Kelly and sends it into the path of new boy, Orstin Tayshus, the short, stocky striker. Now he is bearing down on the English goal, he tries to chip advancing goalie Seph Handys but he snatches the ball out of the air and guides it safely away to Terry Bull on the left-wing, and he's going full pelt towards the German goal line and the advancing full-back, Willi Heff. Bull looks up, sees Ulysses Grant on the right wing and sends a long raking ball right into his path. Grant doesn't even have to adjust his stride; it was an inch-perfect pass. He only has the goalie to beat. This is the first test for the stand-in goalie; will he be up to it? Grant the wing-wizard feints to go left where Hans Bach the central-defender is waiting to intercept, but in the same instant Grant has steered his body back to his right and coolly passes the ball into the German net, leaving Bach and Sheikh on their backsides next to each other. That is three-nil now to England. Can it get any better than this, Jonny?"

"Not for me, it can't! Bin waiting for this for such a long time. I can't believe it, three to nil up against the Germans. Pinch me; make sure I'm not dreamin'. Not just there... that's naughty and you know it. Only jokin', viewers! We are really enjoying this moment."

Colm Nelson carried on where Egar left off. "Such a wonderful feeling, the goal I mean. All they've got to do is to safely play out these last few minutes and then it will be all over for the Germans."

(Echoes of 1966 and Kenneth Wostenholme there I think...*ed.*)

(Oooh! You're on the ball aren't you? ...*me.*)

(Was that an *intended* pun? ...*ed.*)

Moments later the referee blew the final whistle and brought the game to a close. England have beaten Germany by three goals to nil!

Back in the studio there was a buzz about it that had not been experienced by the host, the pundits, or the production team previously. Jurgen Klinsmann was noticeably very quiet. Gary Lineker cheerily picked up where Colm Nelson left off.

"Well there it is, folks, the result that we've all, with the exception of Jurgen I guess, been waiting, hoping, and praying for and for so long. Thanks to Colm Nelson and Jonny Egar for their excellent handling of the game, so to speak, and their professionalism in doing so well to contain themselves. I know what pressure they were under but they acquitted themselves admirably under the circumstances! I have got to say that it was a very good game to watch and not just for the result. What do say to that, Jurgen?"

"Well, as a matter of fact I have to agree with you, Gary. No-one must argue with the result. It was a very good score and well deserved also. I think the Germans did not arrive today, for sure."

Lineker interjected quickly. "Turn up."

Klinsmann answered, "Am I not loud enough? I'll speak up."

"No, what you meant to say was that 'the Germans did not *turn up*'. That was the expression you were looking for, no need to shout at all... unless you want to go and shout at the German players for not turning up."

"Oh I see, thank you for correcting me. That last little bit was funny, or do I mean a little bit funny?"

Gary Lineker smiled and shook Klinsmann's hand, then addressed his next remark towards Alan Hansen. "Alan, as our resident neutral how did you find the game today?"

"Well, I came by tram, a very efficient, clean, and economical way to travel. Then I followed the signs. No, but seriously I am nonplussed at the thought that these English youngsters should come out today and beat possibly the most accomplished and experienced side in world football."

Gary Lineker answered, "Emphasis on *economical* there, eh Alan? And a couple of useful words for you there, Lawro... *nonplussed* and *accomplished*. I think Jurgen and Alan have it right all in all. What do you say, Mark?"

"I'll look those words up later, Gary. In the meantime, all I can say is well done those young lads because they've really done *us* proud today. They've lifted the gloom that has hung over English football for all these years and all I want now is to see them go on to the final and do to the Danes what they have done here today to the Germans."

"Well said there, Lawro, and thanks. Thanks also to Jurgen Klinsmann and Alan Hansen for *their* expert contributions. All I have to do now is to say thanks to *you* for watching and hope that you will join us in three days' time when we bring you the climax to this World Cup when England meet Denmark in the final."

# 49

The former Press Officer to the Queen and owner of the most successful public relations company in the U.K., possibly even Europe, Sir Howard Eyeknow was, for once in his life, experiencing genuine emotions and feelings for a member of the opposite sex. Could this possibly have something to do with the fact that his most valuable client, Ms. Aurora Stafford, had successfully guided the England Men's football team to the final of that most prestigious of competitions in the whole of sport – THE WORLD CUP?

He was playing host to Ms. Stafford's family and friends, Sally Farnham his assistant and quite a few of his fellow professionals. *They* and just about every other football fan in England were celebrating the latest in the long list of achievements attributed to his client and Sir Howard could not be happier. This from the person who in the beginning despised and hated the very being that was Rory Stafford!

He called for everyone's attention. "Ladies, gentlemen, dear friends, one and all. Please can I have your attention? I wish you all to fill your glasses and join me in congratulating Aurora Stafford and her boys on reaching the final of the World Cup. I want you to enjoy yourselves tonight and then come back on Saturday to cheer and encourage her boys to go all the way and bring back that trophy to dear old England!! Everybody... to Aurora and her boys, cheers! Eat and drink now!"

He called Sally Farnham to one side, saying, "Sally, we have to have everything in place on Saturday."

"I have ordered the champagne and the..."

He interrupted her. "I am not talking about the catering! I am talking about the press releases and the 'upping' of the profile of our darling Aurora even further, if that is at all possible. For when her boys actually win this competition and come home with the biggest prize of all!! **We** have to remember that it is all about **her**. We have to prepare the way for her return in glory and see to it that we 'maximise'... I think you know what I mean, Sally." He stared and fixed her with a smile that was almost cynical, then continued. "We have to use these three days to put in place the 'Machinery' to bring about the biggest public relations coup ever! Everyone on the planet will want to speak to him, sorry... *her* and photograph her, be photographed with her, advertise things with her, be sponsored by her and... well... everybody must want to 'get into bed with her'. You know what I mean... don't look at me like that. It was just a turn of phrase. Yes... I'd even get in bed with her myself... I love her that much right now!" He smiled to himself complacently but Sally looked at him askance.

\*

In the three days leading up to the World Cup

Final the English newspapers were full of expectation and hope. Some were openly optimistic about the England team's chances, though others were not so. Several times the phrase 'false dawn' was used and 'raising our hopes and expectations again'.

Sir Howard Eyeknow fed them 'quotes' purportedly from Ms. Stafford herself. He tried to put a positive 'spin' on every call, every text, every email and every conversation in those days leading up to the World Cup Final, at the same time encouraging others to do the same.

Thus the scene was set for what promised to be the biggest ever moment in the history of English football and possibly English sport in general.

It was also a significant time in Danish football's history, since they have *never* won the World Cup, so it would be an incredible landmark achievement for their team and coaches. It has certainly raised their profile tremendously, bearing in mind that Denmark is a country with a population of just over 5,600,000. Compare that with the 53,000,000 plus (And counting...*ed.*) of England, just over a tenth! This puts a bit of 'perspective' on the matter.

# 50

"The day has come, ladies and gentlemen, boys and girls. A day that we all thought could never happen in our lifetimes. Sorry... I got a little carried away there. I mean to say one that we all longed for but never anticipated. No, sorry, same again... I am so overwhelmed by the fact that the England football team is in the final of the World Cup that I am having difficulty expressing myself. Maybe I should ask Alan Hansen to come in whilst I pull myself together... Alan?"

"I can understand where you are coming from, Gary, having experienced so many disappointments in the past. This from a Scot whose national side I don't think has progressed beyond the first round of the competition once, although they did qualify for the finals in the year that England *failed* to do so!"

"Thanks Alan, that makes me feel so much better and helped me to pull myself together! So Lawro, as a red-bloodied Englishman (that should read 'blooded' ...*ed*... Oh... I don't know, perhaps you are right, as you said English... bloodied... it fits! ...*ed*.) perhaps you could express how you feel about it?"

"With great pleasure, Gary. With great pleasure. In

fact that's what I am feeling... great pleasure! I really do believe that this England team can actually win it for us too! I don't mean for the *two* of us, I mean for all of the England fans. It is very exciting and as you say, Gary, it is such a long time since the last time anything that is this big has happened."

Lineker turned away from Lawrenson with eyebrows slightly raised and said, "Yes... I'm with you there, Mark, I think, but before we get too carried away I guess I should introduce someone who I suspect will be 'gunning' for the other side. Popular Danish football commentator and *pundit* for today's game, Mister Kvist Agen."

There was quite a long, pregnant pause as Kvist Agen shook hands with Gary Lineker, then leant over in front of him to repeat the action with Lawrenson and Hansen. When he was finally sitting back in his seat Lineker was able to continue. "Welcome Kvist, and perhaps I could ask you to give us your thoughts on the soccer feast that is set before us."

"Well to tell you the truth, Gary, I saw the half-time sandwiches and I was not impressed. Ha! Ha! Was not exactly a Smorgasbord of delight, which is what your English comedians say, isn't it? Ha! Ha! Ha! That is a Swedish meal, by the way, the Smorgasbord, ok?"

"Oh yes, I see, quite funny but I was alludi... Sorry, referring to the 'feast' of soccer that we have to look forward to. The game between your Danish side and the England lads. What are your thoughts on that?"

"Well you know, Gary, I am looking forward to a game of very skilful and entertaining soccer because of what I have seen so far. These are the two teams that have given us from the 'top drawer', that's what you English say, isn't it?"

"I guess so, Kvist, and I would agree. I'm sure that the other lads around the table think so too."

"As a matter of fact it would have been England that would have held my support if Denmark had not of made it into the final."

"Oh, they impressed you so much, did they?"

"No, no, my mother is English!" After he had registered the reactions of the others, Agen laughed and said, "Not really, I chust wanted to see your faces! Ha! Ha! Ha!"

"Very good, Kvist. You're quite a comedian yourself, never mind the English ones! The 'held my support' bit wasn't a joke then, was it...? I thought not."

Lawrenson and Hansen smiled knowingly as Lineker continued. "Do you think it might be a high-scoring game today, Kvist? I can't help thinking that these two sides are going to be going into it looking for goals."

Agen replied, "I think that too because the way they have played up 'til now is with attacking football, both sides. That is what I want to see, anyways."

Gary Lineker then looked towards Alan Hansen and asked, "Alan, what would you be asking of or telling your players by way of their approach to this game bearing in mind this is going to be the biggest, most important game they have participated in their entire careers so far?"

"Well, I certainly would not be saying that to them! Of necessity, you would have to settle their nerves early on, taking a calm approach, **not** intensifying what they are already going through. You have to lean on the more experienced players like mid-fielder, Paul Bastable, but hey, look, you have the **one** person who has experienced it all at the highest level in men's football and gone all the way in the ladies' equivalent of the World Cup. Surely she will have gone through enough to be able to quote it 'chapter and verse'. So long as they take it all in, eh? Y'know what some of these youngsters are like, and, not forgetting this is the squad with the lowest average age in the competition."

Lineker nodded and answered, "As you say, Alan, they are not the most experienced squad of players whereas the Danes are quite well established... 'battle hardened', we might say. However, we should be encouraged by their excellent displays so far in this tournament. It seems like we are going over the same ground again so maybe now is a good time to hand over to our commentary team who are going to take us through the action out there on the pitch. Mr. Des Kryber and Tony Cottee. Over to you, gents."

Des Kryber thanked Lineker and turning to Tony Cottee beside him, said, "What a game in prospect we have, Tony. There is always the danger of repeating what the others have said so viewers please forgive us if we do and put it down to the excitement and the importance of the occasion. It was good to have the input from Kvist Agen, our Danish colleague, and to him I say, 'may the best side win', eh Tony?"

"As long as it's England, Des. Only joking, but

you know where my heart is, for sure."

(Klinsmann has gone, Goddammit! Don't keep on with that! You know how much I hate it!! ...*ed.*)

(I'm only writing what Cottee said! ...*me.*)

"A true Englishman and ex-England international player to boot! Thanks Tony, and to be fair, throughout this competition I think we have given credit where it was due to the many participants and we have truly seen some memorable moments indeed, that everybody will surely talk about well into the future. But this is the very pinnacle, this is what we've all been waiting for, this is the biggest game of them all. It is all about two teams pitting their wits against each other with the result that one of them brings home, sorry; I meant *takes* home the top prize in the world of international football. The trophy once called the Jules Rimet Trophy... now known as The F.I.F.A. World Cup Trophy!"

Tony Cottee replied, "Sounds like you are just as excited as the rest of us at the prospect of our lads getting their hands on that trophy, Des, and whilst we've been talking the teams have been lining up for the national anthems. Can it get any more intense than this?"

"Thanks again, Tony. There is now a hush over this stadium, the magnificent 80,720-seater SIGNAL IDUNA PARK, home to Borussia Dortmund, the Bundesliga club. We'll acknowledge the silence with the crowd."

\*

With the anthems over, commentator Des Kryber continued. "Only moments now before the kick-off of the twenty-first staging of the football World Cup Final. The England captain, Paul Bastable, has won the toss and decided to kick off, and the Danes have chosen to defend the end where most of their supporters are seated. Viewers we are ready to go. The referee has the whistle to his lips. Mark Thyme stands over the ball. A short, sharp blast and Thyme's first touch sends the ball to his right where Ulysses Grant plays it back to Bastable, always a steadying influence at the heart of this England team. You've heard me say that a few times before, viewers, I know but he's so dependable. The backbone of this England team and an excellent captain. If anyone led by example it would certainly be he. Don't you agree, Tony?"

"Certainly do, Des! He is a great player and fine captain, and as you've said before he leads by example and I can't see anybody disagreeing with you, certainly not me anyway."

"Thanks Tony. That's why we get on so well, ha ha! Back on the pitch, the ball has gone out of play from a Danish foot and England has a throw-in which Terry Bull is lining up to take. He has an extra-long throw-in as his speciality."

Cottee cut across him, saying, "He's got extra-long arms, Des, to match his extra-long legs and..."

Des Kryber interrupted him. "Hold on, Tony, where is this leading? Remember, we have some very young viewers. Don't worry, viewers, you're not missing anything, as you can see Michael Kelly is being jostled in mid-field and the referee is having words with the huge figure that is Theo Rasmussen."

Again Tony Cottee cut in. "Des, I don't know how you managed to resist calling him the... Great Dane, I wouldn't be able to stop *myself*!"

"Ah but that is why I do this job... I'm not a comedian! By the way, I thought it was funny and I'm sure our viewers did too, but as folk always say 'don't give up the day job'! Bull has taken the throw, a long one down the Danes' right. He's found Kelly, Kelly to Mark Thyme, a long looping pass to Leydon Lowe. Having a run from the right-back position, he does a one-two with Ulysses Grant; that is not a dance, by the way, before our resident comic chips in. Grant is bearing down on the Danish goal and the ball comes in from Lowe, too close to the goalie and he snaps it up and clears it upfield. It falls nicely at the feet of striker Brian Larsen; Larsen tries to bring in Arne Helt on his left but Leydon Lowe has read it well and snaps it out to Grant and again moving towards the bye-line, he looks up and sends a lovely curling ball in for Thyme perhaps to test the Danish goalkeeper Theo Rasmussen. No, it was a fraction too close to the goalie and again he was able to gather it up and clear it out to Hans Andersen on the right of the Danish mid-field. Before you say anything, Tony, he's not the same person."

In genuine surprise, Cottee asked, "Same person...? Who...? Same as who?"

"Oh, are you saying you haven't heard of Hans Christian Andersen, the writer of fairy tales?"

"Yes I have, but I thought you said Hans Andersen." Des Kryber let it drop and continued his commentary whilst Tony Cottee sniggered quietly to himself.

"Andersen in the meantime has played it back to Bent Bastrop who gives him a quick return ball, now he finds Hans Colding the holding mid-fielder. The English players are holding their line well and the Danes seem to be bogged down and passing it around in mid-field. This is good from the English lads, eh Tony?"

"Des, as long as they keep their concentration and don't get caught napping, watching the ball."

Play continued in a similar fashion for most of the first half with neither side taking any risks, until the fortieth minute, that is, when things changed. Des Kryber picks up the commentary.

"Hans Colding, not Cans Holding as my friend on my left calls him, the holding mid-fielder – say all that when you're drunk, Cottee – now has the ball at his feet and he has spotted a gap and sent a pass for Lars Ahlberg, left of mid-field, to run onto. He has brought Arne Helt, their left winger in to play, now can he find Brian Larsen? Yes he can, and he has glided past the six-feet four-inch figure of England centre-back Colin Dett, then placed the ball neatly into the bottom left-hand corner of Seph Handys' goal. The Danes are one-nil up!"

"A bit of a lapse there, Des, on behalf of the English defence. Colding was quite canny though, getting the ball through to Ahlberg, and he is very quick for someone as short as him. You can't argue with the finish from Larsen either. Altogether it was great goal. Bit disappointing for the English lads 'cos they've been patient and not forced the issue."

"I agree, Tony, but this game isn't over yet. You

see Aurora Stafford quite animated on the touch-line trying to get the message over to 'keep their cool' and 'use their heads'. At least that is my interpretation of her signals, for what it's worth."

Cottee answered, "I'm guessing she's encouraging them to keep it tight at the back and hold on 'til half-time when she can get 'em back in the dressing room and sort a few things out. I can remember how it would be in Ms. Stafford's former life as *Rory* Stafford. *He* would be 'sounding off' well before the players got back to their dressing room and before poor old Donnie Mclaren, the Barcaster United manager, could get to 'em. Apparently it was the same when he was playing with the England team. And he was well known for the most 'colourful' language, if you know what I mean. Well, not just colourful but numerous too! In fact, if I remember correctly, somebody counted him using the 'F' word over a hundred times in one game and most of those were aimed at the ref."

"I can just about remember that, Tony, and if I can, I'm sure our viewers can too. Thanks for that. Oh, and there goes the whistle for half-time. Is it me, Tony, or was that an extra 'trill' whistle just then from the referee?"

"Well I have to say that that's the 'trillest', if that's a word, whistle I have heard in many a long year. Certainly not heard it previously in this competition!"

"Nor me, Tony. Maybe it was specially made for this game, it being the most important game of the year and of the last four years too, come to think of it, and for the English fans quite a few more years than that, eh? Well on that note we'll hand you back to

Agen's comments and carried on. "It is good to have such a forthright opinion there, viewers. We certainly see both sides of the coin and also a neutral perspective here in the studio and at this point we have to put you back in the capable hands of Mr. Des Kryber and his sidekick Tony Cottee. Over to you, chaps, to guide us through the second half of this, the final of the 2015 F.I.F.A. World Cup Trophy as it has been known since 1974. This incidentally is made of 18 carat gold, or karat with a 'K to use the North American spelling. Stands 36.8 centimetres tall or fourteen and a half inches approx. in old money. It also weighs 6.1 kilograms, which is equal to 2.76 lbs, again in old money, so it says here."

Des Kryber replied to Lineker, saying, "Well thanks very much for those 'nuggets' of information, Gary. Sorry, viewers, I couldn't resist, but for a minute there I thought Gary was going to make us late for the kick-off of this second half. I am sure that the tension is at its very highest right now as the teams await that shrill blast (enough already! ...*ed.*) from the ref's whistle, I know it..."

Tony Cottee cut in. "I thought they'd milked that one at half-time, Des. I can't believe you of all people, and 'those nuggets', please! Seriously."

"Ok Tony, point taken. There goes the whistle and the Danes kick off in the shape of their tall striker Brian Larsen. He plays it out to the right wing where Hans Andersen calmly plays it back to his namesake Hans Colding. He in turn takes a cool look around him and despatches the ball sideways to Bent Bastrop; from Bastrop it goes to Bent Munk at right-back then to Theo Rasmussen in the middle at the back of the

Danish defence." At this point Tony Cottee remarked. "Des, they are playing 'keep ball'...just inviting the English lads to come and take it off 'em and I can see Aurora Stafford at the side calling at 'em to stay calm."

"Yes, I can see with her hand gestures she's saying hold back, keep cool and don't rush in... patience."

Cottee could not hold back. "What, all that from just those hand movements! Can you lip-read what she's saying as well?"

"Not from this distance, no. Alright, Tony Cottee, but I think we can guess what is coming from her generally, if not specifically! Anyway, because of the pressure from England striker Mark Thyme, Rasmussen has had to play it back to Nils Lofgren in goal who launches a hasty clearing kick upfield which has landed at the feet of twenty-one year old Colin Dett at the heart of the English defence. Now it is his turn to take a look around before sending a lovely weighted pass to Terry Bull on his left wing. He takes it past Bastrop and shapes up to Munk at full-back, then shifts the ball sideways to Bastable who plays it just behind Munk for Bull to run onto. He looks up to see Mark Thyme running into the penalty area and places a glorious pass tantalisingly close to Rasmussen, but just right for the speedy centre forward to run onto and guide it into the Danish net. That was a beautifully worked goal and it means that the English lads are level. How about that, Tony?"

"Absolutely beautiful, Des. That was quality football. I'm lost for words!"

"Alright then, let me put it into words for you...

just two... pure poetry! It has stunned the Danes I guess, because they thought that they were in control. Well they are back to level and it opens the game up once more. What a final this is turning out to be and we are only about five minutes into the second half. They are kicking off again but this time there is more 'urgency' in their play. They are shifting the ball around a little quicker now."

"Yes Des, the English lads are closing them down much quicker now and jostling 'em. They're playing it much tighter and that's good 'cos they are the younger team so they have the legs to do it."

Des Kryber picked up on Cottee's observations and added, "Yes they've probably got the energy too, Tony, to carry it off. We shall see as the game progresses. It is getting more interesting as the minutes tick by. The Danes seem to be 'encamped' in their own half. Passing the ball side to side then backwards, to the other side and back. Even striker Brian Larsen has come into his side's half of the field in search of the ball. This is quite uninspiring stuff from the Danes considering what we have seen of them in this competition thus far."

At this point Tony Cottee interjected. "Des, they are playing a game of patience here. Their experience tells them that sooner or later the English lads will overcommit, lunge in, and maybe commit a foul even. You can see Aurora Stafford in the coaching area pointing at her head as if to say 'think and remember what I told you, be patient', but it has to be very hard for 'em to do that. They want that ball to be able to do stuff of their own with it."

"I'm sure you are right, Tony. You can see a bit of

frustration creeping into their game, because even as we speak the referee has blown for a foul on Hans Colding, in the mid-field area. The ref has had to pace out the ten yards and use his foam to keep the English players at bay. What are you laughing at, Cottee...? Never mind. Free kick is taken by Colding himself, Larsen has made a run into the English half of the field but Colding has played the ball to left of mid-field where Lars Ahlberg latches onto it, having moved into space created by Larsen's run. He took two English players with him. This is a set piece that they've worked on I'd say, Tony."

"I agree, Des; you've suddenly got most Danish players in the English lads' half. These lads have gotta stay focused or get caught out."

"Paul Bastable is calling out to his players now and directing them as he intercepts the pass meant for Hans Andersen or Bent Munk, who was just behind the Danes' right winger. He has caught the Danes flat-footed with that and fed the ball out to Ulysses Grant on his right wing; he has brought Leydon Lowe, his right-back, into play with a short back pass, now he's waiting for a return ball. He can see Mark Thyme bearing down on goal and signalling. The ball is returned to Grant and he draws the left-back, leaves him for dead and puts in a cross with pinpoint accuracy that Thyme merely has to side foot in to beat the advancing goalkeeper. It is two-one to England! The English lads are in the lead; their patience has paid off, Tony."

"It certainly has, Des. Another brilliantly created goal all thanks to that timely interception by Paul Bastable."

Kryber was quick to respond. "And the pass to find Grant out on the wing. From then on it was clever inter-play that brought the goal, Tony."

"Des, that goal will really bring this game to life now. We might now see some of that classy football that we have witnessed in previous games in this competition."

"I agree, with twenty minutes left of this one I think we are in for a real 'humdinger'. The Danes, in the shape of Brian Larsen have kicked off once more and Arne Helt is racing down his left wing; he's a flyer when he gets going, viewers, but Leydon Lowe is no slouch when it comes to that and he is forcing him out wider. Helt looks up, sees Larsen hovering close to the penalty spot and attempts to find the head of his tall striker but Colin Dett, at six feet four inches, the equal of Larsen, has read it and headed the ball clear."

"That was a mighty clearance from Dett there, Des, the youngster is doing very well, fulfilling the faith his boss has shown in him."

"Very much so, Tony. Paul Bastable has latched onto the header and laid it off to Terry Bull on the left; he brings Bastable back into play and points to where he wants the return. As he streaks past Bent Munk at right-back, he finds Mark Thyme but he's tightly marked and nudged from behind by Rasmussen so threads it out to Grant on the other wing. He in turn finds Bastable who looks up to see Thyme making a clever run, drawing Rasmussen away from his central position, and spots Bull who has continued his run into the gap, places the ball into his path so he doesn't have to adjust. Bull is down on goal now with only the keeper to beat and he rounds the keeper with a neat dip of his shoulders and coolly slots the ball home. It is an unbelievable third goal for this young English team!"

"That's another great goal, Des, and there's a bit of daylight between the two teams now. It is no less than they deserve for the way they've played. They've gotta hold it together for another ten minutes or so and the trophy is theirs."

Des Kryber took a few deep breaths before continuing. "It is very difficult to hold it in but as a commentator I have to not let my emotions get the better of me at this stage, Tony."

"I know, Des. I want to jump up and down myself but I don't know how safe it is, this high up in the stadium."

"Are you questioning our hosts, the Germans' engineering, designing, and building skills, Tony? Of course not! Meanwhile, back down at ground level we have another restart by the Danes. Larsen plays it left towards Arne Helt who passes it to left mid-fielder Lars Ahlberg, onto Hans Colding in the centre, over to his right for Bent Bastrop. The English lads are still not giving them any room to manoeuvre, they are marking them very tightly again."

"It is good to see, Des. They've gotta keep it tight to get through these last few minutes."

"Hans Andersen is in possession at the moment and he is contemplating his next move but Bull is back in support and harassing the right winger. He wins the ball and gives it to Michael Kelly who's had a quiet time filling in at left-back. He calmly plays it back to his goalkeeper Seph Handys, whose first touch sends it out to Leydon Lowe, who has been the busiest of the English full-backs. Lowe sends it back to Handys who moves it out again to Kelly. Bull collects it from him and brings Dett into play. This is very good keep-ball, Tony."

"It is cool. They're not being too clever and not in a rush to go forward. The Danes are running out of time but all credit to 'em they are not getting dirty like some of the teams we have seen so far."

"Ooh, just as you say that, Tony, Brian Larsen has lunged in on Dett as he played the ball out to Grant. The ref has blown for a foul."

"Yes, he was a bit late and took the man's leg, no contact on the ball at all. It looked dangerous and Colin Dett has stayed down and he's not one to make a meal of it, I can tell you."

"The referee has shown Larsen a yellow card as a result too, Tony. Total frustration on his part. He had been starved of the ball for so long. Dett is getting treatment but he's wanting to get up and get on with it. His team-mates are telling him to take his time and make sure he's okay to carry on but he is brushing it all off as he gets to his feet. The crowd are clapping in appreciation of his actions. It's good to see, Tony, when so many players these days would do the opposite."

"It's good for the game, Des, especially at this level, the greatest stage of all. It does spoil the game as a spectacle when you see the histrionics and play acting from some of these very fit, highly trained and extremely well-paid athletes! All credit to the lad and anyway there are only about three minutes on the clock plus any added for this stoppage."

"Correct Mr. Cottee, and as they line up to take the free-kick a gentleman on the touchline holds up a board showing that there is one minute of extra 'injury' time to play. It is Colin Dett himself who is shaping to take this kick. He's urging all his players forward as if he is looking for another goal to round it all off!"

Tony Cottee edged forward on his seat and remarked excitedly. "What a finish this would be if we... er... *England* scored a fourth goal!"

"Don't hold your breath there, Tony. The big centre-half is stepping back. The rest of the players except himself and Handys, the goalie, are in the Danish side of the pitch. There is total silence in the stadium. You could hear a pin drop."

Cottee quipped, "Not on the grass you couldn't!"

"Thanks Tony. You're wasted here. Back to the action. Dett has lofted the ball right over to the right-wing position where Ulysses Grant trapped and moved it infield immediately to where he knew Mark Thyme was waiting for it. He took a first-time shot that bounced off the shins of Nils Lofgren in the Danish goal right into the path of Bull tearing in from the left-wing, who hits it into the top right-hand corner of the goal. That is an unbelievable four-one to this young English team."

"That's absolutely incredible! What a finish! What a result! They've totally blown them away!"

"Who would have thought it? From one-nil down at half-time to four-one. As results go they do not come any more convincing than that! Pinch me,

Tony, because at the beginning of this competition not many people would have given this young English team a chance in hell of going all the way, but there you are, they have won the World Cup, the F.I.F.A. Trophy 2015. Congratulations to them and the Danes of course for making such a good game of it!"

"Yeah, let's not forget this *Great* Danish side. No pun intended there, Des."

"None taken, Tony. Might have been better if you had said 'this side of Great Danes' though. Well, perhaps not, and with that I'll hand you back to the studio whilst we prepare for the Award Ceremony."

Gary Lineker excitedly picked up where Des Kryber had left off. "Speaking of Danes, *great* or otherwise, apologies to Kvist Agen for that."

"No need for apologies. Your boys scored some very good goals and deserved to win. It was a great game to watch and of course I am sorry our boys didn't win but give credit to the English boys, a good young team. They will be hard to beat anywhere if they are to be judged on this game."

"I was apologising for... well it doesn't matter. I can see that Lawro is anxious to give us his reaction." Lineker chuckled then continued. "But in the meantime I will just ask Alan Hansen for his views on the final result and that second half in particular. Alan, the neutral's response please."

Hansen smiled at Lineker and with a sideways look at Lawrenson, who was doing his best to contain himself, said, "It was a thoroughly enjoyable game and the excitement was raised beyond all my expectations in that second half. As Mr. Agen said it was a thoroughly good performance all round from, as he reminded us, a young England team. Well done to the Danes for playing their part too."

"Almost complimentary there, Alan. I guess you are saying that this side could be around and successful for a few years then." Lineker deliberately kept the focus on Alan Hansen. "Do you see any particular weaknesses in this line-up?"

"No, not really, but it's necessary to back up each position with good cover because injuries can be an issue of course. It also keeps this current line-up on their toes and looking over their shoulders, y'know what I mean, healthy competition for places helps keep complacency at bay."

By now Mark Lawrenson was becoming agitated and was shifting about in his chair. Lineker took this on board and carried on, keeping his gaze on Hansen but at the same time, smiling, said, "The producer says that we can go down for an interview with the winning coach, Ms. Aurora Stafford." Lawrenson leant forward, sighing in frustration. Lineker continued. "But before we do we have time for a quick word from Mark Lawrenson. Lawro, anything to add to what Alan has already said?"

Lawrenson started in earnest. "I think you know how I feel, Gary, but just a few words cannot explain it. We have waited so long for this moment and it has surely been really worth it. For *many* it has exceeded all expectations, I'm sure. To see this young team achieve what they have achieved in this, the biggest competition in world football, is absolutely incredible. I mean they only came together a short while before the start of the World Cup. If they carry on there'll be no stopping 'em. If you ask me they'll win the European Nations Cup and then be back in four years' time to take today's trophy home again. I can't see an end to their success. I just hope that Aurora Stafford is gonna carry on in the job 'cos I'm sure *other* folk will be looking at what she has achieved with them and will covet her qualities, strengths, and lack of weaknesses. It has never taken her that long to get success with whatever set-up she has been involved in. Just like Brian Clough with his different teams, we might not have had to wait this long if he had been made England manager but that is history. This is now! England has won the World Cup again at last."

Lawrenson paused to take a deep breath and Lineker took the opportunity to say, "Thanks for those *few* words, Mark. I think you captured the mood perfectly. Now it seems we can go to our man on the ground, Mr. Adam Sayle, in the Signal Iduna Park Stadium, Dortmund, for a chat with Ms. Aurora Stafford. Over to you, Adam, and please give our congratulations to her and her boys."

Adam Sayle was quite taken with the tall, statuesque, blonde beauty that was Aurora Stafford standing next to him in what looked like a 'designer' England tracksuit that did nothing to hide her superb figure.

Gary Lineker had to jog him. "Adam, over to you, ok?"

"Oh yes, ok, thanks Gary. Well... er... folks, I have the great pleasure of introducing the lady of the moment. Aurora, congratulations from all in the studio and the commentary box and I guess the millions of viewers back home and all over the world

I daresay."

Adam Sayle waved the microphone shakily near Ms. Stafford's face.

"Thank you so much. I'm glad we were able to do it for you all. We know it means so much!"

"Yes, well, one of our pundits in the studio, Mark Lawrenson, used many words to say what we are all feeling. For me it's all summed up simply by saying with only three words – we're 'over the moon'! Thank you and your boys for giving us England football fans something to celebrate after being so long 'out in the cold'. I can confidently say that *you* have the respect of everybody in football now. I won't keep you much longer as the Trophy Presentation Ceremony is soon going to be under way and I know that you'll want to be there with your boys. But if there is anything you want to say to your adoring fans and faithful followers, carry on."

Again Sayle nervously put his microphone close to Ms. Stafford's face, this time so close that he narrowly missed her chin with it. He was not helped by the fact that she 'towered' over him, of course. She smiled and held his microphone hand to steady it. Which if anything, made him even more nervous, though he enjoyed the closeness, almost to the point of 'arousal'?

"Thanks Adam, I would just like to say that whatever else I have achieved in my lifetime this is definitely the very biggest, most memorable, and most enjoyable of the lot. I would like to thank the players and the coaching team around me for their input too. Without their hard work and dedication we would not be here today! Not forgetting the English fans for their support, of course. Thank you all, every one of you! Oh, and could I just say at this point that I'm really looking forward to getting home to see my lovely family again. We've been a long time apart, I've missed them so much and I can't wait to get back to them. Meanwhile, Lisa, Gavin, Fiona... I love you so much and I'm really looking forward to seeing you very soon." Ms Stafford then blew a kiss and a wave to her family.

It seemed that Adam Sayle was quite moved by Ms. Stafford's statement and was slow to react when she stopped and let go of his hand, nearly losing the microphone altogether in the process. That is when Gary Lineker cut in to say thanks to both of them.

"I'm sure they all look forward to having her back as well. Now over to you, Des, to take us through the final proceedings."

Des Kryber thanked Lineker and carried on. "That was Adam Sayle, of course, with the England coach Aurora Stafford. Our thanks to both of you too. Now, the two teams have shaken hands and are lining up for the presentation and who should be handing over the trophy to the England captain? None other than the German Chancellor... Angela Merkel! There is a roar from the crowd as Ms. Merkel steps up to hand over the runners-up medals to the Danish team first. She smiles briefly at each player as he moves forward. There is a very warm reaction from the crowd. Then, as the last Danish player steps down from the award platform the volume in the stadium increases. The English fans' chanting is getting stronger and stronger. At this level I wonder whether the roof will stay on its supports!"

Tony Cottee jumped in. "Now who's questioning the stability of the structure, Des?"

"I know, Tony, but I have never heard sounds like this before. There will be quite a few sore throats in the morning but who cares? Let them indulge themselves, let them enjoy the moment I say."

Cottee replied, "Des, this is a heck of a moment for them all, and anyway I'm sure they'll be able to take advantage of our refrifracal, recifrical medical..."

Des Kryber came to his friend's assistance. "Reciprocal Medical Agreement to sort out their throat problems, is what you're trying to say I think, Tony."

"Yes. Ta, Des."

"You're welcome, my friend. Meanwhile there is a separate roar as each of the England players receives their medals from Chancellor Merkel. As Paul Bastable, the inspirational captain of this England team, steps up and gets his, he pauses briefly before receiving the F.I.F.A. World Cup Trophy. Then as he raises it for all to see, suddenly it feels like the roof of the stadium is going to be lifted by the sustained almighty roar coming from this eighty thousand plus crowd, the vast majority of which it seems are English fans. What a sound, Tony?!"

"You said it, Des. I reckon it is gonna get louder still when they take the trophy round the ground to show it to the fans!"

"If that is at all possible, Tony?"

"You've heard of Phil Spector's 'Wall of Sound'. Is

there such a thing as a 'Roof of Sound', Des?"

"Now I think you are getting carried away, Mr. Cottee. Still, enjoy the moment eh! *They* all are. The players are passing the cup around between themselves and even bringing in the coaching staff to take their turn as they very slowly make their way around this beautiful stadium..."

Tony Cottee interrupted Des Kryber to say, "I can hear a new sound from this crowd now... singing... and they're singing the national anthem. They're all singing 'God Save the Queen'!"

"You are right, Tony; thousands of them are joining in and singing it too! Quite significant, eh? Bearing in mind the suggestion that like the other countries of the U.K. maybe England should have its own individual anthem. They are singing it with real 'gusto' as well."

Tony Cottee was visibly moved by it all. "That is music to my ears, Des. That was not a pun by the way. I am really touched by the show of passion. I'm guessing that they won't be singing many German drinking songs in the Bier Kellers tonight, judging by this performance."

"Tony if they keep this up, there won't be any singing at all tonight, just a lot of 'wetting' dry, sore throats."

"Good luck to 'em, I say. I'd say they deserve it for their sheer patience. I reckon the English players will be doing something along those lines as well. Eh, Des?"

"You bet, T.C., and *they* thoroughly deserve it too. Though with so many youngsters in their number, maybe someone should keep an eye on them!"

"I think they have the very person in Ms. Aurora Stafford to do just that. Talk about experienced. She's *been there, done it* and has *bought the T-shirt* on many occasions, it's well documented. I say *she* but I mean primarily in her former life as Rory Stafford of course, when we are talking about behaviour and celebrating!"

"We are with you there, Tony, and to be sure with that kind of experience she'll want to keep them in check. And to be fair to them they've hardly put a foot wrong thus far. Don't want to spoil it now. Well then, the team has been to every part of the field showing off their prize and are about to disappear up the tunnel to their dressing room with Paul Bastable and Aurora Stafford herself bringing up the rear whilst the two of them take turns in sipping champagne from the now 'brimming' F.I.F.A. World Cup Trophy. There is still a 'buzz' around the stadium. The crowd seem reluctant to leave and even as I say *that*, singing has once again broken out."

"This is amazing, Des, they are singing 'You'll Never Walk Alone' over there and I think I can hear 'Roll Out the Barrel' down this end. That's all *before* the drinking has started!"

"It's a great atmosphere, Tony, but I think they are going to be moved on soon for the cleaning up to begin."

The singing continued as the crowds flowed out into the city of Dortmund until the last fans had left and the stadium fell completely silent.

*

In no time at all, the bars, Bier Kellers, cafes and

restaurants were absolutely 'buzzing' as the celebrations continued. This carried on well into the night and the early hours of the next morning.

Meanwhile, after they had enjoyed the celebratory banquet and the toasts at the Stadthalle with F.I.F.A.'s top officials and their German hosts, the England players were driven back to the team's hotel and bed. But some of their number considered that the night was still young and so remained in the Lounge Bar at the hotel to enjoy a few 'toasts' of their own in the company of the coaching staff and under the 'watchful eye' of Ms. Aurora Stafford and team captain Paul Bastable.

# 51

The following morning at his home in London, Sir Howard Eyeknow was up 'with the lark'. Keen to read the headlines and learn how the media was reporting and reacting to the England football team's amazing win but more importantly to him, his favourite client Aurora Stafford.

He had hardly slept a wink but he had insisted on going to bed to try to get some rest at least. He knew that his assistant Sally Farnham and he would have their hands full with the arrangements for press calls and dealing with the increased media interest and the like.

It was around 6.30. The papers had not been delivered yet so he made himself a coffee and turned on the television. What he saw next made him keel over backwards and land on his sofa.

Because emblazoned across the screen was:-


ENGLAND SOCCER COACH HAS SEX ROMP
WITH VICTORIOUS TEAM CAPTAIN!!!!!!!!

The England Football Team coach Ms. Aurora Stafford and Team Captain Paul Bastable were caught indulging in drunken sexual activity in the lounge of the team's hotel in Dortmund during the early hours of this morning. CCTV footage of the episode was secretly leaked to the German T.V. service who confirmed the identity of the participants though they withheld the footage.

As Mr. Rory Stafford she was subject to a gender change during a complicated and invasive operation which was the result of a serious road accident in which...

# THE END

Printed in Poland
by Amazon Fulfillment
Poland Sp. z o.o., Wrocław